W9-BZW-957

COLD

ALSO BY JOHN SMOLENS

Winter by Degrees

Angel's Head

My One and Only Bomb Shelter

SHAYE
AREHEART
BOOKS
New York

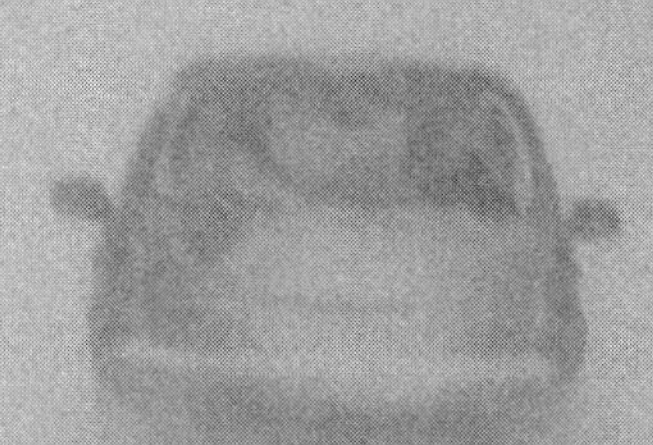

COLD

A NOVEL

JOHN SMOLENS

Published by Shaye Areheart Books/Harmony Books, New York, New York. Member of the Crown Publishing Group.

Random House, Inc. New York, Toronto, London, Sydney, Auckland
www.randomhouse.com

Shaye Areheart Books and colophon are trademarks of Random House, Inc.

A portion of *Cold* first appeared in *Columbia: A Journal of Literature and Art*, published by Columbia University, New York, and in a collection of short stories, *My One and Only Bomb Shelter*, published by Carnegie Mellon University Press, Pittsburgh.

Printed in the United States of America

Design by Lynne Amft

Library of Congress Cataloging-in-Publication Data

Smolens, John.
Cold : a novel / by John Smolens.—1st ed.
1. Upper Peninsula (Mich.)—Fiction 2. Triangles (Interpersonal relations)—Fiction. 3. Fugitives from justice—Fiction. 4. Middle-aged women—Fiction. 5. Murderers—Fiction. 6. Revenge—Fiction. I. Title.

PS3569.M646 C65 2001

813′.54—dc21 2001022268

ISBN 0-609-60794-4

10 9 8 7 6 5 4 3 2 1

First Edition

To

my wife, Reesha

and

my mother, Mary Burke Smolens

and

In memory of John Harrison Smolens Sr.

ACKNOWLEDGMENTS

Thanks, as always, to my family; G. G. Gordon, Assistant United States Prosecuting Attorney, for her technical assistance; friends and colleagues at Northern Michigan University; my agent, Noah Lukeman; and my editor, Shaye Areheart.

I saw a thousand faces after that,
All purple as a dog's lips from the frost:
I still shiver, and always will, at the sight

Of a frozen pond. All through the time we progressed
Toward the core where all gravity convenes,
I quaked in the eternal chill

THE INFERNO OF DANTE, XXXII, 67–72

PART One

CHAPTER
One

Liesl Tiomenen saw the man from her kitchen window. It was snowing so hard that he was barely visible, standing at the edge of the woods. Staring toward the house, he kept his arms folded so his hands were clamped under his armpits. He wore a soiled canvas coat and blue trousers, but no hat. His stillness reminded her of the deer that often came into the yard to eat the carrots and apples she left for them.

Liesl went out into the shed and took Harold's .30-.30 Winchester carbine down off the rack, then opened the back door, holding the rifle across her chest. The man didn't move. The north wind chilled the right side of her face; her fingers on the stock felt brittle. He was young, not more than twenty-five, and she could see that he was shivering.

"All right," she said. "You can come inside."

He began walking immediately, his legs lifting up out of the deep snow.

"Slowly," she said. "And put your hands down at your sides where I can see them."

He stopped and watched her. Then he dropped his arms to his sides and continued on toward the house.

When the door opened, he had expected an old man or woman. Something about the house suggested that retired people lived there, the way it looked simple but well maintained. There were recent asphalt shingle patches on the roof, the wood storm windows had been freshly painted, and at least a cord of firewood was stacked against the shed. It was the smell of chimney smoke that had drawn him toward the house.

But it was a woman, maybe in her early forties. She was tall, and her long blond hair was tied in a thick braid that hung over her left shoulder. Her hands were large, and one thumb appeared to be smeared with mud. When he reached her, she pointed the rifle at his chest and he stopped. She stared at him a moment, her blue eyes showing no panic or fear, only determination. He tried to quit shaking, but it only made it seem worse.

"Okay," she said, stepping back into the shed. This close he could see that there was something odd about her mouth; her lips seemed out of kilter. When she spoke there was a kind of sag to the right side of her face, as though the muscles were lax. "Kitchen's that way."

He stepped into the shed and opened the door to the warm, heavy air of the house. There was the smell of burning wood, and something else that he couldn't identify—a pleasant scent of damp earth. It made him light-headed, and his shaking only got worse.

He fell to the floor, his palms slapping on the wood, and didn't move.

Liesl walked around him, watching his face. There was a small cut beneath his eye, and twigs and pine needles were entangled in his short black hair. She poked him in the shoulder with the rifle, but he didn't respond. He wasn't faking. She went to the stove and turned on the burner beneath the teapot. From the pocket of her flannel shirt, she took out a cigarette. She held the tip to the flame for a moment, then raised the cigarette to her lips and inhaled.

When he opened his eyes, she was standing at the wood-burning stove, smoking a cigarette, the rifle tucked beneath one arm and angled down. Not exactly pointed at him, but not far off, either.

"Can you get up?"

"I think so."

"Then sit in the chair by the radiator and keep your hands on the table."

He watched her raise the cigarette to that mouth, and then the tobacco glowed. He inhaled through his nose, and the smoke helped revive him. For a moment she looked pleased as she reached in the pocket of her flannel shirt. She took out the pack of Winstons and tossed them onto the kitchen table.

"Thanks," he said. There was a book of matches beneath the cellophane. His hands were shaking so bad that the first match waved out; the second he had a hard time holding steady to light the cigarette. When he got it lit, he watched the match flame burn down to his fingertips. After it went out, he said, "Nothing. Can't feel a thing."

"Rub them," she said. "Rub them together."

He did, working the palms slowly against each other.

"When'd you break out?"

"Two days ago. Musta walked fifty miles."

She smiled crookedly around her cigarette. "You're not twelve miles from the prison."

"I bet I walked fifty."

"Why do you think they put prisons in the Upper Peninsula? You think you're the first one to try to walk away? They usually turn themselves in—you're lucky you haven't already frozen to death."

The teakettle whistled and he nearly jumped up from his seat.

She did everything with one hand, hardly taking her eyes off him. When she placed the mug of tea on the table, she said, "Have you eaten anything?"

"No."

"You drink that. I'll feed you, but first I got to be able to put this thing down."

"I won't do nothing."

"If you had done nothing, you wouldn't be in that prison." She opened the shed door, reached around the jamb, and took something that rattled off a hook. It was a chain, the kind used for towing, coiled up like rope. She unlocked and removed the padlock, then put the chain on the kitchen floor by his feet. "Now, you wrap that around your middle a couple times, then run it round that radiator foot." Putting the padlock on the table, she said, "Then lock it."

He chained himself to the radiator. As he picked up the mug, the heat from the tea stung his fingers.

She leaned the rifle in the corner by the stove and began to make him some eggs. Three scrambled eggs, with dark rye toast. When she wasn't watching him she listened to him; he was quiet and he hardly moved. When he finished drinking one mug of tea, she made him another.

She sat down across the table and watched him eat. There were acne scars on his neck, and his nose reminded her of boxers who have had the cartilage removed. She was surprised that he ate so slowly, that he didn't just eat like a dog. But he seemed to have trouble swallowing.

"Been so long since I ate," he said when he was halfway through the eggs, "my stomach hurts. But they're good. They just go down hard." He glanced out the window frequently, toward the driveway, and she could see when it registered in his eyes. He tried to conceal it, but the next time he looked at her he was shy, like a child with a secret.

As she lit another cigarette she looked out at the snow where the drive was—the banks were over six feet high, and there was at least two feet of new snow in the drive. "My plowman came night before last," she said, "but it's been coming down so fast he can't get up the hill now. It's been like this all winter."

"Last year, after we set the record for snow," he said, pushing away his empty plate, "we all thought this year couldn't be so bad."

"It's worse," she said. "We're ahead of last year. At this pace they say we might get three hundred inches."

One corner of his lips tucked in, creating a dimple. "My friend Bing was right. Said all people do outside is talk about the weather." He picked up the pack of cigarettes on the table and tapped one out. "You can't get out of here and the police can't get in. How you going to get me back?"

"That's what you want, right?"

"I stay out there any longer, I'm dead." He touched the cut beneath his eye a moment. "I know what you're saying. Guys inside tell you about other escapees, how they walk away, then give themselves up because of the woods and the weather. I didn't believe them."

"You're from downstate."

"No, I'm a Yooper. From North Eicher."

"Oh sure."

"That's why I thought I could walk out. I know the winters up here. But I just couldn't get out of the woods. And the snow, it just kept falling."

She went to the sink, soaked a washcloth, and gave it to him. "You better clean that cut."

He daubed at his face, wincing and only smearing dirt. "It's fine."

"Right." She came around the table and took the washcloth from him. "Hold still." She put one hand on the back of his head and cleaned the cut. He stared up at her and didn't move, though when she touched the wound she could feel the muscles in his neck tighten as he tried to pull his head back against her hand. "How'd you do this?"

"Saw some coyotes on a ridge. Maybe they were wolves? Hard to tell from a distance through the trees. Then I tripped over a downed tree under the snow."

When she was finished she looked at the wound a moment before letting go of his skull. His clothes smelled bad, and his hair was wet and dirty. "Where'd you think you were going?" she said as she went back to the sink to rinse out the washcloth.

"Don't know. Into Marquette and steal a car, I guess. Got lost instead."

"I guess you did." She turned and leaned against the sink, drying her hands on a towel. He smoked and gazed out at the snow. "You been in long?"

"Three years, three months, eleven days."

"Why?"

"Bunch of stuff."

"Like what?"

"Like assault. Shot a guy, too." He drew on his cigarette, then crushed it out on his plate. "Guess I had a bad day. I used to do a lot of stuff, you know? Get really fucked up. My brother, Warren, he has connections down in Milwaukee, and he kinda has a business going over our way. I just lost it."

"What happened?"

"Well. I had a girlfriend, my fiancée. Say I beat her."

"Did you?"

"Sort of." He touched the cleaned wound with his fingertips. "I don't remember everything too clear."

"Who'd you shoot?"

"There was a hunter named Raymond Yates."

"This Raymond Yates, he and your girlfriend were up to something?"

He shook his head. "Wasn't that simple. No, she was up to something all right, but it wasn't with Yates. He's older. Noel—that's my girlfriend—she was up to something with my brother, Warren."

"That's why you lost it."

"Guess so."

"How long you in for?"

"Ten. But I coulda got out after seven, maybe."

"You couldn't wait another few years?"

"Guess not. Now, when I go back, I don't know what I'll get." He turned his head from the window. "What happened to you?"

"Car accident. My husband and daughter were killed."

"I'm sorry."

"Are you?"

"Yes, I am."

She went to the phone on the wall and picked up the receiver. There was no dial tone. She hung up.

He was watching her. "Dead?"

"I'll try again in a while."

He leaned back in the chair and the chain rattled. "So you live way out here alone?"

"Harold and I built this house together, when we were your age. It was about all I had afterwards."

His eyes wandered toward the door to the living room. "There's a smell—it's not the smoke, but something else." A puddle of melted snow had formed around his boots.

She picked up the rifle and put the padlock key on the table. "Come in here and take those wet things off."

He unlocked himself and put the key next to the plate; then he coiled the chain up, gathered it against his stomach, and led her into the living room, which opened onto a large studio with skylights. He looked at the shelves of clay sculpture and pottery, the wheel, the work-benches, the kiln. "You can smell it way out there in the woods." He bent over and began unlacing his boots. "What if that phone doesn't come back?"

"We can always walk to the store down at the crossroads."

"How far is it?"

"A ways."

"Walk?"

"You ever wear snowshoes?"

"Not in a long time."

"We could ski out, if you'd rather."

"The snowshoes'll be fine."

She stepped into the bedroom to get him some wool socks. When she looked up at the bureau mirror she saw that he was asleep on the couch, cradling the chains on his stomach.

When he awoke he lay beneath a wool blanket. His feet stuck out the other end; she had put wool socks on him while he slept, and his toes were slightly numb but warm. "I thought I'd never feel my feet again."

She was sitting across the living room, the rifle resting against the arm of the stuffed chair. "You stayed out there much longer and you wouldn't have."

"I tried not to think about the cold, but it's all you think about. Same as being inside, really."

"What do you think about, inside?"

He gazed at the ceiling a long time, then he smiled. "I know what most of the guys would say."

"I do, too."

He turned his head on the armrest of the couch. She had put on a green sweater that made her breasts seem full. He couldn't take his eyes off them. When he raised his eyes to her face, she watched him with an even stare. He realized she was accustomed to men looking at her that way, that it was something she had endured for a long time. It appeared to bore her.

"Bing, he read a lot and he told me stuff. He had a theory: If you think about how some people have it worse, you won't find your situation so bad."

"Not a bad theory," she said. "What's he read?"

"All sorts of stuff. Lot of history. Tells me about battles and conquerors. For a while we were into tortures. Bing found a whole book just on torture techniques. The Inquisition, Ivan the Terrible, Vlad the Impaler."

"Wasn't he the one Dracula's based on?"

"That's right," he said, staring at the ceiling again. "As a boy he had been a hostage of some sultan in Constantinople, and he was butt-fucked a lot. So later, when he's this fierce military leader he scares the hell out of his opponents because he impales his captors. He used a long, thin needle—greases it, then shoves it up their ass until it comes out their mouth. Did it in a way that it would take days to die. He'd do thousands of people at a time and stick them in the ground outside his camp to ward off the enemy. Like a forest—thousands on a skewer."

He turned his head on the armrest. She was staring very hard at him, and her cheeks were flushed. "And Bing thought it took your mind off prison?"

"Yeah, but it only works for a while. You actually have to concentrate on that sort of thing, and it gets old. Out there in the woods, it didn't work after a while. I tried to think of everything, believe me, but I was just too cold."

"So much for theories."

He couldn't tell by her voice whether she was making a joke or being serious. Her eyes were just as steady as when she'd first opened the shed door.

"When you came outside with the rifle and pointed it at me, what would you have done if I had, you know, tried something?"

"What would you have tried?"

"Take the gun away."

Turning her head, she seemed to be searching for something in her studio. "I'm not sure. Suppose you had gotten the gun from me, what would you do?"

"Unload it."

She continued to stare at her shelves of pots and clay animals—eagles and deer and bears, mostly—so long that he began to wonder if she'd heard him. "Well, you didn't, and I didn't, and it stays loaded." She looked at him. "Don't lose sight of that fact."

"I'm not dangerous or anything."

"Not now you aren't."

They didn't talk for a while. He stared at the ceiling. What he had thought were shadows he realized was smoke residue from the kiln. The wall and ceiling surfaces all had faint smudges built up around the slightest raised edge, whether it was a small imperfection in the wall, along the edge of molding, or around a light switch plate. It gave flat surfaces relief as though someone had taken a pencil and shaded everything carefully, first using the side of the lead point, then smearing the gray with a moist fingertip. On the wall by the door to the bedroom there was a small rectangle of white where a photograph had hung. His eyesight was good, and he could even see the small black hole where the nail had been driven into the wall. It was like her life here: a white rectangle surrounded by not so white, two shades so close that you don't notice the difference right away.

"You try the phone again?" he asked.

"Twice while you were asleep," she said. "Still out."

"What're we going to do?"

"You feel like you could walk out there again?" she asked. "This time properly dressed and with snowshoes."

"I'm not in any hurry to get back."

"I suppose you're not."

"It's nice here. Warm. I see why you stayed after—I see why you live here."

"We have to go soon if we're to get out before dark."

She gave him some of Harold's clothes: long johns, corduroy pants, a second pair of socks, a flannel shirt, a heavy sweater, good insulated boots, gloves, parka, a wool hat that could be pulled down over the ears. She let him use the bathroom to change, telling him that the window had been stuck for years.

When they were both dressed they went out to the shed and buckled on the snowshoes. Then they started down the drive, which was a wide, snowbound path through the woods. He led and she followed with the rifle. He walked slowly, with his head down, concentrating on each step.

"I'd forgotten about how you kind of waddle," he said over his shoulder. It was hard to hear him because the wind was at their backs. "I feel like a baby in diapers." There was some joy in his voice, something she imagined he seldom expressed now.

"You're doing fine," she said.

"How far is 'a ways'?"

"We should get to the store at the crossroads before dark, if we take a shortcut over that hill."

He looked to his left. "It's steep."

"It's that or walk five miles around it."

His snowshoes were old, the varnished wood frame worn and splintered and the mesh broken and mended in several places with dirty white shoelaces. The snowshoes allowed him to sink down in the powder a good half foot; then he could feel the snow compress and support him. It was hard work, deliberately lifting his leg up and out of the snow with each step, and soon his groin muscles ached. By the time they were at the bottom of the drive, he had broken a sweat beneath the layers of her dead husband's warm clothes.

The road hadn't been plowed, either, and they walked down the middle of it, toward the hill. They were now heading east, and the wind and snow struck them from the left. She kept to his right and a full stride behind, carrying the rifle across her chest. The wind was so steady that the snow was horizontal.

"You mind if I ask your name?" he asked.

"Liesl."

"Mine's Norman. How long ago was your accident?"

"Five years ago this April. It was during a spring blizzard."

"What did Harold do?"

"Lot of things. Carpentered. Drove heavy equipment. Hunted and fished for much of our food. There's a freezer locker in the shed that used to be stocked with venison, smoked whitefish, and coho salmon all winter."

"You're one of those live-off-the-land people. He hunted and you did your pottery."

"Something wrong with that, Norman?"

"No. Where I come from a lot of people live like that, except they don't bother with the pottery. What grade was your daughter in?"

"Wasn't in a grade." He turned his head until he could see Liesl. The left side of her coat and hood were covered with snow. Her eyebrows were white, and her face was red from the cold. They made her eyes an even brighter blue. "We home-schooled Gretchen. She was seven."

Liesl stared back at him, and he couldn't keep his eyes on her. Finally, he lowered his head against the wind and watched his snowshoes.

They walked down the road about half a mile, then began to climb the hill. Liesl explained that in order to get up the hill they would have to zigzag, ascending very slowly. It was rough going. The woods were dense, and they often had to push through branches. At times it was so steep that they had to grab hold of a tree and pull themselves up to the next step. Liesl had slung her rifle over her shoulder so she could use both arms. Norman continued to lead, and occasionally he would set himself, holding a branch, then reach back and lend her a hand as she stepped up.

Once he lost his balance, and for a moment he had the gut-hollowing sensation that he was going to fall backward and sail off the side of the hill. But he managed to fall forward awkwardly, and his arms went into the snow all the way up to his shoulders. "It's deep," he said, laughing.

Liesl had to help him to his feet. "See, you can't run away," she said. "And I wouldn't recommend trying to fly."

It took over an hour to reach the crest of the hill. Liesl said they should rest. She had brought some chocolate and they sat on a granite outcropping, eating. They could see down through the trees to the next smaller hill. Norman kept scanning the valley.

"Where's the road?" he asked finally. "I don't see a clearing down there."

"It's on the other side of that hill."

"You didn't mention a second hill."

"Didn't I?"

"So, it's going to be like that?" he said, nodding.

"Like what?"

"All my life it seems people tell me half of what they know. I believe 'em—then suddenly they tell me there's another hill." Norman took a bite of chocolate. "What kind is this?"

"Semisweet. It's one of my favorite things to eat."

"We don't get this in prison."

"I used to eat a great deal, particularly in winter. Harold and I were both large people. My jaw was fractured in the accident, and my mouth was wired shut for a long time. I couldn't eat solid food, and I lost nearly sixty pounds. I don't eat like I used to, but in cold weather like this I love semisweet chocolate." She turned her head so she could see around the edge of her hood with one eye. He had the blue wool cap pulled taut over his skull so his ears were completely covered. He raised a gloved hand and tugged his cap farther down his forehead, so it came over his eyebrows. There was something about his eyes that was alert, even startled. She got out her cigarettes, and after several attempts they both got one lit. "Norman, what do you mean you 'sort of' beat your girlfriend?"

"I don't know what I did for certain," he said. "I was really fucked up. Told you, my brother, Warren, deals a little, so I always had access. No question I was thoroughly whacked out. Noel and I were engaged, but then I found her—you know."

"With your brother."

"Yeah. Warren. A few weeks before the wedding, we were all out at this old lodge her father owns. He takes hunting and fishing parties out there—mostly businessmen from Detroit and Chicago—and we all worked for him. We drove 'em in and out of there, cooked, kept the fire going, kept the assholes happy. When the season was over Warren, Noel, and I stayed on a few days and partied. I found them in the woods, going at it in a storage shed. Warren and I never got along so good. He's a couple years older, and here he was doing my girlfriend and I—I did what they say I did, I guess. I knocked her around, and then Warren and I really got into it. I really don't remember too clear. I went off into the woods and that's when I shot this hunting guide Raymond Yates—and, like I said, I had a bad day."

"He die?"

"No."

"I suppose it was self-defense."

"It wasn't like they said."

"How was it?"

"Yates was hunting me. When Noel's father came back to the lodge and found what I did to her, he sent Yates out after me. But—" Norman hesitated a long moment, and Liesl wasn't sure if he was going to continue. "Strange thing," he said finally, "is that before my trial began Yates disappeared. He never testified at my trial, and if he did, I don't think things would have gone so bad. Yates was okay, really, a true hunter, and I was just beginning to learn to guide from him. So Noel's father, he got their lawyer to make a big deal about how if I hadn't been let out on bail until the trial, Yates would still be around."

"What happened to Yates?"

"Told you, he disappeared."

"Never came back? Never was found?"

"Nope. They kept suggesting at the trial that I had something to do with that. Couldn't pin it on me, but it was enough to convince the judge to nail me good." Norman adjusted the cap around his ears. "I should've left Noel alone. If I was going to get sent away, I should've just gone after my brother, period."

"Where are they now?"

"Oh, they got married and were living like I never existed, but I hear that they've split up now. Guess they thought that getting married would make it all right what they did to me, but it didn't work out that way."

"If you had managed to escape, I mean, to really get out of the woods, what would you do?"

"I don't know. I didn't really have a plan. I mean, my escaping was something that I just did, right then. I'm what they call a trustee. It's the level fives, the crazies, that they keep really locked up. Nobody has contact with them except the guards. A bunch of us trustees were unloading supplies in the kitchen, then we were told that one of the trucks got stuck in the snow on the road out to 41, so we went out to dig and push the thing out. The snow became an absolute whiteout, and I suddenly realized I could just walk into the woods and no one would notice right off. So I did."

"You're not answering my questions. Where would you go?"

"Home, maybe. But if I was smart, I'd go away and try to be someone else."

"That, Norman, is impossible to do."

"Then I'd try to be who I was before any of this happened." Snowflakes had built up on his eyebrows and lashes. She thought it was a beautiful image on his hard, lean face. "Why couldn't I do that?" he asked.

"I don't know, that seems pretty hard, too. Maybe it's just impossible, to go back like you say. I know it's what we all want." Liesl stood up and slung the rifle over her shoulder. "Ready? Going downhill in snowshoes is tougher than climbing."

Norman led the way down through the trees. The strain on the legs was worse, and it was harder to keep balance. He often felt as though he would pitch forward and roll down the hill. He never took a step without having at least one hand on a tree trunk or branch.

They came to a trail in the snow, deep narrow tracks, frequent patches of urine, and small pellets. When they rounded a knob on the side of the hill they saw half a dozen deer standing in the snow. They were scrawny, their coats ruffled by the wind. All the deer started to move off, except one, a smaller deer, which simply stood still, with its head turned toward Norman and Liesl.

She stepped past him. "Winters like this a lot of them starve. It takes a long time to do that, and they're so cold eventually they can't move. I see them around my house. They just stand there."

She walked toward the deer and stopped when she was perhaps ten yards away. The deer only watched her approach. Liesl took aim with the rifle and shot the deer in the chest. It fell over, its blood seeping into the snow.

Norman walked up to the deer. Though its eyes were open, it was dead. Small dark pellets issued from its anus into the snow.

"I used to watch the weak ones die." She came up and stood next to him. "But finally, a couple of years ago, I went out and shot one. Now I do it when I'm sure they're not going to make it."

"There was a photograph on the wall by your bedroom door. It's gone now." She looked at him, surprised, then curious. "It was of your husband and daughter?"

"No, it was a photograph Harold took of the Château Frontenac."

"What's that?"

"It's a huge old hotel in Quebec City, on a cliff overlooking the St. Lawrence. We went there on our honeymoon, then we went back with Gretchen when she was five. It's odd, photographs of Harold and Gretchen aren't so bad. I have several in the bedroom. I like looking at them. I do for long periods of time. But photos of places we'd been, especially Quebec, they're much harder. Maybe it's because they were places we visited and liked, and they're still there, in the world, so to speak. Places I'll never go to again. Something like that."

"The only thing I know about Quebec is that they speak French and the Nordiques moved to Colorado and became the Avalanche. And Noel's father's ancestors came from there. Her name's Pronovost."

They left the deer and continued down the hill, zigzagging slowly through the woods.

"Everything is in French," she said from above and behind him. "And the architecture is—well, I've never been to France, but it *feels* like being there. Very old buildings, many with these tall steep roofs covered with copper, which over the years has turned a bright green called verdigris."

"I've seen that," he said.

"And even if you don't speak French, you quickly pick up enough to manage in shops, restaurants, and cafés. Some Americans complain that Quebecois pretend not to understand them. But we never encountered that. We always found them friendly. I think that when they first look at you they make a distinction—something about body language or maybe our eyes—and determine if you're American or English Canadian. If you're American and you don't walk in expecting them to speak your language, they treat you fine. And the food! All you'd do is eat, then walk, then eat, then walk some more. *Moules et frites*—mussels and French fries, that was our favorite lunch. And when you're not eating or walking, you make love in a room with a view of the river—with French music on the radio."

Norman stopped and looked over his shoulder. Half of her mouth formed a smile, while the lax side hardly moved.

"Perhaps your friend Bing's wrong," she said. "Rather than thinking of tortures to forget the cold, you should think of things like good food and a long afternoon of fucking." She laughed. "Don't look so shocked, Norman, and let's get down this hill before dark."

They reached the bottom of the hill, crossed a narrow valley, and climbed the smaller hill. It was not nearly as steep, and they made good time. It was late afternoon when they descended, and below through the trees they could see County Road 644. They didn't talk once they were in sight of the road, and Liesl began to worry about ending this. When Norman had first approached her outside the shed, she would have shot him if he'd tried anything. Now she wasn't sure she could. She wondered if he knew that.

As they neared the bottom of the hill, there were frequent rock ledges jutting through the snow. They were walking along the edge of one when Norman felt Liesl suddenly clutch at his arm, but she couldn't hold on, and she fell off the ledge. It was only about six feet into snow, but she lay still and looked up at him with an expression he didn't understand. He walked around the corner of the ledge, then made his way down to her. She hadn't moved. Lying in the snow, she looked as though she'd been dancing, then suddenly froze in midstep.

"It's my back," she said. "I've had problems with it ever since the accident."

"Can you get up?"

Slowly she raised an arm toward him. "Pull."

He positioned himself over her, took her arm, and helped her up out of the snow. Her body leaned against him, and he held her as she breathed heavily.

"I don't know," she said, her voice shaking. "I don't think I can walk."

"It's not far to the road. I'll carry you. Let me get your shoes off."

As he crouched down, she kept both hands on his shoulders to keep herself upright. He removed his gloves and unbuckled her snowshoes—the leather straps were caked with ice, which he had to break off with his fingers. It took a long time to get her boots free of the harnesses, and his fingers were frozen. Finally he got his gloves back on, then put his arms around the backs of her legs.

"Are you sure about this?" She eased herself down as he stood up, so that she hung over his shoulder.

"I'm glad you lost those sixty pounds," he said.

"The rifle," she said. "It's way down in the snow."

"Fuck the rifle," Norman said. "Bambi'll have to starve."

He began walking. Her weight compressed the right side of his body, causing pain down through his hip and knee. It was less than fifty yards to the high snowbank on the side of the road, but he had to stop after each step and get his balance. Once he put her down so he could shift her to the opposite shoulder. When they were almost to the snowbank he lost his balance and fell forward. When he landed on top of her, she let out a cry.

"I'm sorry," he said. His face was against hers, and they both lay still, exhausted. Finally he raised his head and looked at her. "I can't carry you any farther."

Her eyes were watery and she whispered, "Go get help." She kept one hand on his shoulder for a moment, then dropped her arm in the snow.

He couldn't get to his feet—there was nothing to push off of because his arms sank into the snow. He took off his snowshoes, crawled the rest of the way to the snowbank, and rolled over the other side into the road. Standing, he could barely see the store down at the crossroads. There was a truck, an eighteen-wheeler, parked by the gas pumps, its taillights two beacons in the snow. He began walking, which now felt strange without the snowshoes.

After a while Liesl closed her eyes against the incessant flakes. Cold seeped into her back and shoulders. Her arms and legs were outstretched as though she were floating on her back, and she tried to imagine a lake with the blue sky of a hot summer's afternoon above her. But it wouldn't hold, and she opened her eyes again to the snow. The cold had worked its way up into her rib cage, causing her to shiver. She closed her eyes again and saw bearded men in robes and fur hats. They spoke a foreign language and watched her with interest. She smelled grease. When the sharp thin needle stabbed into her anus, she remembered Gretchen's birth. But instead of descending, the pain ascended, moving slowly up through her bowels, her stomach, her lungs, her esophagus, the back of her throat, then finally, as she opened her mouth, the warm steel slid along the end of her nose, its bloody tip stopping right before her eyes.

CHAPTER Two

The space heater beneath Sheriff Del Maki's desk was going full blast. It rattled and vibrated and seemed on the verge of burning the hair off his shins. His back, chilled by the draft coming from the window, felt about fifty degrees cooler. This had been his dilemma every winter since he'd turned forty—he was rarely able to get every part of his body warm. There was always some place—his hands, his feet, that spot between the shoulder blades—where the chill resided no matter how many layers of clothes he wore, no matter how close he sat to the source of heat. He had hockey knees, and the cold ache where cartilage used to be was as persistent as a toothache. There was paperwork he could do, but he had given up on it.

When the phone rang, his deputy didn't answer on the first two rings—either he was dozing on the sofa out in the front office or he'd stepped out the back door to suck on one of those cheap cigarillos—but on the third ring the hardwood floor creaked as he went to his desk and picked up the receiver.

"Yellow Dog Township Police, Deputy Price speaking," he said. "Hold on, Tooley, I think the sheriff's on line two, but let me check." Louder, he said, "Can you pick up on line one?"

There was no line two—a township with a year-round population of less than eight hundred didn't need more than one—but Del and Monty maintained the illusion of line two for the benefit of the public. It also allowed them to dodge calls from people who felt it was their civic duty to nag the local constabulary. "Find out what he wants."

Del swiveled around in his chair so that the space heater could do his back for a while. He found that about eight minutes on a side worked best. His ankles had already begun to cool.

"Easy, *easy*, Tooley—what're you all exercised about?" Monty said into his phone. "A woman? What woman? In the *snow?*" Del reached behind him and picked up the phone. "Oh, he's off line two now," Monty said joyously, and he hung up. The front office floor creaked and the bathroom door closed. With this weather he might be cracking the window in there and lighting up his cigarillo.

"Tooley, what's going on?"

"We got a-a sit-situation here, D-Del." He sounded more worked up than usual.

"Take your time. What kind of a situation?"

From the bathroom Monty grunted, "Situation? *I'm* in a *sit*uation."

"Somebody drive off without paying for the gas?"

"N-no."

"You haven't been robbed again?"

"N-no."

"Good, because we're not chasing anybody in this stuff."

"N-no. D-Del? Just c-come out, 'kay?"

The snow was horizontal, with the wind out of the north off Lake Superior. Del could see only the white roof of his Land Cruiser parked beyond the snowbank. A plow came down Trowbridge Street, sending a low vibration through the old brick municipal building.

"*Oh!* The earth is *moving!*" Monty shouted from the bathroom.

"Tooley, you just hold on," Del said. "I'll be right out." He hung up, switched off the space heater, and went into the front office. "Monty," he said, standing in front of the bathroom door. He couldn't smell tobacco. "I'm going to take a run out to Stop and Go. You answer the phone, hear?"

"All these sailing magazines with glossy pictures of tropical islands and palm trees," Monty said. "I never thought it was too healthy keeping 'em in the bathroom, but they got this picture here on page eighty-six—Del, she's got a yellow bikini on and she's lying back in a boat deck, all slicked up with tanning butter, and you can see her—"

"Monty."

The bathroom door opened and Monty stepped out, still putting himself together. "Someday I swear I'm going to live in a place where I'll *never* need long johns," he muttered as he buckled his belt. "I mean someplace where they don't have them on sale eight months out of the year at Shopko. Someplace where if you mentioned your long johns, they'd think you were referring to your tall uncles, one from each side of the family."

"Monty."

"Yeah?" He looked up at Del.

"Stick by the phone."

"Sure thing, Delbert."

It had been a problem in school: Delbert. The first week of school every year the teacher would call roll, and being one of the Ms, Delbert Maki's name would come somewhere in the middle of the list. When the teacher got down to the Ls, Delbert would sense the tension developing around him—a little stiffness in the postures of the other boys, a descent into a more complete silence as his classmates waited for his name to be called. After Delbert would say, "Present," there'd be the faintest snickers. Or maybe a cough. He'd turn—it always seemed to be boys seated behind him—and find the source. One year it was Tommy Lebeau and his pal Nick Thornton, a team. Another year it was a fat kid named Jimmy Nugent. It was always kids with names like Tommy, Nick, or Jimmy. Eventually there'd be a fight, usually outside during recess; once, with Nugent, it was in the basement during lunch. Delbert didn't always win—boyhood fights rarely ended in clean decisions—but afterward he was left alone for the rest of the year.

Then there was the song "Runaway," by Del Shannon. A number one hit in 1961. He was a rocker, he was from downstate Michigan—all the kids thought it was the coolest song, and one morning in the schoolyard a kid had an autographed photo of Del Shannon, and looking at those three letters, *D-e-l,* Delbert saw something else. The kid holding the photo whispered, "Look at this guy. Look at that hair! Del's so cool." So from then on he insisted that his classmates and teachers call him Del. For years "Delbert" seemed to have vanished; even in the official class rosters he was "Del Maki." Only his Marquette High School diploma stated his full name, "Delbert Esa Maki."

At Tooley's Stop & Go Del parked next to a county snowplow, which was still running, its yellow lights rotating on the roof. The truth was he went into law enforcement because as a boy he had always wanted to drive vehicles with flashing, rotating lights. There were no cars at the gas pumps. An orange ambulance from Marquette General Hospital was angled so that its back was just outside the door to the station. Inside Del found Tooley and the plow driver, Viekko Rupp, watching as two paramedics worked on a woman lying on a gurney.

"S-she's still alive," Tooley said as his fingers pulled nervously on his gray beard. "But v-very cold."

Viekko probably weighed over two-hundred-fifty pounds, and with so many layers of clothes on under his brown snowsuit, he might have been mistaken for a bear in this snow. But here inside, under the fluorescent lights, he had the soft, pale face of a boy, startled blue eyes, and a slack mouth that revealed teeth that were already going bad. The earflaps on his hat stuck straight out sideways, like stubby airplane wings. "Found her up the road a couple hundred yards," Viekko said. "She was in the snow, on the other side of the bank, eh?"

The woman wasn't a snowmobiler; they always wore jazzy snowsuits and helmets as if they were riding motorcycles through the great white. She had on brown corduroy pants, with the wale worn thin at the knees, heavy gray socks pulled up over her calves, and an old soiled blue parka. Del looked at her feet, expecting to see cross-country ski boots, but she wasn't wearing them. "What was she doing out there?"

"Snowshoes," Viekko said. "They're back where I found her, ya know."

Del nodded. He knew the female paramedic, Mona Lottke, who had been working at Marquette General for several years. "Mona, how long she been out in this thing?"

Mona, who was not thirty and wore her brown hair in a ponytail, shook her head. "Two, maybe three hours."

"She going to make it?"

"The real concern is cardiac arrhythmia," Mona said. "She seems a healthy woman. All we got to do is get her warmed up—and get through this stuff back to Marquette."

Del glanced out the plate glass windows at the snow. "Looks pretty chancy at the moment."

"She was just lying there, eh?" Viekko said. "About twenty yards in behind the snowbank. Nobody else would've seen her but me, up high in the plow cab. The banks out there are a good eight feet now."

"If she was out there several hours," Del asked, "wasn't she covered with snow?"

"Just about, eh?" Viekko said. "When I made my pass down the other side, something caught my eye, but I thought it was just downed branches sticking up out of the snow. I came down here to the crossroads, made my turn, and started up the other bank. Then I see it's the rounded tip of a snowshoe, ya know. So I climb over the bank and pull her out. Stuff's so deep I could hardly get out myself. I went back to the truck, got some rope, waded in again—it's really more a crawl in the snow, eh?—then I manage to drag her out. I called the dispatch, and by the time Tooley and I got her in here, the ambulance had arrived."

"The snowshoes are still back there in the snow?"

"Not quite two football fields, maybe," Viekko said.

The paramedics raised up the legs of the gurney under the woman. She was perhaps in her mid-forties, large boned; her mouth was crooked, and Del suddenly thought he recognized her, but he wasn't sure. He removed his gloves. First he took the long blond braid that hung off the side of the gurney and draped it over her shoulder so that it lay on her right breast. He put his hands in the cold pockets of her parka.

"She's l-local. That artist no one ever sees much. I see her in here sometimes. Buys g-gas. Lives up in the hills s-somewheres."

Del removed the key chain, which felt like ice, and from the other pocket he found a wallet. A man's wallet; worn leather. He opened it and read the Michigan driver's license: "Liesl Tiomenen." There were a few credit cards, a business card for her sculpture, pottery, and ceramics, and twelve dollars in cash.

"Any injuries?" he asked.

"Nothing we can see," Mona said.

"She just collapses in the snow two hundred yards from the crossroads," Del said.

"Her f-face," Tooley said. "What about that?"

The other paramedic, a man in his late thirties with a trimmed black beard, said, "Naw, it's old. From something else. I'd say she had some broken bones in there, and the jaw, the cheek, and the muscles never quite returned to their original shape."

"It was from a car accident," Del said. He remembered his search for the green truck, the months he'd tried to track down a vehicle that she'd said had caused the accident. He never found it. He had been deputy sheriff then. "I haven't seen her in years."

"When?" Mona asked.

"Five years ago, maybe," Del said. "Happened during one of those spring blizzards. She swore there was a green truck coming the other way that caused her husband to lose control. Looks so different now, I didn't recognize her at first. Lost a lot of weight." He stepped back from the gurney. "All right, Viekko, you lead the ambulance back into Marquette."

Viekko held the door open as the paramedics began pushing the gurney. Del watched the woman's face, the blue white of her skin. Her eyelids were large, with long blond lashes. It was hard to believe she was the same woman whose husband and daughter had been killed in that accident. He was trying to think of a painting by Andrew Wyeth he'd seen once, long ago, in a magazine, or in one of those large coffee table books. Wyeth had painted a woman, a woman with Scandinavian features, painted her many times. There was one painting that this Liesl Tiomenen reminded him of—a woman sitting at a table in an old farmhouse, wearing a heavy turtleneck sweater, her head turned aside. There was in this woman's face the same sense of quiet, of patience, of looking to the side of things. But there was something else—a sense of endurance, and perhaps resignation. He wished he could see her with her eyes open. They must be large, under those lids. Her license said they were blue.

Del sat in his Land Cruiser while the paramedics secured the gurney and Liesl Tiomenen in the ambulance, then the truck led them out onto County Road 644. Viekko went slowly, the blade of his plow throwing new snow up on the bank along the side of the road. It was accumulating at least six inches per hour; if the plows didn't keep working, this road—perhaps all the roads in Marquette County—would be shut down soon. About two hundred yards from the Stop & Go, Viekko's arm came out of his cab window and his gloved hand pointed toward the snowbank on the right.

Del pulled over and watched the plow and the ambulance lights disappear in the snow. He put on his flashing lights and climbed out. The wind came down the road, straight out of the north. The snowbank was at least eight feet high, but it was angled so that he could get enough purchase to climb up and kneel on the crest. From there he could see Viekko's tracks leading up to where he had found Liesl Tiomenen. There was the tip of a snowshoe, but no sign of what might have caused her to collapse at that point. The tree line was a good fifty yards back, and the hill rose steeply from there. He could see the trail she had left as she had come down from the hill; the depressions were now softened, filled in by new snow.

He kept a small pair of binoculars in one of the pockets of his coat, and he took them out. Through them he looked more closely at the tracks, following them from the depression where she'd collapsed back to the tree line at the base of the hill. Then Del lowered the binoculars and carefully got to his feet on top of the snowbank. After putting the binoculars to his eyes again, he refocused and looked toward the trees. It was nearly dark beneath the evergreens, but it looked as though she might have fallen a second time in there.

He went back down to the Land Cruiser and got his snowshoes out of the back. They were wood shoes that he'd bought at a garage sale years ago. The lacings were still good. He kept them in his Land Cruiser six, seven months out of the year, and during the summer he hung them on the coat rack by the front door. Just in case.

He climbed back to the crest of the snowbank, put on the snowshoes, and began walking across the snow. He walked wide of the first depression where Viekko had found the woman and continued on into the woods. There had definitely been another fall there. Del followed the tracks up the base of the hill and found a third depression below a granite ledge. It was different from the other two depressions—deeper. He stared up at the top of the ledge, maybe seven or eight feet high. The snow there had been broken, too—here in the woods the impressions were sharper because less new snow had fallen. If she had fallen off this ledge, which was what it looked like, he wondered why there were also tracks that came down around the left side of the ledge.

Del began to climb the hill off to the right of the ledge, pulling himself up by grabbing on to tree branches. Climbing stairs bothered his right knee and hip, and this was much worse. He did most of the work with his left side. It was slow, difficult going. This had not been a recreational walk in the snow for Liesl Tiomenen. No one would choose to take this route just for the hell of it. He was sweating by the time he reached the top of the ledge, and he paused to catch his breath. It was nearly dark here in the woods, and he took his flashlight out of his coat pocket. Looking farther uphill, he could see that the tracks descending to the ledge were much wider, and at times they appeared to diverge. It looked as though there had been two snowshoers coming down the hill, and here one of them, Liesl evidently, must have fallen off the ledge. Or been pushed. Del shone the light on the depression below the ledge. It was difficult to tell how she had landed, though if it were face first, there might be deep holes where her arms went into the snow in an attempt to break the fall. Then he saw the outline of an arch just beneath the snow a few yards from the depression.

Del climbed back down off the ledge. He reached down and pulled a pair of snowshoes out of the powder. They must have been Liesl's. He studied the depression again and the single set of tracks that led out of the woods. Deep tracks, because someone was carrying her after she fell. Someone who had carried her out beyond the tree line to where Viekko had found her. Someone who had left her there, about twenty yards from the road. What Viekko hadn't noticed were the tracks leading away from where Liesl lay in the snow. He was too intent on the woman, getting her out, and he must have waded through those tracks. The other person—a man strong enough to carry a woman of her size on his shoulder—took off his snowshoes where he left Liesl and then somehow made it out to the road. If that was so, why did he bother to carry her out from the woods at all?

Del went back to his Land Cruiser. Once he was inside, his face stung from the wind. He picked up the microphone on the Roadmaster unit that was perched between the bucket seats and called Monty at the station.

"I'm on line two," Monty said. "Please hold."

"Knock it off." Del could hear the television on in the background. "Any calls?"

"Nope. Just the usual cancellations. Schools, clubs, meetings, high school sports. Days like this I don't know why they don't just make one announcement at six A.M.: 'Today has been canceled in the Upper Peninsula.' "

"There was that thing from the prison the other day," Del said. "A walkaway. They haven't found him?"

"Haven't heard anything. Anybody who walks away from there in this stuff won't be found till the snow melts. Won't be a pretty sight, particularly if animals get to him first."

"Call over there and get a full description."

"Really? Think you got him?"

"No. I just want to know who he is."

"What's going on out there?"

"A woman in the snow."

"Dead?"

"No. Just real cold."

"Car wreck?"

"Snowshoer, found under the snow."

"Know what does those people in?" Monty asked. "*Boredom.* They get out in all that snowy natural beauty and they get *real blissful.* Then, Del, they just get bored. I swear it's more dangerous than drunk snowmobiling."

"Monty, call me back when you get something on the walkaway."

The coffee at Stop & Go was lousy. When he was out on the road, Del seldom stopped there for coffee. He preferred the Four Corners Cafe at the next crossroad, nine miles south, or Louise's Dinette, in the village, where he often ate meals. But Tooley had brewed this pot fresh, knowing that Del would be coming back, so if nothing else, it was hot.

"You have much business this afternoon, Tooley?"

"N-no, not in this stuff. Truckers, mostly. Some gas-ups."

"See anything odd?"

He shook his head. "Like w-what?"

"I don't know."

Tooley opened up his cash register and studied the roll. "Gas, mostly g-gas. Some food, c-canned goods 'cause people don't want to get stuck driving into Marquette."

"Anybody on foot?"

"On foot?" Tooley shook his head. He closed the cash register, then said, "W-wait, there was a hitchhiker."

"In this stuff? When?"

Tooley had worked for years out at the Tilden mine, until he was hit in the head by a falling beam. The injury had caused him to stammer; he went on disability, and he and his wife bought the Stop & Go. "Young fella," he said. "Got a lift in a rig."

"He come inside?"

Tooley shook his head. "Just caught a glimpse of h-him, climbing in the passenger d-door of the cab."

"What else do you remember?"

"Nothing."

"Come on, Tooley, what else?"

"Nothing. 'Cept the rig was an eighteen-wheeler. Took a right here at the crossroads."

"West."

"Yeah, that one w-went west."

On County Road 810 Del didn't get out of second gear, but his four-wheel drive kept him moving down the middle of the snowbound road. He called in to Monty at the station.

"Well?"

"The walkaway's name is Norman Haas, H-a-a-s. Twenty-five. In for you name it. Aggravated assault, battery, and if that wasn't enough, he shot someone. Nobody's seen him in two days. I'll bet he's buried under three feet of new snow."

"Or he's in a rig heading west," Del said. "Are the roads still open that way?"

"So far only the stretch of 28 between Marquette and Munising is closed. That sucker always goes first, being right along the lake; I don't know why they don't just shut it down in winter. Want me to call the state police? If it's Haas, he could be headed for Sault Ste. Marie and they could pick him up when he crosses the border. But the Soo's east. Did you say he was headed west?"

"In this weather maybe he couldn't be choosy about the ride. Who'd he beat up?"

"His fiancée," Monty said.

"Who'd he shoot?"

"Doesn't say. The other guy, probably."

"Where?"

"North Eicher. Didn't their hockey team win the state championship once?"

"Thirty years ago," Del said. "When I was in high school, they were the team to beat." Like many towns in the Upper Peninsula, North Eicher started as a logging camp with a railroad running through it. When logging became mechanized—when it no longer employed hundreds of men in each camp—the town nearly disappeared. Chances were there weren't more than a thousand residents now. Yellow Dog Township was smaller, but it was a handful of miles outside Marquette, the biggest town in the U.P. North Eicher wasn't near anything. "I think I remember reading about this Norman Haas and his fiancée," Del said. "It wasn't long before their wedding, and I don't think it was the other guy. Shot some other guy, who disappeared before the trial." Del began to hang up the mike, then punched the button again. "Go ahead and call the state police. But they won't do anything in this weather."

"I betcha they're sitting in their warm offices, playing with their radios, too!"

"Bet you're right."

"You comin' in? Bring something big and round to eat, with pepperoni on it."

"I'll see what's still open. If anything, this stuff's getting heavier."

CHAPTER Three

The trucker's name was Eldon Waters, and he wouldn't shut up. Norman figured it must get lonely in this cab day in, day out. Everything was a question with Eldon, as if he knew deep down that nobody really listened.

"I live in Michigamme—been there?"

"No, just passing through."

"But know where I spend most of my time when I'm off the road?"

Norman said nothing, and when Eldon looked over at him he shook his head. "I got a camp up in the Huron Mountains. You never saw better country. Lots of moose and bear, and more deer than you can believe. But know what the best part is?"

Norman gazed out the side window at the snow. The rig was doing about thirty-five, and he could feel the trailer sliding back there, tugging on the cab.

"Guess?"

"Haven't a clue, Eldon."

"You like a sauna?"

"You mean the thing you sit in and sweat?" He turned and studied Eldon. Queers in the joint said strange things, to get your attention. Eldon must have weighed close to three hundred pounds, and Norman couldn't imagine him sitting naked on a bench in some hot little room.

"Yeah, that heat! It comes from wetting down these very hot rocks, you know? And you sweat it all out of your pores, and you feel great after, eh?"

"What're you asking me about a *sauna* for?" Eldon turned his large head toward Norman, his small dark eyes confused. His whole body shook as the cab bucked over a frost heave under the snow-packed road. "You a cocksucker, Eldon?"

"Hey, *what*—"

"You're such a fat shit, you couldn't get your hands on a woman if you tried? Christ, she'd never find your prick in all that."

"Jesus H, didn't I give you a lift in this storm? What you doin' talkin' that way?"

"Boys, Eldon. You like boys?"

"Boys, my ass. I'm gonna stop and throw you out right here and let you walk twenty miles to the next town."

"Yeah, that's it, isn't it?" Norman said. "You like boys that are lean, got some muscle on 'em. Hard little dicks to suck on in your sweatbox camp."

As Eldon began to let up on the gas, his right arm came off the steering wheel and reached across the cab toward Norman. "Instead, how 'bout I shove my dick up your—"

The cab lurched to the right as the rig began to jackknife. Eldon got both hands back on the steering wheel, but the cab was sliding diagonally toward the snowbank on the other side of the road. The rig bucked, causing the cab to lift off the ground, then it hit the snowbank, and Norman raised his arms. First he hit the windshield, then the trailer slammed into the rear corner of the cab on the driver's side, causing sparks to fly out from under the dashboard.

Norman wasn't sure how much time had passed. There was the smell of burned rubber. His left forearm hurt, and his face was wet. He opened his eyes and touched his forehead with his right hand. He expected to see blood on his fingers, but it was only sweat. There was nothing but snow outside the windows, and somewhere from the engine came a hissing sound.

Eldon was slumped over the wheel. The windshield in front of him was cracked, all the streaks fanning out from the point where his forehead must have hit the glass. There was a lot of blood—on the side of his face, dripping from his nose, pooling around his boots. He didn't move, except for the faint, rhythmic swelling of his huge, arching back. Laying his head against the door window, Norman looked out at the snow, then closed his eyes again.

It was the sound of an engine that brought him up and out of it, and he opened his eyes. A brown van had pulled over by the snowbank on the other side of the road. The snow was so heavy, Norman couldn't tell whether it was a man or a woman who got out. Turning his head carefully, he saw that Eldon hadn't moved, but he was still breathing.

It was a man walking back toward the truck, a bearded man wearing a down vest and a Packers cap. Behind him, the van's engine was idling and white exhaust drifted out of the tailpipe. He kept his hands in the pockets of his jeans, and he seemed to favor one leg. He reached up, opened Norman's door, and shouted against the wind, *"You all right?"*

Norman nodded. "I'm not sure about him, though."

The man was in his mid-forties, and he had a full dark beard. As he raised himself up on the cab step, Norman realized what it was about his walk: he had something wrong with one leg—either he couldn't bend his knee much or he was wearing a prosthesis. "He doesn't look good at all," he said.

"I can't get him out," Norman said. "He's too big."

"His door'll never open, the way it's caved in. Here, let me help you out—think you can stand?"

"I don't know."

Leaning into the cab, the man took hold of Norman's shoulder, then helped him to turn until his legs were outside the door. His breath was sweet, and there was the slightest click in his mouth. Norman recognized the smell of Certs.

He helped Norman ease down to the snowy road. "That's right," he said, "keep a hand on the door. Now let me see how he's doing." He took hold of the back of his left knee, lifted it until the leg bent enough for him to plant his foot on the floor of the cab; then, using his arms and his good leg, he swung his body up and onto the seat. He leaned over and placed a hand on the back of Eldon's neck. "He's breathing." He took the microphone off the CB radio and switched on the unit, but after adjusting a few knobs, he shook his head. "That *smell*—the wiring's fried. We got to get him out—this thing, it might catch fire and *blow!* He's got to come out this side, but, God, he's *big!*" The man leaned over and tried to lift Eldon's arms off the steering wheel. But he was having difficulty, so he rolled down Eldon's window. "Go around to his door, maybe you can push, and I'll pull, and we can get him out of here."

"Sure." Norman walked around to the front of the truck and stopped. He stood still, his back to the snow and wind, staring down at his boots. It was like the moment, two days earlier, when he had been on the access road outside the prison. Something told him he should just walk, walk, and not look back, and in that moment he didn't know if he could do it, and then suddenly he was walking. It was as though he were watching himself, disappearing into the snow. He had been outside himself somehow. And he realized that at the time he was walking away from the prison, he kept saying to himself, *It doesn't matter, it doesn't matter, they could shoot me, but it doesn't matter, I just got to keep going, keep walking.* When he finally looked over his shoulder, he could no longer see the other prisoners. There was nothing around him but the snow and the woods.

Now, Norman raised his head and stared through the cracked windshield above the hood of the truck. The man had his arm around Eldon's shoulders. There was an earnest expression on his bearded face, as though getting Eldon out of the cab were a math problem, something abstract that had to be solved only because it was there, as a challenge. Eldon's face was covered with blood, and his lips were loose, making him look stupid. When Norman had first seen him coming out of the gas station, Eldon was eating a Mounds candy bar. Norman had been standing next to an eighteen-wheeler at the diesel pump, where he was protected from the wind. He figured he could go in the Stop & Go and just say to the guy behind the counter that he thought he saw something down the road—maybe an overturned snowmobile. Just enough so someone would go look for the woman, and then he'd get out of there fast. But Eldon smiled, a fleck of coconut and chocolate on a tooth, and said, "You look like a guy who could use a lift." He climbed up on his rig and opened the driver's door. There was something playful in his voice. He had probably offered a lot of young guys rides, asked them a ton of questions. "Better hurry," he said, " 'cause I'm outta here before this blizzard closes all the roads down."

"Which way you headed?" Norman asked.

"It matter to you?"

"It matters."

"West—Duluth."

Inside, you're not offered much of a choice. There was rarely that moment of hesitation before making a decision. Now, standing in front of the jackknifed rig, Norman felt it again, and he was keenly aware of the position of things. He could hear the van idling behind him. He could just walk to the van, get in, and drive off. With that bum leg, the bearded guy would never get down from the cab quick enough to stop him. It was just like the moment he'd walked away from prison: *You don't think about it, you just go.* You don't look back, and suddenly there's nothing around you but woods and snow. But Norman simply stood there in front of the cab. He couldn't make up his mind.

"Come on!" the bearded man yelled. "Give me a *hand.*"

"Yeah, sure." Norman started to climb the snowbank so he could get around to the driver's door.

But something sprung loose in the engine, and there was a hiss that grew louder. Norman slipped and rolled down the snowbank, and for a long moment he wasn't sure what had happened. His hearing was gone. His face was in cold snow, but there was intense heat pressing into his left side, and he realized that the engine had blown.

Raising his head finally, he looked up at the flames that now engulfed the cab. He could barely see the two men; they were motionless and appeared to be huddled together. The heat was incredible. He could see the bearded man's mouth open in a silent scream. Norman turned and crawled away in the snow. When he got to his feet he looked at the cab again, and now he couldn't see the two men at all through the fire. He kept backing away from the heat, his arm raised to protect his face. A tire blew, and immediately after that something in the engine began knocking until metal buckled under pressure.

Norman turned his back to the heat and walked toward the van. He opened the door and climbed in behind the steering wheel. It had been almost three years since he'd driven. As he pushed in the clutch and shifted into first gear, he realized there was a familiar smell in the warm van. The ashtray was full of rolls of Certs; he picked up one and began peeling back the paper. In the rearview mirror he could see the burning truck. The flames now rose high above the cab, and thick black smoke blew into the trees alongside the road. Norman put a Certs in his mouth. The taste reminded him of inside, where he'd sucked on Certs all day long. Wintergreen.

PART Two

CHAPTER Four

Noel Pronovost had taken two more pills, downers now, and was just dropping off to sleep when the phone rang. Because there was no longer a phone on her nightstand, she had to get up from bed and answer the wall phone in the kitchen. Afraid that the ringing would wake her daughter, Lorraine, from her nap, Noel walked quickly in her slippers, one hand touching the wall. Since she'd lost her hearing in her left ear, her balance had never been the same.

"Hello?" She could hear music in the background, the sound of men talking, a cash register. "Warren?"

"You in la-la land? Sound like you're half-asleep."

"I was *trying* to sleep, thank you."

"Three o'clock in the afternoon—"

"I was up half the night with Lorraine and I have to work tonight."

"I remember that drill."

"*Right.* Like you ever got out of bed to check on her." She waited a moment, but he couldn't be bothered to argue the point. "What do you want?"

"What do I want," he said. "What do I *want?*"

"Warren. Don't start." She sat at the kitchen table and turned her head so she could see her reflection in the toaster. Her face there was bulbous, one eye grossly larger than the other, like that cartoon character Bill the Cat. With her free hand she gathered her short blond hair and smoothed it down the side of her skull. When she lifted her hand away slowly, her hair raised up again, as if by magic. It was because it was so cold—she was afraid to touch anything for fear of getting a static shock.

"It's snowing like hell." He was barely whispering into the phone.

"You called to give me a weather report?"

He took in a long breath—a drag on his cigarette—and as he exhaled he laughed that tight, wheezy laugh that came out of him when he was half in the bag. "It's snowing so hard, it'll be to his advantage."

She stopped playing with her hair. "What?"

"Use your good ear. Remember which one still works?"

"Fuck you. Advantage? *Whose* advantage?"

"They won't find him in this shit. Probably won't even try."

"Find who?" But she knew now.

"That's right," Warren whispered.

"This is about Norman?"

"Isn't it always about Norman?"

She didn't say anything. Her large purse was on the kitchen table. Aged black leather; the gold plating had chipped off the buckle. For over a year she'd been telling herself she needed a new bag. She reached inside and took out the brown plastic vials, one slightly larger than the other.

"Isn't it, Noel? It's *all* about Norman." The clink of glass against his teeth, a pull on his beer.

She nestled the receiver between her ear and her shoulder so she could use both hands to get the safety cap off the smaller vial. She tapped out a white pill into her palm. She thought of them as her see-saw days: uppers followed by downers followed by uppers, until she could hardly remember what she'd taken last, and all that was achieved was this blanked-out neutrality where she was too tired to sleep, too wired to think straight. She put the pill down on the Formica counter and said, "Will you just tell me what's going on?"

"What's *been* going on, is the fucking question," he said. "I've seen the letters."

"What letters?"

"The ones he's written to you. The ones you keep in a shoebox in the closet."

"Fine. You've seen the letters. You ever hear of something called privacy?"

"No wonder you were so in love with the guy. Who writes love letters anymore? You could ask every guy here at the Blue Antler and not one of 'em would tell you they write love letters."

"Those guys have no one to write *to,*" she said. "Some of them probably don't even know *how* to write." She studied her bloated reflection in the toaster as she put the pill in her mouth and worked up enough saliva to swallow.

Warren was laughing. "Maybe, but inmates got all that time on their hands."

"I'm hanging up now, Warren. I'm hanging up and unplugging the phone here in the kitchen. There isn't a phone in the bedroom to unplug anymore 'cause you broke it against the wall. Remember?" He was laughing again. Now it was the laugh that said "Come on, dump more shit on me," the one she hated most. "Phones, cars, light bulbs—"

"Light bulbs? You still on that?"

"*Light bulbs,* Warren. You just won't admit to that light bulb thing, will you? You come in here while I'm out and remove *every fucking bulb* in the apartment."

For a moment she thought she was going to begin crying—something she had promised herself she would not let him see—or hear—again. The night she had come back to her apartment and found all the bulbs gone, it was after eleven o'clock. She found the flashlight she kept in the kitchen, its batteries barely working, and she called her father. He told her to just get out of there, but she couldn't—it was exactly what Warren wanted, to make her feel as though she couldn't even stay in her own apartment anymore. Her father then told her to stay put and he'd be right over with bulbs. She waited in the bathroom, sitting on the toilet seat, terrified. Fortunately, Lorraine slept through the whole thing in her arms.

Noel put her finger in her left ear and tapped gently. Nothing. For a long time there had been a dull ache on that side of her head, but now the ear was just useless. She used to love to listen to her CDs through headphones—the Cranberries, Smashing Pumpkins, and old songs by Billy Joel—but now music meant nothing to her; she played tapes in the car only for Lorraine, who liked to sing along with certain country and western songs. She closed her eyes, and the darkness was soothing. The speed was kicking in; a pleasant tension seemed to clutch at the backs of her eye sockets. "Listen, Warren, I have to be at the motel by six, and I need to give Lorraine a bath before I take her over to Daddy's." She started to pull the phone out of her hair.

"He walked away," Warren said. He sounded almost proud.

Out the kitchen window she could see the snow in the driveway behind her house. She lived on the second floor, above an elderly couple named Kapala; her father owned the house, and he covered her rent. He owned the house across the street, too, and the convenience store at the end of the block. What her father owned used to impress Warren, but she couldn't care less. "What do you mean, 'walked away'?"

"I mean Norman got out." Warren didn't say anything for a while. There was nothing coming over the line except the sound of a cash register drawer sliding closed. "Tommy Lovell called me and told me."

"Tommy Lovell?"

"State police."

"Oh, the fix-your-speeding-tickets guy."

"Tommy grew up on our street," Warren said. His voice had lost its humor now. "He keeps tabs on Norman for me, and he called to say he walked away in the middle of this blizzard."

"Where is he now?"

"The fuck should I know. Thought maybe you would."

She ignored this. "They'll find him?"

"Eventually. Though Tommy says this blizzard's so bad nothing's hardly moving anywhere in the U.P. The state police just keep indoors like everyone else and wait for it to pass."

Noel stood up. She could hear her breathing through the phone, and she knew Warren could, too. She held the receiver away from her mouth and took a long, deep breath.

"Just go about your business," he said.

She could hardly breathe. "That's exactly what I'm going to do."

"You believe it?" Warren whispered. "He fucking walked away in this shit."

"Hey!" Monty said when Del came into the office. "Marquette got top billing on the Weather Channel! We could get over four feet before this thing passes. And there's more coming in off the Pacific." He turned back to the television that sat on the file cabinet.

Del put the pizza box on Monty's desk, unzipped his coat, and sat on the sofa. The blue vinyl crackled beneath his weight. The splits in the material had been taped with gray duct tape, which after a while had split also. He shrugged out of his coat, which was heavy because of all the things he carried in the pockets. Outside pockets, inside pockets; some closed with zippers, some with Velcro. One leather pocket he had sewn in on the left side especially to hold his .38 Smith & Wesson automatic. Shoulder holsters were too binding. He had a system for his pockets so that he knew where everything was: wallet, keys, notebook, binoculars, Swiss Army knife, handcuffs, cellular phone. He didn't like anyone touching his coat. In old western movies cowboys often had a thing about anyone touching their hats—Del felt that way about his winter coat.

Monty opened the box and carefully removed a slice of pizza. "I like Lucinda," he said, nodding toward the television. "Something about her walk. But that Darlene, have you noticed what's happened to her since she had her baby? She lost that weight and now she's *all* woman." He took a bite out of his pizza slice. "But this new one—I don't know. Somebody oughta teach her how to dress. Looks like she's in the school marching band. Lotta reds with brass buttons, and those epaulets on her shoulders. Kinda got a military thing going there."

The pizza had smelled so good in the Land Cruiser that Del had eaten a slice as he drove back to the station. It went down fine, but when he belched now the pepperoni came back hot and a bit rancid. "You call the state police?"

Monty didn't look away from the set. "They faxed over a sheet on the walkaway."

Del went to Monty's desk. "That's it—Noel Pronovost," he said, looking at the fax. "That was that girl's name."

Monty was working on his second slice and didn't look away from the television. The map of the United States was on the screen. There were snowstorms in the Pacific Northwest, in the Rockies, over the northern Great Lakes, all along the New England coast. It was raining from Texas to Florida. Even central California was wet.

"I remember the other thing about this kid's trial," Del said. "It was in the papers—something about a missing witness. The guy he shot disappeared, and they wanted to pin that on him, too. But they couldn't, though they put him away pretty good." He watched the Weather Channel a moment. "Look, it's sunny and eighty degrees in San Diego." He dropped the fax on the desk. "San Diego has the most perfect harbor you'd ever want to see. It's huge. Most of the Pacific fleet's there. The whole harbor's protected from the open ocean by this long spit of land called Point Loma. Eighty degrees and it's January. You could keep your sailboat in the water year-round."

Monty turned from the television, chewing pizza. He seemed about to say something, but after taking a look at Del, he just turned and faced the set again.

Norman kept checking the rearview mirror. No one was behind him, and no other vehicle came out of the snow from the other direction. The van was a Dodge, about six or seven years old. There was an overcoat next to him on the passenger seat, and after fishing through the pockets, he found the guy's wallet. It contained forty-three dollars, a couple of gas credit cards, and a license for Rodney Franklin Aaberg.

In good weather North Eicher was less than an hour's drive from where Eldon Waters's truck had jackknifed; but in near whiteout conditions Norman couldn't do much better than thirty miles per hour. Snowplows hadn't been down this way in hours, and there was close to a foot of new snow covering the hard-packed ice. The two-lane county road was bordered by dense woods, which occasionally gave way to a pasture or a clearing with a small house, set back off the road.

Norman frequently took one hand off the steering wheel. Each time his fingers shook and he couldn't keep them still. For long periods of time he just concentrated on driving, on keeping the van centered between the high snowbanks, but at times he suddenly felt a euphoria, even a silliness, seep into his thoughts. He'd been inside so long, and now he was going home. In such a blizzard this could be almost anywhere in the Upper Peninsula, which stretched from the northern Wisconsin border to the Canadian border at Sault Ste. Marie. Lake Michigan, the Mackinac Straits, and Lake Huron lay to the south, Lake Superior to the north. Forest, lakes, rivers, streams bore Ojibwa names, French names, or simply names of a tree or wild animal. Several centuries ago, through some political deal with Ohio concerning Toledo, the U.P. became part of Michigan, and it's still the most sparsely settled region in the continental United States. Yoopers like it that way. A fair number of them believe that they ought to secede from

Michigan and claim statehood: Superior. Just being out here on the land again caused Norman's adrenaline to surge. He was going home.

This time Liesl opened her eyes when the voices drifted near her bed, as hands touched her wrist, forearms, and face. Two men stared down at her. One wore a white smock, the other a bulky winter coat.

"Liesl, this is Sheriff Del Maki."

"How you feeling, Liesl?" He had blue-gray eyes that looked right into hers. "You took a fall from that ledge in the snow, and now you're in Marquette General. You remember anything about that, the fall? Why you were out there on snowshoes?"

She looked away from his stare, at the doctor, who was writing on a chart. "We're going to get you out of here soon," he said. "Your limbs respond, which is good. No serious spinal damage, apparently. You'll probably experience some discomfort and be stiff and sore for a day or two. But the sooner you get up and about, the better."

She closed her eyes. "You never found it, the green truck."

After a moment, Sheriff Maki said, "No, I never found it."

"For a long time that really bothered me," she said. "But right now it doesn't seem so important." The song came to her, but she couldn't remember all the words. Instead she tried to hum the melody. Then she remembered part of it, and she sang, " 'A run-run-run-run-runaway.' "

"You got it," Del said.

The doctor, who wasn't thirty-five, didn't get it. He was too young. More and more of them were all the time.

When Lorraine woke from her nap, Noel bathed and dressed her; then she drove to her father's house. The girl was almost three, and she sat in her car seat, singing along with the tape. She could carry a tune already, and she knew all the words. She liked Faith Hill; she liked Garth

Brooks; but lately she only wanted to sing "Crazy" with Patsy Cline, so they played the song four times in a row. Noel sang along, too, and several times she had to touch her daughter—brushing blond hair off her cheeks, pulling her red wool cap down over her pink ears. The sense of movement helped. Before leaving the apartment, Noel had taken another pill from the vial of whites, and she felt as though she could sing and drive through the snow forever.

After her mother died, her father had built an addition onto the farmhouse for his taxidermy business. He had done it himself; Rejean Pronovost did most everything himself. He had a Ford 150 pickup, a backhoe, two snowplows, and every conceivable hand and power tool ever invented. He owned houses and buildings in North Eicher; he owned property, much of it undeveloped timberland and lakefront acreage, throughout northern Michigan and Ontario. Her mother used to say he was the most self-sufficient man in the Upper Peninsula, which was one of the last havens for self-sufficient men. His self-sufficiency was what had first drawn her to him, and Noel was convinced that it was what killed her of a heart attack at forty-three.

He was in the workshop, sitting at the wood bench, scraping down the skin of a pheasant. He wasn't a tall man, but he was still muscular and barrel-chested. His hands were slick with animal fat. He didn't look up when she came in but put down his knife and began to brush on the Lutan F solution. Overhead, dozens of complete and incomplete bird and fish trophies hung from the ceiling beams, and the walls were covered with mounted deer, elk, moose, and bear. There were chandeliers made of antlers, fox pelts, and raccoon hats. Oak boards listed prices for birds, turkeys, fish, game heads. Lake trout was $7 an inch; king salmon $9. Mounted antelope was $250; bobcat $200; bear $300; half bear $425; three-quarter bear $475. Russian boar was $300; Russian boar with armor $350. Open mouth on all mounts was an additional $50.

Once she was out of her coat and boots, Lorraine ran to her grandfather and he wiped off his hands as she climbed onto his lap. He talked like Donald Duck, which always made the child laugh. It was one of the few joyful things Noel remembered from her childhood, Daddy talking like Donald Duck.

"I should get right back into town," Noel said, her voice echoing up into that dreadful ceiling hung with dead animals. "The roads are really bad."

His nose was crooked from a hockey game he'd played in high school. One side of his trimmed white mustache lifted as he said, "I guess so. Carol called and said she'd be late."

"Carol. Do I know Carol? No, not Carol, Doug Harbaugh's ex-wife?"

"She's bookkeeping part-time for me."

"She have any ex*per*ience?"

"She does the books." He put a long pheasant's feather in Lorraine's hair.

"With what, those boobs?" When he looked up, Noel said, "Daddy, you never let anybody count your money. Who could? It would be easier to count the trees in the woods."

"Attend to your own business, Noel."

"Funny, how you've never wanted to teach me the business."

"I helped you mount that owl when you were, what, fourteen. You didn't like it."

"Carol get to mount an owl?"

"You've never seemed interested." He raised his eyes to the ceiling. "In this."

"Right, and now I just get to clerk nights at the motel."

"It's more complicated than that."

"Is it? Daddy, you're so close to being totally *self-sufficient.* There's just this one little *need* that requires Carol Harbaugh's assistance."

"*You're* talking to me about needs?"

"Daddy, I don't care who you mount, but it confuses Lorraine."

For a moment he looked as though he were going to throw the child aside, get up off the stool, and rush the length of the bench at her. But he didn't, and something quickly changed in his face as he spoke Donald Duck to Lorraine, whose hands were playing with his mustache.

"Fine," Noel whispered, pulling on her gloves. Getting past her father was the toughest part of most days. The little feints and dodges for Lorraine's benefit. Usually Noel was buzzed on something, and her father was drinking bourbon by late afternoon. But he was good with the child, and since Noel had split up with Warren there was no one else to take care of Lorraine during the nights she worked at the motel. "I hope Carol can cook, at least. Better than that Jamie, anyway."

Her father continued to talk Donald Duck, ignoring her. "Carol cooks just fine," he quacked.

"I'll bet that's probably why Doug Harbaugh married her in the first place."

"Next time I see Doug, I'll ask him."

She could tell that he hadn't heard about Norman. There was that, at least. If he had, he'd be telling her that it was all her fault. Norman. Warren. Even Lorraine was her fault, a mistake. "Okay, sweetheart," she said. Lorraine turned her head. "I'll be back for you in the morning. Come kiss Mommy good night."

Warren had been talking about the Red Wings with a salesman from downstate who had bought a round, but now the guy was gone and the Blue Antler was empty except for the two waitresses, who were at the end of the bar going on about their kids. Something happened to women after they had babies. Since she'd had Lorraine, Noel had become a first-rate bitch. When Warren returned from the navy, his brother was going out with this nice piece, Rejean Pronovost's daughter, Noel, and Warren saw it right away. Even after she and Norman were engaged, it was still there. Sometimes Warren would look at her and her eyes would hold his a moment too long. And he noticed that she looked at other guys that way as well. Norman never seemed to notice, which was no surprise because Norman had always missed a lot of things Warren instinctively picked up on—Norman was just somewhere else. Their mother always referred to him as the methodical one, but Warren thought that just meant his brother got lost in the details and missed the obvious.

With Noel it was more than obvious. Particularly the night they had gone to a place called the Depot. They were having Mexican night, burritos, enchiladas, refried beans, rice, salsa, margaritas—fare intended to make you forget you were in the U.P. on a cold winter's night. Norman didn't like Mexican food—thought it was always the same. So while Warren and Noel ate, Norman drank tequila and beer. Later they shot pool, and about midnight Warren went looking for Norman and found him asleep in the back hall, outside the men's room. He and Noel got Norman back to her apartment and into bed. When Warren started to say good night, Noel got a couple of beers from the kitchen and turned on the television. *Raiders of the Lost Ark* was on, and Noel loved Indiana Jones. So they sat on the sofa, drinking beer, smoking Warren's last joint, and watching the movie. That's how it started—how she started it. It really had to do with that movie. She knew every scene, and during the last part, where all the Nazis get fried and melted by the thing in the ark, she was leaning against Warren. She didn't have to say anything; it was all in the way she pressed against his arm and leg. He worked his hand up under her sweater, found a nipple, and she kind of sank down on the sofa, sort of went all loose. As soon as the movie was over, they were pulling each other's clothes off, very quietly. After that night they couldn't help it—they kept finding ways to get to each other. Noel was the one who really wanted it, which was why Warren didn't understand what happened to her after the baby. It changed her, that was all.

The next time Liesl awoke it was because of pain. There was a young nurse in the room. She left and came back with the officer whose name was Del something. He'd taken off his coat; he wasn't wearing a uniform, just a plaid flannel shirt, with the sleeves rolled up to expose the thermal shirt that stopped halfway down his forearms. He must have weighed close to two hundred pounds. His hair was short, going gray on the sides, brushed straight back from the high forehead. His face seemed accustomed to dealing with people in pain, in trouble, or both; his expression was sincere, concerned, yet there remained some professional detachment.

"I just called over to my station out in Yellow Dog," he said. "You were with a young guy, mid-twenties, dark hair." He waited, and when she didn't speak he went on. "Marquette Prison faxed us a mug shot." He unfolded a sheet of paper and held it up close to her face. "That's who you were in the woods with, a walkaway?"

Liesl was surprised to find that she couldn't talk. The pain was worse than before; it seemed distant, but approaching. Or perhaps it was rising, like a tide. It was concentrated in her lower back but ran up her spine to her neck. Her intravenous solution had a timed drip for pain relief, but it was too soon, and when she pressed the button nothing happened. She opened her mouth, but she couldn't speak.

Del leaned down to her, and she closed her eyes and opened them.

"That's a yes? A young guy, mid-twenties, dark hair?"

She blinked again, slowly.

"Thought so," he said, folding up the sheet of paper. "He must have come to your house? You live alone up on in the hills above the crossroads? You must have been snowed in, so the two of you walked down to the Stop and Go. I don't understand what you were doing, but that seems to be where you were both headed. Do you remember your fall?"

He waited, but she was becoming rigid with pain and couldn't even blink. The doctor had called it *discomfort;* it was one of their favorite words. She kept thinking about the button pinned to her bedsheet and how long it would be before she could get another hit.

"I know this is hard," he said. "If he pushed you off the ledge, why would he then carry you almost out to the road? Maybe you just fell?

And he thought he'd help, then he got tired—and then he realized that he just had to get away and not worry about you? I don't know."

Del rubbed his cheek with one hand. He hadn't shaved in a day or so, and his whiskers crackled. For some reason Liesl thought it a pleasant sound, and she tried to concentrate on it. He was asking good questions now. She wanted to talk to this man about Norman. She wanted him to understand Norman—he wasn't just a mug shot. But the pain was overwhelming, and with great effort she turned her head toward the monitor beside her bed. The small yellow light went off and she pushed the button. Closing her eyes, she felt herself falling away.

Now, the sensation of falling was slow, pleasant.

Dark and warm.

Not white. Not cold.

CHAPTER Five

As Noel drove to the Deer Run Motel, heavy snow fell through her headlight beams. She thought of it as driving at warp speed. The snowflakes—planets, meteorites, and asteroids—streamed toward her Isuzu Trooper, then rose up along the windshield and hurtled back into the darkness, their moment of illumination fleeting and hypnotic. They seemed to possess the infinity of the galaxies.

She hated driving to work in the dark, knowing that she was going to spend another night stuck in the motel office—she thought of it as her own version of doing time. She used to blame Norman. For leaving. For being sent away to do time. But it was her fault, too—she knew that—because neither of them saw what Warren and her father were really about. She had been working at Getz's Auto Supply for several months, answering phones, keying inventory into the computer. She'd gotten the job on her own, and it was the kind of work that made her want to go to college so she could get a degree and a decent job—a job somewhere outside the U.P. Every day the parts delivery drivers came into the office and always had a line for her. Always something about her tits, about her ass, about what they could do for her. It had been that way since she'd been in high school, boys and men making references to her body. And those who didn't say anything simply stared, averting their eyes just as she looked at them. It was usually harmless, and throughout her teens there were always boys willing to do anything for her. Girls usually hated her.

Norman was a couple years older, and she vaguely remembered him from high school. He was quiet, so there wasn't much to remember. He didn't seem to take notice of her at work, not like the other delivery drivers, which was why she found him interesting at first. He'd come into the office, lean on the counter, and when she'd hand him some paperwork she'd wait. Some joke. Some look. Something that would give away that he noticed what the other guys noticed. There was nothing, and finally she asked him if he was married.

He seemed baffled by the question. "No. Do I look married?"

"You sound like it's a disease, something that might leave you, I don't know, *disfigured.*" She laughed as she laid the paperwork on the counter—triplicate: yellow for the customer, pink for the driver, white for the office. "I just thought you might be married. Don't know why."

He said nothing, just picked up the white and yellow copies and went to the door.

"Pink," she said. "Yours is pink."

And he came back to the counter and handed her the white copy. She'd never seen him smile before. She didn't trust guys who smiled all the time. Or worse, grinned. But he smiled at his own stupidity, and she laughed again.

At first Norman was unlike any other boy she'd ever dated. He didn't talk about himself all the time. He didn't want just to have sex. He was polite. He talked about going to school downstate. Within six months they had decided to get married and go to school together, at Central, Western, or maybe Michigan State.

Then Getz's Auto Supply went out of business. Noel found part-time work at Ron's IGA, and Norman began doing jobs for her father. He plowed the driveways and parking lots of her father's rentals. He did yardwork; repaired windows, doors, sinks, bathtubs. He hung

Sheetrock. He painted apartments when they were vacant. Daddy seemed to like him—as much as Daddy liked anyone. In the fall, he took Norman north to Big Pine, his turn-of-the-century hunting lodge overlooking Lake Superior. Hunting parties consisting mostly of business executives flew in on private planes from Detroit, Chicago, and the Twin Cities. Daddy and several locals acted as guides; Norman was all around gofer. They were gone for weeks at a time. Occasionally Noel would drive up and help out with the cooking and cleaning. Norman seemed increasingly uncomfortable about the hunting parties at Big Pine. Noel thought it had to do with his working for his fiancée's father. She liked that about him.

When his older brother, Warren, returned from San Diego, where he'd been in the navy, everything changed. Warren talked about himself all the time, which meant he usually talked about sex, and he wasn't polite. He had some kind of hold on Norman, some big brother thing; Noel saw it the first weekend Warren was back in North Eicher. They partied day and night. She thought that it might last a few days, but it went on and on, and soon she was talking to Norman about how manipulative his brother was, how she'd never seen Norman like this. They were like Warren's entourage; he couldn't go out at night without bringing them along, buying rounds, providing the weed, and, increasingly, offering pills or a vial of cocaine.

She thought of Norman and Warren as a variation on the same theme. Warren was a few years older, maybe a couple of inches taller. His hair was a lighter brown, straighter than Norman's. Both were lean and hard muscled. Norman's limbs were more compact; his forearm muscles shifted beneath his skin, raising beveled edges effortlessly. Warren's face was longer than Norman's, the proportions spread out and somehow less coherent. You looked at his eyes. You looked at his mouth. One thing at a time. With Norman you took in the whole at once and saw the eyebrows raised in relation to the mouth. The first night she slept with him she had cupped his face in her hands, feeling the ridges and hollows, the bones beneath the taut skin.

That winter Warren became an issue. That's how she thought of him at first—an issue that was coming between her and Norman. It was as though Warren were watching her all the time, waiting for her to do something. The three of them would be driving somewhere, or in a bar or restaurant. Finally—it was in the Green Flannel Tavern, when they were doing shots and beers during a Red Wings game—she stared back at him, hoping her expression was asking, "What the fuck do you think you're doing?" Perhaps she thought that he might just back down. But Warren simply grinned, and his eyes had something in them that Norman's didn't possess. Something dead-on, something that didn't flinch. So they stared at each other in the dim light of the bar as though it were some kind of a duel; Noel eventually gave up and went to the rest room.

She stayed there a long time, staring at the mirror, trying to see what men saw in her face. It was a wide face, with a good jaw and a mouth that she knew was too big. Her eyes were green beneath the strong arc of dark eyebrows. There was something in those eyes that seemed to be asking for it, and that's what they saw. *Fuck me.* Leaning closer to the mirror, she tried to make it go away. But she knew that your eyes never really changed; you could laugh, smile, pout, whatever, but if you just looked at the eyes, there wasn't really much that changed.

Noel went back out to the bar, to a new round of beer and schnapps. The Haas brothers always bought a new round when the Wings scored. She did her shot, drank some beer, and they watched and talked about the game for the rest of the second period. She didn't look at Warren, and the longer that she held off, the more she felt the need to, because she was certain he was waiting. It distracted her, sitting between the two brothers, her fiancé on her left, his older brother on her right, all of them with elbows on the bar, leaning forward watching the Wings-Canadiens game. Nothing more should be going on, no one should be waiting for anything more important than another Wings goal. What distressed her was that she was certain Warren thought he knew what it was they were waiting for.

Of course, Norman didn't know any of this was going on. He had a sense of clarity and purpose that she had never seen in a man before, and it made him oblivious to things. She never really understood this about him until his brother returned from the navy; then she came to realize that she hadn't known Norman at all because she hadn't known his brother. Occasionally Warren would say something that suggested that Norman's view of things was simple; it both aggravated and intrigued Warren. He seemed even jealous at times. He understood that this was a quality Norman had that might be attractive to a woman and that he didn't have it.

When the second period ended, Norman went to the men's room. Noel kept her eyes on the bar. The colors from the television reflected off the wet rings her shot glass left on the wood. She kept waiting for Warren to say something, something about the Wings, something to break the silence.

Finally he said, "We're going up to Big Pine Monday."

"We?"

"Your father's got this hunting party flying up from Minneapolis in a seaplane."

"You and Norman?"

Warren nodded.

"You're working for Daddy now, too?"

Warren finished his shot and placed the glass on the bar. "Call it a partnership."

They didn't speak again until they could hear Norman's boots coming down the hardwood floor. "Let me know," Warren whispered as he raised the bottle of Labatt to his mouth. "You let me know when, Noel."

She didn't say anything.

It was at that moment that she began to blame Norman.

Even during a blizzard, Warren liked to cruise around in his Ford Ranger, listening to the radio or a tape, drinking from the pint of schnapps he kept in the glove compartment with his .38. He had an appointment at seven, a couple of kids he'd told to meet him in the public rest rooms behind the skating rink in Hiawatha Park.

Warren had to admit he was impressed: Norman had walked away. In a blizzard, no less. Chances were very good he'd die out there, freeze to death in the woods. Every spring, bodies were found once the snow finally melted. He could see the expression on Norman's face; even badly decomposed, there'd be that determination in the set of his mouth. Norman never really believed in failure, his failure. He couldn't accept it; he always figured there must be some other way, and he'd set out to find it.

A little after six, Warren pulled into the parking lot next to the skating rink, which was closed because of the blizzard. There was only one vehicle in the lot, an old Camaro with Bondo on the fenders, which belonged to a kid named Buck. Warren waited in his pickup a few minutes, finished his cigarette, and took a last slug of schnapps. Best thing for his stomach, though sometimes he cut it with Pepto. The navy really should have put him on disability for what they'd done to his stomach.

After a few minutes he was satisfied that it was all clear. He put the .38 in the right pocket of his long leather coat, got out, and walked through the snow to the small brick building that housed the rest rooms. He stopped a minute outside the men's room door. He could hear them talking inside, their voices echoing off the tiles. "Buck," he said.

"Hey, Warren!"

"Who you talking to, yourself?"

"Nah. It's just Pete."

"Just you and Pete?"

"Just me and Pete."

Warren pushed open the door and went inside. There was the smell of cold, wet concrete, and he could see his breath in the overhead fluorescent light, but at least it was out of the wind and snow.

"Hey, Warren," Buck said. A tall kid in a grimy parka, scraggly blond hair.

Pete was leaning against one of the sinks, smoking a joint. Pete had been a pretty good wrestler in high school—had the shoulders for it. Now he did roadwork for the county.

"Hi, girls," Warren said.

Buck came over to Warren. "Fuckin' snow, eh?"

Pete stayed where he was, finishing the joint.

"Yeah." Warren had both hands in his coat pockets. Buck kept smiling, trying to get friendly. "Let me see it," Warren said.

Buck hesitated, and Pete looked toward them for the first time. The bill on his worn Tigers cap was tightly curved; you had to work on a hat to get that look. After a moment Buck shifted his weight and dug a wad of bills from the front pocket of his jeans. "Here's the thing," he said. His voice seemed high, nervous. "We're a little shy."

"What do you mean, *shy?*"

"Yeah. Pete was supposed to get paid today, but fuckin' Mr. Townsend calls in sick."

"*So?*"

"So it means I get paid tomorrow," Pete said. "Nobody got paid today."

"I was nice and warm back there in my truck," Warren said. "You work for the county, right? That's like the government. You know they're supposed to pay people on time. You mean nobody in the county got paid because Mr. Townsend stayed home to bang his wife?" Pete just stared at him. "I mean, when I was in the navy we got paid on time. Didn't matter if the captain was on board ship or whether we were in port or out on maneuvers. It didn't fucking *mat*ter, it was the *gov*ernment and we got *paid.* So what is this shit with the *county?*"

"Sorry," Buck said. "Didn't know how to reach you, and Pete only picked me up a half hour ago."

"We got sixty." Pete took his weight off the sink and came over. "We'll owe you the twenty. I'll have it tomorrow, soon as I get paid."

"Tomorrow," Warren said.

Buck nodded and said, "We're not going to, like, skip out on you or nothing."

"Listen," Warren said very patiently, "I said it was eighty."

Buck stared down at the puddle of melted snow around his boots. Pete hadn't taken his eyes off Warren.

"Jeez," Buck said, "I'm sorry. We'll do this tomorrow, if that's what you want."

"What?" Warren said. "You want me to come back *here* tomorrow?"

"We'll have all eighty then," Buck said. Pete was still staring at Warren.

"Eighty is today's price," Warren said. Pete nearly smiled; he understood already. "Tomorrow—I don't know, it's probably going to be more like ninety. Maybe even a hundred. Who fucking *knows?*"

"Why?" Buck said, his voice real high now.

"Lots of reasons," Warren said. "I'll give you one: There's a blizzard coming across the U.P., and you know in weather like that supplies get scarce—bread, milk, newspapers—and nothing gets delivered, and pretty soon the store shelves are bare and you're sitting home lucky if you're eating Campbell's soup and Bumble Bee chunk light tuna fish." He took the vial out of his coat pocket, toyed with the white plastic cap a moment, then tucked it back out of sight. "Who fucking *knows* what this might be worth if we *really* get snowed in."

Pete nodded his head slowly. "Come on," he said to Buck. "He's just fucking with us. Forget it. Let's go."

Buck now seemed alarmed and confused. His eyes followed Pete as he walked toward the door. *"Wait,"* he said. "Will you wait a minute so we can work this out?"

Warren heard Pete's boots stop at the door. He turned, and no one said anything for a moment. Warren went over and leaned against the nearest sink. It wasn't anchored firmly to the cinder-block wall, so he moved over and rested his haunch on the next one.

"I don't fuckin' be*lieve* this," Pete said to Buck.

Suddenly it was as if Warren weren't there. They started shouting at each other, swearing, their voices echoing off the walls. This went on for several minutes. Twice Warren said, "Boys," quietly. Normal speaking voice. Real calm. But they kept at it, and it seemed about to get out of hand.

Warren said, "Boys," once more, and when they didn't stop he took the .38 out of his other coat pocket, aimed it at the raised toilet seat in the stall directly ahead of him, and fired. The water tank shattered and gallons of water spilled onto the concrete floor amid the shards of porcelain. When it was quiet again, when the echoing stopped, Buck and Pete were silent. Buck had taken several steps backward; Pete remained where he was by the door. Warren rested the gun against his right thigh.

"You two are as bad as my brother and me when we were little shits. I mean *really.* I was bigger and I'd always pin him down and tell him to give, and finally he'd say, 'Give,' and I'd get up and walk away because it was over, but then he'd jump on my back or something and start strangling me—because he never understood what it meant to be over. Done." He tucked the gun back in his pocket and started for the door.

Pete didn't move from in front of the door. Warren stopped and looked at the kid's broad chest.

"What're you doing?" Buck asked. "You're just going to leave?"

"I should have walked out of here five minutes ago. Now tell this guy to get the fuck out of the way."

"Pete," Buck said. "Come on, Pete."

Warren shifted his weight.

"Pete."

After a moment, Pete stepped aside. Warren opened the door and paused. "Don't ever pull this crap again," he said without raising his head. "And, Buck? Next time you come by yourself." He went outside, and as he walked to his car, he leaned to his right, into the snow and wind.

When Liesl awoke she had no idea how much time had passed. The pain wasn't so immediate; it was kept at a distance by the morphine. She lay perfectly still. Still body, still mind; this was, she knew, the necessary first step. Her recovery after the car accident had been slow and required such stillness. Once Harold and Gretchen were buried, she tried to maintain the stillness in her mind, even as she became more active physically. When she worked on her house, when she sculpted or shaped pots on the wheel. She learned to think through her hands as she worked with clay. The curve of the spinning clay changed subtly beneath her fingers, until she found the form that she saw in her mind. But it went further. She came to believe, after years of working, that there was a union between her mind and the clay, that each piece sought its own shape, and she was there only to witness the discovery. It was a form of predestination, and it was her job to help the clay find that form, using her mind, her eyes, her hands. That predestined form was what she believed people saw when they looked at her finished pieces, when they complimented her on them. Many times she'd watched someone, in a gallery or at a crafts show, examine her work. It was as though they were looking for something they'd lost, and they knew they'd recognize it as soon as they saw it again. Usually, when the person chose a piece to buy, they would often seem assured, saying, "This is it. This is the one."

But there were times when this stillness overwhelmed her. She would be frozen in time for only a few moments; then she would continue with what she'd been doing. And sometimes she would be incapacitated for days, even weeks. The first years after the accident the stillness came in long waves, and she learned to recognize the signs, to anticipate and even prepare for the peak of their cycle. And the better she became at anticipation, the better she became at controlling the stillness. She could not avoid it or fend it off, though sometimes she thought she could encourage it to go away sooner than it wanted. The trick was not to fight it, but to ease it on through. Let it pass. In recent years she had learned to live with the stillness, and as she did so, it seemed to visit her less.

Now it gripped her mind so that all she could do was continue to stare at the place where the linoleum floor disappeared under the radiator. There she could see the smallest straight line, perhaps an inch long, left by the knife that had been used to cut the linoleum in and around the foot of the radiator. And she just wanted to close her eyes; she just wanted to be horizontal so that all effort, all strain, all exertion, was removed from her body. For just one moment she wanted to be weightless. She wanted to float in darkness.

The sheriff was standing in the doorway. "How're you doing?"

She had no idea how long he'd been there. Somehow his expression suggested that her stillness had been revealed. It took her a moment to remember his name. "It's better, Del Maki. They want to send me home. Would you put me down a bit?"

He adjusted the bed so that she could no longer see the linoleum under the radiator. Handing her the sheet of paper again, he said, "I think you were a little preoccupied before to make a definite ID."

She looked at the mug shots of Norman Haas. "That's him."

"You're sure?"

"I'm sure." He didn't seem pleased. He didn't have any more questions, and she realized he wasn't telling her everything. "What?" she asked.

He pulled the one chair over next to the bed and sat down, leaning forward so that his arms rested on his knees. "There's a report of a jackknifed truck. We don't have many details yet. Only that the cab burned badly, and there were two men in it. They won't be identified without some labwork done, but I think he was one of them."

"Where?"

"Headed toward North Eicher. He was from there."

"I know," she said. "He said he might just go home." She tried to read what was written under Norman's mug shots, but the morphine made it difficult for her to follow the text. There were statistics—height, weight, eye color, race—but they seemed to have nothing to do with the man who had appeared outside her house in the blizzard. Closing her eyes, she said, "I wonder what we'd be like if the automobile hadn't been invented."

Some time passed; she wasn't sure how long. She kept her eyes closed as the tears streamed down her cheeks.

Opening her eyes, she saw that she had crumpled the piece of paper in her hands. "Confused," she whispered. "Not criminal. Norman seemed confused." She turned her head slowly on the pillow until she could see Del Maki's face. "He had a girlfriend. I don't know—I got the sense she meant a lot to him, that she still did." She wiped a tear from her cheek.

"This is something." Del Maki took a tissue from the box on the nightstand and handed it to her. "He left you for dead in the snow, and you're crying."

"But don't you see? He gave me Vlad the Impaler." Del tilted his head; it was clear he didn't know what she was talking about. "It was this 'theory' he had that he tried to use to get through prison. He gave it to me, and I tried to use it when I was lying out there in the snow. I tried to use it against the pain. It worked. He gave it to me and it worked."

She handed him the tissue. His hand was warm and dry, and something in his face revealed that he was embarrassed. "I don't know about any theory," he said. "But not everyone would feel this way about someone who left them for dead."

"You think it's odd?"

"Let's just say it's unusual."

It was slow at the Deer Run Motel, even for a weeknight in January. There was more weather coming, so hardly any traffic was moving through from the west. A trucker who checked in said Route 2 was closed between Iron Mountain and Duluth.

A little after eight, while Noel was checking in a couple from Manistique, Warren came into the office and sat in one of the lounge chairs so he could watch his reflection in the plate glass window. He often did this, ever since he'd moved out of their apartment. Usually he would just sit there, not saying a word to her. Once or twice, when he was really drunk, he'd nod off in the chair. When they'd first been married, he would sometimes come in with the baby; he was okay with Lorraine then, it seemed. But he was overbearing, and it frightened the child. Noel would give him a key and he'd take Lorraine down to a room, put her to bed, and watch television. Sometimes, in the early morning hours, he'd call the front desk and talk Noel into coming to the room, where they'd make love quietly to the flickering light of the TV with the mute on and the sound of the child's breathing rising from the other bed. They rarely touched each other in their apartment anymore, and soon she didn't let him near her at all.

Now, once the couple from Manistique had left the office, Warren continued to stare at the plate glass. She could smell peppermint schnapps. He had a cigarette in his mouth, but it wasn't lit.

"Eighty dollars," he said finally.

"What about eighty dollars?"

"They couldn't get it up."

"Warren, I don't know what you're talking about."

He didn't speak for a while. Once, several months ago, he'd come in after the bars had closed and he was angry. She'd had no idea what he was talking about; some argument he'd had in the Blue Antler. He was pacing around the office, shouting at times, so finally, when he refused to leave, she called her father. He left before Daddy arrived. She didn't see Warren for several weeks after that, and when he did come in again he acted as though nothing had happened. She told him not to come to the motel anymore; but he still did; she knew he would, and she knew she couldn't call Daddy every time. Since that one time, though, he'd usually just sit, maybe drink some of the complimentary coffee, which he spiked with schnapps. He often didn't say anything to her and after a while would leave.

"Where are you living now?" she asked.

"Where?" He thought it over. "I stay over at Bobby's house, usually. Now there's a guy with an understanding wife. When they split up she had the decency to leave Michigan so he still has a house." He raised his head so that she knew he was watching her reflection in the plate glass. "It worry you that Norman's out?"

She only stared back at his reflection in the glass.

"I'd be if I were you," he said. "Look what happened to Raymond Yates—disappeared and nobody's heard from him since."

"You think that's Norman's doing."

"Yes, I think it's Norman's doing. But I'm not so sure you're worried. Marquette's what, over an hour's drive from here? In decent weather. He's walking. And there's a blizzard." He took out his matches and lit his cigarette. "I think that you're pulling for him. Hoping that somehow he'll get out and stay out. Maybe come and find you. I read his letters."

"I don't want to talk about any letters."

"I guess the real question is, what did you say in *your* letters?"

"What letters?"

"You've sent him letters since he's been inside."

She didn't say anything.

"He still loves you." Warren got out of the lounge chair. He stood with his back to her for a moment and then came over to the counter.

"Unfucking real. You help put him away for *years*—and he *still* loves you. Not a lot of women can pull that off, you know?"

After a moment, she said, "We did."

"We did, what?"

"We put him away, Warren. When he found out about us, what did you think would happen? What did you think he'd do?"

"I don't have to think. I *know* what he did—he went com*plete*ly nuts."

"That's right, Warren. We knew it would happen eventually."

"Yeah, well, you seemed to like it there for a while."

"A very little while."

"You used to like a good fuck, Noel. Noisy, too."

"Let's just say I wasn't thinking then," she said. "We drove Norman to it."

"Oh, that's right. You and me. You and me and your father's lawyer. And Raymond Yates disappearing—let's not forget that, how that influenced things. We *all* put Norman away, but only *you* feel guilty. Guilty enough for the rest of us. But—" He raised both hands. "But I know, it's not that simple." He went to the office door and, before he let himself out, said, "I know what it's like when all you want to do is get out of something. Me out of the navy. You out of our marriage. Norman out of prison. Everybody wants to get out of something. Ever wonder why that *is*? All over America, the land of the *free,* and everybody just wants to get *out* of *some*thing. Yeah, *right.*" He pushed open the door, got in his car, and drove off, toward downtown.

Noel picked up her magazine and tried to finish an article about an ancient mastodon found frozen in the Arctic Circle. Scientists hoped to clone a new animal that would be a hybrid of musk ox and mastodon. She put the magazine down.

Sent. Warren had said *sent.*

She'd written Norman plenty of letters, but she'd never sent them.

Except one, and she wasn't sure if she'd ever sent it.

CHAPTER Six

It was almost ten when Norman reached North Eicher. The town appeared to be the same as ever. The snow was a veil, which kept the edges soft. Rooflines of houses. Small brick buildings downtown. St. Luke's steeple. Store signs: Ron's IGA, Hautamaki's Tru-Value Hardware, LeSerge's Game & Fishing. John's Pizza was now Joey's Pizzeria. Hair Apparent had been replaced by Bo Tangles. But Erma's Bingo Shop was still in business. The bars were all the same: JD's, the Blue Antler, Sally's Pub, the Green Flannel Tavern. All of them had neon signs in the front window advertising nonalcoholic beers because someone down in Lansing had introduced a law that prohibited neon signs that promoted alcoholic beverages. At the corner of Hemmila and Linden, Pierre's Pasty Shop was now Thai Princess. Before Norman went away, you couldn't even get an egg roll in North Eicher.

On the far side of town, the road approached the intersection of Linden and County Road 337, which locals called Laughing Pike Road because it went north through the woods for about forty miles and terminated at Laughing Pike Point on Lake Superior. It was the one road in and the one road back. At the intersection was Jacques' Diner and the Deer Run Motel. Norman pulled into the parking lot of Jacques', which was closed. He felt close now and he needed to be patient, careful. It was how he'd survived inside, keeping everything slow and to a minimum. You appear to be a threat, you'll be treated like a threat. He could never accept that he was where he was, and after about a year inside, the life he thought he should be leading here in North Eicher became a distortion. Occasionally he would talk to his friend Gary on the phone. Gary had moved down to Escanaba for a job manufacturing storm windows and doors, but his family was still in North Eicher and he helped Norman keep up. Gary told him that Warren had married Noel and that she had had a baby girl. She was named Lorraine, and she was born on March first. Norman also knew that nine months before the child was born he and Noel had gone down to Door County in Wisconsin for Memorial Day weekend. It was his child, he was certain. And it was his life Warren had been leading, which apparently Warren had screwed up. Gary told him that Noel and Warren were on and off but now had really split up. Her father owned the Deer Run, and she was working the desk nights.

There was a cot in the small storage room behind the front office, and around ten-thirty Noel lay down and closed her eyes. Through the nights at the motel she read a lot, surfed the Internet on the computer, and dozed. But it was never really sleep. And the fact that she'd taken all those pills earlier wasn't helping. She was tempted to take another white, just to get her up off where she was now, a dull, alert state that tended to cram her thoughts together so that nothing seemed interesting. Finally she was able to lie down and close her eyes, but her mind was still going. So when she heard the front door open it wasn't a matter of waking suddenly. Getting up, she pulled her sweater down over her hips and went out the door to the front office.

Norman stood across the counter. His face was pale, his cheeks hollow in a way she could never imagine; but it was his eyes—how deep they were in their sockets—that caused her to gasp. She exhaled slowly. "I heard you got out."

He simply nodded.

"You walked away in the blizzard?"

He nodded again.

Suddenly her knees seemed to quit and she had to support herself by placing both arms on the high counter. *"Oh, Christ,"* she whispered.

He watched her, looking uncertain; then he went over to the coffee machine and filled a Styrofoam cup. "You got to sit," he said, bringing the coffee to the counter. She took the cup in her right hand and, keeping the other hand on the wall, lowered herself until she was seated on the carpeted floor. She couldn't see him, until he appeared at the end of the counter. He seemed afraid to move too quickly, to come too close.

"I'm shaky," she said. "This is *so* weird."

He reached into the pocket of his overcoat and took something out, something small enough to conceal in his palm. Stepping toward her, he looked like someone testing lake ice. When he was close enough he leaned over, extended his arm, and opened his palm, which held two white pills. Certs. "I think you need sugar," he said. "There was a guy inside who got the shakes all the time. They gave him candy bars."

"They're not the ones with that Nutrasweet?"

"No." He smiled, and it did something to soften his face. "They're the real thing."

She took the Certs and put both in her mouth. Her hand was shaking so much, she had to put the cup on the floor. After she chewed and swallowed the first two Certs, he gave her the rest of the roll. "It's working," she said finally. "It's like I'm slowing down."

He knelt on the floor and sat back on his haunches. "I could get a candy bar or juice or something. Is there a vending machine?"

She shook her head and ate the last of the Certs. "I'm all right, really."

For a moment she thought she was going to cry; she could feel the muscles around her eyes and mouth tighten. Instead, she shook her head furiously until it made her dizzy; then she slammed the back of her skull against the wall and closed her eyes. "It *works,*" she said, laughing. She banged her head again. "It works. When I was a girl my friend Amy said that if you do that when you think you're going to cry, you won't." Opening her eyes, she said, "But I don't recommend it too often—because it makes you see those little stars off in the corners."

Warren left the Blue Antler with Bobby's ex-wife's cousin Leah. She waited tables at Jacques' Diner and spent most nights over at Bobby's house since her husband had moved down to Chicago. Warren drove around town slowly while they split a joint and passed the schnapps. Leah was in her early thirties, but she could pass for twenty-five in dim bar light. She kept her hand on his thigh as they drove. He knew she was really angling for a hit of coke.

When they finished the joint, he pulled his truck into the parking lot at Jacques' Diner. He pulled up between the Dumpster and the side of the small building, so that he could see across the street and through the plate glass of the Deer Run Motel's front office. Sometimes he sat here throughout the night by himself and watched Noel work behind the counter. The office appeared empty now, which he knew meant she was in the back room on the cot, reading or sleeping. Or maybe she was just lying there in orbit. Seemed that when he saw her lately there was usually that quickness in her eyes. Though she gave him all sorts of shit when she saw him, he still kept her well supplied. It might help bring her back.

"Whyn't we just go back to Bobby's?" Leah said as she tipped the bottle of schnapps up to her mouth.

"Got something for you." He took his vial out of his coat pocket. "There's not much left, so I think Bobby'll have to miss out on this party."

Leah took the vial. Her fingernails were long and painted dark purple with little flecks of silver. She held the vial, which was shaped like a clear plastic bullet, up to her right nostril, pinched off her left nostril, and inhaled quickly. *"Oooh, yeah."*

She held the vial out to him, but he shook his head. "Not much left. Finish it."

"Thanks, baby." Leah worked the vial into her other nostril, inhaled, and then laid her head back against the seat. She put the empty vial on the dashboard and then rubbed her forefinger over her gums. "How 'bout something in return?" she said.

"What a concept."

"Uh-huh. I give great concept."

They both laughed, but Warren kept his eyes on the motel as Leah undid his belt and zipper. The fluorescent ceiling lights in the office seemed painfully bright. Once, several months after they were married, when he had stopped in at the motel in the middle of the night, he'd found Noel dozing on the cot, and as soon as she saw him she began undoing his belt.

He glanced down at the top of Leah's head. Her blond hair was so fine that it seemed to float above his lap. He placed one hand on the back of her skull, and with the other he took a drink of schnapps. The snow that passed through the light from the motel office was absolutely horizontal, as though there were no such thing as gravity.

It was hot in the office, and Norman had worked his coat off. He was sitting on the floor now, his back against the cabinet door under the counter.

"I got your letters," she said. The color had returned to her face. Something about her skin was different—it wasn't as plump and smooth as he remembered, though the way it was now suited him fine—and he suspected it had to do with having a child. "Why'd you stop sending them?"

"I don't know," he said. "Guess it seemed pointless after a while."

"They made me mad at first," she said.

"They were true."

"Maybe, but they pissed me off. I thought, What happened happened, and there's no changing it. You can't go back and pretend it turned out all different."

"That's not what you said."

"What do you mean?" she asked.

"What you said in your letter—"

"*My* letter?" She seemed frightened for a moment. "I sent it to you?"

He nodded. "One letter."

"Oh, God, I don't remember—I mean, I wasn't sure if I actually mailed it."

"I understand."

"You do? What did it say?" She leaned toward him slightly. "Did it make sense?"

"Sort of," he said. He put his hand in his back pocket, then withdrew it quickly. "Shit," he whispered.

"What?"

"These aren't my pants—and I left your letter in them." She put her head back against the wall and closed her eyes, relieved. Her throat looked strong, two thick cords beneath her skin, with a deep hollow between them. He couldn't stare at it any longer. "But I read that letter so many times I know it by heart," he said. There were small white circles in the blue carpet pattern, and he put his forefinger on one. "It was unreal, how you were saying the things I'd been thinking." He knew she'd opened her eyes, but he continued to trace the white circle with his finger. "Inside, time becomes something else. You start to wonder why you can't just move back and forth somehow. I mean, I know what happened happened." He put his middle finger in another circle and walked his two fingers on the carpet, always touching white circles.

"But you wonder why you can't just go back to a specific point in time."

"Yes, that's what you said, too. In your letter."

He raised his head and watched her put a hand over her mouth. "I was *so* whacked *out,"* she said, almost pleading, "that I wasn't even sure I really *wrote* that, and I had no idea I actually sent it to you, with an address and a stamp and all."

"I got it." Suddenly he put his hands in the front pockets of his corduroys.

"I kept your letters," she said.

"Thank you." After a moment he added, "I think I came just to hear that."

"I wrote you a lot." Her hair was flattened on the side where she'd been leaning against the wall. "I didn't send them except for that one, I guess. I began writing them last summer, when things with Warren were getting very strange. And I was here at work, and I just started writing to you. I hadn't heard from you in several months, and I didn't know what that meant."

"It meant I was coming, I guess," he said. "It meant I was going to do like you said."

"What did I say?"

"In your letter—you said that somehow we would be able to go back to a specific point in time. You really believe that?"

"Well, yeah," she said. "Not physically. Not like in some time machine."

"No, but just you yourself. The way you think and feel about things."

"I guess I do, though it's been hard lately. Since Lorraine—and, well, since your brother moved out." She looked up at the clock on the wall. It was nearly midnight. "You hungry?"

He nodded.

"There's only one place in town now that stays open this late. Joey's Pizzeria has a new owner, and they deliver. Sometimes I call them and the kid comes over on the way home and gives me a deal on whatever's left over." She stood up; her jeans were tight around her thighs. "Let me call before he closes up."

"He sweet on you?"

"Yeah, sure. They're all sweet on me. That's been the problem all along."

Warren opened his eyes. He had dozed off, and now he could see Noel behind the counter, talking on the telephone. Leah's head was heavy on his right thigh, and she was snoring softly. He still had his hand inside her panties, where she was warm and wet. Noel hung up the phone and turned to her left. She seemed to be talking, though no one else was in the office. It was difficult to tell from this distance. Warren drank the last of the schnapps, put his head back against the seat, and closed his eyes again.

"Jimmy was just closing up," Noel said. "He'll be over in two minutes—you should get in the back office." Norman started to get to his feet. "No, I'd stay down," she said. "Be just your luck that somebody would drive by and recognize you."

Norman got on his hands and knees and crawled into the back office. When he was beyond the desk he sat on the cot next to the computer station. "The cops," he said. "They ever come in here at night?"

She leaned against the doorjamb and folded her arms. "Not unless I call them. Sometimes we get a party in one of the rooms and they come and check it out. Happens a lot in the summer. During the fall it's hunters on the weekend, mostly. And now packs of snowmobilers are starting to invade every weekend. A few times I've had to call the police because someone was—" She felt her face flush. "Someone was getting out of hand."

"You mean some guy's beating up on his wife or girlfriend."

"I haven't seen it the other way around yet."

"I suppose not," Norman said. "I just came from a place full of guys like that."

Warren was awakened by the sound of an engine. Across the street he watched Jimmy's delivery truck pull up in front of the motel office. Fucking Jimmy wasn't twenty; wore those real baggy jeans that looked so stupid. Ball cap backward. Just a happy guy delivering pizza. A million kids like that got sucked into the navy. It would be something, he thought, if Jimmy were delivering more than pizza, if he went in there and Noel put her arms around his shoulders, kissed him, then took him into the back office. Warren could see himself driving over there, going into the office, catching her going down on the kid. Snap a photo and give her a ton of shit over custody. Just to make her sweat.

But Noel came around the counter, opened the front door, and never let Jimmy out of his truck. She leaned over and talked to him, her arms folded under her breasts because of the cold. Fucking crazy to be out in that. Hair blowing all around. Then Jimmy handed the pizza box out his window. She tried to pay him, but Warren could see that the kid was refusing it. Always looking for an edge. Maybe the kid wasn't so stupid. He drove off, and Noel rushed back inside. She walked through the door to the back office and went out of sight.

They ate quickly at first, while the pizza was hot, but after her second slice she stopped. Norman kept going, though he left his crusts in the pizza box now. When he stopped, he looked as if he were about to fall asleep. "You look exhausted," she said. "I could give you a key and you could go down to a room and get some sleep. Maybe clean up."

"I stink, huh?"

After a moment, she smiled. "Yeah, kinda."

"All right." He sat up on the cot.

"Then what, Norman?"

"I don't know. What you said in the letter really bugs me."

"There's nothing you can do about it," she said. "You got to keep going now."

"But what you said in the letter, about your father and this guy Woo-San. I wish—"

"You *can't* stay here, Norman. You *know* that."

Reluctantly, he nodded. He sat forward and rested his forearms on his knees. "Bing, a friend inside, he said if he ever got out, he'd go across the border and head out to the Canadian Rockies, maybe British Columbia."

"Sounds like a good plan," she said. "Last summer I went across to Soo Canada a couple of times, and customs never did much at all. Same thing every time—where are you from, where are you going, what nationality are you, are you carrying any firearms? Didn't ask for my license or anything. But they'll be looking for you, won't they?"

"I don't know. I got this van and I just don't know."

"Where'd you get it?"

"Jesus, you ask a lot of questions."

"I know. You stole a van?"

He took one arm off his knee and touched his forehead a moment. "I was thinking I could get another car. I don't want to, but maybe I could do that just to get across in something they might not be looking for." He got up off the cot. "I don't know. I got to lie down, I think."

"I'll get you a key, and I'll call your room in a few hours." She stood up. "This is *so* strange."

He was closing the lid to the pizza box, tucking in the side flaps. He wouldn't look up. There were grease stains on the cardboard, and he traced one with his finger. "No, it's not," he said finally. "Not really. This is just like I thought it would be, and it's just like you said in your letter. We're the same. We haven't changed. All that stuff that happened didn't happen."

She stood there a moment longer, watching his hand. For a moment she thought she would cry, but then he turned to her.

"You really believe that, right?" he asked.

She pressed her lips together and tried to hold on, but the tears were there and she could feel them. Releasing all the air from her lungs, she whispered, "I do. I *really* believe that."

CHAPTER Seven

Warren became aware of bright light coming from behind him; opening his eyes, he squinted against headlights reflected in the rearview mirror.

Leah was sitting up, brushing the hair out of her face. "The fuck is this, cops?"

"I don't know." The lights were right behind his truck. He checked his side-view mirror, but all he could see was glare. He looked at the motel office a moment, then put his car in gear and pulled out into the snowy street. The headlights stayed right behind him. He drove slowly through town toward Bobby's house. After a couple of blocks, he said, "It's not the cops."

"Who is it?" She was tucking her blouse into her jeans.

"A couple of kids in a Camaro, I'll bet. Buck and Pete."

"Pete, the wrestler?"

"Yeah."

"That kid, Jesus," she said. "Last fall he got in a fight with some guy, a hunter from downstate, right in the parking lot behind Sally's Pub. Took three guys to pull him off. I mean, that guy should be on *WrestleMania.*"

Noel gave Norman the key to room 12 because the heat was on and it was around back. Norman went outside and drove the van behind the motel, and suddenly the motel office seemed inordinately empty and quiet. The only sound was the ticking noise coming from the baseboard radiators. She sat at the counter and tried to finish the article about the mastodon, but she kept staring up at her reflection in the plate glass window. She wasn't tired. And she wasn't wired. She felt absolutely even, and it was so odd. A few minutes ago she'd been fighting back tears, but now it felt as if something were moving again. It was not an unpleasant sensation, though it was a bit frightening. She felt on the other side of something, some emotional abyss that was necessary for her to cross. Occasionally a gust of wind would shake the plate glass. All she could see above the counter was her head and shoulders. The sign on the front of the counter was backward in the glass: "!ꟼЯAA ɘmoɔlɘW."

Warren turned into Bobby's driveway, and the Camaro pulled in right behind him. He leaned over and got his .38 out of the glove compartment.

"What the fuck now," Leah whispered.

"Shut up." He opened his door. "You just go in the house and I'll take care of it."

He got out and walked back to the driver's side of the Camaro, holding the gun against his leg. The car window rolled down and there was the smell of stale beer; Pete was behind the wheel, and he was alone. Warren glanced across the roof of the car and watched Leah go in the front door of Bobby's house. Looking down, he saw Pete's arm come out the car window. He touched Warren's crotch with the barrel of a pistol. "Hey, want another blow job?"

Warren dropped his gun in the snow and didn't move.

"Now drop trow."

"What?"

"You heard me."

Slowly Warren unfastened his belt and his fly, and then he let his jeans and shorts fall down around his knees.

Pete touched the head of his cock with the cold muzzle of the gun. "Cute." He smiled. "What was the price of that shit? Did you say it was going to go up or down when this next storm comes in? I think you said down, right? Down, like way down." Pete opened his door, knocking Warren hard in the shoulder. He got out and kicked Warren's gun into the snowbank alongside the driveway. Tucking his gun in his belt, he said, "I hate these things. They're for chickens."

His fist came up out of the dark and caught Warren on the left cheekbone. Warren broke his fall with his hands in the cold snow, and he scraped his right palm.

"Give it to me," Pete said.

"I don't have it. It's gone."

"What do you mean, *gone?* You sold it?"

Warren was on all fours, and he stared down at his blood in the snow. He thought it was coming from his nose, but it could have been coming from his mouth, too. "No," he said. "We just used it up."

He waited, and after a moment he thought perhaps that would settle it. Then Pete leaned over and punched him again, this time behind the left ear.

"Free?" Pete said. "*Free?* Christ, if she starts expecting free hits of coke every time she goes parking, a lot of guys will end up just staying home and whacking off. You got no sense of civic responsibility."

Rolling on his side in the snow, Warren reached into his coat pocket, took out the plastic vial of pills, and held them up. Pete took the vial, and Warren heard it rattle as it was stuffed into the pocket of his jeans. Pete's leg swung out and his boot caught Warren in the ribs, knocking the wind out of him. He lay on his back, sucking in air. His eyes were closed, and it seemed that Pete was walking away. Then the car's door opened and closed, and the headlights passed over him as the Camaro backed out of the driveway.

Though Warren lay still, he had the sensation that he was turning slowly to the left. He hadn't felt this bad since one night in the Gas Lamp Quarter of San Diego. He kept his eyes closed and tried not to think about throwing up.

Suddenly Leah was kneeling over him in the dark. She swore as she tried to help him pull his pants up, but he pushed her away. He crawled toward the snowbank and searched in the snow until his hands were numb with the cold. He couldn't find the gun.

The phone was ringing, and when Norman put it to his ear Noel said, "It's five-thirty."

"Okay, thanks."

She took a breath and he waited for her to speak, but she didn't. When they'd first started seeing each other, he had been nervous on the phone with her. Some guys could pick up a phone and talk to a girl for hours, but not Norman. She understood that, and she did a lot of the talking at first, asked a lot of questions. But most of all there were times when they just wouldn't say anything over the phone. There was an intimacy to her breathing as it came through a telephone that was like nothing else. It was as though her mouth were right there next to his head. Once they started sleeping together, he would sometimes lie on his back with his ear almost touching her mouth, so he could hear her breathe.

"I was thinking," she finally said into the phone. But she didn't go on.

"Yeah?"

"A good time for you to cross the border might be a little before eight in the morning. When businesses open. People go to work. Trucks make deliveries. You know. Maybe they'll be a little busy and won't pay as much attention."

"Maybe."

"But in this weather—I don't know how much traffic there'll be at the border."

"Yeah." She was leading up to something. "But what?"

She inhaled. "You really think you have to go, to Canada?"

"Can't exactly stay here in North Eicher."

"I wouldn't recommend that. For anyone."

They didn't speak for a while, and he held his breath so he could hear her better.

"Why don't you ask me things? Norman?"

"Like what?"

"Like what was I doing with your brother. Like what happened at the trial." Her breathing had changed. She sounded slightly winded now, and there was a quiver to her inhaling that he recognized.

"I've thought about those things—a lot," he said. "I've had the time. After a while they don't seem that important. I've known my brother's—well, I've known *my brother* since we were kids. You didn't know anything about him. Then he returns from the navy and he's like worse than ever. I could see it, but how could you? He conceals it pretty good, at first anyway."

"You think he's bipolar?"

"What's that?"

"It's like manic-depressed. I read about it in a magazine."

"Uh-huh. I don't know any medical terms for it. I just know that we never got along. Even when we were real little, and it wasn't just some *brother* thing, you know, fighting over toys and stuff. It's strange. We could get along on a certain level—a surface level. You know, we could do stuff, go out, have a beer, talk, and everything seemed just fine. But on this other level, I don't know, there's something else going on. After Dad took off for good, it was just us and Mom, and she couldn't control us at all. I never understood it." There was silence for a while, then he said, "All right, why did you and Warren, you know—"

"I don't know," she said. "He just seemed to offer something I thought I needed. It's like he convinces you that he's got something no one else has."

"Yeah, I first bought into that when I was about four."

"This probably sounds—I don't know, weird—but at first I thought I had to go *through* Warren to get to *you*. There was always a part of you that was closed off. You're a very tight person, Norman. I loved that about you, but I wanted inside of it. And when your brother shows up, and he's all, all *big* and *out there,* and . . . well, I thought, This is the part of Norman he won't let anyone see. You know?"

"Yeah, I guess I do."

"And it had to do with sex. Obviously. I can say that now, Norman. I don't know what it was, I don't want to make excuses, but at some point it seemed necessary. I don't know what it is with me and men. It wasn't something I wanted, really, not in a conscious way. It was like I had no choice. I really thought I could sort of get *through* Warren, and then it'd be over and done with."

Norman took a long, deep breath.

"I'm sorry."

"It's okay."

"No, it's not," she said. "You were so fucked up then. We *all* were, but *you* were out of control. Warren was always giving us stuff. It was part of *his* control. Take this, smoke that, snort this, drink that." She caught her breath, and for a moment Norman thought she was going to start crying. But she continued, her voice now rushing swiftly through the phone receiver. "I got taken in, Norman. Completely. I wasn't forced to do anything; I wanted to do it. Before you found us together, I was seriously considering telling you that we had to call everything off, the wedding, everything. But something told me that that's not what Warren really wanted. He didn't *want* me the way you *had* me. He wanted me because he wasn't supposed to, because it was secret, because we had to do it on the sly."

"At the trial it came out like it was all my fault." He waited, listening to her breathing. "I know I really lost it, but a lot of it's still fucked up in my head. *I* was fucked up. I don't remember everything. Some things, yes. I know I hit you. I have images of you, of my brother, of the shit that happened out in the woods—the stuff with Raymond. No one believed me—that Raymond was hunting me, and because he had suddenly disappeared, it only made it worse."

"I was angry during the trial," she said. "I really *did* lose the hearing in my ear, you know, and I still get these incredible headaches a lot. I have prescriptions for them, and your brother, he also keeps me well supplied—it's that con*trol* thing he has. I really wasn't faking that business about my head, which I know you thought during the trial. You know what it's like to hear out of only one ear? You think it's all silence—no, it's noise. You hear all this *noise* inside your head. It's like you can hear your *blood* moving and your *brain* working, and when you eat a po*ta*to chip it's enough to drive you *nuts.* At the trial I was just—I was just *so* angry that everything had fallen apart."

"At the trial," he said slowly, "everybody made like I was the reason why Raymond Yates didn't testify, because he had disappeared. Afterwards I got sent away and you married Warren." She didn't answer, and he couldn't hear her breathing. It was like she'd disappeared. "You there?" She hung up, and he knew that now she was crying.

Warren lay on the couch in the living room, listening to the mattress springs in Bobby's bedroom squeak and groan and twang. Sometimes they sounded like a dying animal. The ice Warren had wrapped in a towel had melted long ago, but he still held the cold, damp cloth against his swollen cheek. When he inhaled a sharp pain jolted through his ribs. Closing his eyes again, he tried not to listen, but the mattress springs began moving faster, and Leah's moans seemed to be pleading for understanding, and Bobby grunted as though he were trying to clear his throat, and the headboard knocked against the wall, and then the bed legs thumped the carpeted floor.

Then the whole noisy contraption came to a halt, leaving silence.

Until the furnace motor kicked on in the basement.

The phone rang several minutes later, and at first Norman considered not answering. He still lay on his back in the bed, thinking he should get up, take a shower, and go.

Go.

Vanish.

Disappear.

Coming back to North Eicher had been something he'd thought about since his first day inside Marquette Prison. It was connected to time somehow. If he could return here, he could turn back time like Noel had said in her letter. Make it new. Go back to before all this happened.

Before what happened happened.

The phone kept ringing. When he finally picked it up, she said, "I thought you'd already left." He didn't answer. "I want to try and explain the marriage to you."

"Don't." She held her breath. "Don't," he repeated. "I don't want to hear it. I know why you married him." He waited, listening to her breathing. "You thought it would make everything right."

"Yes," she said. "Otherwise, you would have gone to prison for nothing. I'm sorry."

"It's funny," he said. "I'm the one who's been in prison, I'm the one who was found guilty, and you're the one saying you're sorry. You don't have to, you know." He realized now that what he wanted was not to undo what had happened, not to go back in time, but to stop it altogether. He wanted this moment only: lying in a dark motel room, listening to her breathing.

Finally she said, "Can I come down?"

"Sure. Let me get a shower first. Give me twenty minutes."

"Okay. I have something for you." She hung up.

Warren's whole face hurt, and the ribs under his left arm ached. He sat at the kitchen table, eating Cheerios with his left hand because his right palm had scabbed over where he'd scraped it. He put down his spoon, which felt awkward in his left hand, and got up from the table. He went into the living room, where his seaman's chest sat on the floor next to the couch; he unlocked it and raised the metal lid. He removed a pile of shirts and jeans and picked up the knife, which lay on newspapers lining the bottom of the chest. Standing, he drew the knife from its sheath and gazed down the hallway. Bobby's bedroom was at the end, and through the open door Warren could see the bedpost. Bobby and Leah were both already gone. Every morning since he'd moved in here, he'd wake up and listen to them get ready for work. They had shit jobs—Bobby worked for an electrical contractor, and Leah waited tables at Jacques' Diner—but they still showered, brushed their teeth, made coffee, and worried about being late. Like it fucking mattered. Holding the knife by the tip of the blade in his left hand, Warren cocked his arm and concentrated on the straw cowboy hat that hung from Bobby's bedpost—Bobby loved country and western, and the hat had been signed by several favorite singers he'd seen in concert. Warren took aim at the crown of the hat and threw the knife—in the empty house it made a fine, whirling sound as it traveled down the hallway, until the handle struck the bedroom doorjamb and fell to the floor.

Warren went back to the kitchen and finished his Cheerios. He probably wouldn't have hit the cowboy hat with a good right hand. What he needed was a weapon that would send a message, something that didn't require a high degree of hand-eye coordination.

Noel let herself into room 12 with the master key. The room was dark, though the light from the bathroom was on and the door was ajar. She could smell soap, and the air was steamy from the shower. He was standing in front of the mirror, scrubbing his hair dry. She caught a glimpse of his bare shoulder.

Sitting on the bed with her back to the bathroom door, she said, "I have some clean clothes for you. People leave stuff behind, and they get tossed in the laundry with the linen. I'm laying them here on the bed—underwear and a nice turtleneck shirt." After a moment, she added, "You can come out for them. I won't look." She listened to his bare feet on the carpet as he came quickly into the room, picked up the pile of folded clothes, then retreated to the bathroom. "And I have an idea," she said.

"Yeah?" She could hear him pulling on his pants.

"That van of yours. The police, they may be looking for it?"

"I suppose."

"Take mine. I have this Isuzu Trooper with four-wheel drive. Daddy got it for me because it's good in the snow. And after Lorraine was born—"

"Whose idea—" Norman came to the bathroom door. She looked toward him. He had the green turtleneck shirt in his hands. Light fell across his bare shoulders. "Whose idea was it to name her Lorraine?"

"I don't know. Mine. You don't like it?"

He seemed embarrassed all of a sudden. "No, it's fine." He raised his arms and pulled the turtleneck down over his head.

"I'll hold off reporting the Isuzu missing," she said. "That should give you enough time to get out of the U.P."

"I don't know." Norman came into the room, where he picked up his gray sweater from the bureau and pulled it on over the turtleneck. "Then they'd know I had come here. It would only make trouble for you."

She was afraid of what was coming, so she said, "You can't see her. I leave her with Daddy when I work nights here, and you can't go near him. You know that."

Norman went to the other bed, sat down, and began pulling on his boots. "Warren, how does he treat her?"

"At first, when she was small, he was all right with her. As things got worse between us, he ignored her mostly. Unless she cries, then he tells me to shut her up." She thought that was enough, but it wasn't everything, and she decided to tell him the rest. "When it got to the point where I started telling him I wanted him out of the apartment, he was more upset about losing Lorraine. He's very possessive."

"He's never given up anything in his life," Norman said. "Never."

"Look, I mean it about my car."

"I know. Thanks." He finished tying his laces and straightened up. "I don't want your Isuzu." He was going to continue, but he didn't. She knew he wanted to but couldn't.

She went over to the bed and sat next to him. "Say it," she said.

"What's the point?"

"Because you want to."

"It doesn't make it any good."

"But say it, Norman. Just *say* it."

"Okay. I wish you and Lorraine could come with me."

"No, that's not it." She kept her eyes on his boot laces. They were brown with flecks of green. "That's not what you want."

"All right. I want you and Lorraine to come with me."

"Thank you."

"You're welcome."

CHAPTER

Eight

The snow had stopped. At first Del told himself that he was just driving around, checking for storm damage. Even when he was on Route 28, headed into Marquette. After his divorce eight years ago, he'd gotten into the habit of cruising at night. Karen had moved to Green Bay, four hours south; when she remarried a year later, she and her new husband moved to Georgia. He was a dentist and she said he was a nice guy, and that seemed to explain everything. He was a nice guy dentist and he got her out of the cold. Del had been south of Chicago only a few times. He still lived in the log kit house he and Karen had built on ten acres in the late seventies. At this point in his life he had expected the house to be full, with Karen and pets and several teenage kids. But since the last of his dogs died, the house had been empty. He'd had two long-term relationships with women, but both had withered and ended quietly after a few years. The past year or so he hadn't had a date, nor had he really wanted one. What he had, what mattered, was work. The long winter months he was at the station early, and he seldom left before Monty, who had a family and tried to be home most nights for dinner. Ordinarily there was no official night shift in Yellow Dog Township. If someone had a problem, they called Del out at the house. In most cases it could wait till morning.

It was not yet daylight outside her hospital room when Liesl saw Del Maki through the open door. As he stood in the hallway talking to the nurse, he kept both hands buried in the pockets of his overcoat. He remained perfectly still while she spoke, and it was this stillness that Liesl found interesting. She realized that it was designed to get people to say more than they wanted, because they knew he was really considering what they were telling him. It must be a useful trait for a sheriff, to get people to talk.

When he came into the room he was almost smiling, and she was certain that for him that was a rare thing. "They're releasing you this morning, and I was wondering if you need a lift home," he said.

She decided not to answer. See just how still he could get.

In the ceiling there was a metal track for the privacy curtain that could be pulled around the bed. She knew this track as well as any sculpture she'd ever done. Dull metal that curved above the end of the bed. When she was on the morphine drip, she'd thought of it as the tracks of a miniature train.

Del moved into the room, but she kept her eyes on the track in the ceiling. He stood at the end of the bed, and they remained that way for some time. She wondered if he knew what she was doing, if he was on to her game. She glanced at him finally and then returned her gaze to the ceiling. Hard to tell. His face was slightly flushed from being out in the cold, and his eyes seemed determined to make some impartial assessment. As though she were a drunk he'd pulled over on the road.

"Would you rather not go home yet?" he asked.

"How long have I been in here?"

"Overnight."

"It feels a lot longer." She closed her eyes and after a moment said, "It seems like I've been in this hospital bed for weeks. I'd like nothing better than to go home. Besides, my cabin isn't like modern houses. It needs constant attention—wood stove fires, for instance."

"I'll take you, if you'd like. I've arranged to have your driveway plowed by a county truck so we can get in." He waited, and finally she opened her eyes, though she only stared at his left shoulder. "You should have someone stay with you at first—" He shifted his weight so that his chest was in line with her gaze. She raised her eyes just enough to see his chin. Firm, broad, unshaven for a day or two. She liked the way that looked on some men. On him. The faint shadow of a beard, but not enough to obscure the line of his jaw. "There someone who can come in and help you out?"

She nodded. "I called my nearest neighbor, and her daughter, Darcy—I help with her home schooling—she's supposed to be tending to the stoves. It'll be good to get back to the house, my studio, my woods."

"Good."

He didn't move for what seemed like a long time, and it was making her nervous. She was used to being the one who was still, but he had his own stillness, and it was both disconcerting and splendid—something about the trim of that jaw, the flatness of his lips. For a moment she imagined his face as clay, how with her thumb she would make the sweet curve where the brow descended into the bridge of his nose.

She took a breath and said, "What?" He turned and went over to the window. She sat up slightly, feeling a twinge in her lower back. Her room faced east, and he was staring at the gray horizon above the blackness of Lake Superior. There were at least a dozen shades of gray out there. He seemed now preoccupied, as though he were alone in the room. "What is it?" she asked.

"The walkaway."

"Norman," she said. Del continued to face the lake. "What about him?"

Every moment the sky seemed to be getting brighter, the grays shifting, and Del seemed content to witness this transformation from night to day.

She whispered, "He's alive?"

"Apparently."

"Then who was in the truck? You said there were two bodies—or maybe I didn't understand you. This med they had me on, it makes you see choo-choo trains in the ceiling."

"There were two bodies all right, but neither one was the walkaway."

"His name is Norman Haas," she said. "How do you know this?"

"The labwork came back, and I asked them to call me as soon as they were certain. Your Norman wasn't in the truck."

"My Norman," she said.

"A man from Menominee was reported missing by his wife, and according to the dental records he was in the truck with the driver."

"Then Norman's free."

"In this guy's car," Del said. "A van, actually, a brown Dodge van. I don't know how Norman managed it. The truck that burned was headed west, but now that he's in the van he could be in Wisconsin, Minnesota, or maybe Canada by now. Hard to say in this weather. Not much is moving out there except the snowplows."

Liesl sank down in her bed. "What happens now?"

"State police put out the word, but they're not moving much in this weather, either."

"They catch him and he resists, they'll shoot him, right?" Del turned from the window now. "Can you tell if Norman *caused* the truck accident?"

"No, I don't know that for certain. Seemed like a typical jackknife in a blizzard."

"He hasn't *done* anything—except walk away from prison. But they think he has."

"And you're in the hospital." She shook her head. Del came over to the side of the bed now. He still had his hands in his coat pockets. His forehead was slightly pinched, creating a small bunch of flesh to rise up between his brows. "What are you saying?"

"More than I had intended." She stretched her left arm out on the blanket and turned her palm up. "I'm saying I fell. It was an accident."

"Right, and he left you for dead."

"He tried to carry me out—at first, that's what he tried to do. But we fell in the snow. Then he went for help, and I guess he just—" Liesl had to avoid Del's eyes now. "I guess he just decided it wasn't worth it. I wasn't worth the risk. But I fell by accident; I'm not here because he tried to harm me. It's like the deer in winter."

"What about the deer in winter?"

"We saw one while we were snowshoeing through the hills. It was dying, starving and freezing to death. You could tell—the others walked off when they saw us, but this one deer just stood there and watched us. It couldn't move." She raised her eyes now, and for a moment she was surprised by something in his eyes. They went beyond the necessary curiosity and skepticism of a small-town sheriff; they were trying to comprehend. She then did something that surprised her even more: she reached into the front pocket of his overcoat and took hold of his hand, which was pleasantly callused and warm. "The deer," she said, "I shot it. It wasn't going to make it, so I shot it. Norman understood that. It wasn't something I caused. It was just the circumstances of nature. Or call it fate, if you want—but whatever, it dictated that there was no reason to let that deer suffer any longer. I told him how it took me years to understand that about the deer I saw dying in the woods around my house. I told him that when I was certain one wasn't going to make it now I put them down with Harold's carbine." She looked past Del now. Out the window the sky had turned a bright oyster color, and the lake was its darkest blue, the color of ink. "Circumstance, Del—he didn't leave me to die in the snow, he just found that once he was out on that road, no longer wearing snowshoes, no longer accompanied by this woman who had a rifle, the circumstances had changed. He did the logical thing: he was free and he kept going in the blizzard."

At dawn Noel stood at the bottom of her father's driveway, which was about twenty yards long going up a slight grade. A set of antlers hung above the front door of the house. When she was small she had stood in the front yard, expecting them to move, for a buck to suddenly burst through the door. In summer, when it turned very humid and buggy, the smell of Borax and the stench of tanned skins from his workshop, which was then in the basement, filled the summer nights. Even from this distance, she could see that the antlers were now dried out, bone white.

She turned toward Norman, who sat behind the wheel of her Isuzu Trooper, but she could barely see him through the reflection off the windshield; then she started to walk up the driveway, which had already been plowed—if it wasn't by the time her father was up in the morning, he would call Marchoud's Garage and let them know about it. Lately, upon returning from a night at the motel office, she had often imagined this particular walk—though never under these circumstances, never with Norman waiting in the Trooper. She saw herself slipping quietly into her father's house and taking Lorraine without his waking. It was possible, because he was a heavy sleeper and frequently hung over. If he woke, if he spoke to her, she knew she'd give away her real intention, not to simply take Lorraine back to her own apartment, but to flee. He'd see it in her eyes; he'd hear it in her voice. He was remarkable in that way. This would work only if she left while he was asleep, if when he awoke he thought nothing of it—an ordinary morning where Noel had come in early and taken his granddaughter home.

But she had difficulty imagining what would happen after that, after she'd pulled away from the driveway. If she went north, there was nothing but Canada. If she went south, it would be hours before she even got out of the Upper Peninsula. She was certain that before she reached Menominee, which was over two hours away on the Wisconsin border, or the Mackinac Bridge if she tried to cross the straits to the Lower Peninsula, her father would awaken, realize what she had done, and call the state police. He would use the same voice with the police as he used with the plow driver at Marchoud's Garage. Never really angry; more like old friends, and he was embarrassed to have even bothered them—but beneath that there was something direct and explicit in his voice that caused people to do as he asked. And that was his secret: to get people to believe they were doing something because they wanted to—her mother and she had both stayed because he'd led them to believe that's what they had chosen to do.

But no longer. Noel realized that last summer: she no longer wanted to stay in North Eicher, near Warren, near her father. It was not a great revelation. What surprised her, however, was that she understood that her mother went through it as well, years before she died: that she too had finally realized that she was staying with her husband not because she wanted to, but because he had convinced her that she *thought* it was her own choice.

At the top of the driveway Noel went in the side door, which let her into the kitchen. Once in the warmth of the house, she moved slowly—just as she had imagined—not removing her boots, but walking on the beige carpet that her father tried to defend against snow and dirt. It was one of the things he was adamant about, keeping the carpet clean, and more than once he'd lost his temper when Lorraine had stepped on the carpet with muddy boots. Noel walked through the living room and then down the hallway, past her father's bedroom door, which was open only a few inches. She smelled the tobacco and bourbon. She smelled the scent that she associated with her father's laundry, when she washed his bedsheets and T-shirts. Not entirely unpleasant smells, and she wondered if she might even miss them. Her father was not an unclean man; it was more that he fully invested himself in everything he did. He never had just a drink. He never could stop smoking. He bought good clothes and wore them until they broke through at an elbow or knee. His T-shirts often had small holes up along the shoulders from years of wear and washing. When she'd suggest that she throw them in the ragbag downstairs, he'd say first, "But they're just getting good and comfortable." And then he'd say, "Throw them out, if you want."

If you want. Once he said that, you couldn't do what you wanted.

The bedroom door at the end of the hall was open, and Noel went in and picked up Lorraine from the crib. Her weight was heavy, familiar. The child didn't wake, her blond eyelashes encrusted with sleep, yet something in her arms and legs suggested that she knew her mother was back. Noel carried her down the hall, but just as she approached her father's door she heard the bedsheets rustle. She stood perfectly still and listened. The box springs groaned, but she didn't hear his feet on the floor. After a moment there was silence again, and she walked by the door without daring to look into the room.

She went through the living room, somewhat disappointed to see that her boots had not left clear footprints of melted snow and mud on the carpet. In the kitchen she put Lorraine into her snowsuit; though the child was still asleep, her limbs responded automatically so that she helped her mother dress her. It wasn't until Noel carried her out the kitchen door and into the smarting early morning cold that the weight of Lorraine's head came up off her shoulder. The girl's body became more alert as they went down the driveway. When she spoke her voice was small and sleepy. "Mommy, we going home?"

Noel stopped walking halfway between the house and her Trooper. She had never imagined this part, never thought that if she did leave North Eicher, it would be with someone.

No, occasionally she had imagined that it might be with a man. Sometimes when a man came into the office at the motel to check in, there'd be something about him that she would keep with her after he'd gone out into the night to his room. Something about his face, his eyes, some kindness in his expression. Or, during the summer when tourists passed through the Upper Peninsula, there'd be some man in shorts and a T-shirt who had firm arms and tanned legs, and she'd hold that image, so that in the middle of the night, when all the rooms had been let and the neon "No Vacancy" sign was lit, she'd lie on the cot in the near dark in the back office and put her hand down on herself, holding that image in her mind until it was all released.

The fact was she often imagined leaving North Eicher with strange men. There was the guy from Minnesota. And a man, easily in his late thirties, who had a scar on his right cheek. And a college kid named Jeff, who was in North Eicher working on a road crew for the summer. After one of them checked in, she imagined going down to the room because this guy was funny, that guy was sexy, or this guy was *really* sexy. But she always imagined going to the room for the primary reason: *This guy might take her with him.* And she would lie for hours on the cot in the office, imagining her life in a strange place with this strange man. A perfect stranger.

But she never imagined leaving with someone she knew.

Definitely not Warren.

And now, she realized, she had kept Norman as much a prisoner in her mind as he'd actually been in the facility in Marquette. She could never imagine him out, free. She could never see him come back into her life. It simply wasn't possible. Yet there he was, sitting behind the wheel of the blue-and-gray Trooper.

She never imagined that it was possible to run away, to flee with Norman.

Perhaps that's why she was here in the driveway, her daughter in her arms. She knew that it made no sense to go away with him, that in fact it was dangerous, but that knowledge seemed far off, crowded aside by the moment. It made no sense, and she felt she had to act quickly before she talked herself out of going.

Her mother must have thought this, too: If I don't go right now, I'll never go.

"We're just going bye-bye," she said to Lorraine as she continued walking toward the end of the driveway.

"Bye-bye?" Lorraine's eyes searched Noel's face, and then she sang, "Bye-*bye!*"

When they had left the motel, Norman followed her Trooper in the Dodge van, and he left it in the parking lot behind Hautamaki's Tru-Value Hardware. Abandon a vehicle on a county road, a snowplow is going to report it in no time; leave it in a lot where cars come and go all day, it'll be a while before anyone realizes how long it's been parked there. Now, sitting behind the steering wheel of the Trooper, Norman wondered again if he should just go. Put it in gear and go, vanish, disappear. If he did, he knew that Noel would cover for him, at least for a while.

And she'd be hurt.

But she'd make up some story about her car so that her father wouldn't call the police right away. Perhaps Norman would have until the afternoon before anyone realized that he was now driving a Trooper. By then he could be out of the state. With luck, he might get through the border into Ontario.

But that wasn't why he had returned to North Eicher. He wasn't *running away.*

He was headed in the other direction.

Watching the house, he began to wonder if something was keeping Noel from coming back out with the child. He was anxious to see Lorraine. Perhaps Noel's father was awake—though she'd assured Norman that he wouldn't be—and he was already on the phone with the police. Or perhaps he was loading one of his hunting rifles and about to come out of the house firing. Or maybe once Noel was in her father's house she simply knew that she couldn't go through with it. For her, this must feel like running away.

When she finally came out the door with the child in her arms, bundled in a red snowsuit, Norman was about to put the vehicle in gear and roll up to the end of the driveway. But halfway down to the road, Noel stopped walking. Her face was pale except for the cold blush on her cheeks, and he understood that she still hadn't quite made up her mind. So he stayed where he was; she had to walk.

She had to decide for herself.

She had to walk away.

She was at *that* moment—just as he had been outside prison, and again standing in front of the jackknifed eighteen-wheeler. He knew he had to leave her alone right now.

He had to wait, and that was one thing he'd learned how to do. Wait.

So when she continued down the driveway to the road, speaking now to the child, he knew she had made her choice. He still didn't put the Trooper in gear. She had to walk all the way to him, get in; then they could go. Together.

Del drove Liesl home from Marquette General, and when they were in her driveway, he came around to her door, opened it, and helped her get out. Walking on the snowpack wasn't easy; her back was still stiff, making her balance precarious. When he offered her his arm, she whispered, "Thank you, kind sir."

Her neighbor's teenage daughter, Darcy, was there, so the house was warm and the teakettle was heating on the stove. Darcy was a plump redheaded girl in a green-and-gold Green Bay Packers sweatshirt that hung almost to the knees of her jeans. She helped Liesl get set up on the couch with pillows and a blanket, then went back into the kitchen.

"Darcy was my daughter's best friend," Liesl said to Del. She seemed tired from the trip. "Her mother runs the kennel down the road. She's home schooling her, so I'm her art teacher, and she spends a lot of time working with me here. I know people think I'm the recluse of the northwoods, but that's not exactly accurate."

Del walked into the studio and looked at the shelves of clay pieces: eagles, wolves, bears, dozens of pots, bowls, and mugs. On the wall there were framed awards and posters advertising her shows in galleries in New York, Chicago, and Minneapolis. "I never understand how someone can do this," he said, his back to her. He was studying the wings of a bald eagle. "See something at a distance and reproduce it on a sheet of paper—or, like this, in three-dimension."

"Method," Darcy said, coming out of the kitchen with two steaming mugs of tea. She was obviously mimicking what Liesl had told her many times. "You must first determine what your *method* is, then the image can be *realized.*"

"I see." Del came back to the living room as Darcy put the mugs on the coffee table.

"Darcy realized these mugs," Liesl said.

"Yeah, but I got to work on my handles. They're crooked."

Del picked up his mug of tea. "Mine seems to be working just fine."

The girl ignored him as she went over to the chair and picked up a loose pile of clothes. "And I found these on the bathroom floor—*a man's clothes!* Liesl, does this mean that you have a boyfriend? A *lover?*"

"I do." Liesl sipped her tea. "But he melted away in the heat of passion."

"Or disintegrated," Darcy said, pinching her nose. *"Pee-you."* As she dropped the pile of clothes on the floor next to the chair, a wad of folded notebook paper fell out of one of the pants pockets.

"Let me see that," Liesl said.

"Love letter?" Darcy went over to the couch and started to unfold the pages. "Hot, dirty sweet nothings, whispered in your ear? Oh, yes, yes, *yes!* I *want* you! I *need* you! I *crave* your, your—"

She started to open the pages, but Liesl snatched them out of her hand. "Be gone, pain in the ass, and don't come back till suppertime."

"Ha!" Darcy stalked into the kitchen. When she had her coat on she came back to the doorway and said, "You going to make *him* melt, *too?*"

"Out!" Liesl said.

Darcy laughed hysterically as she let herself out the kitchen door.

"Twelve," Liesl muttered, opening the pages.

Del sipped his tea from the mug, which had a good heft and a slightly crooked handle.

"Those were Norman's prison pants," she said. "I gave him some of Harold's old things." She looked through the pages until she came to the end. "This is from the girl, from Noel."

"Read it." Del sat on the armrest of the chair across the living room.

Liesl stroked her long braid with one hand while she tilted the pages toward the light from the window. " 'Dear Norman,' " she read. " 'I get your letters and put them in a shoebox. I've written back, but I never send them. I don't know, I just can't. I won't send this to you probably. It's just that sometimes I get like this and I'm so—' I can't make out this part. It might be 'fucked up'? 'I'm so'—yes, it's fucked up—'so much of the time now, and it just makes me sad thinking of you in there. And I don't think we're any better off out here. I thought for a while that I could put it all behind me. Having Lorraine helped me do that, and I suppose to be honest there was a time when I thought that getting married would help me forget, too. But things have gotten so strange between me and Warren. I don't want to go into details. It wouldn't be fair to you. He doesn't live here anymore, which is good. I don't know where he lives really. He just sort of exists, though I think he stays over at Bobby's house a lot. He still comes around more than I wish. And Daddy may be worse than he was. Warren stopped working for Daddy because something's happened between them, and sometimes when I'm talking to one of them I suddenly get scared because all that stuff up in the woods seems to be getting worse. Sometimes when he's drunk Daddy starts talking about the old logging camp and about Raymond, too, he says he was always one with the bears.' " Liesl raised her eyes from the page and said, "All that stuff up in the woods? What old logging camp?"

Del shook his head.

"Raymond? He's the hunter."

"Yates. Went missing before Norman's trial."

"And 'one with the bears'?"

"I don't know," Del said.

Liesl continued to read: " 'There's an Asian guy named Woo-San here now and he's in on something with Daddy. He works days at the motel in the off-season. I usually work nights. But last fall he was up at the lodge for months at a time. He's the new caretaker, and I think he lives in Yates's cabin. I didn't go up there once during hunting season. Daddy kept me busy here in North Eicher.' "

"Woo-San is now caretaker," Del said. "Why an Asian? Why not someone who's familiar with the northwoods?"

"I don't know." Liesl turned the page over and read, " 'I've written about all this stuff to you before, but of course I don't send it. There's nothing you could do, so why worry you, I figure. Maybe I should just go away. I imagine living somewhere else, some city, where I have a job, though I'd really like to go to school sometime. Live there until you get out. I think about how we could start—' There's something crossed out here," Liesl said. " 'No. Instead we could go back so that we are like before, like none of this ever happened. When I talk about what we did to you, how we put you in there, Warren just says what happened happened. Like it was written in the Bible or something. I want us to be able to go back to before what happened happened so we could be like that again. But I don't even think that's possible, though sometimes I do when I read your letters. So I just save them and I write back to you like I am right now and I never mail them to you. I wish you could just somehow *know*. Just know how I wish what happened had never happened no matter what Warren says. Or what my father thinks. He thinks everybody gets what they deserve and so you ought to be where you are. I wish you would just know how sorry I am and how scared I get sometimes lately. I wish you would lie beside me on these long cold nights. I wish you would know what Lorraine looks like. Maybe I'll send you a photo? But that might be hard, looking at her picture all the time. I just don't know. This is just so stupid I'm going to stop now. Maybe I'll send it so you can see how bad things are with me. But I won't. It wouldn't do any good. I hope you're well and that you continue to remember how it was before. Love, Noel.' " Liesl laid the pages in her lap and picked up her mug of tea. "She was 'fucked up' when she wrote this, so much so that she sent this one."

"Probably before she could reconsider."

"What's she afraid of?" Liesl asked. "What's 'out in the woods'?"

"I don't know."

"I think Norman knows, whatever it is," she said. "Or, if he doesn't know, he wants to find out. When he was here I just got the feeling he's running *toward* something."

"What are you saying?"

"I'm saying he needs to be brought in." She sipped her tea and stroked her thick blond braid as though it were a pet. "He's a troubled boy," she said. "Will the state police understand that?"

Del put down his mug of tea. "Now that the snow's stopped it'll turn real cold."

"You're going to go look for him." It wasn't a question.

Del stood up and went over to the window next to the sofa. The sun was on the new snow. "After your accident, I really looked for that green truck. I know that you were counting on it being found, but, I'm sorry, I never came up with a thing." He waited, but she didn't say anything. Finally he said, "I'll see what I can do."

"You'll let me know if you find something out. Won't you?"

"Sure," he said, turning from the window.

"I mean it."

"I know. Thanks for the tea."

He didn't move. She reached across the armrest and took hold of his hand. "Been a long time since I held someone's hand. I could get used to it."

"I could, too."

She smiled up at him then, her eyes large and blue. "Must be those meds they gave me. What's your excuse?" She squeezed his hand a moment and released him.

"You'll be all right? By yourself?"

"Have been for years." She leaned back and closed her eyes. "Darcy'll be back later to help with dinner."

"Good." He watched her a moment longer. She didn't open her eyes, and he knew she wouldn't until he was gone.

He went out through the shed and drove down off the hill. With the sun up now, he wore his sunglasses because of the glare off the snow. His Land Cruiser was a '76 that had been rebuilt from the axles up. With four-wheel drive engaged, he could get down snowbound roads where few other vehicles could go. When he reached the county road, he called Monty at the station in Yellow Dog Township.

"Alberta clipper's coming across Superior," Monty said. "Big time."

"No word about the walkaway from the state police?"

"*Nada.* Why go out looking for the kid when you can stay inside where it's warm? He's going to freeze his ass eventually, and it'll either kill him or he'll turn himself in."

This was true: Marquette Prison dated back to the middle of the nineteenth century, and there were numerous incidents where prisoners had escaped, only to turn themselves in owing to the severity of the Upper Peninsula's climate and terrain. Those who didn't usually died.

"Check that sheet we got on the kid," Del said. "What was the last name of the girlfriend in North Eicher? P-something?"

"Hold on." Monty rummaged through some paperwork on the desk. "Okay, here, it's Pronovost, Noel Pronovost."

"Right," Del said. "I'm heading over that way. Now that the snow's stopped, it shouldn't take me much more than an hour."

"If the roads have been plowed," Monty said. "You have any idea how cold it's going to get? The wind's going to come up as the Alberta clipper comes in off the lake. Lucy on the Weather Channel was talking about windchills of sixty below."

"Monty?"

"Yeah?"

"That cigarillo you got smelling up the office—put it out right now."

"Have a nice trip." Monty hung up.

The second time Warren drove by Noel's apartment, Noel's Trooper still wasn't in the driveway. It was after ten in the morning, which probably meant that after leaving the motel, she'd gone out to her father's to pick up Lorraine and she was still there, scrubbing the kitchen floor, cleaning the bathroom, doing laundry. Countless times Warren had told her that she was nothing but her old man's maid, that she should break free of him. But she couldn't. She was too weak. As long as her father took care of the rent on her apartment, as long as he paid the electric bill, the phone bill, the gas credit card bill on the Isuzu Trooper he'd bought for her, he was going to have a clean house, clean clothes, a vacuumed wall-to-wall carpet.

Warren kept driving, and each time he inhaled on a cigarette a twinge of pain swelled up through his ribs. He'd taken a pounding like this once while he was in the navy. It was over a hooker in the Gas Lamp Quarter of San Diego. This sailor from the sub base, a big kid from Alabama, decided he liked Warren's hooker better, said it was because she had a pierced tongue with one of those little gold studs for giving head. By the time the military patrol van came, the sailor was gone, and Warren had had his face rubbed in gravel out along the curb and it felt as though all of the ribs on his left side were broken. It took him over a month to find out who that sailor was, but by then his sub had gone out on maneuvers. Long after his bruises healed and he had stopped pissing blood, it still bugged Warren that the kid had not gotten back what he deserved. Warren looked again in the rearview mirror and inspected his swollen left cheek. The purple bruise reminded him of sunsets he had seen while on tour duty in the Pacific.

CHAPTER

Nine

As they drove through North Eicher, Norman avoided eye contact with the girl. Noel had strapped her in the car seat in back, and he couldn't help but see the child's face. She was shy and quiet, and she tended to stare at the back of his head instead of into the mirror. He assumed she was confused; he must look like Warren to her, but she knew he was someone else. Noel had simply told the girl that his name was Norman and that they were all going bye-bye.

After that, Noel said little since they'd left her father's house. She stared out her side window mostly, and occasionally she turned to check on the girl.

"You had a moment back there in your father's driveway," he said when they reached downtown. "You made a decision."

She didn't say anything.

"You want, I can still let both of you off right here."

Her head was turned so she was gazing out at the new high snowbanks in front of the stores. "I've been trying to make that decision for a long time, Norman. My mother made it once too and left my father. Years ago. She was from downstate outside Grand Rapids. Everyone over there seemed to be Dutch. Towns like Zeeland and Holland. Daddy's from up here, and his parents came over from Quebec. When

I was eleven I knew there was something different about my mother, but I didn't understand until I came home from school one day and found her suitcases opened on their bed. I asked her where they were going—somehow I understood that I wasn't going on this trip. It was maybe three in the afternoon, and she was having a drink. Before that day I'd never seen her drink anything more than a glass of wine with dinner. She sat on the bed and started crying. Then she told me that I should go over to Ellen's, my friend who lived down the street, and stay there until dinnertime. She said she was going to visit a friend who was very ill. I believed her, but somehow I knew I wasn't getting the whole story."

Once they were out of town, Norman drove faster. A strong gust of wind hit the left side of the Trooper and he had a hard time keeping away from the snowbank. Noel turned around and put her hand on the girl's cheek a moment. "It's okay, honey. Just a little wind."

Norman made a whistling sound through his teeth. The girl watched him in the mirror until he stopped. Something in her large blue eyes said that she knew she wasn't getting the whole story.

Noel faced forward and said, "My mother was a model before she was married. I've seen ads that were in Sunday newspapers in the seventies. Dresses, sweaters, bras. She could have had a career if she hadn't met my father and moved up north."

"But she got away."

"For three days. She ran off with a guy and was back in three days."

"You never told me this. What guy?"

"Later. Let's talk about this later." She turned to him and waited a moment; he knew she had something on her mind. "I should drive through customs," she said. "It's my car. I have my license, in case we get stopped."

He took one hand off the steering wheel, and for a moment he wanted to reach out to her—just hold her arm or her hand. Instead he ran his fingers through his short hair. "I thought you were going to say you wanted to get out."

"I don't want out, Norman," she said as she shook her head. "I know this is crazy, and I keep waiting for that to really sink in, but I'm *not* going back. Not now. I *can't.* I really have been trying to do this for a while. You don't know what it's been like, between your brother and my father."

He glanced up in the mirror. Lorraine's eyes were getting heavy, and she'd be asleep in a few minutes. He realized it was their talking—adults talking—coupled with the drone of the engine that would put her out.

"When we get around this bend," Noel said, "pull over and I'll drive."

"I don't know."

"It only makes sense that I drive until we cross the border."

When they came out of the bend, there was nothing ahead except woods along both sides of the road. Norman stopped the Trooper and turned to her. "We're not going to Sault Ste. Marie," he said. "The cops'll expect that. They can just wait for me at the border."

There was a twitch in Noel's cheek, just below the ear. He recalled that it meant that she was grinding her teeth because she was frightened. "That's why I should drive. Even if we did manage to get across to Canada, they'd still be looking for me. How long do you think it would take the Mounties to find us? Noel, at least if I'm driving and we get stopped, you can tell them I made you come with me."

"No."

"It only makes sense."

"I won't *do* that."

"I hope you don't have to. Right now they're looking for the brown Dodge van."

They sat in the Trooper, staring out at the empty road, both sides lined with snow-covered trees. The road here was straight for several miles, and the woods seemed to converge at the horizon, as though at that point the road would simply end.

"I never realized how *hard* it is to get out of Michigan." She was almost shouting over the heater blower. "It's big and surrounded mostly by water. I don't know, Norman. What are we going to *do?*" There was a fierceness in her expression that made her profile seem sharp, focused, yet in the glare off the new snow her green eyes were incredibly pale. Again, Norman had to keep himself from reaching over and touching her sleeve.

"I have an idea," he said, speaking quietly now. Lorraine had fallen asleep in her car seat, her face slack and a strand of drool hanging off her lower lip.

"What?" Noel said.

"I've been thinking about where we *should* go. Up into the woods." She turned her head and stared out at the road. "You want to go back, you really want to go back to *before* what happened happened," he said, "first you got to go where it *happened.*"

"Norman."

"Like you said in your letter."

After a moment she said, "You know what this means?"

"Maybe—I'm not sure. It probably means I'll get caught. But at least it won't be caught running. And maybe—maybe I can find out exactly what they've been doing out there in the woods. Look what they've done to me—to us. If I do, maybe that'll count for something, I don't know." She didn't say anything. "Look," he said. "I've been thinking about this ever since I got your letter. I wanted to come back and see you, see Lorraine. But I didn't plan on this, on you coming with me—not out there. I thought I'd do that alone."

She turned to him finally. "All right, Norman. This is nuts, but all *right.*" She didn't seem frightened now, but angry and perhaps determined. "*You* go out there, we *all* go."

As he drove to North Eicher, Del saw nothing but snowplows. The wind was building out of the northwest, blowing new snowdrifts across the road. He made a call on his cellular phone to Monty.

"Anything?"

"Nada," Monty said. "I called this guy I know with the state police over in the Soo. Nobody's seen anything, and you can bet nobody's looking very hard in this stuff."

"Anything else?"

"Only thing is I had to run over to Hasslebrink's Repair."

"He finally had a heart attack."

"If he did, you'd owe me five bucks. No, he had two customers who wanted to go duke city right there in his shop. One wanted his snowmobile fixed pronto. The other had brought in his snowblower. It was a no-brainer. I said the snowblower gets looked at first. I tell ya, that snowmobile guy was pissed."

"I bet."

"You should have seen the snowblower, Del. It was a Toro eight-horse. Must have been at least thirty years old and in mint condition."

"I bet. Call me if anybody finds Norman or this Dodge van."

"You bet."

Halfway to North Eicher, Del stopped at a crossroads diner called Koski's Korner, which was known for its pasty: beef, potatoes, rutabagas, onions, and carrots all cooked in a crusty pouch. Miners took pasties to work because they stayed warm for hours and could be held by their crust. Del's grandfather had worked in the copper mines up in the Keweenaw Peninsula, and his grandmother had made pasties Sunday through Thursday night. When his grandfather took Del and his father bow hunting, they brought pasties. He hadn't gone hunting since he was twenty-eight, the year his father and grandfather both died, and he now ate pasties only when it was extremely cold out. The radio said the windchill was thirty below and falling, so he indulged himself. There were two schools of thought concerning pasties: to eat them with gravy or with ketchup. Del favored ketchup, except when it was this cold; then he went with gravy, because it would give him more to burn.

When he was back on the road, he called directory assistance. There were two Pronovosts listed in North Eicher, Noel and a man he presumed was her father. Del called Rejean Pronovost, who answered on the second ring. It was almost noon, and he sounded as though he'd just gotten up.

"Sir, this is Del Maki, sheriff of Yellow Dog Township."

"Uh-huh," Pronovost said. He cleared his throat, then inhaled: smoker.

"I was wondering if you'd heard about Norman Haas?"

"What about him?"

"He escaped from prison."

"Uh-huh." Pronovost inhaled. "Thought you were going to say he was dead."

"Just wondered if anyone's contacted you, or your daughter."

"You mean the police?" Pronovost snorted. "Nope."

"Thought it might be possible that he'd go home to North Eicher."

"Now that wouldn't be too smart. But I don't know if that kid's capable of doing the smart thing. Where the hell are you?" Pronovost asked. "What's that noise?"

"I'm driving, sir."

"What you got?"

"Old Land Cruiser."

"Sounds like a friggin' Zamboni."

"Yes, sir."

"Goes in anything, those Land Cruisers, eh?"

"Just about. I was wondering about your daughter. Is she there, in North Eicher?"

"Yeah, she clerks nights at the motel and leaves her daughter with me usually. She's already been by to pick her up. Came and went before I got up." Pronovost hesitated a moment. "I'll give a call over to her apartment, just to check. Let me have your number so I know how to reach you."

Pronovost called back in less than two minutes. "She didn't answer," he said. He sounded more alert than before. "She might be out shopping, but I called her neighbor, who often looks after the child, and she says she hasn't seen her or her car all morning."

"Still, they might be doing errands," Del said.

"Might be."

"I'm almost to North Eicher," Del said. "Mind if I stop by?"

"I'll be in my shop. Let me give you directions." There was something halting in the man's voice now, as though he were trying to remember something while he was speaking. He inhaled deeply and often.

Warren still had a key to Noel's apartment, and sometimes he went there while she was out. He used to play with her mind a bit, stuff like removing all the light bulbs. That was the best one—it absolutely freaked her out to come home to an entirely dark apartment. But now he usually just watched television and kept an eye on the road for her Trooper. She'd returned only once while he was there, and he'd been able to slip out the back door and walk to his truck, which was parked a block away.

Today he was restless, and though he had *Regis and Kathie Lee* on, he paced in and out of rooms. When they were first married, Warren liked it—sharing a bedroom, a bathroom, sitting in the kitchen having eggs for breakfast. And the baby—he'd tried, but Noel had said he'd tried too hard. Overbearing, she'd said. As if he wanted Lorraine all to himself, except when it came to the work—the feedings, the diapers, the laundry, the cleaning—he just couldn't hack it. So the more responsibility Noel took on, the more he ended up watching television while she'd be in the bedroom or the kitchen, always doing something for Lorraine. It had *all* become about Lorraine. He went into the bedroom and opened the top drawer of Noel's bureau. He took a pair of blue panties into the bathroom, squeezed some toothpaste into the crotch, and then put them back in the drawer. In the baby's room he arranged a set of plastic blocks on the floor into letters that spelled *P-U-S-S-Y.*

Back in the living room he looked at the photographs on the bookshelf. There were fewer than when he'd lived there because she'd removed the photographs he was in, but one that he'd taken of her was still in the corner by her high school yearbooks. On their honeymoon they'd taken a tour boat over to Mackinac Island and walked from the village up to the Grand Hotel. There was a kid working for the hotel who sat at a card table in the driveway, collecting a fee from anyone who wanted to walk on the famous porch that ran the length of the hotel. The fee was three dollars per person, and Noel said it was ridiculous to pay money simply to walk on a porch, so they started back down to the village; but then Warren led her through some bushes and across the front lawn of the hotel, and it was quite easy for them simply to go up onto the porch as if they owned the place. He took her picture, leaning against one of the wide, white columns. Her blond hair, longer then and bleached by the sun, was blown across one cheek, and she was wearing a yellow tank top, no bra. Warren knew the taste and fineness of that hair, the color and shape of those nipples. When he thought of Noel he saw her as she looked in this photograph. Something about her mouth, about her eyes—innocent, but with a definite touch of "fuck me."

Warren took the photograph off the shelf and sat on the couch. He undid his belt and jeans and started to beat off slowly. He stared at the photograph, and occasionally he'd look up at Kathie Lee on the television because she had nice tits. But his face hurt, his ribs ached, and he wasn't really into it. He'd been a lot harder last night when Leah had sucked him off.

Ted Danson was telling Regis and Kathie Lee about his new show when the phone rang. Warren kept going, and after the fourth ring the answering machine went on—Noel's father had recorded it, telling callers that *we* were not available. When the message was over, there was the beep, and her father's voice came over the line.

"Noel? When you get in, give me a call at the house." Warren let go of himself. He scaled the photograph across the living room. The plastic frame broke when it struck the television screen, but Ted kept on talking and Regis and Kathie Lee kept interrupting. "I've heard that

Norman's loose, and I just want to know where you and Lorraine are," Noel's father said. "You call me." He hung up.

Warren zipped up his jeans and got off the couch. He buckled his belt as he walked through the apartment to the back door. Noel wasn't here and she wasn't at her father's, cleaning his toilets or whatever. The bitch wasn't where she was supposed to be, unless she'd gone shopping.

As they drove north, the snowbanks were so high that Noel could seldom see over them to either side of the road, so they were traveling down a long white furrow beneath a blue sky. "It's making me queasy," she said. "The snow—it's so, I don't know, claustrophobic. And the sky, doesn't it seem *empty?*"

"Yeah, it does," he said. "Good thing we're not on drugs or something." She laughed. It was the first time he'd made anything close to a joke. Or perhaps he was on to her? Perhaps he could tell that she had several vials of pills in her bag and that there was hardly a day anymore that didn't require some combination of pharmaceuticals.

"It feels more like we're on a treadmill," he said. "We're moving, but it doesn't seem like we're getting anywhere."

"That's what it's been like day after day after *day* in North Eicher."

"Really? Try prison."

"Was it awful?"

Now he laughed.

"Your cell, it was tiny with no window?"

"I wasn't in a cell. Trustees sleep in a barracks kind of thing, a big room with beds."

"No cellmate?" She hesitated. "It was you and all these other men?"

"Was I raped? Is that what you're asking?"

She knew he had turned his head to look at her, but she kept her eyes on the road, on the whiteness of the snow, the blue overhead. She was suddenly tired; she had hardly slept last night. She picked up her bag off the floor and opened it. "I have a headache," she said, taking out one of the vials.

"Are you asking if I was raped, Noel?"

"It doesn't matter," she said. "No. I mean it doesn't matter—to *me.*"

He had looked back at the road. "What are those?"

"These? They're for headaches."

"Aspirin?"

"No, they're a prescription. I get a lot of headaches, and aspirin doesn't help."

"What, migraines?"

"Yeah, I feel one coming on." She unscrewed the plastic cap on the vial and tapped out a white pill.

"I knew a guy inside who got migraines all the time," Norman said. "He got these auras, too. Something happened to his vision, so there was sort of a hole in the middle. He could see all around it, but not right in the center. They'd come and go. He had white pills for them—sort of like that one—but it wasn't any prescription from the doctor."

Noel looked at the pill in her palm a moment, working up saliva in her mouth. "I get auras too sometimes. Between my headaches, my auras, and being deaf in one ear, sometimes I get the impression that my head just doesn't work too good. Like it malfunctions, and I feel very—very disoriented." She took the pill and swallowed hard.

Turning her head, she saw that Norman was watching her carefully. "I want you to understand something," he said, looking back at the road. The snowpack was slippery, and he wasn't going more than thirty miles an hour. "Things inside, they're different than outside. I'm still the same me. Understand? I'm still the same me."

For a moment she thought she was going to cry. She made herself busy by closing up her bag and putting it back on the floor. "Did they hurt you?" she said quietly.

"No. No, I didn't get raped. And no, because after what they did to Bing I finally walked away."

"Bing? He was a friend? What did they do?"

"Doesn't matter now. It's done. And I walked away."

"Okay." Noel stared out at the snow and sky. The Trooper kept moving forward. The furrow seemed deeper now, the blue sky even bigger. But it wasn't as threatening. It was easier to be lost in all this glaring light, easier than at night when she'd sit alone in the front office of the motel, staring at her reflection in the plate glass window. Sometimes she'd put on her coat and go outside. She'd walk away from the building, until she was out of sight of the motel's amber lights. On clear nights there were so many stars. She'd stare across the field toward the hills that rose above that side of town. On moonless nights the hills were perfectly black, and sometimes she was able to stare right into that blackness until she couldn't stand the cold any longer. It frightened her, this total darkness with the stars above, and because it frightened her she felt she needed to look at it as long as possible. She thought of it as preparation.

"Your father," Norman said. "He'll assume we've gone to Canada."

Noel wasn't sure how much time had passed. "I doubt he'd think that we'd come way out here, to Big Pine Lodge." She felt her lower lip with her fingers. "The thing with Daddy is he never wonders how someone *else* thinks. He never understood why my mother came back after three days."

"Why did she?"

"For me," Noel said. "I understood that right away. In fact, though I was frightened, I knew she was going to come back. I don't know how, but I just knew it. And when she came back she had this look on her face, like she'd seen this in*cre*dible horror. In a way, she never lost that look until she died."

"Didn't she leave with another man?"

"He was a friend of my parents'. Afterwards, he moved out of the state." She smiled briefly. "I think Daddy persuaded him to *think* that it would be a good idea to just disappear."

Norman glanced up in the mirror as Lorraine stirred from her nap. Noel turned around and saw that Lorraine was staring back at Norman earnestly; she didn't seem frightened, only confused. Noel knew she wanted to know why this man looked like Warren.

"Honey," Noel said, and waited until Lorraine looked at her. "Honey, this is your father. He's been away a long time, but now he's come back to us." Suddenly Noel's eyes misted over, and Lorraine watched her with absolute fascination. "It's all right, Mommy's not *sad.* Daddy's come *back* to us. Somehow I *always* knew he would—isn't that *strange?*"

Norman slowly reached into the backseat until his fingertips touched Lorraine's cheek. She stared at him and didn't move away.

CHAPTER Ten

Del found the house just outside of North Eicher. The sign at the end of the driveway read:

REJEAN PRONOVOST
Real Estate
Home Appraisal & Inspection
Land Survey
Taxidermy

Pronovost met Del in the neatly plowed driveway outside his workshop. As they shook hands, he stared right at Del. A lot of people didn't look at a police officer in the face, not right off, anyway. He was six or seven years older than Del, very fit, compactly built—the thick shoulders and short legs of a hockey player. Since childhood Del had seen a lot of guys like this skating on ponds and rinks. His curly black hair went gray at the sideburns, and he had a trimmed white mustache beneath a crooked nose that might have been broken more than once. His handshake was a polite contest of strength. "Folks just call me Pronovost."

"Del Maki."

"Anybody ever call you Chico?"

"No. Delbert was bad enough."

"Uh-huh. Wayne Chico Maki was a good steady player for the Blackhawks. Never understood how a Finn got the name Chico."

"Me neither."

"I appreciate you driving out here, Sheriff." He was wearing a good overcoat with a fur-lined hood. "You know, this whole business will probably seem pretty silly when it turns out that Noel's been buying groceries all morning."

"I suppose. When's the last time you saw her?"

"Last night. She dropped her daughter, Lorraine, off before going to work at the motel. Picked her up this morning."

"You didn't see her then?"

"No, I was still, you know, asleep." Pronovost tilted his head to one side, and Del understood he was referring to his drinking the night before. "Nothing unusual about that." He led the way into the garage. "I just got a call from Woo-San, who works days over the motel. I own the place, and he's bought a piece of it. How 'bout we go over there a minute? Small town—it's only a few blocks."

"In Yellow Dog Township we don't really have what you'd call blocks."

Pronovost laughed as he got into his Ford pickup. It was so quiet, Del could hardly hear the engine. "Fuckin' cold," Pronovost said once they were on the road. "Supposed to really get down there today, then more snow tomorrow."

"That's what I hear."

"You know, smart guys our age go live someplace like Florida or Arizona, come back up here for trout season, and head south again after hunting season's over. Call 'em snowbirds."

"I've never missed a northern winter," Del said.

"Me neither." Pronovost laughed. "Guess we're just not smart guys, eh?"

When they reached the motel office, an Asian man was sitting behind the counter. It was impossible to tell his age—somewhere between forty-five and sixty.

Pronovost said, "Woo-San, tell Sheriff Maki what you just told me on the phone."

Woo-San hesitated a moment. He did not look toward Del, but spoke to Pronovost. "The girl who make up the rooms says that lights are left on in number twelve, so she went in and found that the bed has been slept in and someone take shower." His thin lower lip quivered suddenly, and he seemed personally insulted as he tapped his finger on a book that lay open on the counter. "There *no* name for number twelve."

"What're you saying, Woo-San?" Pronovost asked.

"No mystery to me."

The two men stared across the counter at each other. Del felt almost embarrassed, as though he'd walked in on the middle of a family squabble.

"Your daughter work here last night," Woo-San said. "Room get used and there is *no* entry, *no record* that someone stay there. We don't get paid, and we have to do laundry, pay electricity and hot water." Again Woo-San tapped the book. He had inordinately long fingernails, which made his wrinkled hand seem oddly feminine. "Man," he said, his voice shaking now. "She let a man stay there. Why she do that? You tell me—*you* tell *me.* Your daughter. She go see a man in room twelve. *Your* daughter."

Pronovost had gone tight in the face and shoulders. Del had seen it countless times, often during arguments in bars or after fender-benders. Pronovost looked as if he were about to reach across the counter and take hold of Woo-San. On a hockey team he would be the player known as the enforcer.

"How do you know?" Del asked quickly. Woo-San regarded him as though he hadn't noticed him before. "How do you know it was a man in the room last night?"

Woo-San's mouth opened and he was about to say something, then he just shook his head as though it weren't worth explaining.

"The toilet seats," Pronovost said. He laughed tensely. "It's this theory Woo-San worked up. If the toilet seat's left up, a man stayed in the room. He's done research, I swear. He's checked the names in the register against the raised toilet seats. What do you call that—inductive or deductive reasoning? I can never keep 'em straight."

Woo-San now looked at Del as though he were appealing to someone reasonable and just, someone who was his intellectual equal and could see the significance and logic of his assertion. "There no question, *no question!*"

Pronovost took a step closer to the counter and took his hands out of his coat pockets.

"Woo-San," Del said, "would you mind if I had a look at room twelve?"

Woo-San studied his nails a moment, as though he were wondering how they'd gotten so long. "Doesn't matter if you FBI." He now seemed weary of the whole thing. "The room's made up already. There no *evidence.*"

"Jesus." Pronovost turned and started toward the office door. "Come on," he said, "we're wasting our time with this."

Woo-San folded his hands on the counter, as though he were praying. "If you're sheriff, why not in uniform?"

"Ah." Del inhaled, then exhaled slowly. He took his wallet from one of the pockets inside his overcoat, flipped it open, and held up his badge. Behind him, Pronovost went outside, leaving behind a cold draft of air, followed by the clap of the storm door.

Del leaned forward slightly and spoke quietly. "So a man stayed in room twelve last night, and he didn't pay—why?"

Woo-San's eyes had what appeared to be an ancient weariness. His voice was so deep that it seemed to come straight from the center of his chest. "Why you think? This what you call no-brainer."

Warren sat in a booth by the window in Jacques' Diner, watching Pronovost walk back across the motel parking lot to his truck. The son of a bitch was pissed off about something—it was evident in his strut, in the hunch of his shoulders. He was like those animals in the nature shows, the birds and reptiles that puff themselves up whenever they feel threatened. They raise hackles, fins, any number of appendages designed specifically to make them look bigger. Some have false eyes and mouths, always larger than the real ones, which are intended to deceive a predator into thinking they're capable of warding off an attack. Some emit a scent or a spray. Some, if bitten, are poisonous, stunning the attacker, which is then devoured. Or, in some cases, such as that of a spider and a wasp, the attacker becomes the host for the offspring of the prey. Noel watched all those animal programs, read about them in magazines. She was a taxidermist's daughter, so after years of watching her father stuff animals, she had developed an interest in live ones. Warren often told her she missed the point of those shows: *Animals eat each other, and human beings are animals, too.* That's how nature works.

Warren watched the other man, who wore a big green coat, come out of the motel office and follow Pronovost. He was taller, a bit younger, seemed more agile. Something about his posture suggested that he was not intimidated by Pronovost's display of anger. Probably had to do with that Chinaman, who worked the desk most days. Things between Warren and Pronovost had gone sour since Woo-San had come to town. It was a different game now. As he crossed the parking lot, Pronovost waved his arms as he spoke, but it was clear that Green Coat was taking control. He kept his hands in his pockets, and Pronovost finally nodded agreement.

Warren pushed away his breakfast plate. Smeared egg yolk, leftover hash browns, a crust of toast. Leah came over to his booth and picked up the plate.

"You don't look so good, honey," she said. "That bruise must be sore."

He leaned back and lit a cigarette. "It's not the bruise."

When she waited tables she always wore her blond hair up. It reminded him of Noel, how she'd put her hair up before taking a bath, revealing the curve of her neck, the little hollow above the collarbone.

Leah took her free hand off her hip, wiped it on her apron, and removed the cigarette from his lips. "You ought to just take it easy today. Go back to Bobby's and lie down." She drew on his cigarette deeply, exhaled. "Get yourself a bit of a buzz going, and I'll be back by two. Maybe we could play doctor?" She held the cigarette out to him and scowled. "You think too much sometimes. I can see it in those deep eyes in your lumpy head."

He took the cigarette back from her. "Really?" She nodded. "And what am I thinking about right now?"

Leah glanced down at his crotch. "You getting a morning hard-on, honey?"

"Yeah, and it's all for you."

She opened her mouth and let him see a little tongue. "Naa. I don't think so."

"No? Who else would it be for?"

"The guy gave you that swollen cheek," she said. "You're thinking revenge."

Warren drew on his cigarette and then he smiled at her, exhaling. "You're a very perceptive woman. And you have a nice ass, too. That's a lethal package."

Leah smiled, turned, and carried his empty plate back to the kitchen. Her apron was snug on her hips. Half a dozen men sat on stools along the counter, eating, drinking coffee, and each head turned to watch her walk down to the kitchen and push through the swinging door. Chain reaction.

Across the street, Pronovost and Green Coat were getting into the truck. No waving arms now, just earnest discussion. Probably negotiating some real estate deal. Maybe sell Green Coat a share of the motel. Or better, hire Green Coat to knock down the motel and build apartments. Better still, condominiums. Condos in North Eicher—right. Warren had heard Pronovost's spiel. The man believed he could buy, sell, or trade anything. He'd bought into Pronovost's bullshit when he first became his son-in-law. But the bullshit changed, and then Pronovost pulled away. He no longer needed Warren's help with his rental properties; and last fall he said he was going to stop bringing hunting parties out to Big Pine Lodge. Woo-San's arrival in town had something to do with it. The guy just shows up and all of a sudden he's working at the motel and he's the caretaker out at the lodge. When Warren was stationed in San Diego, he'd met some Asians. Some of them born over there, some on the West Coast. Why Woo-San ended up in North Eicher, Warren wasn't sure. It had to do with the thing he and Pronovost had in common—not just greed, but absolute greed. You had to admire the purity of it.

As Pronovost drove the few blocks back to his house, Del listened to him work his tongue over his teeth, as though he were trying to dislodge food. After shouting in the parking lot, the man now seemed contrite, though even more anxious. "You don't know for certain that it was Norman who stayed in room twelve."

"I can't be certain of anything. He was last known to be traveling in this direction in a brown Dodge registered to Rodney Aaberg. It's just a possibility: Norman came here, and he left with Noel and the girl."

"Abducted," Pronovost said as he pulled into his driveway next to Del's Land Cruiser. "They didn't *leave,* he's *abducted* her. *Them:* my daughter and granddaughter." He shut off the motor but made no move to get out.

"It's the child that I don't get," Del said. "You're asleep when Noel comes into the house, puts her daughter in her snowsuit, and leaves.

What, does Norman come in the house with her? How's he persuade her? And you said she drives a Trooper? If they left in the van, her Trooper should have still been there at the motel."

"He must have been with her when she picked up Lorraine," Pronovost said.

"Don't know how, is all. It just seems pretty risky, Norman coming in the house, knowing you're there. How can he be sure you're asleep, that you won't wake up?"

"I bet he's armed."

Del considered this a moment. "Where's Norman get a gun?" he asked. "But then, let's give him credit—he's gotten this far. He's walked away from prison. Snowshoed through a blizzard. Ridden in an eighteen-wheeler, stolen a van, and now, well, it's also possible, I guess, that he's in your daughter's Trooper." Del pulled on his gloves. "Maybe he's quick, lucky—and persuasive. That's a tough combination."

Pronovost reached for his door handle but paused. "You're not suggesting she went with him *willingly.*"

Del shook his head. "All I know is they could be together. Let's say it's more than possible—it's probable. Why else would he be headed in this direction?" He opened his door, admitting a blast of cold air, and got out. "I'm going to make a call from my phone," he said.

"Come inside and call. Get out of this wind."

They went up the driveway and into his workshop. Del glanced up at the forest of antlers overhead. There was a phone on the wall at the end of a long bench covered with tools. He called Monty and said, "Anything?"

"Still nothing."

"My guess is that Haas isn't traveling alone now," Del said. "He's with his old girlfriend and her baby. They're either in the Dodge van or her Isuzu Trooper, Michigan registration under the name of Noel Pronovost. She's blond and the kid's about three, a girl named Lorraine."

"I'll call the staties." Monty was silent a moment. "This the same girlfriend that got beat up?"

"Right. And I'm not convinced he's dragging her along by the hair."

"That's interesting. Must be real love."

"Maybe," Del said.

At the far end of the bench, Pronovost was sharpening a knife on a whetstone.

"You think they could get through customs, the three of them?" Monty asked.

"Possible."

"I doubt it," Monty said. "They're checking everybody closely, and he can't hide in the trunk because a Trooper doesn't have one. But in this weather, chances are they haven't even *reached* the Soo yet. When they get there the staties'll pick them up."

"I suppose," Del said.

"You know, you almost sound like you're rooting for this kid."

Del thought about how Liesl sounded when she was still in the hospital. In a way, she was almost pleading that this escapee that left her for dead in the snow be saved. After a moment, he said, "Just call the state police, okay?"

He hung up and walked down to where Pronovost was mixing some chemicals in a plastic cup. Before him was the head of a buck with a ten-point rack. The eyes looked real except that they didn't move.

Pronovost seemed to have found new resolve. "Let's suppose, just for discussion's sake, it's not exactly an abduction."

"Do you think that's possible?"

"My daughter's a woman. How the fuck am I supposed to know why she does what she does? I'm trying to think this through, is all."

"The Soo is at least four hours from here in good weather. Or they could go west, through Duluth, and head up into the Boundary Waters region. You can get real lost in there. But they may have gotten stuck, or the road may not be plowed all the way. If they try to cross the border, they'll be picked up, most likely."

On the far wall there was the upper torso of a black bear. Its arms were raised as though prepared to claw a victim and its jaws were wide open, revealing false teeth and tongue. The head and protruding snout were huge, and the eyes possessed a fierce certainty. Below was a plaque, an award from a national competition. It reminded Del of the awards on Liesl's wall, one for an eagle she'd done. Taxidermy and sculpture—both came from the same impulse, which was to preserve an image.

In the corner was a small color photograph of a woman, smiling and stark naked.

"Nice, huh?" Pronovost said. "Some years ago I get a call from a guy downstate. Says he read about my work and he had a once-in-a-lifetime job for me that would pay well, if I did it right away. I told him I had enough work to keep me busy at least a year. But he insists it's got to be right now. I say, What is it, fish or fowl? He says he'll FedEx me a photo, then call. Next morning that picture is delivered, and I think it's a joke, but he calls up not an hour later and asks will I do it. The day before, his thirty-two-year-old wife was killed in a car accident. So he offered me ten thousand dollars to do the job." Pronovost took a moment to light a cigarette. He'd told this story before and knew the pause was part of the effect. Exhaling, he said, "I told him I don't mount women for money. So he offered me fifteen." Leaning over the deer head on the bench, he seemed so preoccupied, as though he were alone.

"And?"

"Oh, and I hung up."

Del studied the owl and the bear again. Pronovost was now so calm, where fifteen minutes ago he was having a fit at the motel. When people got bad news, the kind that usually involved the police—accidents, deaths, missing persons—their behavior would often be erratic, ranging from hysterical to nearly comatose. Pronovost, hunched over his workbench, now seemed to have taken shelter in the routine of his avocation. "I think that maybe I've followed this as far as it can go for now," Del said.

Pronovost placed a hand on the buck's neck and smoothed down a tuft of fur. "I see."

"If I hear anything, if they show up at the border, I'll let you know."

"I'd appreciate it, Sheriff." Pronovost leaned closer to his work.

Del went out into the cold, got into his Land Cruiser, and drove back through town. He kept telling himself to keep driving, to get back to Yellow Dog before dark, before the cold really set in—cold like this caused machines to just lock up; get stuck fifteen miles away from a town and you could freeze to death. On more than one occasion he had found stranded motorists frozen in the seats of their cars. Their faces were blue white and they looked less authentic than the animals in Pronovost's workshop. When he reached the motel he turned in and went into the office.

"I want a room," he said to Woo-San. "I want room twelve."

"Room twelve?"

"You said it had already been cleaned."

Woo-San bowed his head once.

"Okay, then I want it." Woo-San placed a registration card on the counter, which Del filled out. "And I saw a Chinese take-out place down the street. They deliver?" Woo-San bowed his head again. "What do you recommend?"

"Recommend?"

"What's good there? You know them, what they cook?" Woo-San seemed confused. "Related? They family?"

"Family? Restaurant? No. But dumplings okay. You try dumplings." As Del pushed the registration card across the counter, Woo-San grinned. "Cash or charge?"

After his umpteenth cup of coffee, Warren was about to leave Jacques' Diner when he saw a Land Cruiser pull into the motel lot across the street. Green Coat got out and went into the office. On the door panel of the Land Cruiser was a small chipped and faded insignia, beneath which read: "Sheriff, Yellow Dog Township."

Warren turned toward the counter, where there were only two other customers now. "Where the fuck is Yellow Dog Township?" he asked.

Guy Marchoud, who ran the gas station down the street, didn't even look up from the sports section of the *Milwaukee Journal Sentinal.* "Township? I don't know about any township, but there's good fishing on that river." He tapped cigarette ash on the side of his plate and turned the page of the newspaper. "Somewhere outside Marquette."

Now Warren lit another cigarette as he gazed out the window toward the motel. Green Coat, sheriff of Yellow Dog Township, wasn't one of Pronovost's real estate deals. And he wasn't any hunting pal. It had to do with Norman, with Noel and the kid.

CHAPTER

Eleven

Liesl must have dozed on and off for several hours, but finally she found the strength to get up off the couch. Walking was an effort. It was like after the car accident that killed Harold and Gretchen: she had to think through each small step while jolts of pain shot up her spine. Still, she crossed the living room slowly, entered her studio, and carefully lowered herself on her workstool. Some of the pressure was taken off her spine, though a deep ache resided in her left hip.

The studio, beneath the three long, slanting skylights, always felt different from the rest of the house. It was the light, the ability to see. Even now, in midwinter, a clear, pale light from overhead isolated everything: shelves crowded with pieces, finished and unfinished. There was a box of clay on the worktable; Liesl opened it and removed the block. The red earthen color was always soothing to her eyes, and she stared at it for a long time. Finally she placed both hands on the block. The clay felt cool, and its flat surfaces had that manufactured perfection that she was always reluctant to spoil. As a child she'd felt the same reluctance whenever she'd open a new jar of peanut butter or unwrap a fresh stick of butter. The smooth surface in a jar of Skippy fascinated her. It was flawless in a way that seemed to defy her desire to break the surface with her butter knife. Once, using her finger, she had poked two holes in the surface of the peanut butter, then drawn a straight line for a mouth: a face. She screwed the lid back on and returned the jar to the refrigerator. Later her sister opened the jar and complained to their mother that Liesl had put her fingers in the peanut butter. Liesl considered it her first sculpture.

Now she pressed her thumbs into the clay. *Eyes.*

With a forefinger she drew a straight line beneath them. *Mouth.*

Laying her hands in her lap, she stared at the block. The expression was grim, yet it seemed to be holding forth against some relentless pain. Not just an ache, but pain.

"Face," she whispered.

The road had been climbing steadily, and the hills were becoming steeper as they neared Lake Superior. Norman remembered that there was always this sense of anticipation once he had passed the old logging camp, which was down between low hills to the east, only the swayback roof of the sawmill visible from the road. From there it was only a few miles until Big Pine Lodge came into view. He pulled the Trooper over and stopped next to the archway made of logs and decorated with chain saw art: serrated edges, jagged mouths, deep Vs cut out of timbers, presenting a mosaic of northern images—Ojibwa, blackrobes, canoes, howling wolves, eagles, and bears. A row of fence posts, protruding through the snow, ran toward the tree line at the top of a ridge. "I had forgotten," he said. "This is another time, long ago, and you're the only people out here."

"A few year-rounders still live up on the bay," Noel said as she turned around and began to undo the straps that held Lorraine in her car seat. "Otherwise they probably wouldn't even bother plowing this road."

They pulled on their gloves and hats and got out of the Trooper. Noel carried the child on her back in a baby sling, and Norman took the rucksack, which was full of the baby's things—clothes, a blanket, a plastic bottle for juices. They climbed over the snowbank and followed the fence posts toward the ridge. The snow was up to their knees and deeper in some places. Noel walked downwind of Norman and talked to Lorraine, telling her that they'd be inside soon. The girl held tightly to her shoulders and kept her face turned away from the wind.

When they reached the trees they could see the lodge, a long log cabin with a steep-pitched roof. Below the lodge a narrow river wound through marshlands, snow covered in most places, though at one bend the ice had given way, revealing black water. On the far side of the river stood a wall of birch and pines, their branches heavy with snow. The ridge commanded a view of steep, forested hills in every direction, except several miles to the east, where the broad blue plane of Lake Superior seemed to rise up to meet the sky.

Once on the porch they were protected from the wind. Noel got out her keys and sorted through them—she had several for the motel, and they were similar to the lodge key. After trying a couple in the lock, she opened the door and they went inside to a large room with massive timber beams overhead—it was always referred to as the Great Room. The air was musty; though they could see their breath, it was warmer than outside. All the furniture was made out of wood, rough-hewn logs mostly; some chairs were constructed of fine saplings that had been bent and twisted to create backs and arms and legs.

Noel put Lorraine down on the couch and said, "The three bears used to live here."

"No shit." Norman placed his hand on the log wall. Each timber was at least a foot in diameter, and the chinking between was hard, rough, pale gray. "Then the three bears moved back into the woods—reluctantly."

They got to work. The pipes were shut off for the season, so there was no running water. But there was electricity once Noel went out back to the new fuse box and switched on the power. She then began to stack logs in the large stone fireplace in the Great Room and in the wood-burning stove in the kitchen.

Norman took a pair of snowshoes off the wall and put them on; he found a shovel and went back down to the road and dug a space in the snowbank for the Trooper. Then he climbed back up the ridge, but rather than going inside the lodge, he headed down toward the river. The new snow was clean and light, and it didn't stick to the snowshoes. As he neared the stream, he heard something to his left, upwind. Standing still, he turned his face into the blowing snow, but the gust was so strong that he had to shield his face with his forearm. Once the snow began to settle, he could see them walking out from the darkness of the trees: a line of deer. He counted up to nine and then stopped; they still kept emerging from the woods, walking in file across the snow, descending toward the far side of the river. There was a buck with a large rack, and several does that kept close behind. One small deer struggled through the snow, its mottled fur ruffled by the wind. He remembered what Liesl had said about the deer, how sometimes they got so cold they could no longer move, though they were still alive, and how they often died a slow, painful death. Norman wondered about her, how long it had taken for her to die in the snow. He didn't regret any of it except her. He should have dug down in the snow, found her rifle, and shot her. He should have at least given her that.

When the deer reentered the woods, Norman began walking to his left along the riverbank. He came to the footbridge that was covered with untrammeled new snow. As he crossed he gripped the two heavy suspension cables, knocking off long thin sections of snow, and the whole bridge jounced and creaked with each step. On the far side there was the shed, covered with tarpaper. He followed one of the deer paths into the woods. He had walked this same deer path when he and Warren had gone out to find Raymond Yates, who had called up to the lodge on his cellular phone, saying that he needed help bringing in a black bear. They had followed the deer path until they heard Raymond's dogs up a hill. Raymond stood over his kill, his rifle slung over his shoulder. Mud clung to his camouflage and twigs stuck out of his full gray beard. It was early September, and the bear had put on weight for the winter hibernation; Raymond figured she was at least three hundred pounds. She had killed one dog and maimed two others so that Raymond had to put them down. He was angry and, when they got back to the lodge grounds, he wanted more money from Pronovost. They argued down here by one of the cabins below the falls. Pronovost refused to pay extra because of the dogs, and Raymond finally got in his truck and took off down the logging road toward his cabin, firing his gun into the air.

When Norman came to the falls it was silent except for a trickle that seeped out of the frozen wall of water. In summer the rush of water could be heard a great distance through the woods, depending on the wind. The cabin, which had been beyond the pool below the falls, was gone. Norman remembered how they had to shout over the falls, and how when Raymond had driven off, the dogs barking in the back of his truck could hardly be heard. Only the gunshots had rung out over the constant rush of water. Looking downhill across the pool, Norman could see the rectangle under the snow—the stone foundation of the cabin. It had burned to the ground that night. From the lodge up on the ridge, they'd seen the smoke rising above the forest.

"You know, that's fucking Raymond's doing," Warren had said.

"So?" Pronovost said.

"So he's torching one of your cabins. We got to do something about it."

They were passing a bottle of Jack Daniel's. It had been a good day, except for the thing with Raymond. Pronovost took the bottle from Warren and said, "It's just an old cabin in the woods. There are others. Doesn't mean anything. Raymond's hunted these woods over forty years. When someone requests a guide, he's the first one I call. Some of my best customers come back every year just to hunt with him. He's the best there is. He's got no family, and he loves his dogs. This old cabin doesn't mean anything. He knows that."

Warren said, "It means everything."

"No," Pronovost said. "It means we're drunk and he's drunk and there were some unexpected expenses incurred during the business transaction. When he sobers up, he'll understand that that's the end of it."

"We ought to go in there and track Raymond down," Warren said.

"And do what?" Norman said. At that point he still believed he understood Pronovost's logic most of the time. "*You* going to catch him—how? And if you catch him, what do you *do* to him?"

Warren yanked the bottle out of Norman's hand while he was still drinking. Bourbon ran down his chin and neck and soaked his shirt. "Fuck Raymond Yates," Warren said. "What you do is go down that logging road till you find his truck full of dogs. You want to pay Raymond back, you torch that dog pen he's got in the back of his truck. Let him listen to those dogs howl." He took a drink and held the bottle out to Pronovost as though it were a challenge.

"We're not burning anybody's truck full of dogs." Pronovost ignored the bottle and started walking back toward the lodge.

Norman worked his way diagonally down the snow-covered embankment and walked around the frozen pool. Though it was iced over, he could hear running water underneath. He passed the rectangle in the snow and continued on until he came to the next cabin in a stand of birch. Part of one wall still stood above the snow. That first night, the first cabin torched was one thing; Pronovost would let that go—but this cabin, burned the second night, changed things. It was no longer a matter of an angry drunk hunter mourning a few good dogs. It was something that could get out of hand and draw attention to the whole thing—the bear had been taken illegally. As far as Pronovost was concerned, if a man can get close enough to a bear, he has the right to take it, regardless of what the Department of Natural Resources says about seasons and lotteries for bear hunting permits. He hated the DNR and would not acknowledge that their regulations applied to his land. But a man starts burning cabins in the woods, it's going to draw attention to itself eventually.

So Pronovost arranged a meeting and sent Norman out to Yates's cabin. Though it was warm and humid, Yates stood on his front porch in a heavy flannel shirt buttoned up to his throat.

Norman sensed that to even get out of the truck would be undiplomatic. "Pronovost wants to settle up, straighten things out before somebody burns down the entire woods from here to Lake Superior."

Yates was hung over, and he gazed past the truck into the woods. "You want to guide, you want to learn to guide?"

The question surprised Norman. "Yeah."

Yates scratched his beard. He had that look some men get when they think they're explaining the obvious. They seem almost happy about it, but you know they're really just pissed off. "All gonna change, you watch. Pronovost has big plans."

"What're you talking about?"

"Won't be no need for guides. Hunting out here's gonna go the way of that old sawmill out there. Same thing, really, sawyers, hunters—just end up some old black-and-white photos like he's got on the walls up there at the lodge."

"I don't know about that, but I'll tell you something," Norman said. "A hunting party's flying up from Chicago."

"Those aren't hunters."

"Well, they want you to guide tomorrow."

Yates worked his tongue over the corner of his lower lip where he'd stuffed a wad of tobacco. He leaned over and spat black juice off the porch.

"And Noel's driven out from North Eicher, and she's cooking venison steaks outside on the grill tonight."

Yates's eyes drifted over Norman a moment. The man liked his venison.

He came up to the lodge that night, and Pronovost gave him two puppies as a peace offering. By the time everyone sat down to dinner in the Great Room, they were all drunk and friendly.

Beyond the second cabin there was a long, low hill. Norman took the logging road down through a ravine strewn with a lot of deadfall. It was beginning to get dark in the woods, though the sky was still light above the hill. The new snow seemed illuminated from underneath by a soft glow of its own; there were no shadows, no colors, only variations of gray. It was the time of day when there was perfect clarity, and Norman always wished you could just stop things right there. But by the time he reached the old logging camp on the far side of the hill, the light was fading away. Across a small clearing stood the remains of one long brick building, the sawmill. Part of the roof had collapsed and one end wall had caved in, causing the whole structure to lean to the left as if pushed by some invisible force.

Norman entered the building through a gap in the brick wall. He practically knew Noel's letter by heart. It seemed to confirm what Raymond Yates had said: "Warren stopped working for Daddy because something's happened between them, and sometimes when I'm talking to one of them I suddenly get scared because all that stuff up in the woods seems to be getting worse. Sometimes when he's drunk Daddy starts talking about the old logging camp and about Raymond, too, he says he was always one with the bears." And it was that reference to the bears that had haunted him for months.

Norman worked his way down the length of the building. There were chutes and conveyors, an elaborate system designed to turn logs into building materials—along one wall were large bins, some still marked: "Clear," "#1 Select," "Moulding." But after being idle for decades, the roof and sections of brick wall had caved in, allowing shafts of cold sunlight to angle down to the dirt floor. The far end of the building was nearly dark, and there was an open area where the roof had not yet fallen in; his eye was drawn toward something that glinted there—a small round spot of light winking on and off. He circled piles of rubble and crouched under collapsed beams until he saw that the glinting light came from a small metal disk. Quite suddenly he realized that a system of black lines loomed above him.

Iron bars.

He walked on until he was sure that it was a large cage more than twenty feet deep. Still he couldn't make out what caused the glinting; after removing his glove, he took hold of the metal disk. The padlock was cold in his hand. When he let go, the clang of metal resounded up through the iron structure.

Warren parked on Linden Street and walked a block over to Tom's Party Store. Through the plate glass he could see Pete behind the counter, stocking the shelves with pint bottles. Otherwise, the store was empty. Pete's Camaro was parked next to the building, back by the Dumpster. Warren crossed the street and approached the small cinder-block building from the side so that he couldn't be seen from inside the store.

He pulled a long wool sock out of his coat. When he was stationed in San Diego, he and his shipmates often went down to Tijuana. Besides the bars and the women, they liked the Sunday afternoon bullfights in Playas de Tijuana. They would sit in the *del sol* section and buy beer from vendors, who carried the bottles in a galvanized bucket full of chunks of ice. One afternoon the crowd was displeased with a succession of matadors and there was a riot. Though the bulls had been killed, it apparently had not been done correctly. The sailors soon became the focus of the hostile crowd in their section of the seats. None of them had brought weapons across the border. They bought a bucketful of ice from one of the vendors who had sold all his beer; each sailor filled a sock with chunks of ice and used them to get out of the arena. Now, standing next to the party store, Warren loaded up the long wool sock with chunks of a large icicle that had fallen off the roof of the building. He went up to the passenger door of Pete's Camaro and broke the window with the sock. After unlocking and opening the door, he felt around under the bucket seats, and then he checked the glove compartment. There was no vial; there was no gun.

Behind him, an oblong of light spilled across the parking lot. Warren turned around and saw Pete's silhouette in the doorway.

"The *fuck* you do to my *car?*" Pete came out into the lot, blocking more of the light from the store.

"You got something of mine," Warren said. "You got my stuff, you got my gun, all because you and your shithead friend were shy twenty bucks. This crap has to stop, and it ain't going to end on me, I promise you that."

"Look at my car!"

Warren swung the sock, and the ice made a hard, hollow sound when it connected with Pete's skull. He went down on all fours, and Warren worked his back and sides good until the ice started to break up into smaller pieces. When he stopped, Pete was lying on his side, whimpering. Warren knelt down and put his mouth close to Pete's ear. "But who needs guns, right? They're for chickens. But you'll thank me for those pills because it fucking hurts so bad when you piss blood for weeks at a time."

Standing up, he tossed the sock into the open Dumpster and walked away.

Liesl was dozing on the couch when Del called. He said he was in a motel in North Eicher and that he'd just eaten dumplings, hot-and-sour soup, and chicken fried rice, washed down with a can of Vernors Ginger Ale. Norman and the girl were gone, it seemed, and Del had decided to spend the night before returning to Yellow Dog. While he spoke, Liesl stared into her studio at the clay bust she'd worked on for nearly an hour. She'd started with the brows; somehow it seemed necessary to get the forehead and brows right before anything else. In the kitchen, Darcy was boiling pasta, and the house smelled of damp clay, tomatoes, onion, and garlic.

Liesl said, "I think it's real love. Maybe Norman and the girl will get away. Maybe the world will let them go."

"Doubt it," Del said. "This weather's on their side, but it won't last." He paused a moment, and she realized she liked the way he would take a moment to consider what he was going to say next. Too often, men just went on and on. "I don't know where to look next. Norman and the girl were here last night, I think, but they're long gone. State police haven't seen anything, either. I'm sorry. I know you don't want to see him hunted down, but I don't know where to look now. There's not exactly a manhunt going on out here. It's just too damned cold for that."

"Don't apologize."

"Well, I have to tell you something," he said.

"No, you don't. Really. Describing your dinner washed down with Vernors was a remarkably personal revelation, and I wouldn't want you to overdo it."

"This is serious."

"Listen, you already told me you looked for that green truck."

Again there was a pause, this one long enough that she was about to ask if he was still on the line. Finally he said, "I ran a search through the DMV's computer and whittled it down to a list of probables. There're about seventy thousand residents in Marquette County, and I'll tell you a lot of them own trucks. Then I made a bunch of phone calls. In some cases I went out to businesses to talk to people who sounded, you know, vague over the phone. But there was nothing, nothing concrete. I couldn't find anyone who was driving a green truck toward that bridge when—"

"Del."

"What?"

"Will you do me a favor?" she asked.

"Sure."

"Will you put your other hand on your forehead?" There was silence over the phone, except for the rattle of what she assumed was the heater in his motel room. "Just place your fingers at your hairline and run them down to your eyebrows."

He sort of laughed. "Is this like one of those nine hundred phone numbers?"

"Sure, whatever you want. You're the one in the motel room."

"All right. I'm running my fingers down to my eyebrows."

"How far is it, two and a half inches?" she asked.

"Oh, closer to three. Used to be only two, but that was years ago."

"Creases? I recall two that were quite pronounced."

After a moment, he said, "Yeah, I'll go with two."

"And the right eyebrow, it's more prominent than the left."

"Thirty-six stitches in a high school hockey game, a two–one win over Negaunee."

"Of course. Now, let's do the nose. From the bridge to the tip."

"Now you're getting kind of personal." There was silence. "I'd say an inch and a half—maybe three-quarters. And there's an arch to it. Only a slight arch, I might add."

"Yes, I remember the arch," she said.

"Where else?"

"That's all for now."

"That's it? I'm a guy alone in a motel room, feeling his face, and that's it?"

"You've been a big help."

"I couldn't interest you in an ankle?"

"No, really."

"Perhaps a collarbone?"

"That's it, thanks. Gives me a sense of proportion. I like working from memory."

"Don't I get a turn?"

She laughed. "If you want."

"Now I'm blushing. I guess I'd rather wait."

"All right."

"That's a middle-aged thing, isn't it?"

"Waiting can be good," she said. "I didn't appreciate it when I was young. But now I know you can get a lot done while waiting. Will you call me before you start back?"

"Sure. Next I'll give you my earlobes. Would you like that?"

"Perhaps. And I may need help with the mouth."

"I charge extra for the mouth."

She laughed as she hung up.

Darcy was standing in the kitchen doorway, a bowl of steaming pasta held in front of her as though it were a sacrificial offering.

"Phone sex," Liesl said. The girl looked nearly hysterical. "It can be so satisfying. Comes with age. Now bring that over here—I'm famished."

"You were out there a long time," Noel said. "Hungry? There's mostly canned goods in those cabinets. A lot of soups."

Norman sat at the log table in the kitchen. "Starved." She was looking for something in his face, some sign that he'd found what he was searching for out there. But she couldn't tell.

"Hold her while I dish out the soup." She sat Lorraine on his lap.

It was sudden, and at first Norman looked uncertain. He placed one hand on the child's back, the other on her shoulder to help her keep her balance. Cautiously, he bounced his knee, and she laid her head on his left shoulder and giggled.

Noel brought two bowls of beef barley soup to the table. While they ate, slowly at first because the soup was very hot, she spoke constantly in a voice that was intended for Lorraine. Not exactly singsong, but there was a lilt that was playful. Simply blowing on a spoonful of soup before offering it to the child became a special event. Noel never asked if Lorraine wanted to get on her lap, and the child seemed content to be able to look at her mother while she ate.

"Did you see the deer herd?" Norman said.

Noel shook her head.

Norman lowered his face until his mouth was close to the child's skull. "You didn't see the deer, Lorraine? Down across the river?"

The girl looked at her mother, as though for the answer. "When are the three bears coming home?"

Noel laughed.

"Well, not for a long time," Norman said. He too had changed his voice, making it higher, more animated. "We'll be gone before they come back."

"Where did they go?" Lorraine placed her fingers in his bowl, picked out a leftover piece of barley, and placed it in her mouth.

"They went to sleep," Norman said.

Lorraine seemed confused. "In bed?"

"Not exactly," he said, staring at Noel. "In the den. In the ground."

Lorraine laid her hands on the table to each side of the bowl. "Are they dead?"

"No, they're just sleeping. They'll come back in the spring. They sleep all winter."

"That's a very long time."

He nodded, but he could see that she still wasn't satisfied. "What?"

"Do they dream?"

"I'm sure they do."

After a moment, she said, "I would."

Del was awakened by a knock on the door. The motel room was very hot now and quite dark. He threw back the bedspread and crossed the room. When he opened the door the air was so cold that it seemed to push against his shirt. In the twilight it was difficult to see, but he thought he was staring at Norman Haas.

"I wake you, Sheriff?"

"Yes, you did."

"Cold as a motherfucker, isn't it?" the man said, stepping past Del into the room.

Del shut the door quickly. Though he wasn't fully awake, the shock of cold air had made him suddenly alert. "Haas," he said.

"Right." There was the smell of beer and peppermint coming off the man.

"Norman or Warren?"

Turning, the man laughed, and Del already knew. "Well, what do *you* think?"

"Norman's not that stupid."

"Right." Warren Haas fit his brother's description, though he might have been a bit taller and a few years older. He took a pint bottle from the pocket of his long leather coat and unscrewed the cap, releasing a medicinal smell into the warm air. After taking a swig, he offered Del the bottle of schnapps.

Del switched on the light and said, "No thanks." He went to the heater and shut off the fan.

When he turned around, Warren said, "I know why you're here."

"Do you?" Sitting on the bed, Del began to pull on his boots.

Warren Haas fell into the chair by the window, placing the bottle on the small round table. "He's got Noel." Del finished tying one lace and raised his head. "He's got my daughter, too."

"You know that for a fact?"

"No." Haas picked up the bottle of schnapps and took a long drink. "But why else would you be here?" He took a pack of Winstons from his shirt pocket and laid it on the table. "What I don't know is why you're still here."

"I'm not going to be much longer. I'll head out at first light."

"Trail grown cold?" His smile was crooked because his cheek was badly bruised. "It's going way down tonight. *Way* the fuck down. You're smart to wait till morning. I'd hate to break down out there thirty miles from the next town."

Del leaned over and tied his other lace. "I appreciate your concern."

"They're out there, in the cold," Warren Haas said. "Think they'll survive? Can't sit in her Trooper all night. Got to get inside somewhere warm."

"How do you know they're in her Trooper?"

Haas shrugged.

"You seen your brother today?"

He shook his head.

"That's some bruise there," Del said.

"I haven't seen Norman since he went away." Haas turned his head quickly, as though he'd just noticed someone right next to him. He picked up his pack of cigarettes and tapped one out. "Maybe they can keep each other warm. You know? Noel can be a very warm girl. And my brother, he's been out of circulation for a while."

Del got up and came to the table. "This is a no-smoking room."

Warren laid the cigarette on top of the pack of Winstons. "I bet I know where they went." Del stared back at Haas. "I have a good idea, anyway."

"You can tell me. Or you could contact the state police."

Haas took another pull on his schnapps and shook his head. "That's not exactly what I had in mind."

Del sat in the other chair at the table. He picked up the cigarette, held it horizontally beneath his nose, and inhaled. "I smoked for fifteen years. Winstons, Marlboros, and now and then when I'd cross the border into Canada I'd get something like Players, something with the big hit. It's hard to quit. Ever try?"

Warren Haas shook his head. "Only thing I ever managed to quit was the navy."

"You were a sailor?"

"Stationed in San Diego."

"Beautiful harbor."

"I never noticed. Been there?"

"Twice. Law enforcement conventions. One day I skipped all these sessions I was supposed to go to and I rented a sailboat in Mission Bay. There was a steady northwest wind and I sailed right out into the Pacific. It was something, it was really something out there." Del leaned back in his chair, holding the cigarette between his fingers as though it were lit. "Sometimes I still find myself flicking the ashes off a pencil or pen." Haas nodded as though he were sympathizing. "What exactly did you have in mind?" Del asked.

"I'll take you to them."

"Where?"

Haas smiled. "That's my point. No state police. No one else. Just you and me."

"How do you know where they are?"

Haas shrugged. "Maybe you'll find that out when we get there."

"But not before."

"Right."

"Why? What do you want out of this?"

"He has my wife—my soon-to-be ex-wife. He has my daughter, Lorraine. I want to make sure they get out of this safely."

"I see," Del said.

"Listen, that's guaranteed not to happen if you send a bunch of state police out there." Again, Haas looked to the side quickly, then he leaned forward and placed both elbows on the table.

"Out where?"

Warren took a drink from his bottle of schnapps.

"So, you'll lead me to them, in this weather?" Del asked. "What're you driving?"

"We go together. My truck's got four-wheel drive, too, and I'm parked right across the street there in front of Jacques' Diner."

Del shook his head. "If we go, I drive."

Haas raised the bottle of schnapps to his mouth, but he didn't take a drink. He held the bottle against his bruised cheek, tenderly, trying to soothe the skin. "You got that Land Cruiser out there. Good four-wheel drive on those things. Okay, you drive." Haas stood up. He took Del's coat from the back of the chair and held it out. "Heavy. Feels like it's armed." He smiled. "Guess that's a pun."

Del took the coat, got up, and pulled it on. He patted his left side. "I don't like holsters under winter coats. Too bulky. So when I bought this, I had a special holster pocket sewn in here." He looked at Haas's leather coat. "That's not the kind of coat you see much up north. Has more of a city cut."

Haas took a little step, as though he were modeling the knee-length garment at a fashion show. He opened the coat, first right, then left. "See, no holster pockets. Just an ordinary coat with two arms." He turned up the collar and yanked open the door.

Outside, Woo-San backed away from the sudden light cast from the room. He looked startled, embarrassed, and his lips moved, though he didn't say anything.

"Look at this," Haas said. "Listening at your door. Hear anything interesting?"

"I not listening. You—" Woo-San turned toward Haas. He was not a large man, but his shoulders beneath his coat were thick. Something about him seemed forceful and beyond intimidation, as though he had been conditioned by being the outsider, the stranger. "You been told not to come around here anymore."

"Says who?"

"Pronovost say so."

"This man's a sheriff," Haas said. "Register your complaint with him." He walked around Del's Land Cruiser.

"He not suppose to be here," Woo-San said.

"Well, he's leaving," Del said. "And so am I."

"You go? You go together?" Woo-San turned and walked back toward the motel office.

Del got in the Land Cruiser and opened the passenger door for Haas. They drove through the downtown section of North Eicher. Except for a couple of bars, nothing was open.

"All right, where are we going?" Del asked.

"Take a right at this next corner, Sheriff. We want to head up north."

PART Three

CHAPTER
Twelve

Liesl sat at her bench in the studio, her hands covered with clay. "It feels good to have my skin caked again," she said.

Darcy leaned on the stool across from her, eating ice cream, staring at the clay head between them. When she was finished, she put the empty bowl on the worktable and said, "What's wrong with him?"

"He's a work in progress."

"The eyebrows, and that hat, they're too big on one side."

"It's snow. It's blowing from his left. We'll call that north. It's like shadows in a painting. When you look at a landscape, you can see that the artist is always aware of where the sun is. When you sculpt a figure in a blizzard, you need to be aware of which direction the wind is from."

Darcy reached out and ran one finger down the back of the head. "It feels—*gross.*"

"Sometimes I think the feel of clay saved my life after the accident." She had a brief, sharp recollection of when she and Harold had first met, before they were married. She'd just started to do pottery, and she had discovered how fascinating wet clay could be, how it could be spun, turned, molded, formed, and re-formed, and how when it dried hard it held firm the movement of that turning.

Darcy wiped her finger on her sweatshirt. "Mom says that afterwards you were—distracted."

"I was distracted, yes." She thought of Harold, young, thin, naked, covered with wet clay. "I was distracted for a long time," she said vaguely, "until I started working again."

Darcy kept rubbing her finger on her sleeve. "It feels—*dirty.*"

"It is, and that's part of the beauty of it. This is just dirt."

"A 'work in progress.' " Darcy leaned over the table, bringing her face up close to the bust. "That's what Nikki Koivu says—'I'm a *work in progress!*' She's got these incredible boobs already, and I know that she showed them to three boys for a dollar each, and she let Jimmy Hackett feel her up at the Delft in Marquette." Gently she ran her finger over the cap that was tight to the clay skull. "I think sex is overrated."

"You do?"

"Sometimes dogs in the kennel get to each other when they're not supposed to and I have to turn the hose on them, and even with the cold water they stay stuck together." She scratched her cheek, leaving a smudge of clay beneath her right eye. "And once a white lab and this mutt got turned around, butt to butt, while they were still stuck, and they just look at you with these stupid dog grins. God, it's so disgusting. Even puppies, male puppies, are always mounting my leg and going—" Stepping away from the stool, Darcy thrust her hips rapidly. She dropped her tongue out the side of her mouth and panted quickly, until she collapsed, facedown, on the worktable.

"That's pretty good," Liesl said.

Sitting back on her stool, Darcy said, "That's all there is to it, really."

"You're sure?"

"The male part, anyway. Ah-ah-ah-ah-*ah-ahhhh.* Just like the dogs."

"What about the female part?"

Darcy's cheeks flushed slightly. She said nothing; she didn't have to.

The first summer Liesl and Harold lived here in the woods was extremely hot and humid for this far north. They had bought the land together but had not yet built the house, so they were living in a small World War II Quonset hut they'd found in a salvage yard. One night, after smoking some of the grass that they were growing in the woods, they stood naked in the clearing where the house would eventually be built and Liesl began smearing wet clay on Harold, starting at the top of his head, working down through his beard, his neck, his chest, arms, hips, legs. He stood absolutely still, at her insistence. She covered every part of him, and when she did his penis last, slowly, he became large and erect.

"Then there's form," Liesl said.

"Form?"

"Human form."

"Oh, like Jason Knott's arms. He pumps iron every day."

"Something like that, but it goes beyond the physical. When you look at a certain boy, there's just something special about his form. And I'm not just talking about the size of his muscles. It tells you all about him—and about you."

"Form," Darcy said slowly, as though she were trying to commit it to memory. She patted the bust's head. "Is this anyone in particular?"

"No, I don't think so. Maybe it's a composite."

"A composite?"

"Parts may suggest a particular person, but you draw from several sources."

"Uh-huh."

Liesl studied the bust between them on the worktable. She liked the texture of snow as it collected on wool and hair; and the forehead possessed the deep concentration that came with the sudden realization that he was lost. She remembered Norman as they climbed through the hills toward the crossroads. He had a plain honesty, but he also seemed driven in a way that both terrified and intrigued her. Perhaps honesty and evil were so close together as to be indistinguishable. What Norman did, leaving her in the snow, most people would call evil. Liesl didn't think so. It was honest. He walked away from her and realized he would only put himself in jeopardy if he tried to get her help. Any animal would do the same, including a human.

She turned the bust slightly, to get a different perspective on the face. The forehead, the eyes, the nose, the jaw, all suggested an older man. Like Del, but not specifically Del. Someone who if lost in a blizzard doesn't panic, because he's been through it before. That's what she had going here: a man struggling against a cold, brutal wind and blinding snow, a man honest enough to do whatever was necessary to survive.

After the soup, they were all tired, and Noel put Lorraine down for a nap. When she came out into the Great Room, Norman was stacking more logs in the stone fireplace. Noel sat on the couch facing the fireplace and pulled the afghan over her legs. Her cheeks stung, and she could see that Norman's face was badly windburned, too. She watched his shoulders and hands as he set the logs on the andirons, then laid kindling and newspaper beneath the stack. He was no longer a boy; prison had pared him down to something more essential. His face, his shoulders, his hands, were lean, strong, but somehow reduced.

When he had the fire lit, he sat on the couch and she draped part of the afghan over his legs. They watched the fire a moment; then he shifted so she could lean against him. Carefully he put his arm around her. They remained that way without speaking, watching the flames build in the fireplace. Frequently the crackle and pop of the fire was accompanied by the creaking of the walls and roof as another gust of wind hit the lodge.

"What did you find out there?"

He didn't answer.

"You don't want to talk about it now."

"I can't," he said. "Not now."

She watched the logs catch on fire. "I love the way fire creeps along the wood. And I always wonder why part of the flame is blue. When I was a kid I thought I could stare into a fire forever," she whispered. "It's like watching waves on the beach—no two licks of fire are the same. Something soothing, almost like meditation happens, and it seems to empty your mind."

She raised her head off his shoulder and saw that Norman was asleep, his mouth opened slightly, his head turned away as it lay against the back of the couch. Resting her cheek against his shoulder again, she closed her eyes. They were both exhausted, much as they used to be during hunting season, when the work at the lodge was constant, intended to allow the members of the hunting party to relax. Her father used to tell them, "We'll do everything—you just worry about bagging your trophy." There were usually seven or eight men at the lodge at one time, and several other groups occupied the cabins down in the woods. They all wore their expensive outdoor gear, didn't shave, and after a few days they looked like born woodsmen. Noel cooked—eggs and bacon or ham for breakfast and at night meat: black Angus steaks Daddy had flown in from Chicago, duck, and venison. She was the only female in the camp. More than once she had to slap a wayward hand.

Warren and Norman came and went—driving back and forth to Sipson's Lake, where a seaplane would put down to deliver and pick up men, or back to North Eicher for supplies of food and liquor. Norman went about his duties quietly, deliberately, while Warren spent much of the time trying to be one of the boys. Out here he could bullshit with some auto execs and pull it off. They were all so drunk that it tended to level the field.

And Daddy was at the center of the whole event. This was his realm, and he wanted to bring them into it and be well compensated for it—though never appearing to be interested in the money. That was the trick; that was the real game. These downstate fools—trolls, they were often called, because they lived below the Mackinac Bridge—were willing to pay huge sums for the authenticity of roughing it. They were willing to pay so they could go back to Farmington Hills or Brighton or Grosse Pointe and tell people they had been way the fuck up north.

They all requested Raymond Yates as guide. One night at dinner a Ford executive asked, "You really know these woods. Where you from, Yates?"

"Born in L'Anse. Lived out here my whole life."

"A real Yooper, eh?"

Raymond, who was about the same age as these men from downstate, continued to cut his meat. The exec must have been accustomed to having people answer his questions. He kept staring at Raymond.

"Off-season, what do you do for work?" the exec asked Raymond.

Raymond jabbed a forkful of venison into his mouth.

Finally Warren said, "Work?" He looked as though he'd never heard the term. He turned to Norman. "Isn't that that thing Uncle Toivo used to do? Go down in da mine dere and work?"

"You betcha," Norman said. "He did do dat."

"Until it kilt him," Warren said. "Got da black lung dere, eh?"

Everyone at the table laughed.

"No, no," the auto exec said. He spent a lot of time trying to reach people long-distance on his cellular phone, which was not easy out here. "I'm serious. What do you do for employment up here?"

"Oh, em*ploy*ment," Warren said. "Pronovost makes sure we got plenty of dat."

Noel knew the look on her father's face. She'd seen it all her life. What she never got used to was the stillness in his eyes. They just didn't move—no more than the glass eyes in his mounted trophies.

"What kind of employment?" the auto exec asked.

The table was quiet. Raymond appeared confused by the fact that on the one hand these men seemed to be having a laugh at his expense, and on the other he'd been asked legitimate questions. "I hunt," he said.

"You hunt. You just hunt, eh?" the exec asked, and everyone laughed.

Finally Daddy pushed away from the table, letting the scrape of his chair legs bring the party back to order. "Raymond's the best guide there is. No one knows these woods like him."

"So," the Ford executive said. "You're a professional hunter." Raymond simply wouldn't return the man's stare. "Gentlemen, a toast." The exec stood up and raised his glass. "A toast to the last of a dying breed: the true hunter."

The other men stood and joined in the toast. Warren beamed as though he were the birthday boy, while Raymond stared down the table toward Daddy.

As they drove north in the Land Cruiser, Warren Haas drank his peppermint schnapps and did most of the talking. Del was sure that something essential was being left out. What, he didn't know.

In his experience as sheriff of Yellow Dog Township, where most of the crimes committed were motivated by domestic discord, Del knew that the truly dangerous individuals were those who were driven by one clear desire. Often it was revenge. It could be love or deep regret or simply wanting something back. Whatever, it was almost always impossible to steer the perpetrator, usually an angry male, away from the source of his anger, usually a woman or, in some cases, another man who had taken the woman, physically, emotionally, or both, from the perpetrator. On many occasions Del had stood in front yards, on porches, in living rooms, facing an angry man, who couldn't see him at all, who kept looking past him at the object of his anger, standing a few feet behind Del. Often Del would be able to get through enough to persuade the perpetrator to desist for the time being; and usually it was only a matter of time, just a day or two, before Del was called back to the house, where a beating, sometimes even a shooting, had finally taken place. He knew that you never really talked a perpetrator out of the desire to harm the object of his anger because the perpetrator always felt justified, that the wife, the girlfriend, the guy doing the wife or girlfriend—the *object*—deserved what it got. Some perpetrators were so locked in to their desire—and drugs and alcohol often came into play here—that no matter what Del did or said, they could not really see him standing there in front of them, could not comprehend what he was supposed to represent. He was not the law; he was simply in their way. In such cases they would make some move, some attempt to go around or through Del, and then he would have to subdue and handcuff them. He had done this on his own many times, though in recent years he and Monty tried to answer such calls together.

Del thought that he had a better understanding of Norman's desire. He had been sitting in prison gnawing away at the fact that his brother and his former fiancée had married. Warren wasn't just sleeping with her, which would be bad enough; he'd married her. That wasn't something most men could tuck away and forget. It was the kind of thing that caused erosion inside, until one day when there's a chance you just walk away without considering the consequences. Norman was beyond the consequences.

However, as Del drove north and Warren talked about his brother, Warren's desire couldn't be so easily determined. He had said something about wanting to insure the safety of his ex-wife and their three-year-old named Lorraine. But Del suspected that there was more to it. He wondered if Warren felt the need to defeat Norman in order to prove that what he had done to his brother—taking his fiancée, marrying her, having a child with her—was justifiable. No matter how twisted their logic, perpetrators always maintained a deep sense of personal justice. One of the difficulties here was that it was hard to determine which brother was the real perpetrator.

The going was slow; Del could hardly maintain a speed of thirty miles per hour. There were few lights, and the road ahead was pitch black.

"We're headed toward Laughing Pike?" Del asked.

"We are."

"Woods, rivers, lakes. No towns."

"I know, it's perfect." The peppermint schnapps smelled cheap, like an air freshener.

"You're sure they're out there?"

"I'm not wrong."

"How do you know?"

"Because I know how my brother and Noel *think*—that's how I fucking know."

"This is some place her father owns?"

"Right."

"He owns this piece of land, with cabins for hunters and fishermen?"

"Right. It's some piece of land, too."

"How do you know which cabin they're in?"

"Who the fuck said they're in a cabin?" Haas's leather coat creaked as he shifted in his seat. "I'm hungry. You hungry? In a few miles we come to a little roadhouse. Let's stop and get something to eat. It'll be our last chance."

They didn't speak again until they reached a place called the Bucksnort Tavern, with pickup trucks and snowmobiles parked out front. Inside, Warren ordered a venison burger and a beer; Del had the whitefish sandwich and a Vernors Ginger Ale.

"This could be an on-duty thing," Haas said, nodding toward Del's glass. "Or it could be serious alcohol remission."

"A little of both," Del said.

"Divorced, right?"

After a moment, Del said, "Wild guess?"

"I don't see no ring." Haas snorted. "What are the odds that you're not?"

"Right."

"Kids?"

"No." Then Del said, "She had a couple of miscarriages early on." It felt as though he were offering a form of self-defense.

"She remarried?"

"Sure."

"Still sometimes, you think of her as your wife."

"Not too often."

"But sometimes. I know I do."

Del didn't answer.

"Of course you do. We *all* do, Sheriff. We think of them, you know, in the act—fucking another guy. And we avoid it as much as we can, until eventually it creeps up on you and grabs you by the *cojones.* See, I picked up a little Spanish when I was stationed in San Diego." Haas grinned, then took a large bite out of his burger and put it back on his plate. "Noel, she's always liked it—she likes men, has a thing about them. You ask me, I think it has something to do with her daddy, but I'm not professionally qualified to say for sure. I do know this: Sometimes when she's working nights at the motel, a guy will check in and she'll come on to him."

"You know this for a fact?"

"I have observed this, yes. I know her gestures, her looks—remember, I've been a victim myself."

"And you've observed this at the motel."

Haas put both elbows on the table and ran his hands through his hair, feeling his scalp as though he were inspecting it for a lump or a cyst, some physical evidence of disease. This examination occupied him for at least a minute, until he picked up his burger again. "Nights that she's working I often park across the street by Jacques' Diner and watch the motel office." He took a bite out of his burger. In the dim light from the bar, his face resembled a large knot as he chewed. "Voyeurism, it does strange things for you. It's naughty. It's sneaky. But, shit, it's *fun.* People always prefer to watch, even when it's painful. I know she *wants* to go down to a guy's room. Sparks the imagination."

"The schnapps helps," Del said.

"Especially when it's accompanied by a decent blow job."

"I imagine it would."

"The pleasures of a small town, right?" Haas said.

"Uh-huh." Del ran a French fry through ketchup. "This why you're splitting up?"

"No," Haas said. "What gets to you is the whole thing." He finished his beer and stared up at the television. The Red Wings were playing in Boston, and the second period was just starting. "I love their away uniforms, don't you? All that red. Has to have an effect on the other team."

"What 'whole thing'?"

"Oh, the routine, you know. The kid. The mommy and daddy shit. And then there's her father." Haas watched the game a moment. Del waited. "Pronovost. Jesus, the guy, he has all this property up there—calls it Big Pine Lodge. And he has this *hold* on her. Takes care of her—pays for her apartment, her bills, her car—I mean, she works nights at this motel he owns a piece of, and in fishing and hunting season she comes up here to cook for his corporate cronies. She's totally dependent on him." Haas leaned back and finished the last of his beer. "You ever notice how you can tell a lot about a girl's father by the way she sucks your cock?"

Del put down his sandwich.

"How's the whitefish?"

"Fine."

"The venison usually isn't this dry." Warren stood up and went to the men's room.

Del balled up his napkin and dropped it on his plate. He paid the bill at the bar, went outside, and climbed into his Land Cruiser. He got out his cellular phone and punched in Liesl's number but disconnected before her phone rang. Though it was only about eight-thirty, she might be asleep, and he didn't want to wake her.

That wasn't it, not really. He felt soiled listening to Warren Haas.

He kept thinking about how she'd held his hand. Something so simple, but it was everything. It was enough. It was all he needed to know. It was all he needed from her. He understood that it wasn't just affection, but much more. It frightened him a bit, but he liked how it felt—as though he were carrying something inside, something that he'd not had or known for a very long time. He didn't believe it was possible anymore—and that's what seemed so strange, this felt as if it were there all the time, but it revealed itself only now. He recognized it right away, and he knew that Liesl did, too. He wouldn't call her now. They both first had to get used to it on their own.

After Noel put Lorraine to bed, she went into the kitchen and, using towels to protect her hands, carried the first of three large pots of hot water from the stove to the bathroom. While Norman had been out in the woods she had gone out the kitchen door and filled the pots with snow, then put them on the stove to melt them down. As she poured the hot water into the claw-foot tub, Norman brought in the second pot and placed it on the floor; then he went back to the kitchen. She had been anticipating this since they had arrived—the moment when the snow would become bathwater.

When he returned with the third pot, she said, "Want to join me?"

He poured the steaming water into the tub and didn't look at her.

"With the two of us in the tub, the water will be high enough for a decent bath." She sat on the edge of the tub, pulled her sweater over her head, and began unbuttoning her blouse. Norman looked away, embarrassed. "It's all right," she said. "It's just me." She removed her bra, then her socks, jeans, and long johns.

If anything, he seemed more embarrassed. "You rarely see a woman in prison," he said. "They work in the kitchen, places like that, and they're always these older women. Some of them pretty ugly."

"Hot," she said as she eased herself into the tub.

"There were some real queens in there. At night you'd hear bed-springs, guys moaning and shit. Told you, I never got raped or anything. I had a friend, though, Bing."

"Is this like a relationship that should, you know, make me jealous?"

Norman scratched his ear. "No, I wouldn't say that."

"So, you left him behind when you walked away. That must be hard—"

"He got out before I did."

"I see."

"No, I don't think you do."

"Norman, I don't care. I just want you to get in this bath with me. Please."

After a moment he began to undress. She watched him, but he wouldn't turn his head toward her. He came to the tub and got in facing her. *"Holy shit."*

"You get used to it." She smiled. His wet legs touched hers. "We said we wanted to go back to before all this, but it's not easy. There's a lot to get through. I think I've been looking for a man to take me away for a long time, and now it turns out to be you. I never imagined."

Norman seemed deep in thought. Reaching down through the water, he placed his hand on her pubic hair. She slid lower in the tub so she was closer to him, and his fingers went between her legs. She held her breath as they carefully opened her up.

"This isn't at all like before," he said.

"No, it isn't." She exhaled slowly.

"We aren't like before."

She took hold of him under the water. "I'm afraid to move," she said.

"Then don't."

His fingers pressed into her, and she thought she might slip completely under the water.

"Oh, Jesus. I'm going to—Norman."

"Me too."

"Oh, Jesus. Wait. *Wait.*" She closed her eyes, and her mouth dropped open.

They didn't move, and the hot water around her was absolutely still.

She opened her eyes when she felt him go tense. They resembled egg whites swimming up to the surface of the water. She watched them as long as she could, then leaned her head back and closed her eyes, the water now lapping against her chin.

When Warren got in the Land Cruiser, they continued north.

"Yellow Dog Township will survive without Sheriff Del Maki?"

"Somehow," Maki said. "Today there was a near fight at the local repair shop."

As they passed the casino on the left, Warren saw it: Pronovost's Ford pickup, parked in the back of the lot. The sheriff didn't notice. He was still talking about snowblowers. "Half the town owns Ariens," he said, glancing toward Warren, "and the other half owns Toro. Its like Republican and Democrat."

"Which do you drive?"

"I don't. I get plowed by the town. One of the perks of the job."

Warren turned toward the sheriff and smiled.

"And on the front walk I use a snow scoop." They reached the edge of town, and Maki switched on his high beams as they reentered the darkness.

Out of the corner of his eye Warren could see headlights well behind them. He assumed that Pronovost would not be alone, that he would have Woo-San with him. They would be armed. He decided not to tell the sheriff that they were being followed. It was more important that they find Norman, Noel, and the girl. "A snow scoop?" he said. "Sheriff, you're a real traditionalist."

CHAPTER Thirteen

After they got out of the bathtub, they toweled each other off slowly. It became difficult to stand. They lay on the shag rug on the bathroom floor, and Noel knelt above Norman, her legs straddling his head. He took hold of her hips and pulled her down to his mouth, while he felt her warm breath on him. Having come so quickly in the bathtub, they were now slow and methodical, until she turned around and came down on him. He held her breasts, her nipples large after so long in the hot water. Periodically she brought them down to his mouth. Then she got on her feet so that she was squatting over him, and she rose and fell on him, dictating the force and rhythm of his entry. With each descent it was as though she were trying to receive him deeper. She stared back at him through the damp hair that fell about her face. Her expression revealed only the work, the concentration, the physical effort involved. He understood that this was her only sense of escape, these moments when she was engaged in nothing other than the labor of achieving an orgasm. He didn't know that before, and he should have—but he knew that now. And he also knew that the pills she took had created a kind of protective membrane. Her days held no relief, little hope. He could see that in her eyes the moment he had walked into the motel office. They said "I'm buried way deep in here, and maybe you can still come inside far enough and reach me." Now, as she moved above him, a groan was forced out of her with each descent, each sounding like a greater plea for mercy.

The narrow road rose and fell through tight turns. Del kept his speed to about twenty-five, mostly in second gear, and he never touched the brake on turns. Occasionally they'd emerge from black woods and cross a field of blue snow beneath the full moon. But mostly the road was walled in by dense forest, with stretches where overhead branches formed an intricate canopy. There were absolutely no other lights in this landscape.

"We've got to be nearing Lake Superior," he said.

Warren Haas had emptied his bottle of schnapps, and a couple of times he appeared to have dozed off. "Not far now," he said.

"What're we looking for?"

"A lodge on a ridge that overlooks a little river that's not much more than a creek."

"This is Pronovost's land?"

"His haven. During hunting and fishing season he brings customers in wearing Orvis pants with deep pockets. Very exclusive. When I worked for him I was here a lot, but nobody comes out here in winter. I think he wants to get it so exclusive that no one really sets foot in his domain."

"What happened between you and Pronovost?"

Warren snorted. "Has to do with who Pronovost is, who I am, and I suppose the fact that I've been married to his daughter. For a while I thought we had a good business relationship. But his long-range plans have changed, and I'm not part of them. That's the way Pronovost is—look, can I tell you something?" Del nodded. "There's no love lost between my brother and me, but he's still my brother. He's received the raw end of things, and it's not all his fault."

"What things?"

"Things that happened up here at Big Pine that sent him to prison."

"What did happen?"

Warren took out his pack of cigarettes. "Don't worry, I won't light it. I just want to feel it in my hand, know it's there. You know what I mean? Like you said, you still tap the ash off the end of a pencil now and then. You want one, too?"

"No."

Warren placed a cigarette in his mouth and pretended to take a puff and exhale. "What's important here is that we find him and Noel and the kid before anyone else does. I owe Norman that much. You take him back where he belongs."

"What about Noel and the girl?" Warren didn't answer. "You think doing this is going to make her want you back? Sounds like she may have come up here with him willingly."

"After you get Norman back to prison, maybe she'll see things my way."

"What was this raw deal your brother got?"

"He brought it on himself, but I'm not sure he deserved it."

"You mean his time in prison."

"I mean he got a raw deal, and I think he believes he can change things by coming out here. You know, like proving that he shouldn't have gone to prison in the first place."

"Shouldn't he have?" Warren's head was turned toward his side window. "What's he going to prove out here? His innocence?"

Warren laughed. "You are the small-town sheriff. Nobody's innocent here." He zipped up his coat so that the raised collar came right to his jaw. "Nobody's fucking innocent, Sheriff."

"It's so strange," Noel said, lying back on the shag rug, still trying to catch her breath. "You hardly make a sound now."

There was an old Indian blanket hanging on the bathroom wall; he got it down and draped it over them. She snuggled close, her head on his shoulder.

"Your eyes are different."

She raised her head off his shoulder.

"The pills do something to them. Some guys inside look that way."

"What way?"

"I don't know, like you're way inside yourself, trying to keep safe and protected."

Noel seemed about to protest, but then she lowered her head to his shoulder again. "This is all the safety and protection I need. This is the moment where I want it to stop. Right here. It was this way when we first met. You made me feel like nothing else mattered." He held her tighter. "Then it got all crazy. Both of us. I wish we had just gone away together when we first met—remember how we talked about doing that?"

"Sure. But we didn't, and that's why what happened happened."

They didn't speak for a couple of minutes. The bathroom was lit by only one candle and the log walls were the color of honey, the knots black. Norman listened to her breathing lengthen, and by the weight and stillness of her head against his shoulder he knew she'd fallen asleep.

They would always refer to it as "what happened happened." But in fact Norman wasn't sure he understood exactly what had happened. He knew that it started after the last of the hunting parties had left, all the executives who talked in percentages and yields and market shares. They had cellular phones and laptop computers, and it was clear they thought that this was *it,* sitting out here in the woods, hunting or fishing by day, drinking much of the night, and getting on-line with www-dot-something-dot-com.

When they all finally left, it was just Norman and his brother, Noel and her father; they were exhausted, and it seemed they'd earned a few days by themselves at Big Pine. The season was over. But things began to unravel. There was the afternoon when Norman was here in the bathroom, soaking in the tub, drinking some McClellan's Scotch left behind by one of the executives and smoking a joint Warren had given him. He was alone in the lodge. Pronovost had gone hunting with Raymond

Yates. Warren was down in one of the sheds on the river, stowing canoes and gear for the winter. Noel had said she was just going for a walk.

When Norman got out of the tub, he put on clean clothes, something he had not done in several days. It was early afternoon and he went down to the river with the bottle of expensive Scotch, but when he got to the canoe shed it was locked. Norman sat on a tree stump and watched the black water flow between the narrow banks. Then he heard a knocking sound coming from another shed, one farther down the riverbank that was seldom used. He got up off the stump and walked through the woods toward the shed, and when he was within ten yards he could hear them. He knew right away. He recognized Noel's groans, and as things speeded up he could hear Warren gasping, his voice anguished and hoarse. Norman stood still while they finished, and there was only the sound of wet snow falling on dry leaves. Finally he walked back up to the lodge.

He continued drinking, as he lay on the couch in front of the fireplace, and when Noel came in the kitchen door she was alone. Norman got up and said, "How was your walk?" She told him fine as she began to fill a large pot with water, and she was saying something about boiling potatoes. Norman went to her at the kitchen sink, and as she turned toward the stove, he punched her in the jaw. She fell back against the refrigerator and the pot of water fell to the floor. He hit her again, this time catching her above the left ear. After that, he wasn't sure. He may have continued to hit her. But he also realized that she was screaming and crying, and eventually Warren came in the kitchen door and he hit Norman on the side of the head with one of the logs he'd brought in for the fireplace. Norman may have been knocked out, but only briefly, and the next thing he knew he and Warren were grappling on the floor of the kitchen. All the while Noel was screaming and both brothers were shouting. When they were boys they had fought all the time. Being younger and smaller meant that Norman lost more often, but he refused to give in. Once they got into their late teens they avoided fights, perhaps because they both realized by then that they could really do each other damage. But there in the kitchen it seemed as though they'd been waiting years for this, and neither held back as they punched, kicked, scratched, and bit each other.

Finally Norman got free of Warren. He went outside, running down the ridge toward the river. His clothes were torn. Blood ran out of his nose and his right eye was swollen. His right hand was strained and the forefinger felt as if it were broken. He staggered out into the woods, and when he got on the other side of the river, he heard Noel calling for him. He kept going, walking through the forest for perhaps an hour. He felt stupid. As soon as he had heard Noel and Warren in the shack, he knew it was inevitable. He couldn't believe that he hadn't seen it before, hadn't caught some look, some gesture, between them. All three of them had been headed toward this since Warren had returned from the navy. It had to do with the fact that Norman and Noel had made plans, to get married, to try to get into a college downstate—as Warren called it, to grow up. So the shots and beers, the joints, the lines of coke, the pills—it was all orchestrated by Warren because in some way he felt it was his responsibility to save them from dreams of growing up, of leaving, of trying to change their lives. It was because Warren couldn't change his life. He'd gone off to the service and come back saying it was all a lie, it was all corrupt. All a matter of who you salute, whose ass you kiss. In some twisted way Warren believed he was protecting Norman and Noel, saving them from the truth.

Now, he gently eased Noel's head off his shoulder. Sound asleep, she curled her legs up so that she was a soft concentration of breasts, arched hip, and smooth thigh. Getting up, he tucked the Indian blanket around her. He gathered his clothes and went out into the Great Room, where he dressed before the fireplace and then stacked new logs on the andirons.

When Noel woke up she was alone beneath the Indian blanket. Standing, she wrapped herself tightly, though the wool was scratchy, and went to the sink. She leaned close to the mirror to see her face. By candlelight, she looked older. Her cheeks were hollow, her eyes dark and sunken. This was how she would look ten years from now, in her mid-thirties. Lorraine would be going into her teens. It seemed a remarkable length of time, ten years. But ten years ago she had been a teenager in eighth grade. How did she get here so fast? She looked tired and felt exhausted. She considered simply lying down and going back to sleep. Instead, she picked up her purse and looked through it until she found the plastic vials. She knew this had to end, that this wasn't the answer. She knew that pills wouldn't get her through the next ten years. But when do you stop? What day? What time of day? How is that day different from the others? Why on a certain day would you suddenly find the strength to stop? Norman was right. The contents of these amber vials provided her safety, protection. To abandon that would take strength, and she wasn't feeling very strong right now. She took two pills and went back out into the Great Room.

Norman wasn't there, but the bedroom door where Lorraine was sleeping was ajar. Noel pushed open the door and found him standing next to the bed. Lorraine's hair was matted to her forehead, her breathing heavy, her face illuminated by the fire from the Great Room.

"Look at her," he whispered. "She's so beautiful."

"I know. I've already noticed things about her that are like you."

Noel went to him and put her arm around his waist. The flickering light danced on the child's face. Norman reached down and touched Lorraine's hair, brushing it off her forehead. They left the room, pulling the door shut behind them. Noel gathered the blanket around her on the couch. Norman put a few more logs on the fire and sat next to her.

"We need to talk about what happened," she said. "What *really* happened."

He nodded.

She pulled the blanket up around her shoulders. "This is how it looked, Norman. This is how it came out at the trial: You went berserk. You were the wild man in the woods. Remember what that lawyer Daddy brought up from Detroit said in his closing statement—you were less civilized than Big Foot. You beat up Warren so bad that he needed stitches at the clinic in North Eicher. You beat me up so bad I lost my hearing and I still get headaches and auras all the time. And best of *all,* later that day Raymond Yates drives himself down to the clinic in North Eicher with a gunshot wound in his shoulder. They wanted to get you for attempted murder, as well as assault and battery, but then Raymond disappeared just before the trial begins."

"And no one's heard from him since," Norman said. He continued to gaze into the fire. "That Detroit lawyer—one of your father's hunting pals—wanted to nail me for murder, but Yates never turned up again. Still no one knows what happened to him. So they put me away for everything else."

"What I said at the trial was true, Norman."

"I know."

"I was hurt."

"I know," he said quietly. Turning to her, he asked, "Know why I shot Yates?"

The light from the fire danced in his eyes. "You were angry."

"I was scared," he said. "Why else would I shoot Yates—with his own rifle?"

"I don't know. At the trial you said he was after you—it was self-defense."

"That's right, *he* was chasing *me*—out there, in the woods. After I left you and Warren here, I was just wandering around out there, for hours. Your father and Yates came back to the lodge and found you and Warren, right?" She nodded. "Your father took both of you down to the clinic in North Eicher." Norman faced the fire again. "And he sent Yates out after me—your father told Yates to hunt me down."

Norman got up and went over to the fireplace. With the iron poker he shifted the logs, tipping up their glowing undersides, which gave off more light and heat. When he stood and turned around, he was silhouetted against the flames. "You know, at first I didn't even think that Yates was following me. I thought he was out hunting. I saw him from a distance and figured I should get out of his way, so I worked my way off to the east, thinking I'd go wide around him and head back here to the lodge. But the next time I caught sight of him, it was clear he was still following me, so I started toward him. The brush was dense and I didn't want him to mistake me for an animal. I called out to him, but then I saw him shoulder his rifle and he took a shot at me—he missed. And I understood right away—your father had found you back at the lodge and he'd sent Yates after me. So I took off into the woods, and Yates followed me. I couldn't lose him. The man could track anything, and he was patient—he knew I'd tire. After maybe an hour he took a second shot at me and missed—probably because I stumbled. When I looked up I could see him coming down a steep hill. He lost his balance and fell and came rolling down through the brush. When he stopped he didn't move, and his rifle was well below him. I thought he'd been knocked out, or maybe he broke something. I climbed the hill and picked up the rifle. When I looked up he was pulling an automatic from his holster. So I fired first."

Noel watched Norman come around the coffee table and sit next to her. "But Yates never testified at the trial," she said.

Norman shook his head. "You think I had something to do with that? You think that Detroit lawyer, with his suits and those ties, was right—that I had taken care of Raymond Yates so that he couldn't testify against me at the trial?"

"No, I don't," Noel said. "During the trial I wasn't sure, but not now."

"Why not now?"

"Because several months ago I overheard Daddy say something to Woo-San. He said, 'He was always one with the bears.' I think he was talking about Raymond Yates. I said so in that letter to you, right?"

"You did, and that's why I wanted to come up here. For months I've been thinking about that—what's it mean, 'He was always one with the bears'?" Noel leaned against his shoulder, and they watched the fire for a minute. "When I went out there this afternoon," Norman said, "I walked as far as the logging camp. There's something going on out there now. What is it?"

"I don't know," she said. "It has to do with Woo-San. I'm not certain where he's from. At the motel he gets mail from Korea, Hong Kong, China, Japan, and a lot of calls from Vancouver and some from San Francisco. I asked him once and he just said, 'Relatives.' Woo-San and Daddy are planning something—I don't know what. You know that last fall Daddy hardly brought anyone out here—just a few small parties. And he told them that there'd be no more hunting and fishing here next year. That's what seems strange. He wants to keep this so private now, like a kind of preserve. He and Woo-San have found a way to make it pay without the hunting parties."

"If you don't cut timber, if you don't hunt, how do you make land like this pay?"

"I don't know," she said.

"And Warren? Where's he at with all of this?"

"He and Daddy had some falling-out. Daddy does that—he gets close to people, then cuts them off. It had to do with me, but it also had to do with this, too. Warren came out here last fall and helped out with the hunting parties, but I could tell there was something odd between them. Warren would never admit it, but I think he knows what Daddy and Woo-San are up to, and I think it scares him. This was right around when I had told Warren I wanted him to move out, so he was acting strange—more so than usual. He's gone back to dealing like he did before he really got involved with Daddy. He goes down to Milwaukee every so often and comes back with stuff."

"Which you get for free."

"Norman, nothing's for free." Noel turned toward the fire. "He still comes around, and sometimes he's all right. You have any idea how lonely it is, spending my days taking care of Lorraine? I know you've been away and that prison's awful, but it's not so good out here, Norman. That's why I finally sent you that letter." She laid her head against the back of the couch and closed her eyes.

After a moment, she could feel his hand on her shoulder. She didn't feel exhausted now. There was relief, a sense of energy. She got up off the couch. "I made a mistake, Norman. I should never have gotten involved with your brother." Norman stared hard into the fire. She moved over until she was standing directly in front of him. The heat from the fire was warming the blanket, and she was now almost too hot.

"No apologies," he said. "It doesn't matter now."

"No, it doesn't." She let the blanket fall to the floor and knelt on the couch, her legs straddling him. She leaned forward and gently wrapped her arms around his head. "There's my daughter and you—only you, Norman," she whispered. "Nothing else really matters. It's more than enough."

CHAPTER

Fourteen

After a couple of miles, Del asked, "The lodge—how many entrances?"

"Just two. The front door," Warren said, "and the kitchen door in back."

Del tilted his wristwatch so that he could read it in the light from the dashboard. It was just after eleven o'clock. "How close to the road is it?"

"A hundred-some-odd yards. They'll see your lights if they're paying attention."

Del shut off the headlights. The moon was so bright that he could see the snowbound road easily. "Any weapons, hunting rifles?"

"Could be. There's a gun cabinet—I don't have a clue what's left there over the winter." Warren folded his arms, his leather coat creaking. "Listen, what're you going to do? Just walk the fuck in there?"

"No, you're going to lead me."

"Hey, this isn't, you know, my *job.*"

"You wanted to come along, remember?"

"*You're* the law."

"What was it? To help your brother? To protect your ex-wife and your daughter?"

"Well, you know it's about fifty below out there in this wind and there's hardly enough heat in this buggy now while she's running." He exhaled. "Look, I can see my breath. Why don't I stay here and keep the engine running?"

Del smiled. "You'd like that."

"Yeah, I would."

"How far are we now?"

"Maybe half a mile," Warren said. "There's one big bend in the road up ahead, then it falls off and runs toward the ridge above the river."

"You know it pretty well."

"I'm a quick fucking study," Haas said. "Listen, how many weapons do you have? Maybe you could let me carry something?"

"Not on your life," Del said. "Even without that bottle of schnapps in you, I wouldn't trust you with a BB gun."

"Now it's a trust issue? This is Boy Scout shit. I brought you up here, didn't I?" Del said nothing. "You really know how to instill confidence in your troops."

Del pulled over close to the snowbank on the right side of the road and stopped. He shut off the engine and said, "Just stay close to me, keep your mouth shut, and do what I say."

"Or what?"

"Or I handcuff you to your seat there and you sit here in the cold."

"Either way I *freeze* to death. I don't even have a fucking *hat.*"

"Anybody ever tell you you're an awful whiner?" Del pulled the hood of his overcoat up over his head and tied it snug around his face with the drawstrings. He then fastened the Velcro flap so that his face was protected up to his eyes.

Haas looked at Del and laughed. "If it isn't Admiral Fucking Peary. I tell you, my ears are going to *freeze* and *drop off.*"

Del opened the glove box and handed a wool headband to Warren. "It'd be better if your lips went first."

He got out of the Land Cruiser and waited for Warren, who had difficulty opening his door against the wind. Looking toward the ridge, Del could barely see the lodge. The snow rose up on the wind like smoke. He started walking down the road, bent well forward so that the force of the wind struck the top of his head, which he kept turned away to the left.

"Jesus!" Warren shouted. *"Fuck this!"*

Del shoved him hard in the back. "Shut up," he said. "You understand?" He pushed him again, forcing him to walk ahead.

They came to a break in the snowbank by an arch constructed of timbers—animals carved with a chain saw, because hunters often decorated their lodges, cabins, and camps with images of the animals they sought to kill. It was a sign of warning for intruders, of respect for the animals. Monty called it "northern voodoo." Next to the archway was an Isuzu Trooper that was nearly covered with blowing snow.

"You were right about their coming out here," Del said. "I hope you're as good at reading your brother's mind."

"Don't expect him to step outside and give up, Sheriff."

They climbed over the hard rubble of the plowed bank and began to wade toward the ridge, following a line of weathered fence posts jutting out of the snow. The lodge was constructed of logs, and a broad porch spanned the front wall. Del guessed the place had been built sometime in the twenties or early thirties, when such buildings could be assembled cheaply using labor from one of the logging camps out here. The windows in the lodge were dark, and it was impossible to tell if there were blinds or curtains.

Warren turned and looked over his shoulder.

"Go on," Del said.

He walked right behind Warren, stepping in his foot holes. The effort of climbing through the deep snow was causing sweat to run beneath his long johns. He was fine except for the fingers on his right hand. The cold made them feel brittle as glass. He worked his fingers back into the palm of his glove so he could make a fist and try to generate some warmth. He didn't want to have to hold his gun in his left hand.

The climb up the ridge became steeper. A brutal wind rounded the corners of the lodge, sculpting the snow into deep, graceful canyons. Warren stopped and turned his head away from the wind. His eyebrows were encrusted with snow and ice. Even in the moonlight, Del could see that the skin on his cheeks was beginning to freeze. His lips and chin were blue white; they reminded Del of frozen corpses he'd found in vehicles stalled in a blizzard.

"I'm really cold, Sheriff."

"Keep going."

Norman had seen them from the window while he was getting dressed. At first he'd thought they were animals, but when the swirling snow let up for a moment it was clear that they were bent forward, walking on two legs. The second form had more bulk than the first.

Noel came out of the bathroom, pulling on her sweater. "Who are they?"

"I haven't noticed any lights on the road."

"Maybe they broke down. Maybe they were on snowmobiles—they get in accidents all the time." Norman tilted his head slightly. "All I'm *saying* is they might not be after us. They might be lost or in trouble."

"That cabinet," he said. "There a key?"

"It's on top."

"Open it." She didn't move. "Open it, Noel."

He leaned toward the window. They were perhaps thirty yards from the lodge and making slow progress against the wind. He went over to the cabinet. There was enough light from the moon that Noel could fit the key into the lock. When the door was opened, she stepped aside.

"Lorraine," she whispered. "What should I do with her?"

"Nothing. She's better off asleep."

Noel went to the window nearest the front door and looked out through the curtains.

The cabinet was empty except for one crossbow, which Norman took out. It was a Browning, and there were three short arrows in its quiver. He had handled a crossbow only a few times. He remembered that a crossbow arrow was called a bolt or sometimes a quarrel.

"How're they doing?" he said.

"Slow. But they're coming."

Norman put his foot in the stirrup and pulled up the string until it locked in place. "Noel," he said sharply, "pull all the curtains closed now."

She backed up, banging her hip into an end table. A lamp fell on the floor, breaking the bulb. She turned and faced the room Lorraine was in, and Norman remained perfectly still. They could hear the child shifting under her blankets, but she didn't make any other sound. Noel drew the curtains together at all four front windows and then came over to him. She laid a hand on his shoulder. "You can't," she whispered. "You can't just *shoot* at them for walking up here." He closed the cabinet door. "We don't let them *in*, that's all."

"And what if they try to get in, Noel?"

She took her hand off his shoulder.

At the bottom of what appeared to be the porch stairs, Warren stopped again.

"Up," the sheriff said. "It's three steps."

Warren climbed onto the porch. Maki followed and went straight across and put his back to the wall. The snow wasn't as deep and there was less wind here, though to Warren's left came a steady howl as the air cut around the corner of the lodge. Warren stumbled against the log wall, whacking his forehead. "*Shit.*"

He removed the glove from his right hand and felt his forehead. Strange: fingers that barely had feeling touching skin that seemed frozen solid. There was only a deep burning sensation that was penetrating his skin. He tried to scrape off the ice that had formed on his eyebrows, but his hand was getting too cold, so he pulled his glove back on.

He stared back toward the road. He couldn't see it. Their footprints went out from the porch and disappeared in the blowing snow. He could barely make out the arch at the end of the drive. Beyond that, the snow just gave way to darkness, while overhead a milky light bathed everything. No headlights. Perhaps he'd been mistaken. Perhaps Pronovost and Woo-San weren't following them. "What now, Sheriff?" he said.

Maki turned his head. With his hood up and his lower face covered, Warren could see only his eyes. They were angry. Maki tugged off his right glove, and as he pulled open the flap covering his face, there was the ripping sound of Velcro. "*Quiet.*" He unzipped his coat, reached inside, and took out a pistol.

"You remind me of one of those guys in the desert. A sheik."

Maki kicked him in the shin.

"All right, all *right.*"

The sheriff held the pistol against his right shoulder, the barrel pointed at the porch roof. He turned left and walked along the porch toward the windward side of the lodge. He stopped at the first of four windows, got on his hands and knees, and crawled to the end of the porch. He stood up and looked back, jerking his head for Warren to follow. Getting down on all fours, Warren crawled through the path in the snow. When he reached the end of the porch, Maki was already working his way along the side of the lodge. The land fell away gradually, and he walked upright beneath each window. Warren climbed over the porch railing, dropped into the snow, and followed Maki down the side of the lodge.

Noel could hear their boots on the porch, but she couldn't determine what direction they were headed—it had been that way since she'd lost hearing in her left ear. Suddenly she couldn't hear anything. "I don't know where they are now."

"I think they're along that side of the house," Norman said. "We can't hear them 'cause of the wind. I think they're going down the ridge and around the back to see if there's another door." He came over to her and took hold of her upper arm, squeezing her biceps tightly. "Listen, get Lorraine, put on your stuff, and go out the front door."

"What?"

"Noel—*do* it. Just take her and get down to your car and get out of here."

"Norman."

"Look, you can't stay here. The baby can't."

"No."

"You should never have come with me. This is a mistake. We both know it."

"But I did and I'm not going anywhere." She pulled her arm free of his hand.

"All right," he said. "Then go in the bedroom and stay with her. If she wakes up, try to keep her quiet."

Noel walked across the Great Room. Just before entering the bedroom, she looked back at him, her face briefly illuminated by the fire.

Norman went into the kitchen. He figured they would go along the back of the lodge and eventually come to the outside kitchen door. There was a space between the wall and the refrigerator where a plastic trash basket was kept. He pulled out the basket and pushed it over by the counter, then backed into the space and squatted down beside the refrigerator. There was enough room for him to lean back against the wall so he was out of sight if anyone looked through the window in the kitchen door. With the crossbow stock tucked into his right shoulder, he took aim at the door. He had a clear shot.

Del and Warren walked along the back of the lodge and turned the corner out of the wind. There was a door with a small window. Del went up the steps and looked inside at the kitchen, which was dark, but he could make out a log table and four chairs and, beyond that, the dull white of an old refrigerator.

Warren came up the steps and Del turned around. "Call for your brother."

"Yeah, right."

Del grabbed the leather lapel of his coat, pushed him forward, then rapped the butt of his pistol on the door. He nodded his head emphatically at Warren. His back was against the wall, and he held his gun up. His bare hand was numb with cold. He could hardly tell that he was holding a pistol; his forefinger couldn't feel the trigger at all. He rapped the gun on the door again.

"Norman!" Warren called finally. *"Norman! It's Warren! Let me in, I'm freezing my ass off out here. Come on!"* He waited a moment. *"Noel, I know you're there, too. Open the fuck up, will you?"*

Warren folded his arms across his chest. He was shaking badly.

"Who's that with you?" a man called from inside. He seemed close, somewhere in the kitchen. His voice was similar to Warren's, only younger and somehow less cynical. It had to be Norman Haas. "I saw both of you coming up from the road," he said. "Who is that, Warren?"

"It's—" Warren sounded relieved that he didn't have to shout to be heard. He studied Del a moment, then faced the door again. "It's Woo-San. This guy who is in on all this shit with her father now. He figured out that it was you who came to the motel, and he got in touch with me."

"I don't know any Woo-San," Norman said. "I never met a Woo-San."

"You've been away," Warren said. "Out of touch. Let us come in and talk."

"What do you want to talk about?"

"Come *on,* Norman," Warren shouted. "I'm fucking *freezing* out here!"

"Go away, Warren. Just *go away.*"

"I'm coming in," Warren said, bending over. "I can't *stand* this cold anymore!"

Del watched as Warren untied his left boot and yanked it off his foot. He straightened up, put his hand inside the boot, and with one swing broke the glass window. Balancing on his right foot, he hopped to the side of the door. Somewhere deeper in the lodge there was the muffled sound of a child.

"What're you *doing?*" Norman said.

"I'm gonna open this goddamned door now and walk in there where it's warm. You understand me, Norman? It's 'cause of you being out of prison that I'm out here in this crap. *I'm coming in where it's fucking warm!*"

"Don't!"

"We're coming *in,* Norman!" Warren hopped in front of the door, reached through the broken glass, and, after fumbling around, turned a latch. "Now don't get excited," he said as he turned the knob from the outside and pushed open the door. "I'm not armed. I'm just coming in to get out of this fucking weather." He stepped into the kitchen, his boot crushing glass on the floor. "Jesus, I'll be lucky if I don't cut my foot to *shreds.*"

Del waited outside. Nothing happened. There was just the sound of Warren stomping on a creaky wood floor. Del knew he shouldn't risk going in, but he was cold, too, and they'd gotten this far. He stepped into the doorway. Suddenly the refrigerator door was swung open and the small, bare bulb came on, making it difficult to see. Del remained perfectly still, his gun pointed at the ceiling, and after a moment his eyes began to adjust. Warren was sitting at the table now, pulling his boot back on his foot. He did this with a certain poise, as though he'd just come in from a leisurely stroll. Norman was standing behind the open refrigerator door, and he had a crossbow against his right shoulder, aimed at Del's chest.

"Shut the door before you let all the heat out, will you?" Warren said calmly.

Del pushed the door closed with his left hand. Somewhere in the next room, which was very dark, there were footsteps coming toward the kitchen. Del could barely see her until she was in the doorway. She had short blond hair, a wide pretty face, and a beautiful, full mouth. But her large eyes were tired, frightened. Looking at her, Del suddenly felt he understood something about the Haas brothers. She stared at Warren a moment; at first, Del thought she was angry, but then she looked confused.

"*This* guy's Woo-San?" Norman said.

"No," she said. "Woo-San's Asian—does he look *any*thing like Asian to you?"

It was difficult for Del to see Norman's face, but he could hear him breathing and he could see the rise and fall of his chest, which was affecting his aim with the bow.

"Jesus," Warren said as he tied his boot lace, "you two are just beautiful together."

"Shut up," Norman said. He never took his eyes off Del. "Who *are* you, mister?"

Warren grinned at Del. "You want to break it to him, or you want me to do it?"

"Do *what?*" Norman nearly shouted.

"Easy," Del said. "I'm a police officer, Norman."

"He's a regular fucking sheriff," Warren said with delight.

Norman turned his head quickly toward his brother. "You brought a *sheriff?*"

"Christ, Norman, I didn't, you know, *bring* him. Not like I extended an invitation."

Noel took a step into the kitchen, and a floorboard groaned. The sound caused Norman to start, and the crossbow fired. The quarrel pierced Del's coat on the left side. Noel screamed and Warren stood up.

Del couldn't move. His arms were spread out from his sides, and the gun, which he had been holding in his right hand, fell to the floor.

The others stared at him, and finally Warren whispered, "Holy shit."

Slowly Del looked down at his left side. "I'm stuck," he whispered.

Warren came to him and leaned over to inspect the arrow. "You're not hit?"

"No."

"Fuck, if you *missed,* Norman," Warren said, disappointed. "Not eight *feet* away and he *misses.*" Reaching up under Del's left arm, he felt the shaft of the quarrel, and he snorted. "Why, Norman. You've gone and pinned the sheriff to the doorjamb." He turned to his brother and laughed. "You couldn't do that again if you tried."

Norman appeared to be coming out of a trance. "Noel, get that pistol for me."

She stared at the gun on the floor a moment, then picked it up by the handle as though it were something dirty that she didn't want to touch at all. She handed him the gun, and he put down the crossbow and pointed it at Del.

"Mind if I just take my coat off?" Del asked.

Norman didn't say anything, but then he nodded.

Del untied his hood and pushed it off his head; then he unzipped his coat and pulled first his right and then his left arm out and stepped away from the coat, which remained hanging from the doorjamb.

"Christ, Norman," Warren said. His laugh was loud and irritating. "He's the sheriff of Yellow Dog Township. Followed you all the way out here after you walked away. Pretty good on the chase, but he doesn't always get his man, you know?"

"Put on a light, Noel," Norman said. She reached for a light switch that turned on the lamp that hung above the table. Norman closed the refrigerator door and stepped out of the corner. "Now how 'bout some lights in the Great Room."

Noel went into the other room and switched on several lamps.

Warren stood up, rubbing his hands together. "I'll just get in front of that fireplace."

"You brought this sheriff out here," Norman said.

"Well, you can *see* that he was armed." Warren took a step toward the Great Room but stopped when Norman turned the pistol on him. "Look, I just got to get my ass warmed up some." Norman kept the gun pointed at his brother for a long moment. "You know how cold it is out there?"

Norman nodded.

"Well, come on, then. Let me get those logs cranked up."

"How's Ma?"

Warren seemed irked by the question. "Ma's fine."

"Don't hear much from her. Maybe three letters and a Christmas card. Nothing in a long time now. She all religious these days or has that faded away, too?"

"I don't know what she's up to since she moved down to Florida."

"When was that?" Norman seemed genuinely surprised.

"After last winter. I thought she'd let you know."

"Well, she didn't. No one let me know." Something happened to Norman's face, to his eyes, a recognition of some sort. He appeared to make some decision, and Del thought he might shoot his brother. But instead he lowered the gun to his side and said, "Go build your goddamn fire."

CHAPTER Fifteen

Shortly after Liesl sent Darcy home for the night, the phone rang. It wasn't Del, but his deputy, Monty Price. In the background she could hear a television, and two girls arguing over something.

"He's somewhere between North Eicher and Lake Superior."

"He's found Norman?"

"No." Monty paused; the channel on the television was changed. "After this cold front passes through," he said, "we're going to get hit with another blizzard. Should start tomorrow morning."

"Thanks, Monty."

"No problem. You okay up there on your own?"

"Yes, thanks. My phone's working again, and my back's feeling much better."

She hung up, returned to the couch, and lay beneath blankets, fully clothed. When she switched off the lamp, the moonlight came through the skylights. She had pared her life down so that she was unaccustomed to being concerned about someone else. When Gretchen and Harold were alive, it had seemed she was always waiting. When the child was out of her sight, she often imagined horrible things: accidents, rapes, kidnappings, murders. She remembered one fall afternoon becoming so incapacitated with such fear that she sat at the kitchen table for nearly an hour, barely moving, until she heard Harold's truck coming up the drive. Then, as if coming out of a trance, she quickly began cutting up vegetables for dinner so that she appeared occupied when Gretchen opened the kitchen door. She used to tell Harold that she was going to die of a heart attack from waiting. Since the accident, she was still convinced that she would have that heart attack, but it would be from remorse. They were different, waiting and remorse, but either could kill you.

Sleep was impossible, and she got up off the couch. The clock on the kitchen stove said it was a little after midnight. She often worked in the middle of the night, but what she needed right now was not the carving, cutting, layering, and shaping of wet clay. So she pulled on her old parka and went out to the shed, thinking that eventually she'd have to return to this daily activity that was essential to her life in this house in the woods. Had she not just been released from the hospital, had she none of these shooting pains in her back, she would think nothing of it: switch on the overhead light, pick out a log, stand it on the block, and begin splitting. She had a Franklin stove and a kiln that required regular feedings.

But because she was weak, and because there were still these twinges that shot up her spine, she took her time. She pulled on the leather gloves, selected a smallish piece of oak, taken from the deadfall she cleared out of the woods—an infinite source of fuel within a hundred yards of the house. After standing the log on the block, she picked up the ax and waited for the right moment. The Zen of log splitting, Harold used to call it. Waiting for that moment when the universe was ready for the union between the ax blade and this particular log. Not just any piece of wood, but *this* log. This log from the tree that had grown out there for decades, until one day it died; then, years later, the forces of wind and elements weakened the trunk until it fell to the forest floor. And then still later, usually during the summer or early fall, Liesl would cut this dead tree into two-foot lengths with her bow saw, fill up her wheelbarrow, and haul the load back to the shed, where she kept a pile of logs. The proof was in the splitting. Now she raised the ax over her right shoulder, paused to gather strength, waiting for the universe to line up just so, then swung down, driving the blade through the log and into the block. Split neatly into two halves, wood clattered on the cold concrete floor. She wriggled the ax free of the block, picked up one of the halves, balanced it on the block, and raised her ax once more.

She found something exquisite and primal in the rhythm of certain activities, log splitting being one of them. Once her body and mind got into that rhythm, she arrived somewhere else. A true Zen practitioner might suggest it was some higher plane of awareness. Or reality. Or spirituality. And of course the repetition of it was sexual if, for no other reason, there was a sense of exhaustion at the conclusion. But she didn't care about any of these things. What she liked about log splitting, aside from the fact that it was necessary to keep the house warm and the kiln stoked, was that during the act her thoughts often seemed remarkably free and clear. She knew long-distance runners and cross-country skiers claimed to achieve a certain intellectual nirvana in the midst of a marathon or a thirty-kilometer course, but for her it arrived while log splitting at the point where each of her actions was smooth, well timed, seemingly effortless. And she would think of things that she was convinced would never come to mind during any other activity.

Sheriff Del Maki was no stranger.

Liesl had broken a sweat. Her back was tired, limber but not sore. She picked up a new log, raised the ax, and brought it down with all her might. What she knew about the sheriff of Yellow Dog Township was common knowledge. Towns with several hundred year-round residents have little but common knowledge to share. She didn't remember exactly where or when or from whom she had learned it. She knew he was trusted but pretty much left alone. Not entirely understood. He seemed to prefer it that way. He was a loner, his Land Cruiser often seen on the county roads at all hours of the night. He tried to remain impartial. He was no backslapping politician; played no favorites.

Someone—she couldn't remember who—had once described him as the high school teacher that students respect because he brooked no nonsense, and he was fair.

There was a little sympathy for him, too. His wife, who was not a Yooper, had left—not so much him but the place. She had remarried and lived somewhere south. No surprise in that. People who couldn't handle the U.P. simply left, and those who remained felt it was for the best. It was a form of natural selection particular to cold, northern regions. But he had not remarried, had not found a mate who would be content with what the township had to offer: isolation, long winters, and the nearest decent mall five hours south in Appleton, Wisconsin.

And there was something failed about him, too. Everyone knew he had grown up in Marquette, then gone downstate to college. But he had not been accepted into the state police academy in Lansing. His test scores were high enough, but—and this was the part that was always implied, though he would take no part in such explanations—he didn't make the cut owing to the fact that he was white and he was from the U.P. So he had taken the position here in Yellow Dog. The state's loss was the township's gain.

Liesl set the ax blade in the block. Split logs surrounded her on the concrete floor. She could see her breath. Not once had she had to resort to the maul and wedge. After tugging off her leather gloves, she inspected a blister that had developed on her right thumb. Her hands felt good and raw. There was something else about Sheriff Del Maki, something that had been only hinted at years earlier, but she couldn't remember—she was too exhausted. She switched off the overhead light and returned to the warmth of the house, hoping that perhaps now she could sleep.

Noel sat on a wood chair in the corner of the living room, studying the sheriff while Warren stacked logs in the fireplace and Norman leaned against the gun cabinet, his right arm holding the sheriff's pistol at his side. Warren was doing most of the talking, and she had no problem tuning him out.

The sheriff's first name was Del, and he was observant without appearing to be: his eyes mostly avoided direct contact with her or either Norman or Warren, yet she could tell that he was paying attention. His head was large, and there were a couple of deep creases in the back of his neck. She liked his hands: broad palms, thick fingers—strong, but not clumsy. She liked his eyebrows, too, the way they tended to hover over his eyes, protecting them, shading them. But she kept coming back to the creases in his neck.

Though she wasn't listening carefully, she was sure Warren was lying. If not outright lying, then embroidering his story to conceal something, or perhaps simply leaving out some important detail. He was explaining why he and the sheriff had followed them here to the lodge. "The man was armed," Warren said when he had the new logs aflame. "I had to go along. There was Lorraine to think about, Norman. And Noel. He's the law—what does the law care about them as long as they bring you in?"

Norman seemed preoccupied, standing by the cabinet. He'd heard his brother's stories too many times. It took Noel a long time to figure Warren out; now that she had, she understood Norman better as well. When the sheriff first sat on the couch, he made fists, trying to warm his fingers. He wore no rings, which was the first thing she would have noticed if he'd checked into the motel. If he came into the office on a bad night—freezing rain turning to sleet—he would ask what the rate was for a single, and when she'd tell him thirty-six, he'd say fine, though they both understood that he wasn't about to go out and look for a better deal. She was already giving him the deal, that a lot of singles on a night like this—when the weather was lousy and it was after nine o'clock—would start as high as forty-four. He would understand the unspoken.

"Question is," Warren said finally, "what now?"

Norman took his weight off the cabinet and went to the picture window. "Nothing," he said. "Not right now. Not in this weather."

"You want to just stay here?" Warren said, his voice coaxing, skeptical. "What if the sheriff here has been in touch with someone? Suppose they *know* he's out here—they don't hear from him after a certain point, they're bound to come looking."

Norman turned around and studied the sheriff a moment. The sheriff continued to gaze into the fire. He was remarkable in his ability to maintain such a neutral expression. Norman went into the kitchen, yanked the quarrel out of the doorjamb, and returned with the sheriff's coat. He went through the pockets—there were quite a few—putting their contents on the coffee table in front of the couch: wallet, keys, Swiss Army knife, notebook with a short pencil tucked in the spiral hinge, binoculars, handcuffs, worn leather pouch, cellular phone.

The sheriff observed these items on the coffee table as though he'd never seen them before.

Opening the leather pouch, Norman said, "Bullets."

Then he picked up the cellular phone. "Everybody's got these now. Cute." He dropped the phone on the coffee table and went back to the cabinet. "You aren't expected to call anyone, are you, sheriff? No, you came out here all on your own. You got that loner thing going for you."

The sheriff's expression didn't change. He continued to gaze into the fire. But somehow Noel was certain that he knew it was the smart choice.

Warren took the sheriff's coat and inspected the hole made by the arrow. Tossing the coat on the back of the couch, he shook his head. "Yeah, but is it bulletproof?"

He continued talking, but Noel tuned him out and concentrated on the flames leaping off the logs in the fireplace. She had to admit that something about the sheriff appealed to her. Warren often accused her of staring at men, older men. He said she had a daddy-thing about older men, but when she reminded Warren that he was about five years older than she was, he said, "That's not what I mean by older. I mean old old."

She knew it wasn't so much age she was looking for; it was a quality, something she could only describe as "the perfect stranger." New, yet familiar.

Noel sat up in the chair. Warren was standing in front of her, looking concerned.

"What?" she said angrily. "*What?*"

"Food. How's the food supply? Now that we've embarked on this little family reunion, we might be stuck here together awhile, and I was wondering what we have out here to eat. *Get it? Eat?*"

"I'll check." She stood up quickly. The sheriff turned his head away from the fire and considered her for a moment. He seemed concerned, grim. He appeared anything but hungry.

Warren hit the side of his head with the palm of his hand. "I don't know, Norman. Sometimes she just drifts away like that. Maybe it's the loss of hearing."

"Shut *up*, Warren. I hear your shit just fine."

He smiled, first at her, then at his brother. "See what married life has done for her?"

Norman's stare gave away nothing. It was as though he had raised some invisible shield that was intended to deflect Warren's cracks, his jokes. She remembered that about Norman, that he could do that—just let Warren go on and on for a long time, and it would seem not to have any effect. She started for the kitchen, wishing she had developed that ability. But she hadn't—Warren still had an effect on her.

Warren followed Noel, walked past her, his shoulder brushing against hers, and led her into the kitchen. He began looking in the kitchen cabinets, slamming each door shut.

She stopped in the kitchen doorway, and looking back into the Great Room, she explained, "He needs something to drink."

Warren opened the cabinets under the sink. "This place needs to be upgraded to primitive." He kicked the door closed.

"You're going to wake Lorraine."

He knew that tone of voice. She leaned against the doorjamb, and he studied her cocked hips a moment before he gazed around at the walls, looking for more doors, more shelves, more hiding places. Nothing but rough-hewn logs, a mounted ten-point buck, fly rods and creels, a two-man handsaw. "Stuff looks like it was hung in honor of Teddy fucking Roosevelt," he said.

"Try over the refrigerator," she said.

"Show me."

She kept her back against the doorjamb, watching him.

"That big sweater does wonders for them," he said.

She came into the kitchen, reached up, and opened the cabinet doors above the refrigerator. Stepping back, she said, "The crackers and cereal have been there since last spring—they're all stale. We have lots of soup, canned ham, tuna fish, stuff like that."

"What's that in back?"

"I don't know. Take a look."

He pushed aside a box of saltines. In back there was a fifth of vodka, two-thirds full. "Ah," he said, taking the bottle down. "Popov. Jesus." He unscrewed the cap, took a pull, and swallowed. "Not exactly Absolut or Stoly, but it'll do the job."

"Happy now?" She started to turn for the door to the Great Room.

He grabbed her upper arm and pulled her close to him. "Happy? Is that what this is about, *happy?*" She tried to yank her arm free, but he held her closer and whispered, "It was those letters."

"What about the letters?"

"You wrote back." She glanced toward the door and then twisted so that she could lean away and stare up into his face.

"What if I did?"

"So the two of you planned this whole thing."

"We didn't *plan* anything."

"How he'd get away and come for you and the kid. You know, they catch you—and they will eventually—they could put you in prison, too, as an accomplice." He pushed her away. "It'll be just fine, Noel. I'll look after Lorraine, and I'll write you *plenty* of letters."

Norman tucked the pistol in the front of his pants and went to the fireplace, blocking the sheriff's view of the flames. "You came out from Yellow Dog?"

The sheriff nodded. He raised his eyes up to Norman's face for a moment, but he seemed intent on watching the fire.

"Why?" Norman asked.

"Somebody has to."

"How'd you know which way to go?"

The sheriff raised his head again. "You left a trail. Think you wouldn't?"

"The truck, the eighteen-wheeler, that wasn't my fault, you know." The sheriff nodded, but he didn't seem convinced. "I'm telling you, that guy, the driver—Eldon was his name—he was—he was like some guys inside. You know?"

The sheriff hardly moved. "The van. What about the guy who owned the van?"

"It was too bad. I didn't ask him to stop."

"His name was Rodney Aaberg."

"Yeah, he was in the cab, and I was going around the front of the rig to push this driver, Eldon—the guy was *huge*—when the whole thing goes up. I thought of taking off, but I didn't. I was going around to help, I'm telling you."

"You're lucky. Not a scratch, no burns."

"It was hot," Norman said. "Hotter than this fire. The truck went up like *that.* My problem seems to be that people who can back up my story tend to vanish."

The sheriff appeared not to be very interested. He stared through Norman's legs at the fire.

Norman stepped away from the fireplace, leaned over, and picked up the sheriff's wallet. He opened it, studied the badge, the driver's license. "Delbert Esa Maki," he read. "All I wanted," he said, and he waited, but the sheriff didn't seem to hear him. "Delbert, all I wanted was to walk away. Not to hurt anybody. That's all, really."

"Del," the sheriff said without raising his eyes. "People usually call me Del." He leaned back, and his expression changed. He looked Norman full in the face and seemed to be inviting him into some confidence with him. "Norman," he said slowly. "Sure, it's one of those names like Delbert, but not quite as bad. It starts in school, during recess or maybe some jerk sitting behind you in class. And it never really goes away—even grown men, sometimes you see it in their eyes, the humor of it. Your name's a joke, so you must be a joke."

"Yeah, I know that look."

"Which do you prefer, Norman or Norm?"

"Norman."

"Good for you. Sometimes I wish I had gutted it out, too, but it's too late." The sheriff nodded his head as though he were agreeing with something. "Norman, if you didn't want to hurt anybody, why'd you leave her in the snow?"

Norman straightened up quickly. He walked over to the corner and leaned against the cabinet. He could smell something from the kitchen—some kind of soup that Noel was cooking on the stove. His brother was in there with her, and he was talking quietly. Fine. Let him talk. Norman wondered how anybody could be hungry. "You found her?" he said.

"Yes."

Norman waited, but there was nothing more; the man continued to stare into the fire, seemingly content that his view was no longer obstructed. Finally, Norman took a breath and said, "Well, so you found her?"

"We found her, yes."

"Where?"

"Where do you think, Norman?"

"Hey, *look,* don't play games with *me.*" He took his elbow off the cabinet, and without something to lean on he felt unstable, his arms limp and unrestrained. "I asked *you* a question."

The sheriff turned on the couch, just his head and shoulders. "Where you left her."

"In the snow."

"Right—in the snow."

Norman took a step closer to the end of the couch. "How long was she there?"

The sheriff gazed into the fire. He'd clearly made some decision.

"How long, I said."

The sheriff didn't answer.

Norman drew the pistol out of his pants and took another step toward the couch. "How long was she there? Was she *alive?*"

"Why?" the sheriff said. He almost seemed to be speaking to himself. "Why would you want to know? What difference is it to you whether she died or not? Unless you're concerned about facing a murder rap. Is that it?"

Norman's right arm reached back and he swung through fast and hard, catching the sheriff on the side of the head with the handle of the pistol.

At first Noel thought it was Lorraine falling out of bed, and she seized up—her muscles, her heart, everything went tight. It was a hard sound, but there was something fleshy about it, too. She knew this sound from falls Lorraine had taken, and she imagined the child half-awake, trying to get out of bed, whacking her head against the floor or the edge of the nightstand. Noel left the stove, the wooden spoon still in her hand, dripping chicken broth and draped with limp noodles.

But when she reached the kitchen door she stopped. It wasn't Lorraine, and Noel felt a momentary sense of relief before something new and confusing and frightening seemed to pour into her. Norman was standing beside the couch, staring down. He seemed both angry and afraid. The gun was in his hand.

The sheriff wasn't on the couch. He was nowhere in sight.

Suddenly Noel was shoved aside from behind as Warren came out of the kitchen and strode over to the couch, holding the bottle of vodka by the neck. "What the fuck?" he nearly shouted. "What the *fuck,* Norman?" He stopped at the back of the couch and looked down toward the fireplace or perhaps the coffee table. And he whispered, *"Holy shit."*

Noel crossed the living room and saw the sheriff, lying on the floor between the couch and the coffee table. He seemed stuck there, and he didn't move. Blood seeped from his scalp; it pooled in a missing knothole and filled the gaps between the floorboards.

"Norman!" she said. "Norman, what—"

"I didn't mean it," he said.

"Fuckin' great," Warren said.

"I just hit him *once."*

"You're pathetic," Warren said.

He went around the couch on Norman's side, and Norman did an odd thing: he turned to his brother and stood in his way.

"Leave him alone," Norman said. "You don't know—he might be faking it."

Warren tried to go around Norman, but his brother grabbed his forearms. The gun and the vodka bottle both glinted in the firelight.

Noel went around the other side of the couch and knelt by the sheriff. He wasn't moving—he wasn't faking anything. Looking up, she watched the two brothers, locked in each other's arms now, as though they were trying to dance and neither wanted the other to lead. "Will you stop it?" she said weakly.

They kept up their peculiar dance, their feet shuffling, their arms quivering, as they tried to overpower each other. Warren, who was slightly taller, seemed to be gaining the advantage, and he began to work Norman's right arm and the gun down to his side.

"Just stop it!" Noel shouted.

And just as the bedroom door where Lorraine was sleeping swung open, Noel stood up and screamed as the gun went off.

CHAPTER
Sixteen

Once Liesl had the wood-burning stove stoked up, she got into bed. The house was well protected by the woods, though when the wind was out of the north-northeast, it came up the drive with a vengeance. Tonight the house swayed, creaking like an old boat. The first winter after they had built the house, she and Harold lay in bed many windy nights, wondering if they had done something fundamentally wrong, if the entire structure was going to collapse about them. They feared that they had made some essential mistake in designing the house. Because they had framed the house themselves, with the help of friends who were willing to exchange labor for beer and a meal, they knew every stud, every header, every joist. Liesl's shoulders had become firm, her forearms taut and beveled, from days of driving sixteen-penny nails with a framing hammer. By the end of the first winter, which didn't declare itself until late May, they believed that the house would stand through anything. Like a wooden hull, she was built to give and to come back, again and again.

In the ensuing years she and Harold called it the Sweet Ride. A strong wind tended to encourage and enhance their lovemaking. Gretchen was conceived on a day in February when the wind gusted to over fifty miles per hour and there was more than three feet of new snow. Since the accident, Liesl found it difficult to lie in bed alone on windy nights. Tonight was no exception, and after about fifteen minutes she got up.

She remembered the other thing about Sheriff Del Maki, and she padded through the living room with a blanket over her shoulders, into the studio, to her desk. She sat down, switched on the lamp, and opened the lower right-hand drawer: file folders arranged alphabetically. She ran her thumb along the tabs—"Auto," "Building Receipts," "Clients/Pottery," "Clients/Sculpture," "IRS Returns"—until she came to a file that was labeled simply "Spring 1993." She hadn't been able to think of any more appropriate title. She opened the folder on the desk and sorted through it: insurance forms regarding the truck, which had been totaled; forms and bills from the hospital; the invoice from the funeral home; the accident report.

She stared at this, a two-page form with the heading "Sheriff's Office Yellow Dog Township." She had not read the description of the accident again since she'd first received the report, nearly five years ago. It had come in the mail along with so many other documents. So many documents and forms and letters generated by one accident. She looked down the first page, which stated facts such as the time, location, and cause—"extreme blizzard conditions"—of the accident. All typed, with occasional letters sitting in a dried pool of Wite-out. On the second page there was a brief narrative of the accident and at the bottom of the page the signature "Del Maki, Deputy Sheriff." Since then, Eno Turnquist, who had been sheriff since the fifties, had retired. She had never made the connection until now: Del Maki was the last one to see her daughter alive.

Liesl pulled the blanket tighter around her shoulders. Her lips were quivering uncontrollably, and it was impossible to read the report through her tears. The facts of the accident—the time, the location, the weather, the road conditions—were all clearly stated in the report. But facts by themselves are nothing, mere points of observation. Without underlying cause, a fact has no significance. She knew why they had been on that road in the storm. It was Saturday afternoon and they were returning from Marquette, where they had taken Gretchen to Darcy's birthday party. Earlier they had discussed not going because of the weather, but Liesl knew that to keep Gretchen home would lead to heartbreak because Darcy was her best friend. Darcy had lived half a mile down the hill until the previous fall, when her parents separated and she moved with her mother into Marquette. So the girls rarely saw each other. Still, they talked on the phone several times a week, they wrote letters to each other. Gretchen had made her birthday present for Darcy, a dog she had fashioned out of some of her mother's clay, painted yellow with brown ears and tail. Darcy loved dogs. She was eight. All the girls at that party, except Gretchen, were now approaching their teens.

The snow was coming down so hard that Harold insisted they get an early start home before dark. Ordinarily the drive out from Marquette took about thirty minutes; in a storm it could take twice as long. The truck had four-wheel drive, but the new snow was powdery and a good foot deep in the roads. The plows weren't able to keep up. As they climbed the hill toward Negaunee and Ishpeming, they discussed staying in one of the motels on Route 41. But a house heated by wood needed constant tending, and if they stayed away overnight, there was a good chance that the water pipes might freeze.

They turned onto County Road 870 and continued to climb. Harold kept his speed under twenty-five and remained in second gear. There were no other vehicles on the road that wound through the woods, though they did pass one car that had skidded up the snowbank; it was abandoned, an orange flag attached to the antenna.

About ten miles out on 870 they began to descend into the valley to the south of Eagle Lake. They were singing, the three of them, as they often did when they drove together. Gretchen and her friends had discovered the Beatles recently, and in the truck Harold and Liesl and

Gretchen worked on the harmony to "If I Fell." For such a big man, Harold had a sweet tenor, reedy and pitch perfect. Liesl and Gretchen took the bottom part—it was something Liesl had been doing since she had been a teenager, singing John Lennon's part of the Beatles's harmony. The joke was that most girls got to be Paul; she got to be John.

They rounded the bend just before Maud's Creek. The small bridge halfway down the hill was narrowed to one lane because of the snowbanks. When they were within a hundred yards of the bridge, a green truck emerged from the bend at the bottom of the hill, a big, squarish vehicle with a row of amber lights across the top—a delivery truck of some sort. It was going too slow for such an incline, and Liesl could see that it was losing speed.

"He'll never make it up at that rate," Harold said.

They were too close to the bridge to stop before the other truck passed, and at their present speed the two vehicles would meet head-on in the single lane in the center of the bridge. Harold eased the gas pedal down slightly, and they descended a little faster.

Liesl would never be sure, but she believed that at the same time the green truck accelerated, too—she could see the rooster tails of snow flying out behind the rear tires. She glanced at the speedometer; they were only doing thirty, but she could feel the truck fishtail slightly just before it reached the bridge. They would have crossed the bridge before the green truck if it had maintained the same speed, but it was definitely climbing the hill faster. Gretchen tensed and leaned against her. She made sure the girl's seat belt was fastened, and she noticed that her boots were pressed to the floor. Liesl remembered thinking that six months earlier, before *her* eighth birthday, Gretchen's legs wouldn't have reached the floor of the truck. She was growing that fast.

Harold whispered, "What's he *doing?*"

"He doesn't want to slow down or stop," Liesl said. "Afraid he won't be able to get up the hill."

They were halfway across the bridge and the green truck was closing fast on the bottom of the single lane. Harold accelerated a bit more, pushing the speedometer just over thirty-five. The green truck blared its horn and it kept coming.

Liesl saw the next few seconds like a dance or perhaps a figure-skating routine, a carefully choreographed duet. At the bottom of the bridge, Harold steered slightly to the right and his wheels climbed the base of the plowed bank. The pickup tilted to the left and they made it that way, coming off the bridge at an angle, just as the green truck, horn still blaring, passed them. A man was driving, bearded, wearing a hat with the earflaps down. It was a commercial truck—there was gold lettering on the side, but it went by too fast for Liesl to read. Harold could read it; she didn't know how, but she was sure he had registered the name of the company written on the truck. There was a look in his eyes, a look he got when he'd been wronged and he had determined a course of action in response. She knew from that look that as soon as they got home he was going to call information, get the number of the company, and call to register a complaint about one of their drivers.

Once past the bridge, the pickup came down off the snowbank. The cleared road widened and Harold steered right down the middle, but they were going too fast to make the next bend. And the grade was getting steeper, so they were picking up speed. Harold had his foot off the accelerator, but it wasn't enough.

He whispered, *"Grab her."*

As they went into the bend, the tail of the pickup swung to the right, and for a long moment they were sliding sideways down the road. Gretchen was leaning hard into Liesl now, looking out her window. Then the rear of the truck seemed to suddenly gather weight and they went into a full spin—four, maybe five times, they went around, seeming to pick up momentum. Trees and road and bridge and sky raced across the windshield, until the pickup slammed broadside into the right snowbank. The impact caused the truck to roll over, right up the six-foot embankment, and then it fell. There was a moment during the free fall that Liesl remembered as being quiet, almost pleasurable. Yet she distinctly recalled the sound of the engine, now racing. She was remarkably calm, and she was aware of a desire to preserve the moment. Out the windshield she saw distant snow-covered trees above the gray sky. She saw snowflakes rising up. Until they landed, and the roof and broken glass came in on them.

Liesl remembered nothing after that.

But now, staring at the accident report on her desk, she remembered the other thing about Del Maki, the thing that wasn't common knowledge in Yellow Dog Township. Something she had known all these years, that had remained hidden in her confused recollection of everything that had followed the accident. Now she knew what had happened.

After the truck landed, she was unconscious.

Harold died immediately of a broken neck.

Gretchen was still alive, though her lungs were severely damaged. It had been explained to Liesl—she wasn't sure when or by whom, though she suspected it was while she was still in the hospital and heavily sedated—that the first to reach the scene was a schoolteacher in a car with a cellular phone, who called the sheriff's office. The deputy sheriff arrived, and before the ambulance came, he worked hard to try to keep Gretchen alive. When they got her in the ambulance there was still a pulse, but she died before they reached the hospital.

Liesl switched off the lamp, went through the living room to the bedroom. She lay down on the bed, still with the blanket wrapped around her shoulders, and listened to the north-northeast wind cause the house to sway, creak, and moan.

Opening his eyes, Del looked into Noel's pretty face, which was only inches from his, and his first thought was that she wanted to kiss him.

He closed his eyes but was aware of her hands touching his head. Of a tightness around the top of his skull, which he took to be some kind of a scarf or bandage. Of pain that was centered above his right ear and ran down his neck and into his shoulder.

"How do you feel?"

He opened his eyes again. She was leaning back now, and beyond her he could see the roof beams—he was lying on the couch and his right side was hot from the fireplace. He raised his right arm and touched the side of his skull, then pulled his fingers away quickly—pain shot through his head.

"Ouch," Noel whispered as she leaned closer.

He realized she had a smell that he missed. It was the smell of smoke and bark and chicken soup, but beneath all that there was something he couldn't identify. It had been a long time since he'd been this close to a woman, to a young woman.

There were voices—Warren's and Norman's—coming from the kitchen. They were speaking quietly, and the silences were punctuated by the creaking of the floorboards. Behind that there was the sound of the wind outside. Del touched the swelling above his ear again and assured himself that some kind of a scarf was tied about his head. He remembered Norman swinging his arm, the gun in his hand. He couldn't remember what had caused it.

"Is he going to *die?*"

It was a child's voice above and behind him. He raised his eyes—causing pain to sink deep into the sockets—and looked at the upside-down head of a blond girl.

"I think he's going to make it," Noel said.

"What's your name?" Del asked the girl.

She looked nervously at her mother. "Lorraine."

"How do you do, Lorraine?"

"How do you *do?*" The girl placed one hand over her mouth as she laughed.

Noel smiled as she picked up a large plastic mixing bowl that was sitting on the coffee table. It contained a soggy, bloodstained towel. "Lorraine, take this into the kitchen and ask"—she hesitated—"ask for more ice."

The girl took the bowl and held it against her chest but didn't leave immediately. She wore a brown-and-white wool sweater with reindeer; it was too big on her, and the sleeves had been rolled up several times so that only her tiny pale fingers were visible. After staring down at Del for a long moment, she seemed to have come to some conclusion and walked toward the kitchen.

Warren put the bottle of vodka on the table and watched Lorraine enter the kitchen, holding the bowl against her sweater, as though she were bearing a ceremonial offering in a sacred ritual. "We need more ice." She spoke to neither of them, really, and she kept her attention on the contents of the bowl.

"Ice?" Warren said. "Who needs ice?" He raised the bottle to his mouth and before drinking said, "You see me using ice? Isn't it cold enough already?" He smiled at the girl, but she wouldn't take her eyes off the bowl.

Norman was not drinking. He stared at Warren a moment before getting up from the table. Warren suspected his brother's look was meant to be sympathetic, but at this point he didn't give a shit. Somehow, since the gun had gone off twenty minutes ago, Warren wasn't worried about any of it anymore. It was their problem, not his. He was more concerned about what to do when this bottle of Popov was empty.

"I'll get you more ice," Norman said. He reached into the bowl, took out the towel, and carried it to the sink, where he rung it out.

"Thank you," said Lorraine. She kept her gaze on the pink water in the bottom of the bowl, which she still held tight to her chest.

Warren leaned toward the child and put his finger in her ear. She started to pull her head away, but he took her small chin in his thumb and forefinger. She didn't move, and she stared up at him uncertainly. Slowly he worked his thumb up her chin until he touched her warm, moist lips. Her eyes grew large and frightened as he began to insert his thumbnail into her small mouth. Just as he felt her small teeth against the tip of his thumb, she stepped back out of his reach and some of the pink water sloshed over the rim of the bowl, splattering on Warren's boots.

"Son of a bitch," he whispered, looking down at his feet.

Norman opened the refrigerator and took out a plastic tray of ice cubes. "After this we're out of ice," he said. The girl watched as he twisted the tray and emptied the cubes into the bowl. "If you need more, you'll have to go outside and see if you can find any."

He put the towel in the bowl of ice, and she left the kitchen.

"Kid has no sense of humor," Warren said. "None."

"Right." Norman sat at the table again. "Takes after my side of the family."

Noel took the bowl from Lorraine. "Thank you, sweetheart. Now I want you to get yourself back into bed." The child looked at her, pleading. "It's all right now. There'll be no more loud noises to wake you."

"But, *Mommy*—"

"Lorraine."

The child glanced down at Del a moment. "Is *he* going to go back to sleep, too?"

"Eventually," Del said.

"Now you go ahead," Noel said in her flat, no-nonsense voice. "I'll be in soon to check on you." She fixed Lorraine with a stare, until the child turned and walked into the bedroom where she had been sleeping. "Leave the door open a little," Noel said.

Lorraine shut the door.

"I knew that was coming." Noel reached into the bowl and rung out the cold towel. She folded it into quarters and laid it on the right side of Del's skull.

"What now?" he asked.

"They're in there planning that, I guess."

"You came here with Norman—willingly."

"Seems silly, doesn't it?"

"Not necessarily," he said. "In some ways it's enviable."

"I can't explain it," she said. "Everything else seems to have been a mistake, why not this? But I wanted this. The other things, I'm not so sure I knew what I wanted."

"Few of us do." He raised his hand and took hold of the towel. He closed his eyes.

She let their fingers touch a moment before she took her hand away. His face was still in the firelight. He wasn't exactly handsome, but she found his face interesting. There was something unadorned and blunt about his eyebrows and nose. His lips were thin and flat. His eyelids revealed an unexpected delicacy in the way his lashes lay against his cheeks. Working nights at the motel, she had become quite good at guessing the age of older people. He wasn't an AARP member yet. Something about the lashes suggested what he must have looked like as a boy.

"What are you going to do now?" Warren asked.

Norman didn't answer. He paid attention to his brother's hands as they clutched the bottle of vodka.

"You don't have a fucking clue—you *never* have," Warren said, raising the bottle to his mouth. "And now with this shit you've gotten this far, but it's only going to get screwed up in the end."

In some fundamental way Warren wasn't any different from what he'd been before all this had begun, before Norman had gone to prison, before Warren had gone into the navy. Warren was the same as when they were kids. He only looked older.

"Things have been screwed up for a long time," Norman said. "This is all your doing, too, you know. There's a history here, Warren, a very long history that we're dealing with."

"Yeah, well, you're the one who was in jail, and you're the one who walked away."

"You think I should have just stayed put."

"At least you had a chance then." Warren's right hand held the bottle by the neck, his greedy fingers slightly distorted and magnified through the curved glass. "It's about time, not history. Do your time, start over."

"If it was you inside," Norman said, "I doubt that's what you'd do."

Warren took a pull from the bottle. "Now you've screwed it up for *all* of us."

"Somehow I get the feeling you were all doing a pretty good job without me."

Warren lit a cigarette and shoved the pack across to his brother. "What *are* you going to do now?"

Norman took his time lighting his cigarette, and waited. He wanted to take a drink of vodka, but he knew that it would be a mistake. It had been years since he'd had anything to drink. Now wasn't the time to begin again. If nothing else, the gunshot had reminded him how important it was for him to stay focused, to stay in control. The bullet had gone in the wall a few feet to the left of the front door, and the impact had knocked chinking to the floor. The shot was incredibly loud, echoing inside these aged timbers.

"Your best bet," Warren said, exhaling smoke, "is to go on by yourself."

"You'd like that."

"Dragging a woman and a kid along? Come *on!* You got as far as you did because you were on your own. You're stuck here because you picked up all this baggage."

"Is that what you'd like? To see me just go on alone? Disappear out there as though I'd never been back?" Warren flipped one hand, suggesting that the idea had merit. "What's done is done," Norman said. "If I walked out that door right now, it wouldn't help things for you. Noel isn't coming back just because I'm gone again."

"Maybe." Warren had the look on his face that was intended to suggest he knew something no one else knew. Norman used to believe it, that his brother had secret knowledge. But no longer.

"It's about her father as much as her," Norman said. "I know that."

"What do you know?"

"That you thought the way to him was through her. Christ, Warren, you were already screwing her. You would never have actually married Noel if it weren't for her old man."

"You're sure?"

"I'm sure." Norman stood up and went to the kitchen door. They had stuffed a towel in the broken windowpane, but there was still a cold draft. Looking out at the blowing snow, he said, "You married her because you wanted a piece of this—Pronovost's land."

"I admit it crossed my mind. The guy owns a lot of these woods. Think what it would be worth to the lumber companies. Or developers. Pronovost—the man doesn't get it. He just wants to keep it like it is, the forest fucking primeval." Norman turned from the door. "And none of this ever crossed *your* mind?" Warren raised the bottle to his mouth and drank. "Yeah, right."

"But there's something else going on out here now."

"There is," Warren said. "And it's no good."

"This new Asian guy. It has to do with him, and with the bears."

Warren put his bottle of vodka on the table. For a moment he didn't seem to know what to do with his hands. He placed them on his knees, and for once he looked as though he were about to be straight with Norman. "Yeah, this Woo-San, once he showed up Pronovost changed his tune. He wasn't satisfied to just let exec types come up and hunt and fish his land. And there wasn't no room in things for his son-in-law. So I got the shove." For once Warren seemed genuinely remorseful, defeated.

Norman was about to speak, when the light above the table flickered once and went out. "What's that?"

"I think we just lost our fucking power, bro."

Liesl still couldn't sleep, and she lay on the bed listening to the wind.

It was the green truck. It had always been the green truck.

She had been in line at the post office in Marquette, and Darcy's mother, Allison, was there. It was the Christmas after the accident, and Liesl had not put up a tree in the house, or stockings or any decorations. Everyone in line had packages—presents—to be mailed to friends and relatives. Liesl had a bunch of bills to mail and one small package containing a present for her sister in New Mexico. Allison was two ahead in line, but once they started talking she let the old man between them go in front of her. The line was very slow; they all stood in the snowmelt from their winter boots.

Allison talked mostly about her divorce from Glenn. He had taken a job in Minnesota, and she and Darcy were moving back out to the house in Yellow Dog, and they were going to start the business she'd been planning for years, a kennel. Though the divorce settlement was meager, she had enough to have the barn converted, and she figured if they got through the first year, they'd at least break even. She kept referring to "us" and "we," meaning herself and Darcy. Liesl understood her reluctance to mention her daughter by name, but it wasn't necessary.

When Allison was first in line she said, "They never found that truck."

"The green truck—no, they never found it."

"It's like it didn't exist," Allison said. "There's a reason for everything."

"I know," Liesl said. "The accident was caused by bad weather and the green truck."

"Yes," Allison said vaguely. "But there's also a reason for not finding the truck."

Liesl remembered being distracted by a small child who was behind them in line, a boy of no more than two who had been crying. The post office was about to close, and everyone had been waiting a long time, most with their arms full of parcels, and she could see the tension in faces as the boy began to scream.

"I heard from Turnquist's wife that they looked for months," Allison said, shaking her head as she watched for a signal from the next available postal clerk. "Located every green truck in the county, it seems. Went to talk to Mitch Cole at Pomeroy's Garden Shop, I hear. Also spoke to someone who works for the new vet out in Skandia. Nothing checked out." One of the clerks waved her on; she put a hand on Liesl's wrist and said, "Come down to the house when we get settled in—should be by February." And she rushed forward to the counter.

The boy was screaming bloody murder, so at that point Liesl simply couldn't stay a moment longer. She considered going back to his mother and telling her to *do something*, but instead she stepped out of line, though she was next to be waited on at the counter. She walked back toward the large mural of Père Marquette and down the stairs to the double doors that opened onto Washington Street. It was not the first time, or the last, when she suddenly could not remain wherever she was, when she simply had to leave, to go.

During the holidays, Liesl immersed herself in her pottery and sculpting, and over the next few years she ventured from the house less and less.

CHAPTER

Seventeen

With his eyes closed, the three voices seemed in suspension and Del heard things he thought he might miss if he could see them as they spoke. They weren't exactly arguing, but there was no agreement, either. Three voices, whispering so low that Del couldn't understand the words, only the tone. It was the tone of want. Norman wanted something done, and there was no changing his mind. Warren wanted to ignore the issue. Noel hardly spoke. It was impossible to tell what she wanted.

Del wanted to stand. He shifted on the couch and lowered his feet to the floor. Pushing with both arms, he sat up, moving slowly so as not to jostle his head, which felt as though it might crack open like an egg. When he was upright, the pain settled lower, down in his neck. It occurred to him that pain was fluid and subject to the pull of gravity. But then we are made mostly of water contained in sacks of flesh hung from our bones. He gathered strength and got to his feet and walked unsteadily across the Great Room, which was now lit only by the logs burning in the fireplace. Noel was standing between the two brothers outside the kitchen doorway, their enormous shadows cast upon the timber walls, and she seemed to have placed herself between them on purpose, as though she could spread out her arms and keep the two warring titans apart.

"Forg*et* it," Warren said. "*I'm* not going out there."

"It'll take just a few minutes," she said. "*You* helped Daddy run that new electric line in a couple years ago—Norman doesn't even *know* where the box *is* out back."

"Why don't I draw you a map?" Warren said. "Why don't *you* go, Norman, and I'll hold on to that gun till you get back?"

Norman shifted his weight impatiently. If Del didn't know otherwise, he would have guessed that he was the older brother.

"Come on, Warren," Noel said. "Just reset the switch and come back."

"I'm not dressed for that shit out there." Warren's leather coat appeared slick in the firelight.

All three of them turned to Del, their faces in the dim light appearing savage, even demonic. He picked up his overcoat, which lay on a bench next to the doorway. "Try this on."

Warren hesitated, then grabbed the coat and pulled it on. "Jesus, this is one serious article of clothing. Thing's built for the Yukon. Bet it comes with its own *theme* song." He drained the last of the vodka and put the bottle on the kitchen counter. "All *right*—I'll be back in three minutes. Let there be *light!*" He yanked open the door and lunged out into the wind and snow.

Norman slammed the door shut. "You, Delbert," he said. "Sit at that table."

The sheriff seemed about to speak, thought better of it, and sat down.

"That's right. Just sit there where I can see you." Norman went around the table to the window. Noel came to his side. "Where's this electrical box?"

"Down along the back wall."

Norman pressed his face to the glass. Because of the snow and dark, Warren's footprints were visible for only about ten yards. He stood for several minutes, staring out the window.

"I don't know what's keeping him," Noel said finally. "You just throw the reset switch and the power comes back on."

Norman turned to the sheriff. "You're not liking this, are you?"

"What's there to like?"

"We should have power by now," Norman said.

"You'd think so,"

"Could be anything. Maybe something froze up."

"Or maybe he slipped and knocked himself out," the sheriff said. "He's had enough to drink. Before the vodka, he had a bottle of schnapps and a beer on the drive out."

"One thing about my brother is he can hold it. Schnapps—he *still* drinks that stuff?"

The sheriff leaned back in his chair. "If he's unconscious out there, it'll only be a few minutes before he starts to go numb."

Norman turned to the window again.

"I've seen it more than once," the sheriff said. "Drunks slip on the way home from the bar and next morning somebody finds them frozen solid. We usually have to break them out of the ice."

Norman glanced at Noel. "There must be some rope around here."

"Why?" She sounded frightened.

"Noel. Find something to tie him up with."

She sighed dramatically and went into the Great Room.

Del sat in the chair in the nearly dark kitchen, and he and Norman listened to Noel. She had opened a door, Del assumed the one to the closet next to the bathroom, and she rummaged through it, saying, "Raingear, wading boots, coats, canoe paddle—*rope!*" She came back to the kitchen. "Now what?"

"What do you think?" Norman said.

"I don't know how to do this. You tie him up."

"All right. Come over here."

She put the rope on the table and went around to the window. When Norman handed her the gun, she said, "If he tries something, what?" She laughed. "I'm supposed to shoot him?"

"No. Just whack him in the head again." Norman began to uncoil the rope.

"Why don't *I* go out and look for Warren," she said. "And you stay here."

"If he's out there lying in the snow, you going to carry him back?" Norman came around the table and stood behind Del. "Put your arms behind you."

Del did as he was told, and he could feel his wrists being tied together.

"You know, that woman," Norman said, "she chained me to a radiator."

"What woman?" Noel asked.

"This woman I met when I first got out."

Norman began to wrap the rope around Del's chest and arms. It was thick cordage, at least half an inch, and it was stiff and cold. After each turn, Norman pulled the rope tight. Del kept his chest filled with air, but he knew it wouldn't help. "The hard part is keeping still," Norman said. "You get an itch and it'll drive you nuts. Keeping still is—it takes something: concentration. I knew this guy inside, he was into Buddha and meditation and all that, and he'd sit on the floor with his legs crossed and not move—I mean not *move*—for nearly an hour. Then he'd get up, bow, and walk very slowly around in a circle for several minutes. And then he'd sit down and do it again. I once asked why he did it, and he said it was because it didn't matter whether he did it or not. I don't know exactly what that meant, but he was about the only guy that didn't seem to mind being inside. I don't think he cared where he was."

"No wonder you had to get away from there." Noel sat down at the table and said to the sheriff, "You aren't a Buddhist, are you?"

He shook his head.

Norman finished tying the knot. He'd done a good job; Del couldn't move his arms, and his back was strapped tight to the chair.

Putting on his coat, Norman said to Noel, "Just watch him. We'll be right back."

Noel didn't like holding the gun. It wasn't that it was heavy, but its weight seemed so concentrated. The black rubber grip felt larger than necessary; its curves had been well configured to fit the hand, and there was a grid of small bumps designed to keep the gun from slipping.

"Those aren't the stock grips," Del said. "Bianchi Lightning Grips."

"Good for large hands."

"They help accuracy and reduce recoil."

"You ever shoot someone with it?"

He shook his head.

"Ever try?"

His eyes met hers for a moment, and she thought he might actually smile. "No."

Laying the gun on the table, she said, "I use to meditate."

"Really?"

"I only did it for a little while. It's hard, you know? With a baby you only get a little peace when she's asleep."

"I'll bet," the sheriff said. "What kind?"

"Huh?"

"What kind of meditation?"

She turned her head toward the window as a gust of wind hit the side of the house.

"Aren't there different kinds of meditation?"

"I guess so," she said.

"What kind did you do?"

"I don't know."

"There's TM."

"TM?"

"Transcendental meditation. And there's several kinds that Buddhists practice—"

"I don't remember. It was just for a couple of weeks. There was this guy who stayed a week at the motel while his car got fixed—had to wait for parts to be sent up from Detroit. He'd walk out into the field behind the motel and meditate. He showed me how to sit and everything." She leaned back in her chair, watching the sheriff in the dark. He seemed to be waiting. He seemed to know that there was something else she wanted to tell him. "All right, I thought about going to bed with him, if you want to know. Something about him told me that he'd be the longest, slowest fuck imaginable."

The sheriff didn't move. He looked pretty uncomfortable, strapped to the chair. It was hard to see his face in the light that came through the door from the fireplace. "But you didn't?"

"You don't believe me?"

"I didn't say that."

"You think I'm making it up." Noel got up from the table, picked up the gun, and faced the window.

No, it's not that—" He hesitated until she turned around. "Why are you telling me?"

After a moment, she said, "Because you asked about meditation." She came around the table.

"That's right, I did."

Noel shifted the gun to her left hand and held it at her side. With her right hand she reached out and gently touched the scarf around the sheriff's forehead. "How's it feel, baby?" she said softly.

He didn't move.

She ran her hand down his cheek to his chin. The stubble of his beard crackled underneath her fingertips. "It's usually older men like you that notice me. I don't know why. Sometimes I'm in a restaurant or a store or going to the movies, and I'll catch someone watching me. I guess it's because I remind them of twenty years ago." He wrinkled his nose. "What's that with the nose?"

He didn't answer.

"You don't like it that I think about a perfect stranger?"

"It's not that at all," he said. "No, I just have an itch."

"You do, an itch?" He nodded. "Where?"

"The side of my nose. Right side."

"And you want me to scratch it?"

"Would you mind?"

"Maybe you can reach it with your tongue."

"It's not long enough."

She laughed. "You trying to do something? Break *free?*"

"I doubt it," he said. "I'm really tied in this chair."

"You know, if you meditated, you'd know how to deal with itches."

"How?"

"You empty your mind," she said.

"I see."

"And if you start to think of something, you concentrate on your breathing."

"Does it work?"

"You tell me."

Noel turned and walked back around the table to the window. She could see two sets of tracks in the snow running along the back of the lodge, but there was no sign of Norman or Warren. Suddenly she felt very alone. "I don't know how this happened," she said quietly. "I'm standing here in a dark kitchen *way* out there, I have this gun in my hand—with Bianchi *Lightning* Grips—and you're sitting there like that. I just don't *know.* I'm doing this because I love Norman, and because, well, I *really* need to get away." She turned around and faced him across the table. "Do you know what that means?"

"Yes, I do. It happens to people who live up here. It's the winters, the light."

"Has it ever happened to you?"

His head tilted back for a moment. "It did, yes."

"Really? Or are you just *saying* that?"

"It did, really. Once."

"When?"

"A number of years ago."

"Really?" she said. "I mean, *really?*"

"Yes, really. It was after my wife left. For a long time I thought about leaving, going somewhere south. I realized that this is a very hard place to live."

Noel came around the table. "You were alone?"

"Yes," he said.

"And you didn't just go, by yourself?"

"No, I didn't."

"Was it because you were by yourself?"

He thought about this for a moment. "Yes, it was. Because I knew that no matter where I went it would be the same."

"You'd be alone."

"Yes."

"Know what you are?"

"No. What?"

"You are the perfect stranger."

Noel put the gun down in the middle of the table and walked over to his chair. She took his face in both her hands, being careful of the side where he'd been struck with the butt of the pistol, and leaned down to him.

At first, Del held absolutely still. Somehow he'd known this was coming. He didn't know how long he had known it, but when she leaned down toward his face, he felt relief. When he was younger it had usually been the other way around—he had kissed the girl—and he never really appreciated what she must have been going through, waiting for it to come. Noel's mouth was full and forceful on his, and something in the way she pressed her face to his suggested both a dare and a plea. Both seemed to be saying "Accept me." As she worked his mouth open with her tongue, he could feel the moisture and heat of her mouth fill his. There was a hint of salt and perhaps chicken broth. And as though trying to obliterate all these, his very effort at sorting it out, she suddenly kissed him hard, rolling her head so that her cheek first spread across his chin, then pressed against his nose. Closing her lips around his tongue, she seemed to want to climb into his head, but then she grabbed his tongue and sucked it into her mouth, taking it deeper and deeper, sucking on it till his tongue began to ache. When he was about to pull back, to try to stop her, she let go of his tongue and, opening her mouth wide, brought his lips together. Squeezing them tightly, she ran her tongue over them, as though to seal them closed.

And then her head withdrew briefly. Their faces were still so close that he could feel her breath, which was now coming in long drafts, accompanied by a faint quivering every time her lungs compressed.

Her face came toward his again, and her breasts spread across the ropes that bound his chest, and she kissed him once more, quickly, and then she stood up.

Gazing down at him in the dark, Noel wanted to say something about loneliness. Something that would make him understand that she really knew what it meant to be alone. Something that would help him to never be lonely again.

Then the sheriff, this perfect stranger, said, "Thank you."

She was certain that he did understand. "I hope you're not offended or anything."

"No, I'm not."

"You *are* very alone," she said. "But I don't think you mind."

"Most of the time, no."

The light from the fire had grown dim, and she could barely see his face. But it didn't matter. She knew he was there. "It's a form of meditation."

Raising his head, he said, "I suppose it is."

CHAPTER

Eighteen

Once outside the lodge, Norman followed his brother's tracks along the wall, but something had happened. It was all there in the snow. The tracks stopped just after rounding the corner of the building, and the snow was broken up in a large area—and from there a wide trail angled down the ridge toward the river. Leaning down for a close look, Norman saw blood, which in the moonlight appeared black.

He followed the tracks away from the lodge, wading through fresh powder that was up to his knees. The tracks, descending the hill toward the river, were made by two, perhaps three sets of legs. When he was near the bottom of the hill he could see the footbridge and the shed. The tracks went to the shed door, which had been swung open recently, clearing an arc of snow from in front of it. He considered calling his brother's name, but the wind in the trees was so loud that he doubted he'd be heard even from this distance. If it weren't for the sheriff, he would have brought the gun with him.

He crossed the footbridge and followed the tracks to the shed. He placed his gloved hand on the doorknob—it was the soft curve of an antler point—hesitated, then pulled open the door. The shed couldn't have been more than ten feet square, and it was pitch dark. He took a step inside and his foot hit something—looking down, he could barely see a pair of legs lying on the floor. As he squatted down to see, he heard a sound outside, a quick movement through the snow, rushing up both sides of the shed. He began to turn around when the blow caught him on the right side of his head.

Del watched Noel as she stared out the kitchen window. She was gnawing on a thumbnail, and she hadn't said anything for several minutes.

"Noel, something's going on out there."

"I *know* that." Her voice was shaking.

"What do you want to do?"

She wouldn't turn from the window. "I don't know."

"Can I make a suggestion?"

She exhaled slowly. "What?"

"I think you should get Lorraine up, get to your car, and leave."

Noel turned her head toward him. The logs in the fireplace were now only embers, and he could barely see her face, though her hair formed a faint blond arc that cupped the left side of her head. It was getting cold, too, and he could see her breath against the fleeting moonlight that came through the window. "You do?" she said finally.

"Yes. Just get her away from here."

"I don't understand what's going *on*—why aren't they coming *back*—why aren't the *lights* on—it's just *so*—"

"I know. But you have to make a decision. You have to get Lorraine out of here."

"I can't leave without Norman."

"Yes, you can. You've thought you needed someone to come and take you away. But now you know you can go by yourself." She didn't say anything, though her breathing was audible. "Just go, Noel."

"Just go? For a long time I've wanted to *just go.*" She raised her head slightly as though she were watching something in the sky. With one hand on the glass, she tapped out a crisp code with her fingernail. Suddenly she folded her arms. "If I did go, what about you?"

"Well, I'd like you to untie me."

"Yeah, sure. And I suppose you want me to hand the gun over, too."

"No, you keep it, if you want. But untie me. Just do that, all right?"

She walked past him, out of his sight. He listened to her footsteps move across the Great Room, rapidly, though once she stopped and seemed to change directions, and then her footsteps returned to the kitchen. She stood behind him. He could hear that her breathing had become even more pronounced; he suspected that she was asthmatic. He also wondered how many pills she'd taken. It seemed she popped pills the way Warren drank, steadily, with little apparent effect. It was not uncommon for people to go on like that, until there was a sudden, dramatic change—they either simply passed out or, in some cases, completely lost it. More than once Del had been called to a house where the other—the one who wasn't as far gone—would simply say, "He was fine, and then all of a sudden this, a total meltdown."

When she walked back into the kitchen, he asked, "Lorraine's still asleep?"

"Knocked out."

"Maybe she won't even wake up. Just carry her out." He waited, but she didn't say anything. "Just undo the knot," he said. "Leave me wrapped up, if you want. I'll wriggle out, but it'll take me a while."

"Like some Houdini?"

"Sure," he said. "It'll give you enough time to get down to the car and on your way."

"But somebody's out there. Isn't there?"

"Something's going on, yes."

"I might not make it to the car."

"Norman and Warren went out behind the lodge. You'll be all right if you just go out the front door and get down to the road. After about twenty yards no one will be able to see you from here." He turned his head and spoke very quietly, with no urgency in his voice. "You go now, and it will be like you were never here. You never saw Norman. I never saw you. You're free of all this."

"It just didn't happen."

"That's right," he said.

"But it *did* happen."

"It doesn't matter now. It's not that important."

"So, what? I go back to North Eicher? Back to nights in that motel?"

He nodded. "I know, I know. Maybe for just a little while. But you'll go. Soon. You'll get out, Noel. It's your father, I know. You'll get away from him."

"You don't know," she said. "You don't know what he's capable of."

"But I know you'll get out on your own. With the baby. That's the best way to do it, on your own. But you have to get out of here first. Noel, this was a mistake, just an all-around bad idea."

Del waited. His arms were sore, and he had a cramp in his left shoulder blade. He wasn't sure how much longer he could hold still.

At first, Warren didn't know where he was, but as things started to come back to him, he remembered being dragged into the shed across the river. This wasn't an ordinary pass-out. He knew he was drunk, but the pain in his head, particularly toward the back of his skull, was greater than the worst hangover. It was dark, and he was lying on the cold wood floor. He was not alone—another body lay motionless right behind him—and somewhere above and behind him he could hear someone breathing. No, maybe there were two of them, and one had a kind of a wheeze to it that was somehow familiar.

A match was struck. The flame illuminated a hand that lit a lantern hanging from the ceiling. The shed was made of weathered boards and fishing gear hung from two-by-four studs. Rolling onto his back, Warren saw that Norman was lying beside him. He knew then that they were in trouble, in a situation that seemed to have been conceived years ago and had been waiting for them since then, waiting in a place like this on a winter's night like this, and though his head was throbbing and he was cold, he knew it would not help to show his fear.

Raising his eyes, he was not surprised to see Pronovost sitting on the bench that ran along the back wall of the shed. Woo-San was next to him, his knees wide apart, his fingers laced over his stomach. Because Warren was looking at them upside down, their mouths seemed odd, the corners turned up, though there was no joy or humor about them.

Woo-San took a pack of cigarettes from his coat pocket and offered one to Pronovost.

"Come on," Warren said. "Give me one."

Woo-San ignored him. He and Pronovost lit their cigarettes, and the shack smelled of tobacco. Warren started to sit up.

Pronovost held a sawed-off baseball bat across his knees and said, "Easy." The bat was old and used to club fish.

Warren shifted on the floor until his back was against one of the two-by-four studs. Blood had run down from Norman's scalp and pooled in his right ear before it continued down his neck. "You kill him?"

"Doubt it," Pronovost said. "I hit you harder. I thought you were that cop because you got his coat on. With the hood up I couldn't tell, so I gave you a good one." He reached inside his overcoat and drew out a flask; it was silver with some kind of leather, and it looked old and expensive. When he unscrewed the cap he took a drink, didn't offer any to Woo-San, then quickly put it away. The smell of whiskey blended with the cigarette smoke.

"Cold in here," Warren said. "A little snort would help."

"This lamp'll take the chill off," Pronovost said. Friendly as could be.

That was the thing about Pronovost: the real estate agent in him allowed him to be agreeable around clients, and it wasn't until later, after he'd showed a house or a piece of property, after the appointment was over, that he'd make it clear how badly he'd wanted to screw them before they got him. It was how he saw all of his clients: like fish. Dangle the bait. Set the hook. Haul them out of the water. Sap them in the head with a sawed-off baseball bat. Then you clean, cook, and eat them. Pronovost wasn't a catch-and-release kind of fisherman.

"So now what?" Warren asked.

"Good question," Pronovost said. "Since it was you in the sheriff's coat, I gather that he's still up there in the lodge with Noel and the baby. I had hoped we'd get him out of the picture first. Instead I got the two of you—so that part was easier than I thought."

"What part?"

Pronovost leaned forward, cleared his throat, and dropped a wad of spit on the floor. "The getting you two bozos part." He studied Warren a moment. "The real question is who's going to walk out of here. No, no—I'll tell you what the real question is, Warren. What did you hope to accomplish by bringing the sheriff out here? Grab your brother and take him back to prison?" He sat back on the bench and drew on his cigarette. "Or did you have loftier goals?"

"The fuckhead belongs back inside," Warren said.

"That's right," Pronovost said. "No sibling loyalty with the Haas brothers, eh?" He turned to Woo-San and said pleasantly, "This all happened before you came to our fair hamlet, but did you know that my daughter was engaged to that one before she married this one? Now that's a brother for you. Guy goes away to prison's bad enough, but this guy has to think about his girl married to his brother." Looking at Warren again, Pronovost said, "What's that fall under, Haas, brotherly *love?*"

"No," Warren said, "it's more a motivational thing. It got my brother to bust out."

"What's this, familial pride?" Pronovost laughed. "Well, at least he succeeded at something. It's more than you can say." Again he turned to Woo-San. "Warren here managed to fuck up his marriage in just a couple of years. Not even as long as his brother managed to stay in prison. I don't know, maybe it should have been the other way around—Warren goes off to jail and Norman marries my daughter. Then we might not be out here on such a cold goddamn night."

Woo-San nodded his head slowly as he crushed out his cigarette on the bench. "So what we do with them now?"

"That, partner, is the question," Pronovost said. He dropped his cigarette on the floor but didn't bother to crush it out. "In some ways it's up to that sheriff up there in the lodge." Looking at Warren, he said, "What's going on up there?"

"You might say he's under control. Norman's already pistol-whipped him."

"That so?" Pronovost said, pleasantly surprised. "Then maybe he'll be reasonable."

As she stood behind him in the chair, Noel thought about their kiss. What surprised her was that he hadn't pulled back, hadn't resisted in some way. She was convinced he'd actually liked it. Sex was so unpredictable. It was like you became another person. Somewhere she had read that in achieving orgasm, you became who you really were. But she thought most men stopped being who they were—they just turned into these writhing bodies driven by the urgent need to get to the end of it. They grunted, they groaned, they thrust, but they didn't seem to achieve anything other than release. Maybe that's all there really was to men. But she had liked being in the tub with Norman because she had witnessed more than his release. He was quiet, his eyes closed, and for a few moments before he came his face seemed to return to what it had been, long before he had been sent away to prison. When his fingers sought her she'd stopped being herself—*this* herself. His fingers touched her as though trying to remember, which was how the sheriff had responded to the kiss, as though he were trying to remember.

"I've made a decision," she said.

"I see."

"I've decided I'm not going anywhere. I'm not going to just run off on Norman." He didn't say anything. "You don't believe me."

"Sure I do, Noel. If you think it's the right decision, the smart thing to do."

"What do you mean, *smart?*"

"Smart. You know, intelligent."

"You don't think I'm very smart, do you?"

"Did I say that?"

"No," she said, "but that's what you meant."

"Not true, Noel. Not true at all. You're taking what I said and turning it around."

"Am I?" She stared at the back of his head a moment. She knew he wanted to be free to turn so that he could see her. "People come into that motel office and they talk to me like I'm ignorant, like I can't even read or write." She laughed. "Then the husband will say something like 'Ain't there no pool at this motel?' Don't talk to me about intelligent."

He said nothing. It seemed like acceptance. She stepped around in front of him and held up his cellular phone, which she had gotten from the coffee table by the fireplace. "I'm staying. But we're going to need help."

"All right, Noel. But first untie me."

"I'm not sure about that—sorry."

"Look, I'm numb from the shoulders down."

"Then that gun won't do you much good," she said.

"Why, Noel? You know who's out there?" She didn't answer. "You do, don't you. And so do I." She nodded. "Yes, we both know who's out there. Your father—he must have followed you. Or maybe he followed me. I don't know. But somehow he figured out that of all the places you and Norman might go, this would be it. I don't know, but it's him out there."

"They're out there, yes."

"They?" Del said. "There's someone with him?"

"Woo-San. Now *he's* really smart—really intelligent, even though his English isn't perfect. And you know why they're out there?"

"No."

"All right, let's just see how intelligent *you* are," she said. "You know what *junbu* means?" He shook his head. "You know what ursodeoxycholic acid is? UDCA for short." He shook his head. "Yeah, see—you're not so bright, are you. And let's not forget, *you're* the one who's tied up in that chair. Well, a lot of Asians believe in *junbu*—that if they eat an animal, they acquire its physical and spiritual qualities. UDCA comes from the bile in a bear's gallbladder. For like a thousand years it's been used to treat all sorts of things. Problems in the liver, gallbladder, stomach. It's used to treat people with severe burns and broken bones. Jaundice, hepatitis, cirrhosis, diabetes, high blood pressure, heart disease. Even toothache and hemorrhoids. Best of all, it's also considered this incredible aphrodisiac."

"Woo-San told you all this?"

"Not directly. I looked stuff up, too. Most nights at the motel you have a lot of time to read books and magazines, to surf the Web."

"Which is the intelligent use of your time." He smiled, and so did she. "So, good, we have UDCA and *junbu.* Tell me more about Woo-San."

"He understands them, sees them in a way we can't."

"Them? The bears?"

"Now you're getting it," she said. "The bears, dead and alive. To him, they're deeply spiritual. And there's the money part of it, too."

"What about the money part?"

"A bear's gallbladder can be worth over a thousand dollars—here in the U.S. or Canada. I think Woo-San deals mostly through Vancouver—that's where a lot of his mail and phone calls come from. That same gallbladder can be worth a lot more over in Asia. It has a greater street value than cocaine. I read that in a magazine. You know one of the ways they get shipped out? Dates. They put them in boxes of fucking *dates* and they blend right in if you don't know what you're looking for. See, they've depleted the bear population over in Asia, so they're coming here now. And the laws—here and in Canada—the laws are nothing. Even if you're caught, they only give you a light sentence and a small fine. It's highly organized, and some of it involves the same people that smuggle drugs. I don't know this for a fact, but I like to think of Woo-San as this drug lord who ran into problems in the city, so he got into this instead. It's like he's in exile out here. But what *really* frightens me about him is this spiritual thing. Bears are sacred, and he feels like he's on some mission, you know, for his culture or whatever."

"We're going to need help," he said. "If you won't untie me, at least make a call so we can get someone to come out here."

"Who?" Noel went over to the window and looked at the phone in her hand. "It's too dark. I can't see the numbers."

"Just hit the button in the lower right-hand corner—redial. It should get you to my deputy."

Noel found the button and pressed it. She placed the phone to her ear and listened to someone pick up the line on the second ring. A woman said, "Yes?"

Noel turned to Del and smiled. "Your deputy's a woman. *Neat.*"

CHAPTER

Nineteen

Liesl heard the girl's voice over the phone, and then in the background she heard Del say, "Shit, that's the wrong number. Give it to me."

The girl said, "Is this the deputy sheriff?" The connection wasn't clear; there was static and electronic humming that came and went, so at first she sounded as though she might be in her teens, but Liesl thought there was something else in her voice. Older. Perhaps frightened. Insincere. Coy.

"Let me talk to the sheriff," Liesl said.

"I would, but he's tied up at the moment."

An image came into Liesl's mind: a drunk middle-aged man with a hooker in a motel room in Sault Ste. Marie. She considered simply hanging up.

"Liesl," Del said loudly, from a distance, "I thought she was calling Monty."

"Who's Monty?" the girl asked, her voice momentarily breaking into shards of static.

"Noel," Del said, sounding almost like a father, "let me speak to her."

There wasn't any response, and the static disappeared. "Noel?" Liesl said.

"All right. I've taken two steps to my right—can you hear me now?"

"Yes. What's going on?"

"You're not the deputy?"

"Let me talk to Del."

"You're not the deputy, are you? What are you, the sheriff's *wife?*"

"No, I'm not his wife."

"Then maybe you're his girlfriend?" She laughed. She didn't sound drunk, only giddy and nervous. "You know what a good kisser he is?"

"No, I don't. Let me talk to this good kisser a moment."

"Del, she doesn't sound too pleased with *you.*" Noel snorted. "What's your name?"

"She *does* want to talk to me," Del said. "Now bring that over to me."

"What's your name?" Noel asked. "Will one of you tell me what—"

"My name is Liesl."

"You know, it sort of rhymes. Noel. And Del. Liesl, Noel, Del."

"Just hang up," Del said loudly, "and get hold of Monty. Tell him we're about thirty miles north of—"

There was silence for a moment, and Liesl said, "What's happening?"

"I've taken the situation into hand," Noel said. "Before we start giving road directions, I want a little clarification."

"I do, too," Liesl said. "What the *fuck* is going on?"

"I told you. Del's tied up. And at the moment I've got this gun pointed at him."

"Are you joking?"

"No, I'm not joking. It's his gun and you hold it a while, it weighs a *ton.* Now what I want to know is what *your* relationship is to the *sheriff.* Husband and wife? You his girlfriend? Or maybe you're the woman on the *side?*"

"None of those."

"Oh *sure.* I hit *re*dial and *you* answer the phone. You *have* to be one of those."

"This business with the gun—and being tied up—is this really true?"

"Yeah. But I didn't tie him up. And you know *I* didn't hit him in the head."

"I don't believe you would, but you might put the gun down."

"If you're not his wife or his girlfriend, who are you? What do you care what happens to him? I mean, do you even *like* this guy?"

There was a loud burst of static and Liesl said, "Don't *move*—I'm *losing* you."

The static faded away. "What did you *say?*"

"I said I like him."

"This is *great,*" Noel whispered. "Have you told him? Does he know?" She held the phone away from her mouth. "So, Sheriff, how do you feel about Liesl?" There was no reply, and after a moment Noel said, "He's not saying. Strong silent type. It's *so* hard for these guys to, you know, *open up.*"

"Is this why you called?" Liesl asked. "To provide some sort of long-distance matchmaking service?"

"That's not a bad idea! I could get one of those nine hundred numbers and advertise it on late-night TV. Probably make a bundle. Call it something like Matchmakers Anonymous. 'Hi, my name's Michelle and I'm lonely.' What do you think?"

"I think you were trying to call the deputy because you've got a problem." Noel didn't answer, but the connection was better now and Liesl could hear her breathing. She realized that this giddy banter was an attempt to conceal fear. "Tell me about it, Noel. What's going on out there?"

There was a long silence. So long that Liesl was afraid they'd been cut off. She was about to speak when Noel said, "Daddy found us." Now her voice was very faint, small.

"He did?"

"He and Woo-San have Norman and Warren outside somewhere."

"Norman," Liesl said. "He has Norman?"

"Do you know Norman?"

"We've met."

"Really?" Noel asked. "Should I be jealous?"

"No, he was a perfect gentleman."

After a moment, Noel said, "I know, he really can be."

"What do you mean, your father has them outside—outside of where?"

"Here, the lodge." The girl was sounding very distant and frightened now.

"I want to come out and help. Noel, do you hear me? I'm coming out."

"Okay. Alone? Or are you bringing help?"

"Just tell me where you are."

"Hurry," Noel said. "She wants directions." She seemed to be asking Del.

"We're north of North Eicher," Del said. "Take Laughing Pike Road about thirty miles, almost to Lake Superior. There's an old logging camp, and from the road you'll see an old sawmill off in the hills. You'll know you're getting close. The lodge is on a ridge above the right side of the road."

"You coming?" Noel asked.

"Yes," Liesl said to her. "I'm coming."

She heard a click and a dial tone.

Leisl called Monty. It was four-thirty and he was sound asleep. "I've heard from Del," she said. "We have to go after him. There's trouble."

"Okay, where is he?"

"Listen, I want to go."

"Just tell me where he is."

"No, Monty. You pick me up. I'll tell you when you get here." She hung up.

Norman lay on his side, his eyes closed, unsure if he could move. He knew he had been hit in the head, and he was aware of two kinds of cold—the cold that came up off the wood floor and the damp cold that covered the right side of his head. His right ear was clogged and he guessed that it was blood, which had begun to congeal. Still, he could hear well enough, but the voices tended to drift in and out.

At one point he thought that maybe he was still in prison, that the voices were other trustees. It reminded him a little of trying to sleep. It was like being in a barracks; there were dozens of trustees, and it was seldom absolutely quiet. Even in the middle of the night somebody was always snoring or talking or jerking off or whatever. There was always noise, so he'd learned to block it out.

But he wasn't inside, and after a while he accepted the fact that he knew two of the voices. Warren and Pronovost. The third voice he didn't recognize. The man seldom spoke, and it was always just a word or two. He had an accent Norman couldn't place.

"Your brother couldn't just sit in prison and do his time?" Pronovost's voice had that ease, that good humor, that Norman never completely trusted.

"Look, his showing up isn't exactly helping me, either," Warren said.

"He come back for Noel and the girl?" the third man asked. Norman had it now: he was Asian.

"Right," Warren said. "For my daughter."

"And my granddaughter." Pronovost paused, and there was the sound of something being unscrewed, followed by the slosh of liquid and the sharp smell of whiskey. "He and Noel must have planned this," he said. "I had no idea, did you? She hid it so well."

"I don't know if they planned it," Warren said. "It doesn't fucking matter. What matters is that Norman came back and she went with him. She *wanted* to go with him."

"So he must know—"

"I don't think he does," Warren said.

"She must have told him."

Warren didn't answer immediately. When he spoke he was very deliberate. "She doesn't really know what's been going on out there at the sawmill."

"Maybe," Pronovost said, though he didn't sound convinced. "She's my daughter, and believe me she can conceal things well."

"She's my wife—still," Warren said, "and *I* can tell when she's hiding something."

There was the creaking of wood. Someone shifted, and then the Asian voice said, "Why you come out here?"

"Woo-San," Warren said, "maybe we came out just to fuck up your shit, eh?"

Norman opened his eyes and stared up at his brother, who sat with his back against the wall. Warren stared at him a moment but looked away as though he hadn't noticed anything. Norman remembered when they were little they'd play a game they called You're Dead. Warren was pretending Norman was still knocked out for a reason, and it worried Norman. He thought he knew Pronovost's limits, but this Woo-San was another story.

"I read this whole thing from the beginning," Warren said to Pronovost. He was using his confidence bullshit. Norman knew that it really meant his brother was uncertain or even afraid of something. "Right from the start I saw how this was going to go," Warren said. "And Pronovost, you didn't want to hear it. Remember that. I said this thing you and Woo-San have going wouldn't work."

"This is true," Pronovost said pleasantly. "You deserve credit for that." Norman could hear Pronovost get up from the bench, and suddenly he was kicked in the lower back. "Norman, you can stop pretending now," he said. He kicked him again even harder.

Norman held his right side and tried to catch his breath.

Pronovost leaned over Warren and slapped his face with his gloves. "On your *feet.*"

"*Shit!*" Startled, Warren got up off the floor. "Where we going?"

"Talk with this pistol-whipped sheriff you got up there," Pronovost said. "Maybe this can be a simple business transaction."

Warren felt his cheek. "Guys like Maki don't get bought."

"That so?" Pronovost shoved him toward the door. "Everybody gets bought." He laughed. "But I'll grant you that this sheriff's made of different stuff than you."

Woo-San nodded toward Norman. "What about him?"

Pronovost stood in front of Norman as he pulled on his gloves. Norman sat up and leaned his back carefully against a two-by-four stud. "What *about* him? He would have been better off staying in prison." Turning to Woo-San, Pronovost smiled. "Just watch him for now. And if he tries anything, he's raw meat. You know, sushi."

Warren pushed the door open, letting cold wind and snow inside. After Pronovost followed him out into the dark, the door was slammed shut.

Woo-San whispered something in his own language as he opened his coat, revealing a long leather sheaf on his belt. The knife handle was made of bone. Woo-San's face shone in the dim light. Snowflakes hissed as they melted against the lamp.

Del watched Noel put his cellular phone and gun on the kitchen table, and then she walked around his chair and stood behind him. He felt her hands tug at the knot. "Tell me something," he said. "At the trial, you testified."

"Right. I testified that Norman had beaten me up here at the lodge—right here in the kitchen. It messed up my hearing, you know. I told the truth, and at the time I was so angry I wanted them to send him away. He denied knowing anything about Raymond Yates's disappearance, and he didn't say *anything* about finding me with Warren."

"It's called being a stand-up guy."

"Well, that's Norman for you. I didn't realize that he still loved me—after all *that*—until I started getting his letters from prison. I'm having trouble with this knot."

She stepped back away from him as the kitchen door swung opened. Cold air blew into the kitchen. The first one in was Warren, followed by Pronovost, who kicked the door shut. He smiled at his daughter.

"Well, are you tying him up, Noel, or are you setting him free?"

She studied her gnawed thumbnail. "Where's Norman?" She turned and punched Warren hard in the chest. "Where *is* he?"

Warren grabbed her wrists and she struggled to pull them free.

"Knock it *off,* both of you," Pronovost said.

"There's enough fuckin' rope here," Warren said. "I could tie 'em both up."

"Daddy!"

From the bedroom, they could hear Lorraine begin to cry.

"See?" Pronovost said. "You two woke the child up. Go see to her, Noel."

Warren let go of her wrists and she shoved him away from her. She looked at Del for a moment and then left the kitchen, crossed the Great Room, and went into the bedroom where Lorraine had been asleep.

"All right," Pronovost said to Warren. "Go help her."

"What?"

"Go take care of Lorraine. I want to talk to the sheriff."

Warren followed Noel into the bedroom, where the child was sobbing.

"Christ, I'm hungry," Pronovost said. "It's the cold. Need something to burn." He opened the cabinet over the sink. There were boxes of crackers, cereal, and instant pudding. He took down a glass jar. Sitting across the table from Del, he laid his gun—a 9 mm—on the table next to Del's .38 so he could use both hands to tip cashews from the jar into his palm. "Showing up in North Eicher was one thing, Sheriff, but you should have let it go at that. Bad idea, coming up here. That's a nasty bruise on your head, and now you got yourself all tied up."

"Where's Norman Haas?" Del asked.

Pronovost chewed a moment. "Outside."

"With Woo-San?"

Pronovost set the jar of cashews on the table. "Worst thing that ever happened to my daughter is hooking up with either of the Haas brothers."

"This is all about bears, right?"

Pronovost sorted through the cashews, selected a few, and shook them in his fist as though they were dice. "What do you know about bears, Sheriff?" He tossed the cashews into his mouth.

"All I know is that once in a while we hear about some bear that's been taken illegally and the carcass is left to rot in the woods. We go out and find them cut open. I understand the gallbladder's worth a lot of money."

"If you know who'll pay."

"And Woo-San does."

Pronovost worked his tongue back into one of his molars, and he seemed intent only on trying to dislodge a piece of cashew.

"The thing was," Del said, "the bear carcasses are also missing their paws and teeth."

"Funny, you don't strike me as a save the whales, tree-hugging kind of shithead."

"You see a lot of dressed-out wildlife up here, but there's something about a toothless bear with its paws chopped off."

"Woo-San tells me that in Siberia the word for 'honest truth' is *koju-bat,* which means 'bear truth.' " Pronovost ate another fistful of cashews. "Before testifying in court, they give someone a bear paw and make them bite it. And they say something like 'If I perjure myself, the bear will bite me.' It's like our swearing on the Bible. Asians see the bear as a sacred animal. I don't think we can really appreciate it—it's a very deep, cultural thing they have about the bear. Woo-San calls him 'Grandfather,' and he believes his spirit never dies."

"And the paws go into soup?"

"Have to boil them for about three days to make them tender."

"You've sold some bear parts in the past."

"So. What's your point?"

"There's no evidence," Del said.

"No, there's no evidence."

"Then what's the problem?"

"You tell me," Pronovost said.

"If you let me go, you think I'll come back here with help and we'll comb through all these woods till we find something. But we won't find anything that could be used to make a case." Pronovost's gaze was steady. He seemed to be enjoying this. "Besides," Del said, "that's the DNR's business."

"The Department of Natural fucking Resources has no business on my land. This is MNR—*my* natural resources."

"And I'm a sheriff in a small town who doesn't have the time for such exercises."

"This is a family matter. Just between the Pronovosts and the Haas brothers."

"I just want Norman Haas," Del said. "He's all I came for."

"Well, maybe we can all walk away from this and everybody'll be happy," Pronovost said. The child was crying in the bedroom, but Pronovost didn't seem to notice. Leaning over the cashews on the table, he seemed to be counting them. He regarded them as though they were something of great value, infinitely rare, and he would not look up from them. "Maybe we can do business after all."

Behind Pronovost, Del became aware of the change in the light outside the window. He thought it was sunrise—the way first light can seep under an overcast winter sky and illuminate the woods, the falling snow. It usually lasts only a few minutes before the gray closes the seam in the horizon. But it was too early; daylight was perhaps another hour away. The light illuminating the snow flickered unevenly.

Pronovost raised his head, picked up his gun from the table, and went to the window. *"Fuck,"* he whispered.

From his seat Del could see that several trees beyond the river were on fire.

"It's the goddamned shed." Pronovost turned to Del. What casual pleasure he had experienced while eating the cashews at the table was gone now. *"Warren!"* he shouted. "Get in here." He went to the door to the Great Room. Del could hear Warren's boots as he came out of the bedroom. "You stay here and watch him," Pronovost said.

"What is that out there?" Warren said. "A fire?"

Pronovost went to the kitchen door. "I said you stay here."

Liesl was standing at the bottom of her driveway when Monty pulled up in his Jeep. She climbed in and said, "We're going north of North Eicher."

"Christ." He had a broad sleep line running down his right cheek.

"I know." She unscrewed the cap on the thermos bottle she'd filled with coffee. She poured Monty a cup and handed it to him.

"Thanks." He appeared more alert just for having the smell and the steam rise off the coffee. "Another blizzard, a big one, is coming in by daybreak."

"Then let's get going."

He took a sip of coffee, handed the cup back to her, and put the Jeep in gear.

The kid wouldn't stop screaming. Warren tucked the .38 in the outside pocket of Del's coat and went back into the bedroom. Noel kept pacing back and forth, bouncing her, patting her back, cooing and humming patiently. Then she began singing softly "Somewhere Over the Rainbow."

"Great," Warren said, "it's Judy Garland. Can't you *shut her the fuck up?*"

Noel walked past him, the kid on her shoulder sobbing, gasping for air.

"Come on, *do* something."

"I *am* doing something, Warren."

"Yeah, you ran away with her."

"I didn't *run away,*" she said, her voice stony and righteous. "I left. There's a difference, Warren. I chose to leave."

"Yeah? I'll tell you something, Noel. You're going to come back—with me. I don't know what's going to happen with my brother—that's up to your father and this sheriff, I guess—but no matter what, you come back with me. *You* and *her.*"

The child's crying had begun to subside, and without turning toward him, Noel said, "If we go anywhere, it won't be with you."

"Listen," he said, quieter, calmer, "I want us to try to work this out, okay? I want to move back in and—"

Noel turned around. "Forget it." The kid was suddenly silent.

"I just want us to try, that's all."

"There's nothing to try. *That's* all, Warren. Nothing."

He walked over to her. She had that look on her face. "We try," he said, "or this is going to work against you." He had her attention now. "My brother, an escaped prisoner, and you, running off with the kid? You want to keep her, then you do it with me. That's the deal. You got that? She's *our* kid."

Noel suddenly seemed distracted, which was not unusual. Poor hearing and the frequent use of drugs tended to diminish her focus, but she seemed to have made some decision. All she did was turn away, go to the bed, and put Lorraine down. He could hear the child's shallow breathing, her sinuses clogged with snot. It was as if the kid leaked; there was always something running out of her mouth, her nose, her little asshole. Noel tucked the blankets around her, whispering and humming. Then she came around the bed and walked past him toward the door. Pausing just before going out, she turned to him. He could barely see her silhouette against the glow cast by the embers in the fireplace. "Whatever happens, Warren, you'll never get her. Face it, you don't *want* her. You never have."

"*Wrong*, Noel. I know what's mine. This time, we're going to do it *my* way. It'll work, you'll see. And if you don't, I'm telling you I'll get her away from you. Then we'll see how you manage."

"You can't *get* something that's never been *yours!* She's *not* yours." Noel walked quickly out into the Great Room.

He stood for a moment in the dark bedroom and then followed her. She was on her knees, putting logs on the fire. "What do you mean, 'not mine'?"

She arranged the logs with a poker. "Figure it out, Warren."

"Figure it out? Figure *what* out?" He came around the couch. "*Norman.* That what you're telling me? *Norman?*"

She ignored him as she got to her feet. He grabbed her by the upper arm. As she raised the poker in her other hand, he punched her in the mouth. Staggering backward, she fell over the coffee table and her head struck the floor hard. One leg was propped up on the coffee table, and she didn't move.

Warren stared at that leg for a moment and then whispered, "All right. All right, Norman." He walked across the Great Room, took the snowshoes off the wall, and then went to the kitchen.

"You kill her?" Del asked.

"Shut up."

"You're going after your brother."

Warren tucked the snowshoes under his arm. "It's a family thing, Sheriff. It's not just business. It's definitely personal." He took the .38

from the coat and placed the muzzle against Del's left temple. "You understand?"

"Yes."

"Good." Warren waited a moment. "And it's okay if I borrow your gun?"

"Sure."

"And I can wear your coat again?"

Del hesitated. "I suppose."

"You *suppose?* Thanks, Sheriff. That's very generous of you." Warren raised his arm and said, "Suppose *this,*" and brought the butt of the gun down on the side of the sheriff's head.

He went to the kitchen door. Over the years the log walls in the kitchen had been carved and written on—there were names and dates, occasional crude drawings of women, of penises, of killing wild animals with rifles or bow and arrow. There were testaments of love, and there were simply initials. Many were filled with grime and must have been carved decades ago. As he reached for the knob he noticed the words carved deep into the timber above the door: "Abandon all hope, you who enter here."

PART Four

CHAPTER Twenty

Norman leaned against a tree trunk, shaking uncontrollably. He hugged himself, trying to stop the tremors. Through the woods he could see the shed burning, its column of smoke rising above the trees and then dispersing on the gusting winds.

His back slid down the trunk until he sat in the snow. Carefully he touched the right side of his face. The cheek was slit open, the diagonal cut running from below the ear, almost to the corner of his mouth. Taking his hand away, he saw that it was covered with blood. He leaned over and vomited between his knees. It wasn't so much the blood or the pain, but the thought of the blade, the swift parting of his flesh, that made him ill. Before going to prison, he'd cleaned animals, gutted fish. He'd never had a fear of knives until he'd seen too many inmate fights, too many ugly scars—and then the day last summer in the exercise yard: Bing, suddenly kneeling in the dirt, cradling his bloody intestines against his blue uniform. No one was near him; no one approached. No one appeared surprised that it had happened, either. He'd been slit across the belly, and his intestines seemed to have a life of their own, determined to ooze out of his grasp. It was as though they were no longer a part of him, but something determined only to escape confinement. His shaved head gleamed in the sun, and he didn't make a sound—no screaming, no crying out. He seemed baffled by his situation as he used both hands, trying frantically to gather everything together. He was dead before the ambulance arrived in the yard.

Norman knew he was lucky. He realized that he had underestimated Woo-San.

"Why are you here?" he had asked.

At first Woo-San wouldn't answer. He sat on the bench in the shed and stared straight ahead, as though he were alone—as though he were meditating or praying. As though Norman didn't exist.

"You came and stayed in North Eicher. Why?"

Woo-San folded his arms. Questions seemed an insult. The knife with the bone handle was still in its leather sheath, just below his right hand.

"I bet you ran away," Norman said. "You can't go back to wherever you're from."

Woo-San didn't seem to hear him. There was no apparent expression on his face.

"Somebody ran you out."

But then Woo-San's head turned toward Norman and he spoke rapidly, his deep voice bursting from his chest. "Why *you* come? For that *whore?*"

"This is where I'm from. This *is* my home."

"Here! Why you come out *here?*"

"*Here* is why I had to go away in the first place."

"Why you not take whore and *go*—run away? Hide."

"Because they'd find me, and they'd just send me back. I'm not going back. And she's *not* a whore." Woo-San faced straight ahead again. He seemed to be trying to will Norman into silence. "I went out there to the sawmill in the logging camp," Norman said. "I saw the cage—it's your idea. You brought it in, didn't you? What is it, you don't kill the bears right away now? You put them in the big cage—and *what?*" Woo-San's lips were trembling. "What good are they to you alive in a cage? *Look at me!* You have any idea what's it's *like* to be *locked up? Why do you lock up the bears?"*

Woo-San turned his head toward Norman again and shouted, *"You not understand Grandfather. His bile medicine. Give strength. Save lives."*

"Take the bile? From a bear in a cage?" Norman couldn't see this; he could only think of a black bear behind the bars, wild at first until it exhausted itself. He'd seen this in new inmates at the prison. They'd be pissed off at everything when they first arrived, often until they hurt themselves—getting into a fight with other inmates or beaten by the guards—then they'd become quiet because their energy had been used up. They would just sit, some of them, just sit and wait. Then it didn't matter where they were or what happened to them. "How?" Norman asked.

"Belt," Woo-San said. "Bear wear belt with shunt go into gall-bladder."

Norman was sitting on the wood floor of the shed, his arms propped on his knees. He rubbed his face, and he felt the cold dried blood in his ear. "You must have to tranquilize them," he said quietly. "Over and over, from the same bears, a little at a time. You tap them like a maple tree." He knew Woo-San was looking at him now. "You don't kill them till they're sapped dry and they're just so much meat lying in a cage."

"Grandfather never die," Woo-San said, his voice hardly a whisper.

"You don't even pay them the dignity of death."

It was then that Woo-San put his hand around the bone handle and withdrew the knife, and he appeared to enter into a state of prayer. "Grandfather never die." He sat perfectly still, and a low deep hum rose up out of his chest in preparation for something—a ritual, an offering.

It was hard for Norman to look at the knife. He got to his feet quickly when Woo-San stood up. The man was silent now. As he came forward, quickly, even gracefully, Norman felt somehow paralyzed, as though he needed to wait and make sure this was really happening. It was only a moment, but he remembered it clearly. Beneath the dim light from the kerosene lamp, Woo-San's expression had solidified into a kind of devotion that somehow prohibited Norman from reacting. There was no doubt then. No pleading or begging, no crying out. There was no asking for reason. Woo-San had committed himself to the act, and he was obliged to be swift.

Woo-San first tried to stab him in the abdomen, but the blade only cut the bulky material of his coat. Then, swiftly, the knife came up toward his face—for his neck. Norman turned his head away, and the blade sliced his cheek instead. It was only the force of the pain as the knife blade was drawn across his skin that ended Norman's paralysis. He fell backward. Woo-San, too, appeared to have been brought suddenly out of a trance. He appeared confused and perturbed that Norman had resisted him at all. Where there had been patience in his eyes and the set of his mouth, there was now anger, even disgust. It seemed that he was again actually seeing Norman.

As Woo-San lunged a second time, Norman buckled, bending forward, and his forehead struck Woo-San on the bridge of his nose. Straightening up, he watched Woo-San stagger backward and knock the lantern to the floor, where it burst into blue flames, which spread across the wood upon the widening pool of spilled kerosene. Norman pushed open the door behind him, and the rush of air into the shed fanned the flames. Woo-San stamped his boots on the burning floorboards as the flames ran up his pant legs.

Norman slammed the door shut with his shoulder just as Woo-San threw himself against the other side, shouting. Heat was coming through the wood. Woo-San continued to scream and pound on the door, and then, quite suddenly, he stopped and there was only the sound of burning wood.

Again, Norman vomited into the snow. He kept telling himself to stand up, but he remained with his back against the tree trunk. With his eyes closed he listened to the crackling fire, and he thought he might pass out. When a large burning branch exploded and fell to the ground, he opened his eyes. At first he wasn't sure: there seemed to be something dark moving along the far bank of the river, a gray form angling down through the whiteness, almost as though it were flying. When it reached the footbridge he knew it was Pronovost.

Norman scooped up a handful of snow and held it against his wound. The pain made him light-headed. He struggled to his feet, clutching snow to his face, and moved deeper into the woods.

Warren strapped on the snowshoes and followed the trail down the ridge. Across the river he could see Pronovost standing before the remains of the shed. There was no sign of Woo-San. No sign of Norman. Pronovost moved on into the darkness of the trees. Warren continued to the bottom of the ridge, walked alongside the river, and crossed the footbridge. The fire had given way to smoldering charred rubble. He saw the arm; somehow he was certain it was not Norman's.

Following the tracks into the woods, he came to a tree where there was darkness in the snow; leaning down, he could see that it was blood, and he could smell something else—something so vile that it caused his mouth to secrete painfully. He continued on, periodically finding more blood in the snow. He knew they were following his brother. Whatever happened at the shed, he was sure that Norman had been injured.

The wind diminished as Warren went deeper into the woods, though overhead branches creaked and clattered. The snowshoes were an advantage. Ahead of him, they would be moving slowly—Norman because he was injured, Pronovost because he was a cautious hunter. It was like tracking a wounded animal, which was always a mixed blessing. On one hand, there was the adrenaline rush from shooting your quarry. But there was also the hard admission: It had not been a clean shot. Things could get messy. It could take hours before you bagged your kill. Or you could lose him because of terrain or because of nightfall. Warren had never lost a wounded animal. With time they only became weaker.

Liesl knew what Monty was doing when he turned onto County Road 187. Taking this route could cut their time in half—rather than driving west to North Eicher and then turning north, they could head directly northwest and pick up Laughing Pike Road as it approached Lake Superior.

"Hypotenuse of the triangle," she said.

"It's all I remember from high school geometry."

"Provided the road isn't snowed in."

"If you're going to believe in anything up here, it better be your four-wheel drive."

"Otherwise, move to Florida, where it never snows."

"And there's a patrol car on every block." He'd had three mugs of coffee, and he gripped the steering wheel as though it might try to get away. He picked up the microphone to his Roadmaster unit and punched in a series of numbers. After listening to a recorded message, he hung up. "Leo Warra's a friend of mine. He's with the DNR over in Drummond Corner, but if this shortcut gets us through, we'd beat him by a good hour at least. But he'd be a good backup. He's probably stuck somewhere in a snowdrift himself." Monty hung up the mike and shrugged. "We're the closest thing to 'authority' there is out here. Every morning I get up and look in the mirror and I go, 'I *am* the authorities.' "

They were doing about forty, and the Jeep's traction was holding on the straightaways; Monty downshifted going into the corners and often managed a controlled drift in the snow.

Liesl tried to call Del's cellular phone again, letting it ring about a dozen times. When she turned off her phone, she said, "Is it my imagination or is the snow coming down harder now?"

"One thing I am an authority on is snow. Don't need the Weather Channel for that. It's not your imagination—this is approaching white-out conditions." Monty picked up the mike and punched redial but soon hung up. "Warra's probably drunk and stuck in a snowdrift."

Norman reached the logging camp at first light. The bleeding from his cheek had been slowed by constantly pressing compacted snow against the wound. He entered the sawmill and, starting at the cage, walked the length of the building, moving slowly under and around fallen timbers. Near the far end, the earth rose gently. Snow sifted down from overhead, but it was the earthen ground he was interested in—he was standing on a slight mound about twelve feet in diameter. Tools had been left behind, and he took the pick in his hands. He raised the pick above his head and then brought it down on the hard earth. Chunks of dirt sprayed his face. In prison he'd done a lot of roadwork; if there was one thing he'd mastered inside, it was breaking hard ground. He fell into the rhythm of it, using his whole body to swing the pick down on the frozen earth.

Noel's leg dropped off the coffee table, and the knock of her boot on the floor caused her to open her eyes. Directly above her was the armrest of the couch. Her mouth ached and, placing her hand on her lips, she felt a sharp stinging pain in her gums. She pulled her hand away and saw that her fingertips were bloody. Tenderly she inserted one finger in her mouth. Both front teeth had been pushed back and it was too painful to straighten them out.

She got up off the floor and went into the bathroom. One candle was still burning on the sink, and she gasped when she looked in the mirror. Her bloody upper lip had collapsed inward, making her face seem remarkably old. Just drawing air in through her mouth hurt. Her handbag sat on the edge of the sink; she searched through it for the plastic vial. There were two pills left. She took both of them. The vial was empty. Maybe it was about time. Maybe it was too late. She sat on the rim of the bathtub for a while, her eyes closed. Though she held perfectly still, she felt as though she were spinning slowly.

Finally she managed to get up, place both hands on the sink, and look in the mirror again. The blood on her face had dried. The pain in her mouth wasn't gone, but it was tolerable—that was the word her mother often used. If a thing was *tolerable,* that was all you could ask for—it was part of her Dutch heritage, where frugality, decent behavior, and cleanliness were expected. When she was a girl her parents used to drive down to the small town of Holland in the Lower Peninsula for the annual spring tulip festival. Her mother and grandparents always participated in one event that fascinated her: Hundreds of townspeople, dressed in traditional Dutch costumes, washed the main street, using straw mops and wooden buckets filled with soap and water. She liked the clip-clop of their wooden shoes, which sounded like horses' hooves; she remembered her mother explaining that cleanliness was next to godliness. Looking in the mirror, she saw that her face was not clean.

She picked the bucket up off the floor; it still contained melted ice water for the bath. After soaking a washcloth, she leaned toward the mirror and began to daub at the dried blood caked around her mouth. It was careful, tender work, in its own way more difficult than washing a paved street by hand. Slowly her lips were revealed, and she saw again the damage Warren had done. Her upper lip was deflated, and it sagged in a way that placed a greater burden on her jaw. She recognized this aging, defeated, wounded face.

"Mommy?"

Noel turned from the mirror. Lorraine stood in the doorway, a blanket pulled around her shoulders. "You're awake."

"Mommy!" Lorraine screamed. "Your *face!"*

"Yes, it's all right."

"What happened?" The child was crying, but she came closer, timid but curious.

"Nothing." Then she said, "It was inevitable."

"What's that?"

Noel picked her up. The child couldn't take her eyes off Noel's mouth. "This, Lorraine. *This* is inevitable," she said. "But we're going to get out of here—just the two of us."

"We're going *bye-bye?*"

"As soon as we get your snowsuit on."

Noel took Lorraine back into the bedroom, dressed her, and put her in the baby sling; then she put on her overcoat and started for the front door. There was a creak of an old wood joint; startled, Noel turned and saw Del, still tied to the chair in the kitchen. She went to him—fresh blood ran down out of his hair.

"Who did this?"

"Of the two Haas brothers," he said slowly, "I would say Norman has the more natural swing. Still, Warren's no slouch." She got a towel from the sink and daubed at his wounded scalp. "You've changed your mind?" he asked. "You're going?"

"Yes."

"Good. One request?"

"The rope, sure." She began to untie the knot. "I'm sorry I didn't get it undone quicker before. None of this would have happened."

"I think we'd have to go back further than that if we wanted to avoid a lot of this."

She began unraveling the rope around his chest. When he was free he flexed his hands as he stood up. He was unsteady, and he had to put one hand on the back of the chair.

"I've had it," she said. "I've got to get *out* of here. They've all just disappeared in the blizzard. I can't deal with it anymore. I only care about Lorraine. Come with me." For the first time he seemed to notice her mouth, and she put her fingers over her lips. "I look like my mother now. I'm starting to catch up to you."

Del reached into the coin pocket of his jeans and removed a single key. "Here's the spare to my Land Cruiser down there. Take it—you'll have the best chance of making it out of here."

"You're not going to stay? Just come with me."

"It's a tempting idea." He turned his head toward the window and rubbed the back of his neck. "But Warren has my coat."

"Your *coat?* You must really *love* that coat," she said. "I know—*wait.*"

Noel went into the Great Room, to the closet by the front door. She got the old coat down off the hanger and brought it into the kitchen. "It's bearskin," she said, "and it smells, it's so old. But look, the buttons are made of carved wood. This belonged to Yates—actually I think it was his father's, and they say he was the last real mountain man to live in the Hurons. Daddy won it in a card game." She held up the coat so that Del could get his arms in. As he turned and faced her, she said, "It's a good fit." She put her arms up over his shoulders and pulled the hood over his head. "It's a real good fit." She left her arms around his neck and buried her face in the thick, dark fur. "I don't feel like you're a stranger at all. I feel like I've always known you. Why is that?"

He put his arms around her and held her for a moment. "Maybe it's the coat."

She looked up at him and smiled, though it hurt her mouth. He kissed her forehead and let her go. As she turned away, Lorraine said, *"Bye-bye!"* Noel went to the front door and opened it to the wind and snow. She looked back quickly, and Del raised one arm. Lorraine said, *"Bye-bye, Papa Bear!"*

CHAPTER Twenty-one

Once Norman got below the permafrost, the pick sank into loose earth and he then used the shovel. The pain in his cheek was constant. When Bing had told him about Vlad the Impaler, he'd said that physical pain was the greatest power in the world because people will do anything to avoid it. Think of it, thousands of people on skewers—taking days to die, every moment complete agony. Pain was a tool, a weapon. If you could inflict pain, you could get what you want. And if you could master pain, Bing believed, you'd never suffer defeat—you would be inviolate. That was his word: *inviolate.* He'd do that often, come up with a word that nobody inside ever used—and that too was a kind of power. It pissed off other inmates, but they usually left him alone. After Bing had been cut open in the exercise yard, another inmate everyone called Pickleman said: "The man had a big mouth."

What Norman knew now is that no one is inviolate. And maybe this was why the bear is sacred. Something about the bear that's inviolate. The bear lives many lives, sleeping the long winter between each, to be reborn in the spring. Look at a bear and it's like looking at what we might have become: our bodies, protected with dense fur, our eyes, curious yet suspicious. Bears have very human eyes. Norman had seen his first bear when he was eleven. He was walking in the woods when he heard the sound of wood cracking and splintering off to his left. Pushing through the brush, he saw a bear ripping apart the trunk of a downed, rotted birch tree so he could get at the ant colony inside. Looking up, the bear seemed unconcerned, and at first Norman thought he hadn't been seen crouching in the bushes. Its eyes were light brown, and Norman's first thought was that there was a person hiding inside the bear. He knew that didn't make sense, that this was a wild animal. The bear, which was not any taller than a man, lowered his big head and continued to search for ants. Norman didn't move, but he wasn't frightened, which seemed odd. He realized he was in the presence of something powerful but not necessarily harmful. Everything he was seeing was remarkably clear. The bear was pure strength; its paws had impressive dexterity. Though there were long curled claws, the bear gripped the wood much like a person. It dug into the trunk for several minutes before stopping again. This time it looked at Norman with some kind of recognition. But the bear seemed unconcerned. A white curl of bark hung from its mouth, making it look slightly daft. Suddenly, turning on all four thick legs, the bear walked off in the opposite direction, and for a moment the fur on its large rump, which was slick with mud, glistened just before the animal disappeared into the shade.

The rest of that summer Norman spent a lot of time alone in the woods looking for black bears, and he soon realized how rare it was to actually see one. He had no luck and instead decided to build a cave in the side of a hill. For days he'd been digging the hole, using his hands and sticks, making it big enough for him to crawl inside and sit upright; and he'd built a door with branches and leaves to lay over the opening so that the cave was hidden. He went there every day, bringing water, cookies, peanut-butter sandwiches. Once he was in his cave, he could pull the door over the opening and sit staring out through the leaves. Even on the hottest afternoons it was cool inside the cave, and the air smelled of earth. The walls were full of tree roots, which seemed like motionless snakes, but he knew that they made the cave strong. There were often flies buzzing around his head, but he learned to ignore them. Staring out at the woods, Norman knew that no one could find him. He was almost invisible; it was a strange feeling and he liked it, though he wasn't sure why. At times he thought that this was what it was like to be a bear. When he would leave the cave and return home, his brother would always ask where he'd been—and Warren would study him carefully, knowing that something had happened to Norman. Something that couldn't be shared. Something that Warren couldn't take from him. The cave seemed to make Norman inviolate.

Norman slipped away from his brother and the other kids in the neighborhood as often as possible, and only when he was sure he wasn't being followed would he go to his cave. Sometimes he knew Warren was following him and he'd lead him through the woods—the worst parts, like the marsh below White Heron Lake or across the old train trestle. He'd lead Warren in a big circle, one that would make sure he was muddy and bug bitten. By the time Warren reached their neighborhood on the west edge of town, Norman would be sitting on the brick steps of Swede's Corner Store, sipping a Coke. His brother always showed up exhausted and angry.

And once, when Warren was following him through the woods, Norman decided to play dead. Usually in the house or the yard, often in the snow during the winter, they'd wrestle and fight until one of them would suddenly be killed. And if you were killed, you had to stay still and dead long enough for your brother to start to have doubts. Norman was walking along a ridge when he slipped; he let himself fall down the slope, rolling over and over through the brush. When he stopped he hit his head against a rock and for a while he was dizzy, but it passed. He was covered with dirt and twigs, and he was lying motionless on his side. He could hear his brother at the top of the ridge, and he remained still for a long time. Finally, his brother came down the slope, digging his heels in and sending pebbles and dirt ahead of him, until he stood above Norman. "All right," Warren said, "you can get up now. I know you're faking it." Norman didn't move. After a moment, he was prodded in the armpit with Warren's foot. He kept his eyes closed, and as Warren continued to poke him, he kept his mind on one thing: the view through the twigs and leaves from inside his cave. And finally Warren stopped and said, "You didn't go and hit your head, did you?" Norman didn't move. "All right, come on, that's enough." Then, as Warren knelt down and leaned close, Norman opened his eyes wide, and for just one moment he saw real shock, genuine fear in Warren's face. Norman screamed, "Got ya!"

When his shovel struck something hard, Norman leaned over and carefully scraped dirt away with the inverted tip of the shovel, exposing green-and-brown camouflage fabric and pale bone. He whispered, "Got ya."

Noel wasn't used to the steering in the Land Cruiser, but the four-wheel drive made it feel as though the big tires were gripping down through the new snow. When she realized that she'd taken a sharp curve too fast, she turned the wheel so hard that the rear end swung free and she was gliding sideways down the narrow road. It was a complete whiteout now, and the high banks on each side disappeared into the snow only a few yards ahead of her. There was the sensation of being totally adrift, of lacking any purchase—visible or physical—in the world. She wanted to slow down—the Land Cruiser, her body, her thoughts—and she felt an oath forming in her mind that if she could just escape this whiteness, she would vow to change everything. Nothing would be the same again. It had all been wrong up until now, but here in this whiteout she saw what needed to be done to make it right. Cutting the wheel the other way, she felt some control return, and she tapped the brake pedal. The rear tires caught and dragged so that she was beginning to straighten out when a Jeep emerged from the whiteness. She took a deep breath and, dropping one hand off the steering wheel, threw her arm across Lorraine's chest.

Del slung the crossbow over his shoulder and walked down the ridge and across the footbridge. He had seen plenty of fires in subzero weather. Buildings, houses, barns. Old wood burned hot and fast, especially when fanned by high winds. Often firemen would give up on the structure and devote their efforts to containment. Nearby houses and buildings would be hosed down, encased in protective ice. The fire had created its own black hole in the woods. The snow around the smoldering shed was black; the column of smoke was black; the timbers were all black. And finally the shed's two-by-four framing collapsed, revealing its black pearl: a small charred figure, curled in on itself, with one crooked arm raised in the air, beckoning.

Tracks led from the fire to the woods—and occasionally he found long, glistening strands of blood that hadn't quite been covered by new snow. If it were Norman's body in the fire, they would have returned to the lodge. Norman must be injured, and Pronovost, who had the 9 mm, was following him on foot. Warren was behind both of them on snowshoes, and he had Del's .38 Smith & Wesson.

Del had two quarrels in his quiver.

It wasn't like before with Harold and Gretchen. There was no anticipation, no watching a green truck climb the hill toward the narrow bridge.

In a whiteout you don't see it coming.

Liesl didn't know how long she'd been on her side in the passenger seat of the Jeep. She was afraid to try to move. When they'd hit the truck there was the sound of buckling metal, breaking glass. She'd felt the shock in her bones, her spine, but now, semiconscious, she wondered if she might be paralyzed. There was hardly any feeling. She only knew she was lying against her door and something was dripping on her forehead and running down off her nose. The snow sounded like hard pellets striking the chassis of the Jeep. Turning her head, she saw Monty above her, hanging in his seat belt. She was reminded of an image her father used to mention whenever he talked about the Normandy invasion in World War II: dead paratroopers suspended from trees by their parachute harnesses. The skin above Monty's left eye had been torn away, revealing bone, and it was his blood that was dripping onto her scalp and running down her forehead. But he was breathing.

She picked up the Roadmaster microphone—it still worked—and she pushed redial. A man answered on the second ring.

"Leo Warra?"

"Ya? Who's this?"

"My name's Tiomenen, and I'm with Monty Price—we've just had an accident."

"You hurt?"

"I'm not sure. Monty's out, but he's breathing. He hit his head."

"Where are you?"

"County Road 187, heading toward Laughing Pike Road. We're in his Jeep, and it's tipped on its side."

"I'll be out, if I can get through," Leo said. "But it's going to be a while."

"All right," she said. He hung up.

Liesl moved her left arm, found her buckle, and released her seat belt. She reached up and gripped Monty's shoulder. He opened his eyes a moment, and she could tell he was dazed. She decided to leave him strapped in, fearing that moving him might cause further injury. "*Monty.* Listen to me. I'm going out there to see who we hit. Monty, you *hear* me?"

"Yes."

"I'll be back. Leo Warra's coming out."

The windshield was a constellation of cracks, and it had popped its seal on her side. With her elbow she pushed at the glass. It made a loud crackling sound and she leaned back, expecting the whole thing to fall in on her. But it didn't, and with a few more nudges she realized that the windshield was oddly flexible; slowly, she curled it back enough for her to crawl out alongside the hood of the Jeep, the metal still warm. The wreckage blocked the wind and she was tempted to stay put, but when her legs were free of the vehicle, she lay on her back and caught her breath. The pain in her right ribs kept her from inhaling deeply. Getting to her feet, she discovered that her right shoulder seemed locked and she wondered if something was dislocated or broken. She looked at the other vehicle, which was angled up onto the snowbank, and realized it was Del's Land Cruiser. The driver's door was collapsed as though a large bite had been taken out of the cab, and metal had punctured the left front tire. She walked around the Jeep and climbed up so she could see in the driver's window. A young woman lay across the seats. Short blond hair covered her eyes.

"Noel?"

She seemed to be trying to see through that hair, see something under the dashboard. Then there was the slightest movement to her battered lips. "Yes?" she whispered.

Liesl noticed that a tiny hand was clutching Noel's coat collar. The fingers squeezed the fabric, and for the first time Liesl understood that there was a child trapped beneath Noel.

She made her way to the front of the Land Cruiser and climbed up to the top of the snowbank, then worked her way over to the passenger door. Opening the door, she almost fell in on top of them. She knelt down, took off her gloves, and brushed the hair back off Noel's face. Her green eyes were open, staring with determination. Something about her mouth wasn't right.

"Can you hear me? *Noel?*"

"Take her," she whispered.

"We'll get you both out of here." Liesl knew she didn't sound very convincing.

"No. Just take her." Blood trickled out of the lower corner of her mouth. "Before she starts to get cold. Please just keep my baby warm."

Liesl pulled off one glove and placed her hand on Noel's forehead. She gently smoothed her hair so that it swung off to the side. Something in Noel's eyes told her that right now it was important to just have someone touch her.

"There's one thing," Noel said.

"What one thing?"

"That I didn't tell Norman."

"What's that?"

"It's what he came out here for. It was my idea, and I'm sorry. I am sorry."

"What idea? Noel?"

"Please just take her. Please."

"All right," Liesl said. "I'll take her and go for help. How far is it to the lodge?" Noel didn't seem to hear her. "Del—is he still tied up there?"

Noel whispered something that Liesl couldn't hear over the wind. She leaned closer. "He's gone—after them."

"Where? Gone where?"

"Out there."

"Where?"

Noel appeared to be considering the questions when some tension in her face let go. It seemed such a simple transition. Liesl removed a glove and put her hand on Noel's throat. Nothing.

Beneath Noel, the girl moved. Her hair was fine and a lighter shade than her mother's; and it was longer, with soft curls falling out of a red wool cap. Her face was hidden beneath Noel's coat. Liesl reached in with her left arm, took hold of Noel's shoulder, and pushed her toward the dashboard, causing the girl to cry out weakly.

"It's all right, sweetheart," Liesl whispered. "I'm going to get you out of here."

She took the girl by the shoulders and tried to pull her out from beneath her mother's body. The girl was crying now, and Liesl kept cooing and whispering to her as she worked the girl free of the weight on her. The effort was hard on Liesl's back, and though she could use her right arm, she knew there was something wrong with the shoulder. The girl's legs were caught, so Liesl repositioned herself, leaned farther into the vehicle, and gave Noel's body another shove, causing her legs to fall heavily on the floor.

"Mommy!"

Liesl pulled the girl out of the Land Cruiser. "It's all right, sweetheart."

She made her way back to the Jeep and knelt in front of the windshield. Monty had released his seat belt and fallen down into the passenger seat. His eyes were open, and he seemed more alert than before. He was holding the sleeve of his coat against his bleeding forehead.

"We hit Del's Land Cruiser," she said. "But this girl Noel was driving, and she's gone. I've got her little girl here. Can you get out?"

His eyes scanned the interior of the Jeep a moment. "Can't move," he said finally. "You go on and get her out of here. Can you drive the Cruiser?"

"No."

"Go. Take her and I'll wait for Leo." He tried to smile. "I'm fine, really."

She reached for the microphone. "He'll be a while. Call him every few minutes."

"Why? To keep me awake?"

"To give you something to do. Don't want you to get bored."

"What do I say to him? Tell jokes? They're wasted on Leo. He never had much of a sense of humor." Again Monty attempted a smile. "But you know, he loves talking about the weather. Watches the Weather Channel all the time, like me. We'll be all right."

"I know." Putting the microphone in his hand, she asked, "What do you need?"

He closed his eyes. "Last woman who asked me that ended up my wife. And she's home with a couple of girls with the flu and regretting it right now." Opening his eyes, he said, "You go on. I'll be fine. Get the kid out of this. And find Del."

She squeezed Monty's hand around the microphone.

Norman found the bear carcasses, large boned, skulls with broad snouts. Entangled in them, Raymond Yates's camouflage pants and vest were caked with dirt. What gray hair was left had grown to his shoulders. The eye sockets were clean black cavities, and without gums his teeth seemed abnormally long. A neat bullet hole in the forehead suggested a third eye, the knowledge, insight, and spiritual wisdom of the true hunter.

He cleared away the bones. What meat was left on them was frozen rock solid. After lifting Yates's body by the arms, he stepped out of the hole and began to drag it through the fallen timbers. Yates's boot heels carved grooves in the packed earth. When he reached the cage, he put Yates down carefully. He removed the padlock and the gate swung open on squealing, rusted hinges. He dragged Yates inside and sat him up against the bars at the back of the cage.

"You know, I've thought about you a lot, Yates," he said. "It's what you do inside, you know—think about things. You had something a lot of people don't have—you really believed in something. You believed in this place—this land. You believed in hunting and how it connected everything. You believed in yourself, that you could live out here by yourself. No need for anyone else. Except maybe a few good dogs. But then you let yourself become dependent. You know it. You relied on

Pronovost, because all this belongs to him now, and only he would let you stay on it, hunt on it. So you became like one of your dogs: loyal, obedient, hungry. He said fetch, you fetched. And when it was necessary, he just put you down." Norman went over to the gate door and turned back to Yates. "I'm not sure who did the deed. Who put that hole in your forehead? Pronovost? Or did he farm the job out? Maybe Woo-San? Or was it my brother? You know, don't you? You probably didn't even know why—it was just so they might put me away a long time. But look at you, right between the eyes. You saw it coming. What do you think in that moment, when you see it coming?"

Norman went outside the cage, shut the gate, and closed the padlock. As he walked away, it swung against the iron bars, sending a soft chime through the air.

Once Warren got below the frozen falls, he knew they were all heading to the sawmill. From the tracks in the snow he knew Norman had taken the long way on the logging road that circumvented the broad, low hill above the falls and that Pronovost was following him. Warren started up the hill, which would cut his distance in half. The climb was difficult, but the effort helped him build body heat against the cold wind, and he knew he could get to the sawmill well before Pronovost.

It was on the north side of this hill that Raymond Yates had found a bear den. "They like to den on the north side so the winter sun don't melt the snow and flood them," he had said when he came into the lodge. It was still morning, and he was already drinking from a flask.

"This one won't have to worry about snowmelt," Pronovost said. "Let's go get it."

Something was different about all this. Warren said, "It's November. They're hibernating now."

No one bothered to answer him.

They drove out the logging road at the base of the hill and climbed up to an outcropping of granite. Yates's dogs were frantic. Woo-San had a strange-looking pistol and, leaning into an opening between the rocks, he fired one round. It shut the dogs up, though they still milled around, their tails wagging. Woo-San then got down on all fours and crawled into the rock crevice.

"This is nuts," Warren said. "He's crawling into a bear den."

"I'd send you," Pronovost said, "but he fits in tight places better."

"He's had more experience, too," Yates said as he raised his flask to his mouth.

There came another shot, small and muffled.

Woo-San turned on a flashlight down in the hole, which was lined with twigs, leaves, and grass. Leaning down until his face was only inches from the granite, Warren saw the bear. Its eyes were open, but it seemed dazed and the forelegs were crossed over its chest. There was no blood, and he was breathing gently. Pronovost began feeding rope down into the crevice.

"What you shoot him with?" Warren asked, and again no one answered.

Yates removed the flask from his hunting vest and, after taking a long pull, offered it to Warren. "Looks like you could use a little tranquilizer yourself," he said.

Warren ignored him and stared into the den at Woo-San. "That what you did, tranquilize it?"

"You tell us how to hunt?" Woo-San said from down in the hole. He was trussing up the bear's shoulders with the rope.

Warren turned to Yates as he took another pull on his flask. "Hunting? You don't believe this is hunting. I know you don't."

"My father was the last real hunter out here," Yates said, his voice melancholy drunk. "No one *owned* the land then. If you could hang some meat and survive off of it, that was all you needed. It wasn't a matter of possession."

"I own it now," Pronovost said. "You want to stay on it, help us pull him out."

"No way," Warren said. One of the dogs was nuzzling at his crotch, and he pushed it aside with his hand. When the floppy-eared hound sniffed his jeans again, Warren kicked him away.

"Hey now!" Yates said. "You don't be kicking *my* dog!"

The dogs kept swarming around Warren, snouts cold and wet against his hands, tails thumping his legs. Woo-San climbed out of the hole and squeezed through the granite crevice.

"Come on now and cut the bullshit," Pronovost said. "Help us get him out."

"Yeah. Right." Warren started down the hill, and one of the dogs yelped.

"Not my dogs!" Yates shouted, following him.

"Fuck you. Fuck all of you," Warren said. Yates took hold of his sleeve, and Warren turned and pushed him so hard that he fell down.

Yates got to his knees, swearing. He took his rifle off his shoulder, pointed it at Warren, and said, "Where you think you're *going?* I take enough shit from those rich assholes that fly in here."

"You're not pointing that at *me?*" Warren said.

"Somebody kicks *my* dogs, they're looking to get *shot!*"

Pronovost came down the hill and grabbed the rifle by the stock and yanked it out of Yates's hands. He turned to Warren while Yates got up off his knees. Warren walked down the hill without once looking back. It was a long walk, and all he could think about was the bullet that would blow out the front of his skull. He walked deliberately, without haste, and when he reached the overgrown logging road he knew he'd make it.

Now, pausing at the top of the hill, winded, sweat running freely beneath his clothes, Warren could see the logging camp below through the skein of branches. He scanned the valley and saw no sign of Pronovost, who must still be around the western side of the hill. Only one set of footprints—Norman's—crossed the snow to the sawmill, where the carcasses were buried. It was the last thing Warren had done in Pronovost's employ last fall. The trees had shed their leaves after several days of freezing rain blowing in off Lake Superior. The bears had to be killed before the first big snow came, before the ground froze. At dawn Pronovost, Woo-San, and he went out to the logging camp in two trucks. The bears were quiet until Pronovost shot the first one. Then the rest of them moved around in the cage, pawing frantically at the bars, until each was dropped with a head shot at close range. The reports echoed through the building, and it was over in a minute.

Dressing out the bears took hours. They removed what was valuable—gallbladders, paws, the leaner cuts of meat, hides—and loaded them into Pronovost's truck. He told them to clean up and then drove back up to the lodge. Warren and Woo-San spent the late afternoon burying the carcasses. It was hard business, and Woo-San never let up. The damp air smelled of blood and raw flesh. Warren's back ached from digging. After a while he threw down his shovel and went to the door and lit a cigarette.

"You no work hard," Woo-San said.

"I no work period," Warren said. "I'm fed up with this."

"You keep dig."

"I no dig no more."

Woo-San continued to fill in the hole. As he tamped down the last of the dirt, he said something in his own language—a prayer for the bears or perhaps a testament to his deep sense of purpose and industry. With Woo-San it was hard to tell.

Staying up in the woods, Warren circled the logging camp until he was around to the far side of the sawmill, where his tracks wouldn't be detected. Walking out from the trees, he took the sheriff's .38 from the pocket of his coat.

CHAPTER

Twenty-two

Liesl walked slowly, hunched over so her left shoulder bore most of the girl's weight in the baby sling. "What's your name, sweetheart?"

"Lorraine." Her voice was tiny, fragile, hurt. A lovely girl's voice.

"Do you know how far it is back to the lodge?"

The girl didn't answer, and Liesl decided not to repeat the question. The child was about three years old; time and distance were different to her. "I'll bet it can't be far," Liesl said, trying to sound reassuring and certain.

The child's arms clutched her neck tightly.

Liesl walked on, but after about a hundred yards she sat down in the snowbank and took off the sling. The exposed portion of her face hurt, particularly the forehead and bridge of her nose. The ache seemed to penetrate the skin and sink right into the bone. She lay back on the snowbank and held the girl tight to her chest, trying to protect her from the wind.

"Here, come inside."

She moved as quickly as possible: she put the child down, removed her coat, hung the sling with the child in it around her neck, and then put the coat on, zipping it up to her throat. The girl placed her head between Liesl's breasts and tucked her hands under her armpits. Liesl folded her arms over the child and rubbed her back and shoulders. She was reminded of when she was pregnant. She was always thankful that she had carried Gretchen through the winter months, when the child would help keep her warm.

After passing a waterfall, Del found that the tracks went separate ways. The footprints continued down an old logging road, while the snowshoe trail went up through the wooded hill. Pronovost must have thought he could catch up to Norman. Warren was farther behind, but he had the advantage of wearing snowshoes and he figured by cutting over the hill, he'd get to his brother first. Del began to follow the snowshoe tracks up the hill. The bearskin coat was long and heavy and remarkably warm; its smell reminded him of his dogs after they'd been out in the rain.

There was a sound behind Norman—turning, he saw his brother emerge from the shadows and walk slowly around to the front of the cage.

"How'd you know Yates was here?" Warren held the sheriff's .38 at his right side.

"Only made sense," Norman said. "The man disappears just before my trial begins. Of course they suspected that I did something to keep him from testifying. And when he didn't turn up after the snow melted in the spring, I knew he'd be buried where no one would look." He took a step toward his brother. "The idea to make it look like I killed Yates—I know it was Pronovost's."

Warren smiled. "Which one?"

"What?"

"Which Pronovost—Noel or her father?"

"Noel?"

Warren nodded. "She was that mad at first—when she realized that her hearing wouldn't come back. *She* came up with it. My guess is she never thought her father would see it as something that could actually be *done.* You know that bitch has a lot of ideas, but she doesn't always execute."

"So her father did it."

"When you come right down to it, Daddy does most everything for Noel. He did the deed, and it worked. But it was her idea originally."

Norman understood that it was the thing she had been holding back. He knew there was some regret she was carrying. "So, you didn't kill him," he said, "but you went along with it."

"I dug the hole—*that* was my contribution. Seemed every fall these past few years Pronovost has me digging the same damned hole out here. Lot of unhappy bears put to rest. I just got tired of it."

"But you kept your mouth shut—something you rarely do, Warren. You kept quiet just so I'd go away for a long time. Then you'd do all right with Noel, and that meant that eventually there'd be all this land out here. For you. Didn't work out, though."

"I admit it didn't work out the way I thought," Warren said. "And now I've got a simpler plan. Much simpler—I'm just going to take what's mine."

Norman looked at the gun. "The true hunter. At last."

"Noel told me about Lorraine. You really believe she's yours?"

"That's more important than land, isn't it. Blood. You know she's mine."

"I'll tell you one thing," Warren said. "She may be *yours,* but she's going to *believe* she's mine. In the long run, *that's* what counts—not whether it's *true,* but what she grows up to *believe* is true."

"You really think so?"

"I do," Warren said. "I really do, and you fucking know it. You might say it's my creed. We all gotta have a creed, right? What you believe *is* the truth."

"You were never satisfied with just your own," Norman said. "You always had to have mine, too. Ever wonder why that is? Why you can't get enough?"

"I think you sat in prison and thought about things too much."

"I had a lot of time on my hands."

"I got better things to do," Warren said.

"No, you've never had better things to do. That's just it, Warren. You have no purpose. You never have. Since we were kids, if Mom told you what to do you didn't want to do it. If there was nobody to tell you what to do, you'd just sit there, all pissed off. When we got older, you just killed time the best way you could."

"You used to get real fucked up—and for free, thanks to your big brother."

"It's the only favor you've ever done me, and it wasn't any favor. I always knew I wanted out of it. That's the difference—I saw there was something better, and I wanted to get it. You just wanted what I had because you couldn't stand to see me have something. And Noel was the best thing I ever found."

"Maybe you just shot too high," Warren said.

"No, you brought both of us down." Norman took a step toward his brother. "I'll tell you one thing—it won't work with Lorraine. She won't believe you're her father for long. She'll figure it out eventually."

"You believe *that?*"

"I do. I really do, Warren. You know, Noel told me she's already seen something of me in Lorraine, in her attitude, the way she thinks. She gets older, it'll come out more and more."

"I don't think so," Warren said.

"Yeah, you do."

Warren raised the gun and aimed it at Norman, but then he hesitated.

"What?" Norman asked. "You're always so certain. Maybe you just can't shoot." Norman took another step and stopped, not five strides away from his brother. "You could make a clean heart shot at this range, but I don't think you got it in you, Warren. Right?"

Something in Warren's eyes was breaking down, giving way. Suddenly a sheen of tears glossed his eyes, and he seemed almost to be pleading. But then his mouth tightened. "Shit, Norman," he whispered as he raised his arm to sight down the barrel. "We're both so far out in the cold, there's no getting back now."

"Warren!" Pronovost shouted from the dark. "Look at me, Warren."

Reluctantly, as though he didn't want to lose his concentration, Warren turned his head to his right.

Pronovost said, "Allow me the pleasure."

"Fuck you."

A gunshot echoed through the sawmill and Warren's body was yanked backward, his arms lifting into the air as he fell on his left shoulder. Blood issued from a hole in his forehead and ran down through his eyebrows.

Norman's face had been sprayed with blood and bone fragments. The gun lay on the ground near his feet. He picked it up and lunged toward the shadows as another shot was fired.

"You all right, sweetheart?"

"Yes," Lorraine said from inside the front of her coat.

"Good." Liesl got to her feet and began walking, her back bent owing to the weight of the child, her head lowered so that she watched her boots move through the snow. Occasionally she looked up to get her bearings. She was walking uphill, and the wind was coming from the north. She could see hills now, but there was no sign of the lodge on a ridge. "Know any good songs, Lorraine?"

After a moment, the child said, " 'Crazy.' "

"Patsy Cline? Can you sing it?" The girl was silent. "Maybe we could sing it together—I think I remember the words. Okay?"

The small voice inside her coat sang, " '*Cra-zy,*' " and Liesl joined in as she walked. They got through the first verse and got stuck on the second, so they went back to the first. They sang it three times.

Liesl stopped walking. She turned her back to the wind, and among the hills below her she saw a faint dark plane—a roof. It had to be the sawmill Noel had mentioned, perhaps half a mile across a field and through the woods. She looked up the road again and couldn't see the lodge; it could be miles still, and she needed to get out of this weather. She climbed over the snowbank and started across the field toward the woods. Lorraine kept singing.

As he reached the crest of the hill, Del heard two quick shots. He was certain they had come from inside the building down below. At this distance he couldn't be sure if it was from his .38 or Pronovost's 9 mm.

He hadn't handled a crossbow since he was in high school; his grandfather only bow-hunted, and his collection included one crossbow, which Del was allowed to use only on the target out behind the barn. The crossbow wasn't for hunting, his grandfather said; it was a weapon for warfare dating back to the Romans. His was a replica of a design made in Massa Marittima, Italy, in the fifteenth century. It had ornate scrollwork carved into the wood stock and was very heavy. The camouflaged crossbow Del had brought from the lodge was made of light, strong composite materials. He lowered the bow and put his foot in the stirrup and drew back the string, flexing the bow, until it locked in the trigger mechanism. He set one of the two quarrels in the channel groove and removed his foot from the stirrup. The crossbow's stock fit nicely into his shoulder, and the weapon felt taut and balanced in his hands.

The snowshoe tracks that he'd been following veered off to the right, and he followed them through the woods around to the back of the building. Gaps in the roof admitted only thin shafts of light. Chains hung from fallen beams, clinking softly in the wind. There was an odor, pleasant and unexpected in such cold—the smell of freshly turned earth—and he came to a hole filled with pale sticks. In the dim light it took a moment to realize he was looking at a heap of rib cages, thick femurs, scalloped hips, and angled joints bent in a mockery of repose. Some of the skulls faced up, while others seemed to be looking into the ground, dejected. All had been shot once in the forehead. Executed.

"You seem destined to be one with the bears," Pronovost said. "Something about that coat, all that long brown fur." His voice echoed among the timbers, and it was difficult to tell what direction it came from—and, worse, there was almost a joyous tone to it, as though he were playing God. "It appears that someone has disturbed their hibernation," he said. "Or maybe I should say it's been extended."

Del stepped into the shadows behind a long wooden chute. He crouched down and looked along the floor, but he could not see any movement.

"Sheriff, you have to realize that bear farming is legal in places like China. Their government's argument is that it's for the benefit of the species. Helps control illegal activity, poaching. If they had started farming earlier in Asia, they wouldn't have to look for bears over here now. We're what you might call ahead of the curve."

"How much were they worth?" Del asked.

"My cut, something over a hundred grand." Pronovost's voice seemed to come from farther up the length of the building, and Del moved slowly in that direction. "Not bad for a new business venture, wouldn't you say?"

"I wouldn't know," Del said. "Never been much for business."

"Now that I know the contacts, Woo-San isn't really necessary, anyway. From now on I deal direct. It's called eliminating the middleman. Certainly you can understand the business logic in that?"

"I think I'm catching on." Del continued to work his way up the length of the building.

"See what you came all this way for, Sheriff? Nothing but a pile of old bones. That's not evidence. Up at the lodge I had hoped you'd be the sort that can be bought off. But it's different, now that you've come down here. Your problem, Sheriff, is you have scruples, and they don't cost anything. I have responsibilities. Took me years to acquire this land. It's my responsibility to protect it. See, *I'm* the real preservationist. To keep this land as it is—as it should be—you need to understand the principles that it represents. You need to utilize those principles."

"What principles are they?"

"The primary principle—everything dies," Pronovost said. "Everything dies and everything comes back. There's no reduction and nothing really disappears. It all just takes on different forms. Woo-San was right: Grandfather never really dies. His people understand that, just as our Indians do. If they want to pay dearly for pieces of bear, fine. Their spirit's still here, and they will return. But—and this is what's important, Sheriff—they'll only come back if there's land for them, only if I preserve the land. That's my responsibility." He had the voice of a true believer.

Del noticed something at the far end of the building. It was difficult to see through the fallen timbers and collapsed roofing, but after a moment he realized he was looking at a large cage. Pronovost had mentioned the logic of this enterprise, but the sight of the bars went beyond logic. Only a human could confine a wild animal in such a place. The iron bars created a hard geometry in the cold, empty space.

There were two bodies, and the one lying outside was Warren. At first Del couldn't tell who was sitting up inside, but then, realizing he wasn't a fresh kill, he said, "Yates."

"Looks more like the missing link now." Pronovost's voice echoed through the sawmill.

"Looks like evidence," Del said.

There was nothing but the sound of the wind, until Pronovost said, "Sheriff, we are all evidence. Of life. Of death. Of life again."

Norman remained perfectly still. He was squatting behind a large wooden bin. Pronovost was somewhere to his left, and he heard the sheriff to the right, on the far side toward the back wall.

There was the sound of boots scraping the hard-packed dirt floor. Norman stood up and, seeing the sheriff, raised his gun. But at the same time, the sheriff stepped out from behind a timber and aimed the crossbow at Pronovost, who Norman saw out of the corner of his eye—he was about ten yards away, and he had his arm and gun extended toward Norman.

No one moved. Seconds passed and nothing happened. Norman's eyes moved from the sheriff to Pronovost and back to the sheriff. Pronovost was an exceptional marksman. If Norman fired at the sheriff, he would probably not live to see him hit. Besides, the sheriff wasn't important—it was Pronovost he wanted.

"Well, what now?" Pronovost asked calmly. "Somebody want to count to three?"

"Norman," the sheriff said. "Put it down. I have all the evidence I need on Pronovost. Let me take him in and things should go well for you."

"Sure," Pronovost said. "Count on it, Norman. But consider this—I won't be taken in. So I'll take you with me no matter what—you and your brother. At the very least neither of you will ever see Noel and Lorraine again. I consider it my duty."

"Then why don't you just shoot?" Norman said. "What are you waiting for?"

"True," Pronovost said. "I guess I'm a little curious."

When Liesl entered the building, it was a relief to get out of the wind. But immediately she saw a large cage, and two bodies, which gave her a start. The one lying outside the cage looked like Norman, but she knew it wasn't—it must be his brother. And inside the cage—it was horrific, but she couldn't resist looking at the jawbone, the large, grinning teeth.

She walked toward the cage, and then she sensed something—not a sound, not a movement, really—that made her realize she wasn't alone. And turning to her left, she saw them in the shadows: three men forming a strange tableau, each motionless, as if frozen in the act of taking aim. Norman to her left, Del to her right, and straight ahead a man with a white mustache.

"Who's this?" he said. "This some *snow angel?*"

She looked at Del, who was aiming a crossbow at the man who spoke. He wore a long fur coat, and he looked as though he were from another era, some ancient time when hunting was a daily occupation, one of necessity and survival.

Turning to her left, she said, "Hello, Norman."

"You made it," he said.

"I made it."

"I'm sorry, Liesl. Believe it or not, I am. I just kept going—I'm sorry, I really am."

"I know," she said. "That's what Noel said, 'I'm sorry.'"

Though his gun was still pointed at Del, Norman's eyes quickly slid toward her. The other man—she assumed it was Noel's father, Pronovost—also glanced at her. But they didn't lower their weapons.

"You saw Noel?" Norman asked.

"Yes."

"Why'd she say she was sorry?"

"It must have been important. It was the last thing she said." Liesl hesitated. "The last thing before she died."

Now both Norman and Pronovost began to turn toward her, their faces curious and confused, but still they maintained their aim.

"Noel?" her father asked. "Noel's dead?"

"We had an accident up on the road." She turned to Del. "Monty's hurt bad, I think."

There was a moment when all three men seemed to have abandoned or forgotten their intent. They stared at her eagerly, even helplessly, despite their weapons—as though she were some inexplicable vision and they were confronted with the reality of it.

Inside her coat Lorraine began to wake up and squirm. All three men watched Liesl in disbelief—she was being transformed in front of their eyes. The child moaned as she moved her arms and legs. "It's *dark!"* she said, her voice small and muffled. *"Let me out!"* Liesl unzipped her coat so that Lorraine's head and shoulders were visible.

Something happened to Norman's face as he lowered his gun and began walking toward her. She recognized the look on his face—protective, concerned, yet helpless—Harold often looked that way when Gretchen was small.

As he approached her, Pronovost took aim at Norman's back.

Del said firmly, *"Pronovost!"*

But Pronovost ignored him and sited down the barrel of his gun. Del fired the crossbow, and a powerful hissing split the air as red and yellow flickered through the shadows. The force of impact startled Liesl. Suddenly a misplaced boutonniere protruded from Pronovost's chest, just below his left collarbone, and his gun fired.

Norman staggered and fell on the ground at Liesl's feet. Lorraine's scream echoed off the timbers overhead.

The crossbow's release had sent a jolt into Del's right shoulder. Pronovost remained standing, and he still held the gun, though it was lowered to his side now. Quickly Del set his foot in the stirrup, drew back the string, and loaded his last quarrel in the channel groove.

Pronovost stared down at the feathers on his coat, confused, and then he began walking stiffly toward Liesl and the child, who continued to scream. Del moved quickly, stepping in front of Pronovost. He spoke his name, but the man didn't respond—he seemed to be operating according to a different mechanism now, one that was both mindless yet determined. In his hunting days Del had seen this in wounded animals, which seem intent only upon taking one more step.

However, Pronovost's right arm began to come up, aiming the gun. He wasn't ten yards away when he fired, the bullet ringing off one of the cage bars. Del shouldered the crossbow and pulled the trigger. The quarrel passed clean through Pronovost's chest, and the gun at his side was discharged into the ground. He turned sideways and raised his head to the snow that was falling through a gap in the roof. Pale light fell across his face and his eyes were inquisitive, as though he'd never seen any of this before. The gun fired again, kicking up dirt next to his boots. Still, he just stood there, gazing up at the snow. He might have been praying.

Del dropped the crossbow and walked up to him. Pronovost didn't acknowledge him. Blood ran from his mouth. Del reached down to take the gun from his hand. The fingers were stiff, and he had to use both hands to release the weapon. He stepped back and took aim.

Pronovost walked slowly toward the cage. The first quarrel protruded from his back at an angle. His knees buckled and he fell forward against the gate, his head sliding down between two bars until his jaw struck one of the crosspieces. He remained suspended there by his chin, half standing, half kneeling—a kind of genuflection—as blood pumped out of his chest and pooled in the dirt in front of Yates's grinning corpse.

Del turned around and saw that Liesl was kneeling over Norman. She held Lorraine in the crook of her arm; the child was now crying, her face buried in Liesl's shoulder. Norman's left elbow had been struck by Pronovost's bullet, and Liesl was wrapping his belt around his biceps as a tourniquet.

"*Norman,*" she said. "You have to get up, Norman. We have to walk out of here."

"I can't," he whispered. "I can't go any farther."

"Dammit, get *up,* Norman," she said. "Think about how some people have it worse—*remember?*" Norman's face was tight with pain, but he stared up at her now. "That's right," she said. "Remember what your friend said—what was his name? Bing? Think about Vlad the Impaler."

After a moment Norman moved his good arm and began the effort of getting up off the ground. Del helped him to his feet. Once he was standing, he stared at Warren's body. "My brother was always taking other people's stuff," he said. "He took your coat and now there's blood all over it. Want it back?"

"No," Del said. "I don't need it now. We'll come back for him—for all of them—after this storm passes. We have to get out of here."

Liesl came over, and Norman raised his good arm and touched Lorraine's face. She was trying to stop crying. "It's all right now," he whispered. "We'll get you somewhere warm."

Del took the girl from Liesl and slung her up onto his back.

"How far is it to the lodge?" Liesl asked.

"It's not far if we go over that hill," Del said. "Warren crossed it in snowshoes and I followed, so there's a good path now. We should be able to make it."

"He's right," Norman said. "It's shorter than walking way around the hill."

"You're sure?" She looked at Norman, giving him the briefest smile. "Just one hill?"

"Yep," Norman said. "Just one hill."

They left the sawmill and leaned into the wind coming out of the north. Walking single file, Liesl led Norman up the wooded hillside, while Del followed. He was tired, but his legs kept moving. The child buried her face in the thick fur of his coat collar, and he could tell as her arms and legs went slack that she had finally given in to her own exhaustion.

When they reached the crest of the hill, Del stopped and looked back down toward the sawmill, but it was barely visible through the snow, as though it were only an illusion. He had never known such complete fatigue, and he was hungry. But there was also a cleansing sense of relief and the feeling that he was leaving things behind, not just his coat, but things that had not really been his for a long time. He couldn't name them right now. The naming of things could wait. He began walking again, and ahead he watched Liesl and Norman descend through a stand of birch, disappearing into the white.

EPILOGUE

During the course of three warm days in late April, the snow retreated from Liesl's yard, exposing soggy brown grass. Still, it snowed intermittently through the first half of May, and out in the woods patches of snow remained on the northern slopes until Memorial Day. In her constant search for firewood, she and Lorraine often encountered dead carcasses. Usually it was a deer, but they also came upon raccoons, porcupines, and one coyote. Lorraine was fascinated by these discoveries, and though Liesl cautioned her against touching them, she was allowed to inspect the remains at close range. The young robins they found nesting in the woodpile behind the shed seemed an antidote to the winterkill.

The child was unimpressed by the brief flurry of media attention that had hovered around her when Liesl first brought her home. The phone calls from reporters became a nuisance, and for several weeks Liesl seldom answered her phone. The judge who reviewed Norman's case had determined that he would be returned to prison in Marquette, but he received a reduced sentence and would be eligible for parole in nine months. Norman's elbow healed slowly, and he would never regain full articulation of his left arm. He had agreed to let his daughter stay with Liesl until he was released, and they made regular visits to him in Marquette Prison.

Early one morning a young woman came up the drive in a white sedan with a rental sticker on the bumper. Lorraine was at the kitchen table, eating oatmeal. Liesl went out through the shed, and something about her demeanor must have told the young woman that she had better keep her distance. Other reporters said they mostly wanted photographs of a smiling child, but this feature writer from the *Chicago Tribune* started asking questions. Liesl's first impulse was to get Harold's carbine and present her with one feasible option; but Francine d'Orr was the first reporter to offer evidence that she had done any substantial research. She knew that Liesl had lost her husband and daughter in a blizzard five years earlier, and she wanted to know how it felt to have a child in the house again. Liesl suddenly found herself inviting Francine d'Orr inside for breakfast. They talked at the kitchen table for over two hours. The feature article in the Sunday edition of the *Tribune* was done well enough that reporters no longer bothered Liesl. She clipped the piece out of the paper, believing that Lorraine would one day want to read about it because she would only vaguely recall her stay with the woman in the woods.

Del came by regularly in the evenings. When he couldn't he would call. Monty's recovery was slow, and it meant that Del had more work than he could handle, and without Monty in the station he didn't find the work very interesting. The town council dragged its feet over the issue of hiring a temporary replacement, and then it became what Del called a bad case of small-town politics. First, complications arose over insurance coverage of Monty's medical bills, and then the council balked at paying for repairs to Del's Land Cruiser. The gist of their argument was that both Monty's injuries and the damage to Del's vehicle had taken place outside their jurisdiction; therefore, they had not occurred while either officer was on duty. The council also thought it was time to invest in a real police cruiser, an idea championed by the councilman who owned a car dealership outside Negaunee.

The evening of June 21, the summer solstice, the repainted Land Cruiser rumbled up the hill. Forest green with a white roof and four new oversize tires, it looked splendid. Liesl and Lorraine had been weeding in the garden alongside the drive. She helped Lorraine onto Del's lap so she could pretend to drive. The interior of the vehicle seemed different; there were new leather seats, but something was missing.

"Your radio unit," Liesl said. "They removed it."

"I gave it back."

She looked at him and he nodded.

"You quit?"

"I resigned. Monty's sheriff, and he gets a brand-new cruiser. Everybody's happy."

"Including you?"

"I have so much comp time saved up that I'll get paid through the summer."

"Then what?"

"Then comes fall and usually after that winter."

"You look relieved."

"It'll sink in eventually, and then we'll see. It seemed I spent most of my days in that station feeling the cold and waiting—waiting for something to happen. A call, some complaint. Law enforcement is mainly a deterrent. I'm tired of being a deterrent. And I don't want to wait any longer. I want to—" He stopped and said, "I'm not making any sense, am I?"

"You're doing fine," Liesl said.

"All I know is that right now it's okay. You might say I'm even happy, though I've always thought the concept overrated." He picked up a plastic bag off the passenger seat. "So let's celebrate."

Lorraine looked in the bag. "Ice *cream!* Vanilla?"

"Not just vanilla, French vanilla," Del said.

This exotic detail had the desired effect on the girl, and she turned her big eyes on Liesl to make sure that this was indeed as good as she suspected. When Liesl nodded, Lorraine clapped her hands, which lately had been her response to anything that she thought beneficial, desirable, or just plain fun.

They went into the kitchen, and while Liesl doled out ice cream into three bowls, Del told her the rest. "I got a couple of estimates on my house and property. The mortgage is nearly paid off, and I figure I could come out of it with enough money to go—" He hesitated. "To go to the next best thing, to quote an old Warren Zevon song."

She handed one of the bowls of ice cream to Lorraine. "Let's sit by the garden."

The child led them outside, and they sat in the faded canvas lawn chairs behind the shed. The air smelled of moist topsoil.

"What is the next best thing?" Liesl asked. "Or perhaps I should ask, where is it?"

"With the right sailboat, it could be the seven seas." Del kept his eyes on his bowl as he carefully cut away a mound of ice cream. "Just kidding." He stuck the spoon in his mouth and pulled it out slowly, leaving a small, smooth lump. He put the spoon back in his mouth, and as if by magic the lump disappeared. "Over the past few weeks I've been in touch with people over in North Eicher. One thing about this job I won't miss is all the forms you have to deal with. I learned that Pronovost changed his will last fall and he left everything to relatives in Quebec, and they want to liquidate his real estate." He became occupied with his bowl, digging around as though he were looking for something.

"The lodge?" she asked. "You want to buy the lodge?"

He nodded. "It's a lot, but if I do all right with the sale of my house, I should be able to swing it. They're willing to sell it and a portion of the land. My guess is the rest of the land will either be picked up by one of the lumber companies or the government will take it. I can manage the lodge and about sixty acres. I think I'll need a partner."

"A business partner."

"Well, you could put it that way."

She worked on her ice cream. Suddenly she was afraid to look at him. It was ten o'clock, though at this time of year the sky stayed light until eleven. The summers in the U.P. were short, but the days long and the fading light had a Nordic clarity. She realized that she had been wary of this moment. They had become lovers as well as friends these past few months, but there had been no attempt at forging anything that resembled a commitment. "How would you make it work?" she asked. "The lodge, I mean."

"Use it for what it is, a lodge. For people who want to get away. To hunt, fish, simply walk out into the woods. I also wonder if it couldn't be attractive to artists, as a retreat where they could get a lot of work done."

Liesl put her empty bowl down in the grass. She left her hand there for a moment, her fingers touching the slick, cool blades. There came the sound of a splintering twig, and she looked toward the woods. "I've lived in this house a long time. I don't know. I've lived alone for years." Then she glanced at him because she realized that he had not said anything about their living together. He had never spent more than two nights in a row at her house. She was always sorry to see him leave, but she liked her solitude. She knew he did, too.

"Perhaps you wouldn't have to leave here," he said. "My guess is that it'll be seasonal, at least for the first few years." His eyes were steady, and she believed that he was trying not to push her into a quick decision.

"I need to think about it."

"I know."

She glanced at Lorraine, whose mouth was covered with ice cream. The reporter from the *Chicago Tribune,* Francine d'Orr, had understood something that Liesl had been trying hard to avoid. When Norman got out of prison and came for his daughter, she would lose a child—for a second time she would have to give up her life with a young girl. She worried about how she would deal with that.

"I was thinking," Del said. He got up and collected the empty ice cream bowls. "If this works out, Norman might want to come to work at the lodge, at least for a start."

Liesl felt something drop out of the bottom of her stomach, and for the briefest moment she felt nauseated. It was, she knew, because of the sugar from the ice cream. It passed, and she watched Del walk toward the house.

"Can I have more?" Lorraine asked him.

"No, but you can help me clean these up, if you want."

The child turned to Liesl and waited for an alternative opinion.

"It's well past your bedtime as it is," Liesl said.

"But it's still light out."

"It'll be dark soon."

"How soon?"

"As soon as you close those pretty peepers, it'll be dark and you'll have the sweetest dreams," Liesl said as she touched the girl's hair. "Now go help Del and I'll be in soon to put you to bed."

Lorraine stared at her a moment longer. When she had first come to live with Liesl, she was awakened by nightmares almost every night; but as the season changed they became less frequent. Still, the idea of bedtime had become a difficult issue as the summer evenings lengthened. Tonight the child was simply too tired to object. She ran across the grass after Del, and he took her hand just as they walked through the shed door.

Again a twig snapped in the woods, and Liesl got up out of her canvas chair. Though there was a cobalt blue sky overhead, stars were now visible and the woods were nearly dark. She walked the length of the garden and stopped at the edge of the yard. There was a rustling sound, and she stepped in among the first trees. She walked carefully, her arms raised to protect her face from branches. Still she could hear a rustling perhaps ten yards ahead, and there seemed now to be a charge to the air. As she approached an evergreen bush, she smelled a musky damp odor that was not unpleasant. Leaning forward slightly, she brought her face right up to the evergreen, which contributed its own mint fragrance. The rustling ceased and there followed an alert silence that was finally broken by a soft exhale. Then, as footsteps faded away deeper into the trees, Liesl caught sight of a leg, a haunch, dark movement against the dark wood. She held her breath until she was enveloped in complete stillness, a stillness she wished would never end.

ABOUT THE AUTHOR

JOHN SMOLENS is the author of two novels, *Angel's Head* (1994) and *Winter by Degrees* (1988), and a collection of short stories, *My One and Only Bomb Shelter* (2000). His stories and essays have appeared in various magazines, including *Yankee, Redbook, The Massachusetts Review, The William and Mary Review,* and *The Virginia Quarterly Review.* Educated at Boston College, the University of New Hampshire, and the University of Iowa, he is a professor of English and director of the M.F.A. program at Northern Michigan University.